The
FRACTAL
MURDERS

The FRACTAL MURDERS

MARK COHEN

New York Boston

For Tana

Lyrics from "If You Could Read My Mind," by Gordon Lightfoot, © 1969, 1997 (renewed) used by permission of Early Morning Music, Toronto, Canada.

Mysterious Press
Warner Books

Time Warner Book Group
1271 Avenue of the Americas, New York, NY 10020.
Visit our Web site at www.twbookmark.com.

Printed in the United States of America

First Printing: May 2004

10 9 8 7 6 5 4 3 2 1

Library of Congress Cataloging-in-Publication Data

Cohen, Mark.
    The fractal murders / Mark Cohen.
      p. cm.
    ISBN 0-89296-799-4
  1. Mathematicians—Crimes against—Fiction. 2. Private investigators—Fiction. 3. Women college teachers—Fiction. 4. Serial murders—Fiction. I. Title.
    PS3603.O367F73 2004
    813'.6—dc22

2003024031

Acknowledgments

An author's first novel is necessarily a product of his life experiences. It is not possible to acknowledge every person that made an impact on my life, but I would like to recognize three that made me a better writer.

First, my father, an English teacher early in his career. He taught me the joy that comes from creating with words. Second, Walter Broman, a professor of English at Whitman College who gave me permission to ignore convention. He was an inspirational and gifted teacher. Finally, Colonel (Ret.) Al Rubin, my immediate supervisor during my time as a Judge Advocate. Whenever I thought I had drafted the perfect document, he would return it to me with red ink all over it and ask, "Isn't mine better?" It always was.

I also want to thank my agent, Sandra Bond. She believed in *The Fractal Murders* and never gave up. Equally important, she never let me give up. I want to remember Sara Ann Freed, the editor in chief at Mysterious Press when we were looking for a publisher. She took a chance on *The Fractal Murders* while others feared it was too unconventional. Tragically, Sara Ann died before *The Fractal Murders* hit the bookstores.

Kristen Weber at Mysterious Press provided help with the plot and proved a worthy editor, while at the same time giving me the freedom to write "my way" and graciously tolerating my quirks.

Professor James D. Meiss of the University of Colorado and Professor Alex Kasman of the College of Charleston both read the manuscript and offered insight concerning the mathematics of the story and the world of mathematicians. To make *The Fractal Murders* enjoyable for those not mathematically inclined I have greatly simplified some of the concepts presented as part of the story. Any errors resulting from that effort are mine alone.

Writing a mystery while practicing law is no easy task. I want to thank my assistant, Sandy Enke, for her help and encouragement. Her willingness to shift from legal assistant to business manager to dog trainer while also serving as a general problem solver was a blessing.

My wife, Tana, provided love and encouragement while I was immersed in this project.

I want to say, "Woof" to Pepper and Scrappy up in heaven.

Finally, I want to thank Phoebe, Bear, and Wyatt. Their unselfish willingness to keep my tiny allotment of the bed warm while I was writing was critical to the success of *The Fractal Murders*.

The
FRACTAL
MURDERS

1

I WAS HAVING A BAD DAY. I had gotten behind Ma and Pa Kettle on the road down the mountain, and by the time I was able to pass them I was almost to Boulder. I blew past them, then blew my nose. I'd been fighting the Sinus Infection from Hell for a week. We were in the middle of round six and it was ahead on points.

The visitors' lots were full, so I parked my aging F-150 in a faculty lot. I ejected my Creedence tape, placed my "U.S. Government— Official Business" sign above the dash, and set out for the math building. I no longer worked for the government, but I'd paid enough taxes during my legal career to consider myself an honorary employee.

I had spent seven years at the university, but that was long ago and I'd taken great pains to avoid math classes. Now I was a private eye in search of a math professor. Unable to find anything resembling a campus map, I finally asked for directions. The first kid wasn't much help. But for the safety pin fastened to his left eyebrow, he looked like a neo-Nazi skinhead. He had no idea where the math building was and his surly demeanor suggested disgust at the notion that anyone would want to find it. I shook my head and said a prayer for the gene pool.

The next man I approached was a foreigner, probably Nigerian. Skin black as coal, trace of a British accent. He was polite and possessed a wonderful smile, but sent me on a trek that took me past the old field house—where I'd spent many an afternoon running sprints—and ended up at the alumni relations office. I could've sought directions there, but I hadn't contributed to my alma mater since changing occupations and I feared some eager assistant might strike up a conversation that would end with a plea for my time and/or money.

The third time was a charm. She was a studious-looking young woman with dark eyes who stared at her feet and talked to herself as she walked. She wore black jeans, a black vest over a gray T-shirt, and black shoes with crepe soles. Her hair was long, dark, and in need of conditioner. The lost daughter of Morticia Addams. She said she was a math major and gave me detailed directions.

It was the first Monday in May. Seventy-six degrees and not a cloud in the sky. Frisbees flew, stereos blasted, and leggy coeds abounded. I recalled the night Scott McCutcheon and I had sculpted a giant snow penis in front of the administration building. Probably not the first college freshmen to engage in such foolery, but a fond memory nonetheless. It seemed like just yesterday, but more than twenty years had passed. Time passes more quickly as you age, but that's one of the disadvantages of growing up.

The math building, a three-story fortress, was right where dark eyes had said it would be. Not far from where I'd parked. I had expected it to be named the Chester Q. Hollingsworth Hall of Mathematics or some such thing, but the sign above the entrance read simply, MATHEMATICS BUILDING. It was a newer structure, but the design was consistent with that of most others on campus. Exterior walls consisting of long slabs of rough-cut Colorado sandstone, all capped with a red tile roof. This warm architectural style dominated the campus and created an atmosphere reminiscent of a rural Italian village.

I entered unafraid. I was forty-four years old and nobody was going to ask me to bisect an angle or test my ability to solve a quadratic equation. That's one of the advantages of growing up. There aren't many, so I savored it.

The inside was about what you'd expect. The walls were covered with announcements and advertisements of every sort—typing services, bands in town, something about the Gay and Lesbian Student Alliance, a sign touting an upcoming lecture by a visiting professor, and so forth. One bulletin board was devoted exclusively to graduate programs at other universities. It was plastered with glossy posters and brochures. A young man wearing a pocket protector and carrying a beat-up briefcase studied them with interest. Probably the next Unabomber.

The lobby directory indicated the office of "Jayne Smyers, Ph.D., Associate Professor of Mathematics," was on level three. I took the stairs two at a time in my gray summer suit, hit the third floor, and started down a narrow hallway. It looked and sounded devoid of life. I glanced in each open office I passed, but only one man looked up. Tall, blond, and in good shape. The nameplate on his door identified him as "Stephen Finn, Ph.D., Assistant Professor of Mathematics." Papers covered his desk. He couldn't have been much older than twenty-seven, but his wire-rimmed glasses gave him a maturity beyond his years. "Can I help you?" he asked. Not hostile, but not friendly. My presence had broken his concentration.

"I'm looking for Professor Smyers," I said.

"Four doors down, on the right," he said with a forced smile. He pointed for me.

"Thanks," I replied. He did not immediately return to his work, and I felt his curious gaze as I continued down the hall.

I arrived at 3:20 P.M.—five minutes late. She was seated behind her desk and immersed in an academic journal of some sort.

"Dr. Smyers?"

"Yes."

"Pepper Keane." She rose from her chair and extended her right hand. I shook it. She was as tall as me and thin as a rail. Thirtyish. Luxurious dark hair—straight, full of body, and worn short, but not so short as to be butch. She'd been blessed with high cheekbones and white teeth. Bright blue eyes. Small, firm breasts. Smooth, milky skin. She wore designer jeans and a white cotton blouse. Except for pink lipstick, I detected no makeup.

"Thank you for coming on such short notice," she said.

"I'm sorry I'm late," I replied. "It took a while to find a parking space."

"Yes," she agreed, "parking is a real problem here. Sometimes even the faculty lots are full." I smiled, said nothing. She motioned to two sturdy wooden chairs in front of her desk and said, "Please, sit down." Feeling liberal, I took the one on the left.

It was a typical faculty office. Small, equipped with an old metal desk and black filing cabinets. Linoleum floor tiles designed to resemble white marble were partially covered by a Navajo rug. Bookcases overflowing with textbooks and professional journals. She had made an effort to decorate it by placing cacti here and there. National Public Radio was barely audible on the small radio by the window behind her. There was one poster. It proclaimed: "A Woman Without a Man Is Like a Fish Without a Bicycle." I hadn't seen one of those in at least fifteen years.

"Would you like some coffee?" she asked. I noticed a small coffeemaker on one of the shelves to her right. The kind that brews only two cups at a time. There was also an electric grinder and a package of gourmet beans. She bought her coffee at Starbucks. I usually buy mine at the Texaco.

"No, thanks."

"You sound like you have a cold. Can I make you some tea?"

"Really," I said, "I'm fine." I had downed forty-four ounces of diet Coke on the drive down and didn't figure to need liquids for a while.

She poured some coffee into a mug and said, "It's one of my few vices." The mug boasted a colorful Southwestern design featuring a coyote howling at the moon.

"Everyone needs a few vices," I said.

She forced a smile and sipped her coffee. "You're probably wondering what this is all about?"

"Well, Professor, I have to admit you've aroused my curiosity." She'd told me nothing on the phone, saying only that she would prefer to discuss it in person.

"I apologize for the secrecy," she said, "but I've never been involved in something like this." She paused. "Would you mind closing the door?" I reached back, gave it a good push, and listened as the latch found its place in the metal doorjamb. She took a deep breath, leaned forward, extended her long arms across the desk, and clasped her hands together. Her nails were short, but she wore polish and it matched her lipstick.

"Do you know much about mathematics?" she asked.

"Not much," I said. "I took calculus twenty-five years ago and it was the low point of my academic career."

She forced another smile. "My specialty," she said, "is fractal geometry. Do you know what a fractal is?"

"No."

"A fractal," she said, "is a type of geometric shape." She paused. "I don't know quite how to explain it to you." She tilted her head slightly, paused again, then said, "Picture a coastline."

"Okay." I didn't know much about geometry, but I'd been a marine officer for three years and I knew about coastlines.

"If we take a small section of that coastline, we can use a straight line to represent it on a map. But if we look closely at that section, we will see that it is made up of many small inlets and peninsulas, right?"

"Sure, and each inlet and peninsula has its own smaller bays and headlands."

"Yes," she said, "that's exactly right." She sipped her coffee. "And if we continue to look at smaller and smaller sections of the coastline, we'll find that this pattern is always present."

"Right down to the last grain of sand."

"Yes. That's the interesting thing about fractal objects: Their pattern remains more or less the same no matter how closely you examine them."

"So a fractal is just a shape with a random pattern?" I took the white handkerchief from my pants pocket, blew my nose, folded it gently, and placed it back in my trousers.

"Not a random pattern," she said, "an irregular pattern. Strictly speaking, there's no such thing as a random pattern. The two words are inconsistent. It's an oxymoron, like military intelligence." I let that pass without comment, though my high and tight haircut should've suggested I had once served in uniform.

"You're saying the shape of a coastline is not random?"

"Not in a mathematical sense," she said. "Each point on a coastline is linked with the points next door. If it were truly random, one point would have no relationship to the next. Instead of gradual curves, you'd see lines going all over the place. One point might be up here, the next might be way down there."

"Okay," I said, "I'll buy that." I waited for her to continue, confident that sooner or later the reason for my presence would become apparent.

"Did you study geometry in high school?"

"Tenth grade." I wondered what Mrs. Clagett was doing these days. Probably in the Aspen Siesta nursing home suffering recurring nightmares about McCutcheon and me.

"The problem with traditional geometry," she continued, "is that triangles, squares, and circles are abstract concepts. You can't use them to describe the shape of things like mountains, clouds, or trees."

"Or a coastline."

"Or a coastline," she agreed. She was becoming more animated; she clearly enjoyed the subject. "Traditional geometry—what we call Euclidean geometry—has to ignore the crinkles and swirls of the real world because they are irregular and can't be described by standard mathematical formulas. Then, about twenty years ago, a man named Mandelbrot invented something we call fractal geometry."

"Fractal geometry," I repeated. I sensed the lesson was nearing its conclusion.

"Mandelbrot realized that although many natural phenomena appear to be chaotic, there is frequently a hidden order in them. In fact, he called fractal geometry the geometry of nature." Another sip of coffee. "No two coastlines are identical, yet they all possess the same general shape, so there is a certain order there. Do you follow me?"

"I think so."

"Fractal geometry provides a way to identify patterns where there appears to be disorder. It allows us to model and predict the behavior of complex systems. It's a language," she said. "Once you speak it, you can describe the shape of a coastline as precisely as an architect can describe a house."

I doubted that. "Give me an example," I said.

"Certainly," she replied, eager for the invitation. "One of the tools we use to compare fractal objects is the concept of fractal dimension. For example, the coastline of Great Britain has a fractal dimension of approximately one point two-five, but the more rugged coastline of Norway has a fractal dimension of better than one point five-six."

"I'll take your word for it."

"I'm sorry." She sighed. "I've probably told you more than you need to know. I hope I haven't bored you."

"No, it's interesting." Not as interesting as the way her delicate bra straps traversed her bony shoulders, but interesting nonetheless.

"This will all make sense in a minute. I promise." She sipped her coffee, and I noticed a silver Navajo bracelet on her right arm. No wedding ring on either hand.

"Take your time," I urged. Despite my strong preference that people get right to the point, experience had taught me that the best way to conduct an interview was to shut up and listen.

"As I said," she continued, "my specialty is fractal geometry." I noted the Ph.D. from Harvard on the wall to my right. "Last year I began working on a paper I intended to present at a conference this fall. It's publish or perish, you know."

"So I've heard."

"When I completed my draft, I wanted someone else to critique it." She finished her coffee and set the mug to one side. "The last thing you want to do is publish a paper that contains a flaw."

"So you have your colleagues read it in advance to see if they can poke holes in it?"

"Yes, but my colleagues here wouldn't be much help. Fractal geometry is a rather narrow specialty, so I compiled a list of five of the most respected people in the field and attempted to contact them to see if they would be willing to critique it." Her slender neck became visibly tense and I thought she might be having trouble breathing.

"Are you all right?" I asked. She took a deep breath and nodded affirmatively.

"Mr. Keane," she continued, "when I attempted to contact these people, I learned that two had been murdered and a third had committed suicide."

"Over what span of time?"

"All within six months of each other," she said. "Do you know the odds against that?" It was a rhetorical question, but I had a hunch she could tell me the odds right down to the decimal point if she wanted to.

"And you want me to find out if these deaths were related?"

"Yes."

"Did you report this to anyone?" I asked.

"I called the police."

"And they said it wasn't their problem?"

"Yes, because none of the deaths had taken place in Boulder. They suggested I call the FBI."

"Did you?"

"Yes."

"They do anything?"

"Not from my point of view," she said coldly. "Two agents from Denver interviewed me. I explained that the odds of it being a coincidence were astronomical. Six weeks later they told me they couldn't find any connection and had closed the case." Her nostrils flared. She was not a woman accustomed to being taken lightly.

"When was that?" I asked.

"About two weeks ago. I've been struggling with what to do ever since."

"Did you know any of the victims?"

"I knew Carolyn Chang. We met at a conference in San Francisco a few summers ago."

"Did you stay in touch after that?"

"Not really," she admitted. "We exchanged Christmas cards, that's about it." We were silent for a moment, perhaps both recalling the names and faces of people who had briefly been friends but had long since been consigned to the category of memories.

"And," she said suddenly, "she sent me a note last year complimenting me on something I'd written for one of the journals. That's the only time someone ever took the time to do that." She seemed on the verge of tears, and I wondered how long it would take her to remove a tissue from the ceramic dispenser on her desk. Like her coffee mug, it boasted a colorful Southwestern design.

"Did you know the others?"

"Only by reputation," she said. She started to reach for a tissue, but caught herself. She would not cry. "I'd read some of their papers," she continued, "and seen their names in professional journals. You have to understand, these were some of the most brilliant people in the field. Professor Fontaine's textbook is the bible of fractal geometry."

"You never met them or spoke with them on the phone?"

"No."

"Ever correspond with them?"

"No."

I leaned back and laced my fingers together behind my head. "You said you had planned to ask five experts to critique your paper?"

"Yes."

"And three are dead?"

"Yes."

"Who were the other two?"

"Norbert Solomon at LSU and Mimi Townsend at MIT."

A math professor named Mimi? "Did they review it?"

"Yes."

"Anyone else?"

"I've asked several others to look at it. I still expect to present it this fall."

I closed my eyes for a moment to process what I'd learned. "How many people in this country would you say are experts in fractal geometry?"

"I think most major universities now offer at least one course in the subject." My years as a trial lawyer had so conditioned me that my first instinct was to rise and object to her answer as non-responsive. But I didn't. She wasn't on the witness stand and I was no longer practicing law. I rephrased the question.

"Would it be correct to say that not everyone who teaches a basic course in fractal geometry is an expert?"

"Yes, I suppose that's true."

I leaned forward. "How many people really know this stuff?" I asked. "How many people know it well enough to critique your paper or write a textbook?"

"Gosh," she said, "I don't know. Fifty?"

"Okay," I said, "can you think of anything that distinguishes these three from the other forty-seven?"

"Well," she said, "Fontaine was certainly one of the best-known people in the field."

"And the others?"

"They were all highly regarded."

"Any other connection?" I asked.

She opened a folder on her desk and removed some papers. "It may not be anything," she said, "but each of them attended or taught at Harvard." She handed me three biographies she'd apparently photocopied from some sort of who's who in mathematics. I studied them.

"It doesn't appear there was any overlap," I finally said. "Fontaine left Harvard while Carolyn Chang would've still been in high school."

She finished her coffee and poured more. "Yes, I noticed that." Her intellect recognized the significance of the fact, but her voice told me the Harvard connection concerned her.

"I'm sure many experts in fractal geometry spent time at Harvard," I said.

"I keep reminding myself of that, but it hasn't stopped me from having some sleepless nights." I suspected guzzling high-octane coffee late in the afternoon wasn't helping the problem, but I kept that to myself.

"Okay," I said, "each of these people taught fractal geometry, each was highly regarded, and each spent time at Harvard. Aside from those things, can you think of any other connection?"

"No," she sighed, "I've been racking my brain about that, but I just can't come up with anything."

I closed my eyes and massaged my temples. "So," I finally said, "three math professors are dead, two of whom you never met."

"Yes."

"But you're willing to spend your own money to determine if there's a connection?"

"There *is* a connection," she shot back. "Besides, if I don't do it, who will?" I thought for a moment. The same logic had governed my actions more than once.

"How did you pick me?" I asked.

"I was impressed by your ad. Law degree. Federal prosecutor. I didn't see any other investigators with those credentials."

"It doesn't mean I'll find anything."

"Mr. Keane," she said, "I understand that people in your line of work can't promise a specific result, but this was not a coincidence. Three mathematicians with expertise in a very esoteric branch of geometry all die of unnatural causes within six months of each other? Fat chance."

"You should've been a lawyer," I said. I reached for my briefcase and removed my clipboard.

"Does that mean you'll take the case?"

"I'll look into it. If I conclude you're wasting your money, I'll tell you."

"I appreciate your concern for my money," she said coldly, "but let me worry about that."

"I was just trying to—"

"I'm sorry," she said, "I didn't mean to be rude. Obviously, I don't have unlimited resources. But these deaths are connected. And if you accept that, it follows that evidence of that connection exists."

"Assuming that's true," I said, "it doesn't follow that I or anyone else will find it." She pondered that.

"One thing is certain," she said, "we won't find it if we don't try." I gave in to a slight smile and that, in turn, brought a smile to her pink lips, but this pleasant moment was cut short by two quick knocks on the imitation walnut door.

"Come in," she said. The door opened. It was Stephen Finn, Ph.D. He stood about six-three and possessed a sinewy build. Maybe one hundred eighty pounds. Blond hair, parted on the left. Green eyes. Blue veins crisscrossed his forearms like roads on a map, and I guessed he was an athlete of some sort—a cycling enthusiast or perhaps a mountain climber. He wore a white alligator shirt, tan slacks, and cordovan loafers.

"I'm sorry," he said with another forced smile, "I didn't know you were with someone. I just wanted to see if we were still on for tonight?" The question was directed to her, but intended for me. He was marking his territory, claiming some form of ownership.

"Yes," she said, "I'll meet you at seven." She did not introduce us and I made no effort to introduce myself. Clearly curious about my business with Jayne Smyers, he studied me briefly, apologized again for interrupting, and closed the door behind him.

"I won't take much more of your time," I said.

"That's all right," she said, "I want to give you as much information as I can."

We talked for another twenty-five minutes. She told me what she knew about the three deaths and gave me some news clippings she'd obtained when she'd first discovered them. I asked if she'd received any threats since discovering the deaths, and she said no. She also assured me she had not received any unusual phone calls or letters. I told her I didn't think she was in any danger, but gave her a pamphlet Scott and I had written on security for women. I requested a copy of the article she'd wanted the victims to review and she provided one. Eventually we came to the subject of fees.

One of the many things I'd hated about practicing law was having to constantly keep track of my time. No matter how accurate my records, there was always some asshole complaining he'd been billed fifty dollars for what was invariably described as a "two-minute conversation."

"I have sort of a Zen approach to fees," I said. "You and I will agree on a retainer. We'll talk about my progress from time to time. If you think I'm charging too much, you can fire me. If I think you're not paying me enough, I can quit."

"You don't keep track of your time?"

"Too much trouble," I said. "You'll know whether I'm earning my money."

"Interesting," she said, not quite sure how to respond.

"It requires a certain amount of trust," I admitted.

"It requires a great deal of trust."

"Look," I said, "I'd make more money if I charged by the hour, but whenever I do that I seem to spend half my time generating paperwork to justify my fees and the other half wondering if the client can afford to pay me to do what needs to be done. That leaves very little time for investigation."

"That leaves no time for investigation," she corrected. I smiled to signify she'd made her point. In the future I would refrain from using fractions in my figures of speech.

"If you'd be more comfortable with—"

"Will two thousand dollars be enough to get started?" She retrieved her purse from the floor, removed a maroon checkbook, and began to write.

"More than enough," I said, "but I don't want your money if you're not comfortable with the arrangement."

"I'm comfortable with it," she said as she handed me a check.

"Good." Not surprisingly, her checks featured scenes from the Southwest; this one depicted a pastel orange sun setting behind a cactus-covered canyon. I folded it in half, placed it in my shirt pocket, returned the clipboard to my briefcase, and stood up. "I want to read what you've given me and do a little digging. I'll call you in a few days to let you know what I've learned."

"I'll help you in any way I can," she said as she rose from her chair. "I feel better just knowing someone will be working on this." She extended her hand and I shook it.

"By the way," I said, "who else knows about this?"

"Just Mary Pat," she said, "my graduate assistant."

"That's it?"

"That's it," she assured me.

"Let's keep it that way."

"Certainly."

"One more thing," I said. "Do you recall the names of the two agents you spoke with?"

"Just a moment," she said, "I have their names right here." She opened the top drawer of her desk and retrieved two business cards, the gold seal of the Federal Bureau of Investigation visible on each. "Special Agent Gombold and Special Agent Polk." My expression must have changed when she said their names.

"Do you know them?" she asked.

"Yeah," I said, "I know 'em."

2

I⊤ was past ten when I returned to my Nederland home. I let the dogs out, removed my already loosened tie, and noticed the flashing red message light on the phone in the kitchen. There was one message. "Hey, peckerhead, give me a call." I punched in my brother's number. It used to be long distance to Denver, but in a rare example of government disregarding the desires of business, the Public Utilities Commission had recently ordered U.S. West to expand its local calling area.

"Hello?"

"Hello," I bellowed in my best equine voice, "'I'm Mister Eddddddddd.'"

He responded with his imitation of an irate Mr. T. "'I pity the fool that calls me this late in the evening.'" I laughed.

"I guess we both like old TV shows," I said.

"Yeah, but I chose one from the eighties and you chose one from the sixties, so I'm more hip."

"What's up?"

"Just wondered how you were doing."

"Pretty damn good," I said. I've suffered from mild depression since the death of an old girlfriend in a car accident years ago, but little brother still calls nearly every day to make sure I haven't killed myself.

"I tried calling earlier."

"I was meeting a new client."

"Long meeting?"

"I treated myself to dinner and a movie."

"Good, you need to be kind to yourself."

"That's what the self-help books say."

"I never read 'em. I thought I was being original."

"I don't know why they call them the dollar movies," I said. "The ticket cost a buck seventy-five, and I spent another six on popcorn and a drink."

"They hose you on refreshments."

"Yeah, and they won't even let you bring in your own stuff. Probably an antitrust suit in there somewhere." I took the hankie from my pocket and blew my nose.

"You got a cold?"

"Sinus infection."

"Gonna see a doctor?"

"They always say it's just allergies."

"That's what they're taught to say when they don't know what's wrong."

"I've never been allergic to anything in my life," I said.

"Me either," he said. "Real men don't get allergies." We laughed at our own caricatures of masculinity. "So," he said when the laughter had ceased, "tell me about your new client."

"She's a math professor with a preference for the Southwestern motif."

"Divorce case?"

"No, a fractal case."

"Is this where I'm supposed to ask what a fractal is?"

"Yup."

"What's a fractal?"

I explained fractals as best I could and outlined the facts my client had presented. "And," I added, "guess who one of the agents was?"

"You're shittin' me?"

"Nope."

"Be nice to prove him wrong." Troy had never met Polk, but he knew the story.

"Be nice to kill him," I said, "but I may have to settle for a small moral victory."

He allowed a laugh but said, "One manslaughter trial is enough." A reference to a legal problem I'd had some years back.

"It was a joke," I said.

"Not funny," he said. I rolled my eyes. "So, you think there's anything to this fractal thing?"

"It's worth checking out."

"Yeah."

"Besides, she gave me enough money to live on for a month and it beats getting a real job."

"Amen."

"Amen," I repeated. There was a brief pause.

"You coming down here tomorrow?"

"How about three o'clock? I'll work out, then chow down with you and the gang." Troy and Trudi have two kids, Andrew, age thirteen, and Chelsea, age seven.

"It's a deal," he said.

"And bring my Glock with you." I own one firearm—a nine-millimeter Glock 17—and I rarely carry it. There had been a string of burglaries in Troy's neighborhood, so I'd loaned the pistol to him a few months back. The burglars, two ex-cons with a taste for heroin, had since been apprehended.

"You really think these deaths are related?"

"She thinks they are," I said. "If she's right, we're dealing with a highly motivated individual. No use taking chances."

"I'll bring it."

"War fractals," I said.

"Out," he said. It was a sign-off routine we'd picked up from Jim Rome's sports radio show.

I hung up, opened the back door, and yelled, "Ollie ollie oxen-free," whatever that means. Like two Cruise missiles, they flew straight to the door, then positioned themselves at my feet and competed for affection. Tails wagging, they followed me in.

"How are my two favorite boys in all the world?" I asked as I knelt to let them nuzzle me. "Daddy made two thousand bucks today, so he bought you fellas some treats." I handed a foot-long compressed rawhide bone to Buck and a smaller version to Wheat. Buck trotted across the room with his and staked a claim on the couch. Wheat took cover beneath the kitchen table, where it would be difficult for Buck to get at him.

I undressed and clicked on CNN. Wearing plaid boxers and a white T-shirt, I began my stretching routine as an auburn-haired beauty summarized the day's events. A terrorist bomb in the Middle East, Republicans and Democrats blaming each other for the nation's ills, and an assortment of murders, kidnappings, floods, and droughts. Who wouldn't have a little depression? I turned off the TV, leaned back in my recliner, and picked up Heidegger's *Being and Time*.

When I left the practice of law two years ago, I purchased a home in the mountain town of Nederland and began a new life. As part of that I promised myself I'd spend time each day studying philosophy or eastern religions. Those subjects had captivated me in college, and my hope was that immersing myself in them once more might give me some insight into how to deal with my existential pain. So far it hasn't, but at least I'm well read.

The problem is that I am one of those unlucky souls condemned to forever ponder life's unanswerable questions. I don't know whether this is the cause of my depression or the result of it. Either way, traditional religion never worked for me. I've always had a bit of an authority problem, so I have trouble with the concept of God. I go through life with the nagging suspicion that it's all meaningless, but I read philosophy hoping to prove myself wrong.

I began my self-study program by reading the pre-Socratics and had since worked my way well into the twentieth century. Consequently, I now found myself trying to understand one of the most incomprehensible philosophers of all time. Martin Heidegger, a German philosopher, has been variously classified as a phenomenologist, an existentialist, and a mystic. For Heidegger, the fundamental mystery of life was that something, rather than nothing, exists. He spent most of his adult life attempting to develop a philosophy based on this rather obvious fact. Of course, I had spent most of my adult life as a lawyer billing people for my services in six-minute increments, so who was I to judge?

As often happens when I read philosophy at night, I soon found myself half asleep and skimming the same paragraph again and again. Something about "*Dasein*"—Heidegger's term for man, or being. I put the book down. "C'mon, boys," I said to the dogs, "time to hit the hay."

They followed me to the bedroom and we began our nightly ritual. Buck jumped on the bed ahead of me, stood on his hind legs, placed his grapefruit-size paws on my shoulders, and gave me a hug. That done, I slipped under the covers so Wheat could begin my face licking. After a suitable interval I turned out the light, then pulled the sheet over my head to signal Wheat the cleaning process was complete. Buck flopped down on my left, Wheat turned around three times and burrowed in on my right. Some people think I'm nuts when it comes to my dogs, but they're all I've got.

"Mornin', Pepper," Wanda said.

"Mornin', Wanda." She took my Foghorn Leghorn mug from the rack on the back wall and handed it to me. Her blond-gray hair was in a bun, and her white apron was covered with assorted stains. She'd been baking for hours and she looked it. It was seven-thirty on a Tuesday morning and the place was crowded.

"Haven't seen you in a while," she said. "You get tired of gas station coffee?"

"Decided to treat myself today," I said. Ever the diplomat.

"Something to eat? I've got some cinnamon rolls just out of the oven." They smelled wonderful, but I'm insulin resistant and have to limit my carbohydrates or I gain weight.

"Tempting," I said, "but not today." I poured myself some coffee, mixed in a little cream, and placed a faded dollar bill on the glass counter by the register. I found a booth in the back, read the *News,* and listened to the morning gossip. The *Post* might be a better paper, but it's divided into folding sections so large only an octopus with bifocals could comfortably read it.

The gossip was more entertaining than the paper in any event. Wanda's Kitchen is a gathering place for the telecommuting yuppies, aging hippies, and transient bikers who populate this mountain town of fifteen hundred. This morning's conversation centered on a controversial proposal to eliminate the town marshal's office and contract with the county for law enforcement services. The consensus was that this was a bad idea that would ultimately lead to enforcement of such things as building codes, marijuana laws, and the three-dog limit. I agreed with the consensus.

I poured some more coffee and returned to my booth only to find Wanda's black Lab, Zeke, sitting beneath the table. The Boulder County Health Department doesn't make it up here very often. I took a moment to rub Zeke's belly, then began reviewing the news clippings and biographical blurbs Jayne Smyers had provided.

The first victim, Paul Fontaine, had been a fifty-five-year-old professor of mathematics at Whitman College, in Walla Walla, Washington. He'd been shot once in the back of the head during an apparent robbery at his home last September. A Walla Walla native, Fontaine earned a doctorate at twenty-three and had taught at some of the best schools in the country. Michigan, Tufts, Harvard. As my client had mentioned, he'd authored a widely used textbook on fractal geometry.

He was the oldest of three children and the only son; his parents owned an immense wheat farm just east of Walla Walla. His father had suffered a minor stroke in 1977, and he'd taken the Whitman position at that time so he could help oversee the wheat operation. Students described him as an easygoing man with a passion for teaching. An avid runner, fly fisherman, and collector of rare American coins. The photo showed a handsome fellow, sharp features and distinguished silver hair. He had never married and had been living alone at the time of his death. I hoped the same would not someday be said of me.

Victim number two, Carolyn Chang, had been an associate professor of mathematics at the University of Nebraska, in Lincoln. A farmer had found her frozen body somewhere north of Manhattan, Kansas, in late December. She'd been raped and repeatedly stabbed. An only child, Carolyn had been born and raised in Honolulu, where her father was a successful building contractor. She'd done her undergraduate work at Harvard and earned her Ph.D. at Berkeley. Though she'd been teaching in Lincoln only five years, she'd been named acting dean of students during one of them. Colleagues and students alike described her as hardworking and demanding. She was thirty-five years old at the time of her death. Like Fontaine, she had never married.

The same photograph appeared in several articles; it was a professional portrait, probably taken for a yearbook or obtained from the university's public relations department. Despite her Chinese surname and Asian features, her well-endowed front and the baby fat in her cheeks suggested at least one of her parents was of Polynesian descent. She had possessed a wonderful smile, wide and unpretentious. I considered her attractive, and I assumed many of her male colleagues and students had felt the same way. Maybe one of them decided she'd been a little too demanding.

Although her body had been found in Kansas, the location of the actual murder was not known. The lead investigator for the Lincoln Police Department, Detective Amanda Slowiaczek, told reporters Carolyn could have been killed anyplace between Lincoln and the site where her body had been found, approximately eighty miles south of there. Neither her department nor the sheriff in Kansas had any suspects.

The third victim, if you could call him that, had been a thirty-seven-year-old associate professor of mathematics at Harvard. Donald Underwood had hanged himself in his upscale Boston town house on Valentine's Day. He and his wife had been separated ten months, but friends and coworkers had noticed nothing unusual in his behavior in the weeks prior to his death. There was no mention of a suicide note. Because the authorities had treated his death as a suicide rather than a murder, the local papers had not seen fit to devote more than a few paragraphs to the story. All I knew was that he was survived by his wife and two sons.

Three victims, three different states, and three different causes of death. That all added up to three unrelated cases, but all three victims had been mathematicians. And not just run-of-the-mill mathematicians, but experts in fractal geometry. The feds had closed the case, but I had a tough time chalking it up to coincidence.

Another thing I had a tough time with was the paper my client had written. It was entitled "Fractal Dimension: Some Thoughts on Alternatives to Hausdorff-Besicovitch." She lost me in the second paragraph, and after that it might as well have been written using an alphabet created by an ancient civilization from another planet in a solar system that had long since imploded. After twenty minutes of struggling with it, all I knew was that no matter how you measured it, the coastline of Norway was still more jagged than that of Great Britain.

I gathered my papers, gave Zeke one last pat on the head, and walked home. It was approaching ten-thirty, so I donned my running gear and jogged to the post office with Wheat. I live on the outskirts of Nederland—a small town fifteen miles west of Boulder. The postal service won't deliver mail if you live more than two miles from town, so I rent a box and check it six days a week.

There was the usual assortment of junk mail, including yet another letter from the credit gods informing me I'd been pre-approved for some kind of super titanium card because of my "accomplishments in life." Once they know you're a lawyer, it never stops coming. I tore each item in half, dumped the remains into the metal U.S. government trash can, and started home. It was a good day to run, about seventy degrees and sunny. Little Wheat detoured now and then to check out a new smell or leave his mark, then raced to catch up with me. His paws didn't seem to bother him, but they sometimes do and I have to walk. Or carry him.

I never take Buck to the post office. Buck is a floppy-eared cross between a Rhodesian Ridgeback and a Great Dane. He was just a puppy when I found him wandering the streets of Denver four years ago. He wasn't wearing any tags and looked emaciated. I figured anyone stupid enough to let a dog roam the streets without tags didn't deserve a pet, so I kept him. Today he weighs 130 and he's extremely protective, so I have to keep him on a leash when I'm in town. Trying to jog while you're tethered to Buck is a great way to strengthen your lats, but doesn't make for a very enjoyable run.

Wheat, on the other hand, is a purebred schipperkee. He's black, weighs about twenty pounds, and has pointy ears. The schipperkee originated in Belgium and was known as a boatsman's dog. We don't boat much, but the little dog is a joy to run with when his paws aren't hurting. I adopted him two years ago, just before moving to Nederland. I had learned of his plight from a newspaper article. His jerk owner had abused little "Blackie" to the point where the jerk's own roommates had called the police. The jerk had kicked the puppy so often that he had suffered permanent nerve damage in his front paws. Surgery helped some, but the dog needed a loving home. One look at the photo convinced me I had to have him. I drove to the shelter, paid the adoption fee, and took the curious animal home. The jerk was charged with cruelty to animals, but made bail and skipped town.

I finished my run, clicked on CNN, and made a peanut butter and jelly sandwich for lunch. Despite the lack of breakfast, I felt great. They say exercise is the best thing for depression, and in my case that is definitely true, but I add 150 milligrams of Imipramine every night just for insurance. I took one of my patented ninety-second showers, dressed, then sat at my desk to consider the case.

I wanted to see the police files on the three victims. This would have been difficult even if they had all died in Boulder, but the three incidents had taken place in locations where I had no contacts. Unlike many private eyes, I had never been a cop, so I wasn't a member of the law enforcement fraternity. I had been a federal prosecutor, but even that was unlikely to get me past the disdain most police officers feel for lawyers. Well, nothing ventured, nothing gained.

I dialed information for Walla Walla only to learn the process had been automated so that you no longer spoke with a human being. A female cybervoice recited the number and offered to connect me for an additional seventy-five cents. I said, "In your dreams, sweetcakes," then hung up and dialed it myself. The woman answering for the Walla Walla Police Department informed me that Lieutenant Dick Gilbert was handling the Fontaine case. He wasn't in, so I left my name, number, and a request that he call me.

I phoned the Lincoln Police Department and asked for Detective Slowiaczek, the woman quoted in the news clippings. I was transferred three times, but finally got her. "Slowiaczek," was all she said. I identified myself and explained the reason for my call.

"Who's your client?" she demanded. She sounded like she was in her thirties. Her abrupt tone suggested my call was about as welcome as one from a sales rep asking her to switch long-distance companies.

"My client," I said, "is a concerned citizen who finds it hard to believe these deaths were unrelated." I heard some noise in the background.

"Tell that asshole I'll be with him in a minute."

"What?"

"I wasn't talking to you," she snapped.

"You sound busy," I said. "All I'm asking is a chance to see what you've got."

"Out of the question," she said.

"I understand it's an open investigation," I said. "If you don't want copies of documents floating around, how about I fly to Lincoln and review them in your presence."

"I'm sure that would be a real treat for me," she said, "but it's not going to happen." Losing her patience.

"Look," I said, "I was a federal prosecutor for seven years. I know what I'm doing. I need to gather as much information as possible about these deaths."

"Uh-huh," she said, not impressed.

"Don't you think it's strange," I persisted, "that all three of these people were experts in fractal geometry?" It was one question too many.

"In the first place," she shot back, "I see strange every day of my life. In the second place, you're asking me to violate department policy. And in the third place, the FBI already investigated that and I'll be damned if I'm going to go over it again with some limp-dick lawyer turned private eye." I got the impression she didn't like men. I thanked her for her time and hung up before I became a suspect.

The detective who had worked the Underwood suicide was Tom O'Hara. He had the Boston accent and sounded like he was nearing retirement. I envisioned a big, hard-drinking Irish cop with silver hair, a ruddy red face, and a bulbous nose. Probably a flask of whiskey in his desk and a Red Sox pennant on the wall behind him.

"Yeah," he said, "the feds went over my reports. Took about ten minutes."

"That long?"

"It wasn't a Boston case. They were doing legwork for some other office."

"They tell you all three of these people were experts in fractal geometry?"

"Yeah, they told me all that, but you don't need to be Dick Tracy to see this guy offed himself."

"Any way it could've been staged?"

"Anything's possible," he admitted, "but at this point we've got no motive for anyone to do that and no reason to think that's what happened." Time to ask for the records.

"Maybe there's nothing there," I said, "but I'd like to review your file. My client's paying me good money and that's the logical place to start." He thought for a moment.

"You contact the other two departments?"

"Yeah, they're sending me what they've got." He thought for another moment.

"I'd like to help you," he finally said, "but I'll bet we get three or four of these autoerotic deaths every year." I didn't say a word. "The department keeps these files locked up tight; you know, outta respect for the family." I said I understood and thanked him for his time.

So, Underwood hadn't committed suicide. He had unintentionally strangled himself while engaging in autoerotic asphyxia. As a Marine Corps lawyer it had been my sad duty to deal with that sort of thing on a fairly regular basis. Write a report, collect the deceased's belongings, help make arrangements and all that. I had practiced law long enough to know there were plenty of apparently normal people out there who had their own secrets and demons. Or, as one of my former law partners, "Big" Matt Simms, used to say whenever we walked into a restaurant for lunch, "I'll bet half the fuckers in here have bodies in their basements."

I closed my eyes and considered the implications. If Underwood's death had been an accident, then, by definition, it was unrelated to the other deaths. While the killing of even two specialists in fractal geometry still seemed highly coincidental, the belief that Underwood's death was somehow related had given the whole thing a sort of critical mass.

Okay, assume Underwood purposely took his own life. Why make it look like an autoerotic death? That didn't make sense, so the only other possibility was that a person or persons unknown had killed him. Where did that leave me? Each of the victims had been an expert in fractal geometry. Each had also attended or taught at Harvard, but that was probably a coincidence. The three victims had not been America's only experts on fractals, but they were the only ones who were dead. Why them? I punched in my client's number. She picked up on the second ring.

"Jayne Smyers."

"Hello, Professor, this is Pepper Keane."

"Oh, how are you? I didn't expect to hear from you so soon." She sounded more relaxed. "Do you have me on a speakerphone?" I like the speakerphone because it leaves my hands free to find documents or take notes, but I could tell it bothered her, so I picked up the receiver.

"I'm fine, but I have a favor to ask."

"Sure."

"Would it be possible for me to get copies of all the published papers of the three victims?"

"Wow," she said, "you don't waste any time, do you?"

"I'm obsessive-compulsive."

"Most people who achieve anything in life are."

I wondered what I had achieved in life. Aside from being preapproved for a plethora of gold cards. "I'd like to see if I can find any pattern in their writings."

"That makes sense. I'll ask Mary Pat to make copies right away."

"That's your graduate assistant?"

"Oh, that's right. Well, if you don't want her to know what you're working on, I could do it, but it would take a few days. I'd have to do a computer search and scoot over to the library to pull them myself." I hadn't heard anyone other than Keith Jackson use the verb "scoot" in a long time. Keith covers college football for ABC. He likes to say things like, "I tell you, folks, this sophomore can really scoot."

"That's okay," I said, "go ahead and have her do it."

"I could tell her they're for me."

"She'd know what you were up to. Just tell her the truth and emphasize that she's not to mention it to anyone."

"Are you sure?"

"Yeah."

"All right, I'll ask her to get right on it. They should be ready in a day or two."

I thanked her and said good-bye. Jesus, it was almost two o'clock. I let the dogs out for a few minutes, then fired up my truck and headed for Denver. I popped in a tape of old Sam Cooke tunes and made it down the mountain in twenty-two minutes. I love old rock 'n' roll and old country. Besides, radio reception in the canyon is virtually nil; the only signal you can get is an

AM station with a fundamentalist Christian orientation. I'm hoping that's just a coincidence.

My brother and his family live just south of Denver, in Highlands Ranch, a wealthy suburb that didn't even exist twenty-five years ago. It is sixty-six miles door-to-door, but the first leg is mountain driving, so it's hard to do in less than an hour. His gym isn't quite so far. I can make it in forty-five minutes if I don't hit Denver's notorious rush hour.

Troy Keane's Gym is a mecca for serious bodybuilders along Colorado's Front Range. There are no chrome-plated machines like you see in the spas. He doesn't sell memberships; everyone pays by the month. He's done pretty well for a guy who never finished high school. He was giving a tour to two future Schwarzeneggers when I came in, so I waited until I caught his eye, then claimed my permanent locker, changed into my workout clothes, weighed myself, and walked to the back room. The room has no official name, but a weathered black-and-white photo of Ingemar Johansson sits atop the entrance. Ingemar, for those who don't know, was the last white heavyweight champion. And probably always will be.

I worked the speed bag for three two-minute sessions, then switched to the heavy bag. I hadn't thought about Mike Polk in a while and visualizing him helped me hit the bag with a little extra vigor. A former basketball star at one of the PAC-10 schools, he's tall and left-handed, so I worked combinations I thought would be effective against a big southpaw.

A successful amateur boxer, I had flirted with the notion of fighting professionally, but it's hard to succeed as a heavyweight when you're only five-ten. Joe Frazier had done it, but he'd usually had to take tremendous abuse from much bigger men and hope he could weather the storm until his left hook floored his opponent. I thought practicing law would be a more enjoyable way to earn a living, though I later learned you take plenty of abuse in that profession.

A few gangly teenagers gathered around when I really started moving the bag. "The secret's in the hips," I explained. I stepped back to rest and felt a tap on my shoulder. It was Troy.

"I'm sorry," he said, "I thought you were Mike Tyson."

"An understandable mistake," I said as I struggled to control my breathing. "We look exactly alike, except he's black and doesn't have a big fucking streak of white hair sticking out of his head." My hair is straight and black, but I've always had a small tuft of white just above my right temple. It's a genetic fluke known as mosaicism. Some people call it a witch's stripe. I'm told it can be indicative of something called Waardenburg's syndrome, but in my case it's just a fluke.

"You look good," he said. We gave each other a bear hug.

"I've been running."

"What do you weigh?"

"According to your scale, about two-fourteen."

"That scale's a piece of crap," he joked. "The owner's too cheap to replace it."

"How about you?"

"Two-nineteen," he said.

"You're a stick figure," I said, "you ought to be in the NBA."

"Yeah, I might not be able to slam dunk, but when I foul you, you'll damn well know you've been fouled." We were poking fun at our genetic makeup. The men in our family are short and powerfully built—thick bones and limbs. At five-ten, I'm the tallest living Keane.

We took turns on the heavy bag, then laced up the gloves and did some light sparring in the ring at the back of the room. Out of the corner of my eye, I noticed a tall woman enter the room. She had dark hair and a bright future in toothpaste commercials. For a split second I thought it was Jayne Smyers, and in that split second my brother tagged me with a straight left. "Her name's Pam," he said as we continued circling.

"Cute." She wore a scarlet leotard and shiny silver leggings, but on closer inspection I could see she was only a few years out of high school.

"You want to meet her?"

"No, not my type."

"What is your type?"

"I don't know." It was a question I'd often asked myself, but one for which I'd never been able to articulate a satisfactory answer.

"She wants to be a stewardess," he said. "Thinks serving Bloody Marys to horny old men at thirty thousand feet is glamorous."

"They're called flight attendants now," I said. "And don't knock it—most of them take home more than I do." Though I'd earned enough practicing law to ensure my financial security for life, in two years as a private investigator I'd averaged less than twenty-five thousand dollars annually. Jayne Smyers was the first legitimate client in six weeks to seek my services.

"You can always go back to representing killers and crack dealers," he said.

"Not in this lifetime," I said.

We took off the gloves, finished with a quick weight workout, then hit the showers. As a result of listening to Sam Cooke on the drive down, I caught myself singing, "'Don't know much about algebra . . .'"

"Why are you so happy?" my brother shouted.

"I don't know," I said, "I guess it just feels good to be working again."

3

WEDNESDAY BROUGHT LIGHT RAIN. Mountain thunderstorms are usually brief, but steady drizzle had been falling since midmorning and showed no sign of letting up. Buck and I had just returned from a noontime run around the lake when the phone rang. I reached for the cordless unit in my kitchen as I watched a pair of blue jays zoom in and out of the pines behind my log home.

"Mr. Keane?"

"Yes."

"My name is Mary Pat McCormick. I'm Professor Smyers's graduate assistant. She asked me to photocopy some papers for you, and I wanted to let you know you can pick them up whenever you like." Her voice had a slight throaty quality, like a young Kathleen Turner.

"Will you be there in an hour?"

"One of us will."

"Great, I'll come right down." I returned the phone to its cradle and watched the blue jays take off. They didn't say where they were going. Maybe Toronto.

Preferring fountain drinks to canned pop, I stopped at the B&F Market—Nederland's only grocery store—for a forty-four-ounce diet Coke, then headed down the mountain. The visitors' lots were again full, so I parked where I'd parked before. In the exact same spot. I was beginning to think of it as my spot.

My client wasn't in, but the door to her office was open. In surveying it I noticed a five-by-seven photograph of an older couple outside an expensive adobe home. A second photo showed my client and some other women on a rafting trip. A small plaque on the wall to my right thanked her for five years of dedicated service to a local women's shelter. The "Fish Without a Bicycle" poster was still there, but so far she hadn't struck me as a militant feminist. Lipstick and nail polish were usually a good sign in that regard.

"Mr. Keane?" I turned around. The Kathleen Turner comparison continued to work because she was about five-eight and had more curves than Jessica Rabbit. The kind of body my former partner Matt Simms loves—like the buxom movie stars of the 1940s. She was in her early twenties. She had intentionally frizzed her long auburn hair, but on her it looked good. Full lips, green eyes, no makeup. She wore tan hiking shorts, a man's blue oxford-cloth with the sleeves rolled up, and leather sandals. Her wide smile oozed optimism and her erect posture projected confidence.

"You must be Mary Pat?"

"Mary Pat McCormick," she said as she extended her hand. Above her shirt pocket was a button urging others to keep abortion safe and legal. Another Catholic girl gone bad.

"Pepper Keane." Her handshake was enthusiastic, like that of a young woman concluding an interview for her first real job.

"Professor Smyers is still in class, but I have the articles right here." She retrieved a stack of papers from my client's desk and handed it to me. Held together by a large binder clip, it was a good two inches thick. "That's every paper they ever published."

"Fantastic," I said. "How'd you get them so quickly?"

"Just plugged their names into MathSciNet," she said, smiling. "Works every time."

"MathSciNet?"

"It's the standard search engine for mathematical works."

"Oh."

"Sorry. I forgot I was talking with"—she made quotation marks with her fingers—"an outsider."

"Don't worry about it," I said. "I'm grateful for your help. I'm sure you had better things to do."

"Not really. Jayne told me what you're doing. I know how important this is to her."

"Let's talk about that," I said. "Why is this so important to her?" I sat down on one of the wooden chairs in front of my client's desk. Mary Pat took the cue and sat down beside me, then stared at the floor for a moment as she considered my question.

"She doesn't like losing, that's for sure. She wants to prove these three murders were not a coincidence."

"Two murders and one apparent suicide," I said. She forced a polite smile, but she was as certain as her boss that Underwood's death was related to the others.

"I've never seen her as mad as she was when those agents strolled in here and told her they were closing the case. She really read them the riot act." I pictured Jayne Smyers confronting Gumby and Pokey. She's an inch taller than Gombold and I suspected she'd had enough assertiveness training to hold her own with Polk.

"How did they react to that?" I asked.

"One guy took it in stride, but the other was a real jerk."

"The big guy?"

Her eyes widened. "You know him?"

"I've known Polk since law school. We were in the same class."

"Talk about arrogance," she said, "I just wanted to smack him."

"He has that effect on people." I'd wanted to smack him ever since law school, but the closest I'd come was a payback tackle in what was supposed to have been a flag football game. Scott McCutcheon called it the greatest flag football tackle he'd ever seen.

"The other thing is," Mary Pat continued, "and I'm just speculating, but I think Professor Smyers has a thing about justice. Her parents were killed when that airplane exploded over Scotland."

"Over Lockerbie?"

"Yes."

"I didn't know," I said. "Thanks for telling me." We were silent a moment.

"Mr. Keane," she finally asked, "is Professor Smyers in danger?" It was a question I'd already considered from a number of angles.

"I don't think so," I said. "If someone wanted her dead, she'd be dead."

"That's reassuring," she said. Her sarcasm wasn't directed at me; she was just too young and good-hearted to accept the fact that any person can kill any other person at just about any time.

"Look at it this way," I said. "Other than a brief friendship with Carolyn Chang a few years ago, nothing connects her to any of the three victims. And if we assume Underwood's death was a suicide, the last murder took place more than four months ago." She said nothing. "If I find something connecting one death to another, I'll be in a better position to know whether anyone else might be in danger. You have to find the connection to understand the motive. It's a process of gathering information."

"I have an idea about that," she said. She flung her head to one side to prevent her hair from encroaching on her face. It was a sexy little move.

"Let's hear it."

"We use the Internet. We send e-mails to mathematicians at universities around the country outlining what we know. I'm sure we'd receive lots of useful information."

"We probably would," I said, "but we can't do it." I leaned forward and waited until we had good eye contact. "No one else is to know Professor Smyers reported this to the authorities or that she hired me to look into it."

"But," she insisted, "that would be the most efficient way for us to gather information." Her continued use of the plural indicated she considered herself part of my team. I laced my fingers together behind my head.

"Have you ever heard of Heisenberg's uncertainty principle?" I asked.

"Of course." She did a poor job of hiding her surprise that I'd heard of it, but I'd learned some physics in my study of philosophy.

"What is your understanding of it?" I asked. She played along.

"It's a principle of quantum mechanics that holds that it is impossible to measure the position and velocity of an object at exactly the same time because the very attempt to do so affects both the position and velocity of the object."

"That's exactly right," I said, "and that's the situation we've got here. If these deaths are related, someone took great pains to make them appear unrelated. That suggests what in my Marine Corps days we used to call a 'highly motivated individual'—someone who would not hesitate to kill again if he felt threatened. We don't know who the killer is or what his motive was, but the very attempt to find out might alert him to my investigation and put all of us in danger. It's vital that this remains a secret. I want your word on that." I was coming on strong, but I believed what I was saying and wanted her to.

"But," she pleaded, "we'd just be contacting other math people."

"Mary Pat," I said, "if these deaths are related, the killer almost certainly has some link to the mathematical community." She broke eye contact and gazed at the floor.

"I guess you're right," she admitted. "Sometimes I dig in before I've considered all the arguments."

"Me too," I said. "It's a hard habit to break." I unclasped my hands and switched legs so that my left crossed over my right. There was a brief pause, but I enjoyed talking with her and didn't want to leave. "So," I began, "you're working on your master's?"

"I just have to finish my thesis. I hope to earn my doctorate here. I'm from Milwaukee, but I love Boulder."

"Not as nice as Ennis, Montana," I said, "but better than East Saint Louis." That made her laugh.

"You were in the marines?" she asked.

"I was a lawyer," I said.

"Like the lady on *JAG*?"

"Something like that," I said.

"My dad was a marine. I was born at Camp—" She cut herself off when Finn appeared in the doorway. He had evidently just returned from a long run in the rain. He wore a white tank top, maroon nylon running shorts, and top-of-the-line running shoes, the kind with translucent green gel beneath the heel. He was soaking wet.

"Jayne around?" he asked as he polished his glasses with a small white cloth.

"No," said Mary Pat, "but she should be back any minute."

He looked at me, put his glasses in place, then stepped forward and said, "I don't believe we've been introduced. I'm Stephen Finn." I stood up and Mary Pat followed suit.

"Stephen competes in triathlons," Mary Pat explained.

"Pepper Keane," I said. We shook hands. He gave me his triathlete grip, so I gave him my I-can-dead-lift-535-pounds grip.

"What do you do, Mr. Keane?" He tried to ask it in an offhand manner, but seeing me in my client's office a second time had him burning with curiosity.

"Mr. Keane is a private investigator," Mary Pat said. I was ready to thrash her, but she added, "He's helping Professor Smyers design a workshop on personal safety for women at the shelter."

"A private investigator? Fascinating." He tried to sound interested, but his tone was slightly condescending. He felt it wasn't an occupation for the educated. "Anyhow," he continued as he turned to Mary Pat, "I just stopped by to chat with Jayne. Will you tell her I was looking for her?"

"I will," she promised.

"Nice to have met you, Mr. Keane."

"Same here," I said. He departed and we returned to our chairs. "What does he teach?" I asked.

"Freshman stuff, mostly. Baby calculus, things like that."

"Low man on the totem pole?"

"Yes."

"How long has he been here?"

"Two years, just like me."

"He looks so young."

"He graduated from Harvard at twenty."

"Big deal," I said, "I started kindergarten before I turned five." She laughed, then gave her assessment of Finn.

"He can be a bit pretentious, I'll admit, but he's not a bad guy, really. His students love him. His biggest fault is that he tries too hard. He's up for tenure next year and he's obsessed with it." I was about to ask the nature of his relationship with my client, but she walked in before I got the chance. She was still as tall as I was and she wasn't wearing heels. Pink lipstick, powder blue sundress, white sandals. And it wasn't even Flag Day.

"Did I miss a good joke?" she asked. I stood.

"No," said Mary Pat, still grinning as she came out of her chair, "Mr. Keane was just recounting his academic accomplishments."

"Well, Mary Pat," she said in mock seriousness, "it's not polite to laugh. It destroys the student's motivation to learn." We shared a smile as she walked around her desk and began making a pot of coffee. "Did Mary Pat give you everything you need?"

"She sure did," I said.

"If you need anything else, Mr. Keane," said Mary Pat as she neared the door, "just let me know. You can leave a message with the department secretary."

"I will. Thanks again."

"Where are you off to?" my client asked.

"I have a date with the supercomputer," Mary Pat replied. "Oh, I almost forgot, I'm supposed to tell you Stephen stopped by 'to chat.'" They exchanged a knowing look and Mary Pat departed. My client stood at the window behind her desk and stared out at the rain. She had a nice view of the mountains and I had a nice view of her.

"I like the rain," she said, "but if it doesn't let up, I'm going to have to make a mad dash for my car."

"I have an old poncho in my truck, but camouflage might clash with your outfit."

"Oh," she said, "that's sweet, but it's not raining that hard. That's what I get for relying on the weatherman." I had intended it as a joke, more or less, but that's what I get for trying to be funny. She sat down behind her desk and poured some coffee into her coyote mug. "So," she said, "what do you think of Mary Pat?"

"Bright young lady."

"She's one of the most talented students we've ever had. She scored a nine-eighty on the Graduate Record Exam. That's as close to perfect as you get."

"She told me she wants to earn her doctorate here."

"I've encouraged her to keep her options open. She could go anywhere, but she likes Boulder."

"Does she want to specialize in fractal geometry?"

"That's an interesting question. One minute it seems to appeal to her, the next minute she's off on something else."

"If she can't make up her mind," I said, "there's always law school. That's what it's there for." She smiled to acknowledge my keen wit. Or maybe she was acknowledging the element of truth in my remark. Either way, I'd take it. She had a nice smile.

"You don't sound much better," she said. "You should see a doctor."

"It's on my list of things to do," I said. I don't trust doctors. I knew plenty of morons who had made it through law school, and my years defending navy doctors against malpractice claims had convinced me a similar percentage survived medical school. "Anyhow," I said, "it looks like I've got some reading to do, so I'd better be going. Thanks for having Mary Pat get right on this."

"You're more than welcome. If you need anything else, just call."

"By the way," I said, "when Professor Finn stopped by, Mary Pat told him I'm helping you prepare a workshop on personal safety for some women in a shelter. Which one of you came up with that?"

She smiled. "She did, but you have to admit it's a good lie."

"It's perfect," I said. "I am an investigator, and you evidently work with one of the shelters." I pointed to the plaque honoring her service.

"I'm on the board of directors of the Boulder Women's Shelter."

"That's terrific. If you ever do want to put together a workshop, let me know. I've had some training in verbal de-escalation and personal safety techniques."

"Well," she said, "let's get through this first." I was almost out the door. "You know," she said, "when I first met with them, those FBI men asked me not to discuss this matter with anyone else. Even after the bureau closed the case, their boss encouraged me to be discreet—he wanted to protect the privacy of the families—so I haven't mentioned any of this to my colleagues, but at some point you may want to talk with Stephen."

"Why's that?"

"He taught at the University of Nebraska."

"When?"

"Just before joining the faculty here."

"Really? Did he know Carolyn Chang?"

"Yes, he learned of her death from a former colleague. He was quite upset."

"Small world," I said.

4

I DROVE BACK UP THE MOUNTAIN with twenty-eight papers on various aspects of mathematics. I speculated as to the nature of the relationship between Finn and my client as Mick Jagger explained why he had been unable to obtain any satisfaction. It couldn't be too serious if she hadn't shared her suspicions about the three deaths with him.

Arriving home at three-thirty, I let the dogs out into the rain, then watched as they reentered and shook from side to side. Nothing like the smell of wet hounds to make a house a home. I headed to my office to study the collected works of the three victims.

My office is in my home. When I left the U.S. Attorneys' office to found Keane, Simms & Mercante, I purchased, among other things, a mahogany desk, a matching credenza, and an original Robert Batemen painting of an Alaskan brown bear. When I left the firm two years ago, I took it all with me. I had enjoyed the tremendous view of downtown Denver, the plush offices, and the other trappings of success, but I don't miss paying four thousand dollars a month in overhead. I have everything I need right here, including a great view of the Continental Divide. And you can bet I take the home office deduction.

Most of the articles had been published in professional journals, but a few had appeared in publications intended for a broader audience, magazines like *Scientific American* and *Omni*. Surprisingly, Fontaine, who had spent most of his career at a college I'd never heard of, had written fifteen of them. Of the remaining thirteen, Carolyn Chang had published seven and Underwood six.

Twenty of the articles were highly theoretical. Of those, Fontaine had written twelve, but several had been early in his career and had nothing to do with fractals. Five of Underwood's six fell into the theoretical category, and the remaining three had been authored by Carolyn Chang. The terminology was foreign to me. I had never heard of Julia sets, parameter spaces, or the escape time algorithm, and I guessed I'd need two years of college mathematics to have a prayer of understanding them. Except for my inability to comprehend them, I was unable to detect a common thread in the theoretical writings of the three victims.

I stood to stretch and became hypnotized by the rain. The clouds hung low, obscuring the tops of the snow-capped peaks in the distance. Frightened by the thunder, Buck trotted into my office and sought refuge beneath my desk. I gazed out the window until a passing squirrel on an electrical line turned and gave me a quizzical look. We stared at each other for a good twenty seconds, then he scampered on down the line and I went back to work.

The remaining eight papers were more in the realm of applied mathematics; each had something to do with how fractal geometry was being used in the real world. Of those eight, Fontaine had written three, Carolyn Chang four, and Underwood one.

Fontaine's first paper was a dull narrative about the applications of fractal geometry in electrical engineering, but the other two fascinated me. They were nontechnical discussions of fractal image compression, a technique that makes it possible to store tremendous amounts of data in a small amount of space. An English scientist named Barnsley had developed the concept while searching for more efficient ways to send satellite images back to earth.

Barnsley believed that images of natural objects could be broken down into a small number of component parts by finding similarities among shapes. By digitally coding these shapes instead of using the conventional bit-mapping technique, a color image that would normally consume 1.4 megabytes could be described using just 25 kilobytes. Fontaine claimed this was what had enabled Microsoft to put an encyclopedia with six thousand color photographs on a single CD-ROM.

The technique had also been used to create backgrounds for video games and movies. Suppose you wanted to create an image of the lunar surface. To reconstruct the moon as it actually is, wrote Fontaine, would take the combined memory of ten thousand home computers. But fractals offer another way. Though craters vary in size, their basic shape remains the same. All you need to do is describe that shape to a computer and provide a formula (an algorithm) that tells it to reproduce that shape on varying scales until it has generated something that resembles the moon. To make sure no two craters are identical, you throw a few random numbers into the formula. In effect, the computer creates a "fractal forgery" that mimics the lunar surface without worrying about precise details. I didn't fully understand the mechanics of it, but I got the idea.

I stretched again, caught a glimpse of two green hummingbirds as they darted from one of the feeders I had filled with red nectar, then turned my attention to the writings of Carolyn Chang. The four nontheoretical papers she'd authored were exceptionally well written; she'd had a knack for presenting complex concepts in plain English. Three of them addressed the growing use of fractal geometry in medicine. The articles demonstrated how fractal patterns obtained from medical images were being used to identify and classify many types of disease. As an example, she cited several studies that had found correlations between the fractal dimension of heart rhythms and the presence of disease. She predicted fractals would play an increasingly important role in automating the science of medical diagnosis.

Carolyn's other piece intrigued me because it seemed out of place in a professional journal. It was an essay in which she had expressed the view that fractals could change the way artists and musicians portrayed the world. "Fractal geometry," she wrote, "offers a new way of looking at space and form. Just as the discovery of geometric perspective transformed the way Renaissance painters represented depth on a flat surface, fractals may free artists to portray natural objects as they truly are rather than within the confines of Euclidean concepts of dimension."

Underwood had made one attempt to write for a broader audience, and that had been one too many. He had not possessed Carolyn Chang's skill with the written word. His sentences were long and flowed in no logical sequence. His topic was neural networks, computer programs capable of recognizing fractal patterns. Because of their ability to identify patterns, such programs were valuable tools in efforts to predict the future. According to Underwood, they had been employed in fields ranging from meteorology to finance.

By now it was past seven o'clock. It had taken nearly four hours to review all twenty-eight papers, but I hadn't discerned any pattern or common theme in the writings of the three victims. I pushed the stack to one side, fed the dogs, and started to boil water for spaghetti. Then I placed another call to the cop in Walla Walla. It was an hour earlier on the West Coast. "I think the lieutenant is still at the hospital," said the female dispatcher, "but I can take a message." I left my name again and called it a day.

Surveying my stacks of CDs, I selected a collection of old Jack Guthrie tunes. The cousin of Woody and a distant relative of Arlo, Jack had died in 1948, but I just love those old western songs. Jack Guthrie, Patsy Montana, Jim Silvers, and anyone else who can yodel.

I opened a two-pound package of spinach spaghetti, broke the thin strands in half, and placed the entire contents in the rapidly warming water. I chopped up an onion, some mushrooms, and a garlic clove, then sautéed the mixture in a Teflon pan. No hamburger because I've been flirting with vegetarianism for a few years, though I'm not real consistent about it.

I opened a jar of marinara sauce, added some ingredients of my own, including red wine, cinnamon, and clove, and began to heat it. I wouldn't eat it all, but I could save what I didn't eat for another day. That done, I deposited myself in my recliner and clicked on CNN. Wheat jumped up and sat on my lap. Ten minutes later the phone rang. It was the cop from Walla Walla, Lieutenant Gilbert. I picked up the cordless. "Thanks for returning my call," I said as I lowered the volume on the TV.

"No problem, what can I do for you?" He sounded like a regular guy. Maybe a few years older than me.

"I'm a private investigator. I'd like to talk about Paul Fontaine."

"Three-o-three, that's Colorado, right?"

"Yeah." The 303 area code had once encompassed the entire state, but in less than a decade the influx of people from California and New Jersey had forced whoever runs the deregulated mishmash once known as the telephone company to carve the state into three distinct calling areas. Now 303 covers only Denver/Boulder, and they've started using yet another area code for new numbers in the metropolitan area, so you have to dial ten digits even for local calls. "I've been hired to see if I can find a link between the death of Professor Fontaine and the deaths of two other mathematicians."

"You know the FBI already investigated that?"

"I was a federal prosecutor for years. I don't take the bureau's conclusions as gospel."

He laughed. "Lawyer turned investigator, huh? You're movin' up in the world."

"Long story."

"Well, what do you want to know?"

"What I'd really like is to see your file. I've read everything these people ever wrote, but all I know about their deaths is what was in the papers and what I learned from talking with a detective in Boston."

"You probably know more than me. All I know is, I've got a dead math professor, no motive, and no suspects. And this guy wasn't just shot, he was executed. Single bullet to the back of the head at point-blank range. Then I find out two other math nerds are dead."

"Any chance I could see your file?"

"You really read everything these people ever wrote?"

"All their professional papers."

"I'll bet that was fun."

"Gotta start somewhere," I said.

"True enough," he said. "Tell you what, I'll make you a deal. I'm up to my ass in alligators right now, but if you can find a way up here, I'll show you what I've got and we can kick it around a bit." It was an offer I couldn't refuse.

"Sounds like a plan," I said.

5

On Thursday morning I did something I'd been putting off. I called the Denver office of the FBI. I'd been putting it off because I wanted to learn a little about the case before I called. And because I'm not exactly Mr. Popular down there. On their list of least favorite people I'm right up there with Randy Weaver, Richard Jewell's lawyer, and every congressman on the Waco subcommittee.

"FBI." She had the sterile voice of a government receptionist. In my kitchen, wearing only flannel boxers, I was making a peanut butter and brown sugar sandwich for breakfast as the morning sun filled my kitchen. The Sinus Infection from Hell seemed to have weakened.

"Tim Gombold, please." I was using the speakerphone.

"May I say who's calling?"

"D. B. Cooper. I want to turn myself in." That had been the name used by America's first skyjacker. He had parachuted out the back end of a Boeing 727 in 1971 with $200,000 in twenties tied to his waist and hadn't been seen since.

"Just a moment, sir." She put me on hold. I heard a few clicks and listened to forty-five seconds of static. It was just after eight, so I thought I had a good chance of catching him. He'd just gotten remarried a month or two ago—I'd attended the wedding—but old habits die hard. Gumby likes to get to work early, down some government coffee, and read the morning papers before hitting the pavement. He reads both Denver papers cover to cover each morning. Says he likes to know what's going on.

"Jesus, Pepper," he shouted, "you can't do shit like that." I picked up the receiver.

"Have a sense of humor, Tim."

"I ought to drive up there and shoot you myself for that." I struggled to keep from laughing. "What do you want, for Christ's sake?"

"I want to talk about a case you worked."

"And based on the high esteem the FBI holds you in, you thought we'd be only too happy to oblige?"

"Exactly."

"Which case?"

"The fractal murders."

"Oh, Jesus. That math professor hire you?"

"Say she did." I heard a typewriter in the background. Despite the advent of word processing, every FBI office kept a few IBM Selectrics on hand for use in completing forms that aren't easily scanned.

"Look, Pepper, three people with the same specialty died within six or seven months of each other. Stranger things have happened."

"Which office ran the investigation?"

"We did."

"Denver?" None of the deaths had taken place in Colorado.

"Yeah, your math professor was the one who brought it to our attention, and we needed someone who could explain the mathematics to us. The boss figured it would be easier to run it out of our office."

"Did you check the victims' phone records?"

"No," he said. "With all the budget cuts, we've had to stop doing that. Now we just rely on psychics."

"What I meant was, did the phone records tell you anything?"

"Far as we know, they never spoke with each other, never corresponded."

"Three of the best-known people in their field," I said. "Seems strange they never communicated with each other."

"Pepper," he said, "we ran down every lead and couldn't find a connection. Fontaine takes a shot to the back of the head, the girl in Lincoln gets raped and stabbed. Totally different MO. And there's nothing to indicate Underwood didn't commit suicide."

"While he was jerking off," I said.

"How'd you know that?"

"Give me some credit, Tim."

"It doesn't even matter," he said. "Our guys say it was a typical autoerotic death. Happens every day."

"Not to a Harvard professor," I said. He sighed.

"Listen," he said, "if you can make a buck helping this lady satisfy her conscience or curiosity or whatever, I've got no problem with that, but we put a lot of hours into it and couldn't find anything."

"Can I see your file?"

"You must have balls like an elephant."

"Is that a no?"

"I've got work to do, Pepper." He sighed again.

"Had to ask," I said.

"Besides, Dittmer would have my ass. He's canned two agents in the past six months. We're all walking on eggshells." I knew Dittmer had been the agent in charge of the Denver office for about two years. I knew he'd been a Rhodes scholar. I didn't know much else about him, but I'd heard he'd won the Silver Star while serving as a counterintelligence officer in Vietnam.

"I thought you liked Dittmer," I said.

"He's the sharpest guy I've ever met, but he's changed over the past year. He was in line to be a deputy director, but the director chose a woman with nine years on the job. And just after that, he lost his wife to cancer."

"Jesus."

"I think he's bitter," Gumby said, "but he keeps it bottled up inside and throws himself into his work like every other alpha male. He's all business these days. He's perfect and he expects everyone else to be perfect. No mistakes. He's even started auditing investigations on a random basis to make sure we haven't fucked anything up. Including your fractal case, by the way."

"Sounds like he's been through a lot," I said, "but I'm sorry he's making your life miserable."

"Well, he'll probably retire next year anyhow. At least that's what he says. Wants to buy a boat and live in the Florida Keys."

"Like that would be more fun than busting crack dealers and monitoring Muslim extremists in Denver in the winter."

"To each his own," he replied.

"Hey," I said, "let me ask you one more question about this fractal thing."

"Sure."

"If these deaths were unrelated, what was your jurisdiction in the first place?"

"The Chang girl crossed state lines."

"Kidnapping?"

"Kidnapping, possible conspiracy."

"One more question," I said.

"You just said that."

"Any chance Underwood could've done the other two, then killed himself?"

"No, we checked that. He had good alibis for both murders."

"Thanks, Tim, give my love to Polk."

"I think I'll pass on that," he said. "His divorce trial starts in an hour. Probably doesn't need to hear from you today."

"Whatever," I said. "Thanks for the info."

"Yeah. Good luck."

I clicked on CNN, ate my sandwich, downed a protein shake and my daily regimen of vitamins, then took a quick shower. It had been years since I'd left my job as a federal prosecutor, but I'd worked closely with Gombold in those days. He'd done a stint in D.C. after I'd left, but he'd somehow managed a return assignment to Denver and we'd crossed paths now and then while I was in private practice. A few years younger than me, he'd been a certified public accountant before joining the bureau. He was a wiry man known for his expensive suits, all-business demeanor, and methodical approach. I still considered him the best agent in the Denver office.

The batter clearly beat the throw, but the first-base umpire called him out. "He was safe!" Scott shouted. Scott "Two Toe" McCutcheon. I've known him since I was three and love him like a brother. We were next-door neighbors back when Denver was a cow town. You wouldn't know it by looking at him, but the lean six-footer with the receding hairline was a navy SEAL and holds black belts in karate and aikido. He is my best friend and spiritual cut man. Though he holds a master's degree in astrophysics, he earns his living as a freelance computer consultant and jokingly refers to himself a self-employed techno-geek. I jokingly call him chief of my technical services division.

"That ump should be a trial judge," I said. It was a beautiful Thursday afternoon and we were at Coors Field enjoying game one of a doubleheader between the Rockies and the Dodgers. Two mediocre teams. Top of the seventh, home team down by three. One out. We were right behind first base, seated beside a dozen or so Cub Scouts. "Let's talk business," I said. "I'm deducting this as a business expense."

"Me too," he said. I laughed and sipped my three-dollar diet Coke. I had purchased the tickets.

"Fractals," I said. I'd outlined the case during our drive down from Boulder.

"What do you want to know?"

"Relate them to money." He sat up straight, placed his four-dollar beer on the concrete, and turned to me.

"Fractal mathematics has plenty of commercial applications," he said, "but it's no big secret. Some of these software companies have been using fractal image compression for ten years."

"Medical imaging?"

"Medical imaging, meteorology, metals, geology, engineering—you name it. Any object with an irregular pattern can be represented by a fractal model." One of the Rockies hit a solid shot down the line. We rose with the crowd. The third baseman scooped it up, but bobbled the ball, causing the throw to be late. The umpire saw it differently.

"He was safe!" Scott screamed as he rose to his feet. I said nothing. We'd been fairly verbal about five or six bad calls and I had a hunch both the first-base umpire and the den mother had grown tired of our act. Scott sat down and finished his beer.

"Back to fractals," I said.

"A lot of different companies use fractal-based models," he said. "Some use them internally; most are selling software or services that rely on fractal-based software."

"These companies make money?"

"You bet."

"And this has been going on awhile?"

"Depends on what you mean," he said. "Fractal geometry's been around more than twenty years, but it's only been in the past five or ten that industry has started to explore all the potential applications."

"Why's that?"

"Two reasons," he said. "First, the knowledge of fractal geometry is no longer limited to a few mathematicians. As more students and researchers gained an understanding of it, they began to look for ways to apply it in the real world."

The next batter was called out on strikes and the Dodgers came to bat.

"What's the other reason?" I asked.

"Computers," he said. "If you're going to mine vast amounts of data in search of fractal patterns, you need a computer that's up to the task. Today's computers are so much faster and more powerful than they were even a few years ago—"

"More people have the technology?"

"Absolutely."

A pimple-faced beer vendor with stringy black hair passed us as he made his way up the concrete steps. "You have anything in a raspberry wheat?" Scott asked.

Not realizing Scott was pulling his leg, the youngster replied, "Just Coors." Scott grinned at me, handed him a five, and told him to keep the extra buck.

"This fascinates me," I said. "I'd never heard of fractal geometry before Monday, and now I can't look at a cloud or tree without searching for that 'hidden order' she talked about." Scott just smiled and sipped his beer.

"Assuming," he said, "these people were murdered because of their work with fractals, why them? Every major university has someone who teaches fractal geometry."

"That's the question," I said.

"They never had any contact with each other?"

"That's what Gombold told me."

He pondered that. "Maybe the killer is the connection."

"That's where you come in."

He looked at me. "Lay it on me," he said.

"I need a list of people who might've taken classes from all three victims." He nodded, said nothing.

Meanwhile, the Dodgers's leadoff man had walked and the count on the current batter was three balls, one strike. The next pitch looked good from our angle, but the umpire yelled, "Ball four!"

"Jesus!" Scott screamed as he stood up. "That was right down the goddamned middle."

I remained silent despite the call, but one of the Cub Scouts stood and yelled, "Umpire needs glasses." The den mother slapped his arm and shot us a look as if we'd just flashed ourselves in a nursing home. Scott winked at her and took his seat.

"This guy Fontaine had been teaching at the same place for more than twenty years?" he asked.

"Since seventy-seven."

"What's the name of that school?"

"Whitman College."

"Never heard of it."

"It's a liberal-arts school. One of the best if you believe *U.S. News & World Report.*"

"So we're probably looking for someone who went to school up there, then took graduate classes from the others."

"Probably," I said, "but not necessarily. Could even be someone who taught with all three of them." He said nothing, but I saw the wheels turning. "Can you do it?" I asked.

"Yeah."

"Knew you could," I said. I have considerable respect for Scott's computer-hacking skills. I'd seen him access classified defense databases just for fun and didn't figure he'd have much trouble with enrollment records at a few colleges and universities.

The first game ended in an eight-to-three loss and we didn't stick around for the second. We arrived at Scott's South Boulder home to find Bobbi watering her flowers. She owns a condo, but spends most of her time with Scott. They'd been seeing each other for three years and the arrangement seemed to suit them. Scott had been married briefly when he was in the navy and swears he'll never marry again. Which is too bad because Bobbi is what my father used to call "a real peach." A perky dishwater blonde with a great figure, she works as a property manager for a commercial-leasing company. She doesn't have a college degree, but she's a bright lady with a fine sense of humor.

Scott had never been one for gardening, but Bobbi's TLC had transformed his previously barren yard into the envy of the neighborhood. "Next thing you know," I said, "you'll have pink flamingos on your lawn."

"She likes football and doesn't mind the occasional use of words such as 'skunkfucker,'" he said. "Flamingos are a small price to pay." We exited my truck.

"Hi, handsome," she said to me. She put her arms around me and gave me a hug.

"Why don't you leave this guy," I said, "and check out life with a real man?"

"I thought about it," she said, "but he said marines were poor lovers because they were always thinking about shining their shoes." Scott grinned.

"It's an old joke," I replied. "And I told it to him."

6

FRIDAY EVENING. I was on the front deck with my dogs, continuing my laborious reading of *Being and Time* and listening to Gordon Lightfoot. Feeling a little melancholy. A girlfriend once told me I spent too much time thinking about things. It was true, but it only led to one of those ridiculous chicken-and-egg riddles. Did thinking too much cause my depression or did my depression cause me to think too much?

Tonight I was thinking about the fact that I was forty-four and had never been married. Troy had been married for fifteen years and had two kids. I hadn't had a date in six months. I suppose some of that was my own fault. Plenty of people had tried to set me up, but I hadn't met anyone who tripped my trigger. Once you've been in love, it's hard to settle for mere companionship. I'd been in love once, but that was long ago and she wasn't coming back.

The wind picked up, and I stepped inside to get a jacket. Nederland sits 8,236 feet above sea level. Though it was May, the evenings could still be chilly. When I returned to the deck, the song playing was "If You Could Read My Mind." I've always been struck by one verse of that song:

> I walk away, like a movie star who gets burned in
>   a three-way script;
> Enter number two.
> A movie queen,

to play the scene
of bringing all the good things out in me.

Was that what I was holding out for? "A movie queen to play
the scene of bringing all the good things out in me"?

This introspection was cut short by Buck's sudden barking.
Someone was walking up the path to my home. Tall and thin.
Luther. "Hey, Pepper," he said, "how you doin'?" There was no
mistaking that laid-back Texas drawl.

"Fine, Luther, how are you?" Recognizing him as friend rather
than foe, Buck trotted over and nuzzled him.

"I was just taking a walk and saw you out here." He extended
his hand and offered me a joint, but I declined. Don't get me
wrong, I had smoked dope periodically in college, I had inhaled,
and I had enjoyed it, but these days my drug usage is generally
limited to an occasional glass of red wine.

"Hey, Buck," Luther said as he gave the dog a pat on the head,
"you sure are a good boy." Buck licked his hand, and Luther sat
down beside me. I'd found two old rockers at a garage sale and
refinished them using a rustic pine stain. "That dog always re-
minds me of Astro," said Luther. "You know, from *The Jetsons.*"

"'Rastro,'" I corrected him, using my best cartoon dog voice.

"Rastro," he agreed.

Luther is one of the last hippies in America. I live in a newer
log home on the edge of town and he lives in a small house a few
hundred yards west of me. It was built in the thirties as a summer
cabin, but they've added on to it. He and his wife own it, but others live there too and the composition of the group is constantly
changing. I guess Luther and Missy are my next-door neighbors.
Come to think of it, I guess they're all my next-door neighbors. I
don't know how old Luther is, but he must be pushing fifty.

When I describe Luther as a hippie, I don't mean to disparage him in any way. He's one of the nicest guys I've ever met and he's a great musician, but it's the best word I can think of. He wears his increasingly gray hair in a ponytail, and his ragged jeans are covered with patches. He owns two vintage Volkswagen vans, one of which looks like it was painted by hyenas on acid. I'm not sure it runs, but I've seen people sleep in it for weeks at a time during the summer.

A lot of aging hippies live in Nederland. The town is nestled in the mountains fifteen miles west of Boulder. In the sixties and early seventies, Boulder was a happening place. There were regular protests, and everywhere you went you saw head shops and Marxist bookstores. Then Vietnam ended and Nixon resigned. With no cause to unite it, the hippie movement died. As more and more people flocked to Colorado, land prices skyrocketed and yuppies gained control of Boulder's political machinery. Now all you see down there are gourmet coffee shops and New Age bookstores. The diehard hippies moved to Nederland. And now you know the rest of the story.

I moved here two years ago. I'd become increasingly disenchanted with the practice of law. Long hours, high stress, ungrateful clients. I hated all insurance adjusters, most of my clients, many of my fellow lawyers, some judges, and all the politicians who competed with one another to propose ever tougher drug laws while at the same time refusing to appropriate money for prevention or treatment. I was burned out. Then I found myself charged with manslaughter.

Though I was ultimately acquitted, that episode had been the proverbial last straw. Life's too short to do something you don't enjoy. I decided to leave law altogether. My partners were shocked, but they purchased my interest on favorable terms and the deal left me with a nice little nest egg. Interest rates were low and I had always wanted to live in the mountains. With my Marine Corps haircut and a business card identifying myself as a private eye, it took a while for people to warm up to me, but now it feels like home. Up here it's live and let live.

Luther and I talked awhile, then sat quietly, enjoying the breeze and the scent of the pines. "Hey, Luther," I finally said, "you know anything about fractals?"

"A little," he said. "Missy's a big fractal freak. She plays with them all the time on our Mac." When she's not reading tarot cards or consulting with other locals concerning various New Age forms of healing, Luther's wife works as a freelance graphic artist. "She can do some far-out stuff."

"Ever hear of anyone using fractals to make music?" In addition to whatever else he does, Luther plays lead guitar for a band called the Stress Monsters. They're actually pretty good.

"Yeah, now that you mention it. You remember ELO?"

"Electric Light Orchestra?"

"Yeah."

"I remember."

"Their cello player was a dude named McDowell. He used fractal patterns to compose a ballet. It's called 'Tijuana' or something like that. I've got it at home if you want to hear it." I had nothing else to do, so I put Buck and Wheat inside and gave Luther a vague outline of the case as we walked through the pines to his home. "Freaky," was all he said.

There are usually several dogs lazing around in front of Luther's house, but tonight I saw just one. A shepherd mix. The front door was open, but the house appeared empty. I had been inside it only once or twice, so I wandered around while he searched for the tape. The sofa was ready for the Salvation Army and there was an air mattress on the living-room floor. His state-of-the-art sound system consumed an entire wall and I wondered how he could afford it. The Stress Monsters didn't figure to have a great compensation package.

I made my way into the kitchen and noticed a Phish calendar on the wall by the back door. "Here it is," Luther said as he returned to the living room. I sat on the couch and he leaned back in an old recliner. The music was soft and flowing. We could have fallen asleep, but Missy and a younger woman came through the front door before we got the chance. Missy wore an ankle-length skirt, the younger woman wore faded jeans. Both barefoot. "Hey, Missy," Luther said, "what's the name of this song?"

"Teawaroa."

"What does that mean?" I asked.

"It's Maori," she said. "It means 'great river.'"

7

As a marine I had learned that when you assume something, it makes an ASS out of U and ME. I had never been to the Pacific Northwest, but I had assumed Walla Walla was near Seattle. I was wrong. I spent most of Sunday getting there. Denver to Salt Lake to Boise to Spokane, then a puddle jumper the rest of the way. One of those twin-engine jobs where only a flimsy curtain separates the cockpit from the passenger cabin. On the plus side, I had avoided flying United. Call it coincidence, but I got a good view of the Columbia River just before we landed. It looked like a great river to me.

To say the airport was small would be an understatement. It reminded me of one I'd seen on an episode of *Green Acres*. I rented a nondescript Mercury Cougar and drove into town.

It was a surprisingly pleasant little city. About thirty thousand inhabitants according to the sign. Five hours southeast of Seattle and three hours south of Spokane, it sits at the foot of the Blue Mountains. It's wheat country, and the dust from the fields gave the late-afternoon sun a pastel orange glow.

I entered town on what must have been the newer part of Main Street. Every fast-food chain known to man had staked a claim. I continued on through, past the college, and soon found myself downtown, a few square blocks of banks, insurance agencies, Realtors, and mom-and-pop businesses. I located the police station so I'd know where to meet Gilbert in the morning.

Main Street ended abruptly, and I was forced to choose between turning right (three miles to the state pen) or left (seven miles to Oregon). I took the third option, made a U-turn and headed back to fast-food alley. Found a motel offering cable TV and a free continental breakfast, paid cash, registered as J. P. Sartre just for the hell of it, and called my brother to check on my boys. He assured me they were fine, so I walked across the street to a pizza place where a dozen college kids were celebrating the approaching end of the school year. I ordered a small pie with garlic and mushrooms, a dinner salad, and a large diet Coke.

"Is Pepsi okay?" the girl asked.

Not wanting to be a troublemaker, I said, "Pepsi's fine." She handed me a tall glass and told me to help myself. I put some crushed ice in it, filled it with pop, and found a table by the window.

The sun hadn't quite set when I finished my meal, so I took a walk. The lilacs were in bloom and smelled heavenly. The residential areas were beautiful; most of the homes were older and many boasted bountiful gardens. Children played and neighbors chatted. Residents nodded or said hello as I passed. I was in a Norman Rockwell painting.

I found my way to the Whitman campus. Ivy covered most of the buildings and a small creek traversed the grounds. If I hadn't known better, I'd have sworn I was at one of those liberal-arts colleges in New England. Proving once again what happens when you assume something, I had assumed the college was named for Walt Whitman, but a bronze plaque at the base of a statue informed me it had been named for Marcus Whitman, a missionary killed by the Cayuse in 1847 for what they saw as his role in a fatal measles epidemic. Despite my Unitarian tendencies, I didn't know much about Walt, and I'd never heard of Marcus. As Whitmans go, my favorite has always been Slim.

From the campus I continued downtown. It was as dead as a jackrabbit on I-80 on a cold winter night, but I found a tavern I couldn't resist. The decor in McDuffie's was vintage 1945. The newest thing in the place was a faded portrait of John Kennedy in a two-dollar frame above the entrance. I guessed McDuffie was Catholic. A few old-timers sat at the bar. It was a dive, but it had a three-Hank jukebox. I sipped tonic water, ate free popcorn, and spent the evening listening to Hank Williams, Hank Thompson, and Hank Snow.

I bid McDuffie farewell at eleven and began walking back on a street parallel to Main Street, but one block over. I heard mariachi music coming from one of the taverns I passed and saw a few unshaven migrant workers milling around outside the entrance. I took my hands out of my pockets—just in case they harbored any thoughts of mugging the gringo—but they ignored me and I felt guilty for thinking they might try it.

Did some channel surfing at the motel, then climbed into my dog-less bed and picked up *Being and Time*. Having started the damned book, I was determined to finish it.

As I've said, Heidegger felt the mystery of life was that something, rather than nothing, exists. He called this basic condition of existence Being and called everything else beings. He argued traditional philosophy had erred by focusing on the individual. Rather than recognizing our place within the world—our status as one being among all other beings—Heidegger believed our man-centered philosophy caused us to view the world as something that exists for and because of us.

If Donald Underwood had been a poor writer, Martin Heidegger had been a terrible one. Maybe the book had been easier to comprehend in the author's native tongue, but I didn't speak German and five pages was my limit. I caught myself nodding off, put the book down on the bedside table, and turned off the reading lamp.

I woke up around four-thirty. Another dream about Joy. A strange dream. I was plummeting to earth and Joy was soaring like an eagle, carrying a CARE package, and shouting, "Dozen, dozen." Joy and I had lived together for two years while we attended law school. She'd been dead more than twenty years, but still visited me regularly in my dreams.

Unable to get back to sleep, I went for a predawn run and soon found myself on a country road. I reviewed the dream in my mind as I ran. Falling to earth could symbolize how I'd felt since Joy's death, but I couldn't make any sense of the rest of it. A dozen what? After a while I let it go. I could've run forever in the cool morning air—especially at that altitude—but a large and spirited farm dog appeared at the three-mile point and suggested I turn back. I took the hint and reversed course. Shaved, showered, and took advantage of the free breakfast.

The police station, a monument to cream-colored brick, had probably been constructed at about the same time McDuffie had last redecorated. I arrived at nine sharp. Gilbert was a tall man, six-two. Maybe two hundred pounds. I liked him the moment I saw him. His left forearm bore a globe-and-anchor tattoo. He had a full head of hair, but spent a disproportionate amount of his salary on Grecian Formula. He wore navy blue polyester pants, a light blue shirt, and a maroon tie that had seen better days. A black nylon holster kept his nine-millimeter pistol snug against his hip. I guessed he was in his late forties. From the way he was smoking, I didn't think it likely he would make it to his late fifties.

"Call me Dick," he said as he greeted me. I commented on his tattoo and told him I'd been a marine JAG. "Well," he said in a raspy voice, "you get points for bein' a jarhead, but you lose points for bein' an officer." I laughed. He led me back to his office, a nondescript room decorated in early cop. Stacks of papers scattered about. Bowling trophies graced the tops of his old metal filing cabinets. The obligatory picture of the wife and kids sat on a shelf behind his desk.

We exchanged small talk for a few minutes, but the phone rang and he took it. "Shit," he told the caller, "it's gonna be another fine day." When he finished, he put down the receiver and handed me an accordion file. "Listen," he said, "I've got some things to do. Here's my entire file. We don't have room for you here, so take it someplace and come back in a few hours. We'll talk over lunch."

I walked two blocks, to the courthouse, found that there was a small law library on the first floor, and further found that it was unoccupied. I parked myself at a sturdy oak table and began to read.

Paul Fontaine had lived on Boyer Street. When he failed to show for classes on the first Monday of the school year last September, one of his colleagues, Professor Max LeBlanc, made repeated calls to his home. When he didn't appear on Tuesday, LeBlanc tried his parents' farm, then walked the few blocks from the campus to Fontaine's home. Climbed the steps to the porch, peered between the curtains into the living room, puked his guts out, then notified Walla Walla's finest.

The pathologist's report indicated Fontaine had been shot once in the back of the head at point-blank range. The angle of entry, blood-spatter patterns, and position of the body all suggested he'd been made to kneel down. Executed in his own living room. Her best guess was that it had taken place late Sunday evening. He'd been dead at least thirty-six hours when the authorities entered his home.

They had found a slug embedded in the floor near Fontaine's head. It had entered his skull at a downward angle and exited in the vicinity of his mouth. It had been fired from a .38-caliber pistol, but that wasn't much help. You can purchase a .38 at any pawnshop in America for less than a hundred bucks. Gilbert had checked on recent sales around the state, but that had produced no viable suspects.

There was no sign of forced entry and none of the neighbors had heard anything. No appliances had been stolen and not much was missing. Fontaine had favored wearing an expensive watch, and a gold ring evidencing his membership in a mathematical society. Those were gone, as was any cash he'd had in his wallet.

The evidence suggested he'd been composing a letter to his oldest sister on the evening of his murder. The computer in his upstairs study was still on when the police arrived. A police technician had examined it, as well as the computer in Fontaine's office, but found nothing remarkable. Those efforts became significant when the feds entered the case because they had yielded no evidence of any correspondence with Carolyn Chang or Donald Underwood.

Gilbert and his colleagues had interviewed dozens of people. I studied the notes of each interview, but nothing jumped out at me. Nobody knew why anyone would want Fontaine dead. He had been a likable man with a good sense of humor. Bottom line, the killer was still out there. I bought ten dollars in dimes from the county treasurer, then photocopied every document in Gilbert's file.

While at the courthouse, I decided to see if Fontaine's estate had gone through probate. The probate court was on the second floor, and the clerk of the probate court was a blue-hair named Edna who'd probably been working there thirty years. She was gossiping with a much younger civil servantress when I approached.

"Good morning," I said. "I'd like to see a probate file on a man named Paul Fontaine. He died last year."

"Are you an attorney?" she asked. It was a public record and I had a right to see it, but practicing law had taught me that court clerks are among the most powerful people in the world. You piss them off at your peril.

"I hate to admit it," I said with a smile, "but I am." I showed her my plastic American Bar Association card—the one with the Hertz #1 Club logo on the back. I positioned my thumb so she couldn't see my name. The card had expired, but she didn't notice. Or didn't care.

"Not from around here," she remarked.

"Doing some work for an insurance company," I lied.

"Just a moment." She disappeared, and I was left to exchange small talk with her protégée, a wholesome cutie excited about her upcoming marriage to a rodeo cowboy. Edna reappeared two minutes later with a thin file in her right hand. Before entrusting it to me, she slid a checkout card across the counter and instructed me to fill it in. I scrawled something illegible and she handed me the file. "File's due back at four," she said as she tapped a sign with the eraser on her pencil. Attorneys who didn't return files on time would lose their checkout privileges.

"I'll have it back in an hour," I said. I winked at her, took the stairs back down to the first floor, bought a cold diet Coke from a vending machine, and returned to the library. I had never been fond of probate work, but I knew what to look for.

Fontaine had executed his last will and testament more than ten years prior to his death. A will executed shortly before his death might have indicated that he had anticipated trouble, but a will made more than ten years ago suggested he probably hadn't had any reason to believe his life was in danger.

His will left everything to his parents, both of whom were still living at the time of his death. The only other document of interest was the inventory of assets. In addition to a home valued at more than $200,000 and his half-million-dollar interest in the wheat operation, Fontaine had owned stock in nineteen corporations. No mutual funds. All told, the value of his estate had exceeded two million dollars. Not bad for a math professor.

I copied the entire file and walked upstairs to return it to Edna. She wasn't there, but the young girl was. As I handed her the file, a yellow sticky note fell from it. I picked it up to give it to her and noticed a handwritten message:

Fax copies of all documents to
Special Agent Mike Polk
FBI—Denver
(303) 877-8121

"Any idea when that was written?" I asked. She took the note and studied it.

"I remember this," she said as Edna returned to the room and joined her younger colleague at the counter. "He called Friday and I faxed everything the same day."

"Are you working on the same case?" Edna asked.

"Same case," I said, "except the FBI's done with it and I'm not." I asked her to photocopy the note for me, then drove to what had been Fontaine's home as I pondered why Polk would've sought copies of the probate documents after the bureau had concluded its investigation. Maybe the local agents had neglected to obtain them and the bureau just wanted to be sure its file was complete. Or maybe the Denver office had managed to lose them and wanted replacement copies.

Fontaine's residence was an impressive white structure with tall columns. Just three blocks from the college. Probably built in the early part of the century. Similar homes sat on each side of it, but none was separated by more than thirty feet. There was a covered porch complete with porch swing. Roses were in bloom in front of and along both sides of the house. The same home in Boulder would cost half a million dollars.

I walked up the seven wooden steps and peered inside. Toys were scattered about, but nothing in the probate file indicated the home had been sold, so I assumed it had been rented to a family with young children. I rang the bell, received no response, and walked around back. The windows were old and large, but high off the ground. Thorny rosebushes nearly reached the windows. Not an easy way to gain entry.

I was back at the station by eleven, but Gilbert wasn't, so I took a chair and read *USA Today*. Two scruffy teens occupied the bench next to me, their heads down, waiting quietly for their parents. "Is that the Group W bench?" I asked the desk sergeant.

"Huh?"

"Never mind," I said. Evidently too young to remember "Alice's Restaurant."

Gilbert walked in at eleven-fifteen, flicked his cigarette butt into an ash can, and said, "Hope I didn't keep you waiting too long."

"No problem," I said as I folded the paper. He walked to the counter and retrieved his messages.

"Daughter's eight months' pregnant and she's having some problems, so the doc put her in the hospital. Wants her to stay there till she pops the kid. Seems like I spend half my time over there." He placed the pink message slips in his pocket and said, "Let's get some lunch." I followed him out and donned my aviator's sunglasses. With my haircut, they make me look like a Secret Service agent on steroids, but I can't stand bright sun in my eyes.

"How many kids do you have?" I asked.

"Three. Oldest boy's an architect in Seattle." He paused to light another cigarette. "Daughter's twenty-two. This is her second child; she had a rough time with the first. My other boy's a student at the college here; costs an arm and a leg, let me tell you."

We ate at a surprisingly good deli. Sat outside and watched the cars and people on Main Street. Everyone knew Gilbert. Some from Rotary, others from church or the Little League team he coached. He ordered a ham and cheese; I opted for turkey and Swiss. A spinning electrical sign on top of the tallest building gave the time as 11:34 and the temperature as 77.

He took a deep drag on his cigarette and said, "You're a man with a past."

"I'd have been disappointed if you hadn't checked me out."

"I got the police reports from Denver," he said. "I can't understand why they charged you in the first place."

"I was a pretty well-known criminal-defense lawyer," I said. "I'd been a vocal critic of the DA, and it finally caught up with me."

"Fucker comes at me with a knife and I ain't got a weapon, one of us is goin' home dead."

"Water under the bridge," I said. A college girl in jeans arrived with our drinks and sandwiches, and Gilbert switched topics.

"So what do you think about this thing?" he asked.

"No forced entry," I said. "I'd guess Fontaine knew the killer. Or felt no reason to fear him."

"Maybe," he said. "Around here nobody locks their doors, so it's hard to say."

"Pretty pathetic robbery," I said.

"Christ, the guy's credit cards are still in his wallet. Silver candlesticks on the dining-room table."

"Don't forget the nineteenth-century coins on display in the study. It looks like the killer never went upstairs."

"If he did, it was before he pulled the trigger. There wasn't a speck of blood up there."

"If we exclude the possibility of a psycho, somebody wanted him dead."

"Guy had no enemies," he said.

"Girlfriends?"

"Not really. He had a thing with one of his students year before last, but she'd already graduated when he took the bullet. She's teaching high school math in Portland. I talked to her, but she didn't have much to say. He was a sweet man, it was a real tragedy, and all that."

"I didn't see any of that in the file."

"The notes are in my office. He'd slept with some others over the years, but the college doesn't need that kind of publicity. I'll give you copies before you leave."

"I looked at his probate file," I said. "He didn't appear to have had any financial problems."

"No, he'd done pretty well in the stock market. And his family owns the biggest wheat farm in the county. That's big business up here, let me tell you; ain't none of them farmers hurting." The waitress refilled our drinks, and Gilbert extinguished his cancer stick. "People don't know it, but this is one of the wealthiest counties in the nation."

"Why fake a robbery," I said, "unless you're trying to disguise your motive or lead us down a false trail? And if you're going to fake a robbery, why not take those coins?"

"The more he takes, the more he has to carry."

"The more he takes, the greater his ties to Fontaine. If somebody finds those coins in his possession, he's got some 'splainin' to do."

"You do a mean Ricky Ricardo."

"Thanks."

We kicked it around for forty-five minutes, and I explained what little I had learned about fractal geometry. Fractal image compression, medical imaging, and all that. "Sounds like there's money in it," he said.

"There is," I said. "And I'm guessing that's why these people are dead."

"Well," he said, "I'm no math whiz—never went past high school—but if you're willing to tackle that angle, I'll help you any way I can." I finished my sandwich and told him there was one favor he could do for me.

"What's that?" he said.

"Call the homicide cop in Boston. He wouldn't share any information with me, but he'll probably share it with you."

"Probably," he agreed. He finished his pickle, then lit yet another cigarette. The smoke annoyed me—it's one of my pet peeves—but I kept my feelings to myself.

"Tell me about Fontaine's student assistant," I said.

"Ronald Bartels. An aspiring math nerd."

"Mind if I talk to him?"

"No. I interviewed him twice, but that was before the other two turned up dead. He's the one told me about the girl in Portland."

"I'd like to know more about Fontaine's research. Maybe he can shed some light on it."

"Knock yourself out," he said. I paid for lunch, and he gave me directions to Bartels's room. "You'd better hurry," he said, "most of these kids will be leaving town by the end of the week."

It was early afternoon and a festival atmosphere permeated the campus. Loud music and plenty of coeds in colorful bikinis soaking up the sun. I caught myself looking more than once and reminded myself I was old enough to have a daughter in college. It didn't stop me from looking.

Bartels lived in Douglas Hall, a dormitory named after William O. Douglas. A plaque indicated the former Supreme Court justice had attended the school, but the building's cornerstone told me it had been constructed a year before his death. His untimely demise had probably deprived the college of an opportunity to name the building after a wealthy alum in return for a generous donation.

The dorm itself was clean, quiet, and utterly unremarkable. When I'd been in college, you couldn't walk through a dorm without smelling dope, stepping in beer, or seeing Farrah Fawcett. Now pot is out of fashion, the drinking age is twenty-one, and Farrah is over fifty. Times change.

I found Bartels's room and knocked, but there was no answer. I knocked again, hard, but the result was the same, so I made my way to the math-and-science building. It was a newer structure with a copper facade along the roof. A long metal bike rack was positioned outside the entrance. Some of the windows were open, the faculty members apparently enjoying the nice weather and/or the music pouring forth from the dorms.

Max LeBlanc and two other math professors agreed to speak to me, but nobody could shed any light on the mystery. Fontaine had spent the summer running his parents' farm. If he'd been involved with a woman at the time of his death, nobody knew about it. They let me see what had been his office, but it had since been assigned to another mathematician who had rearranged things to suit her needs.

My next stop was the student union. I bought a large diet Coke at the fountain, ignored the NO FOOD OR DRINK sign, and meandered through the student bookstore. I love bookstores. Sometimes I think owning a bookstore would be the perfect job.

"May I help you?" a woman asked. Too old to be a student, but not bad looking. There was something sultry about her in spite of her glasses. Maybe the bored wife of a faculty member.

"Just browsing," I said. Wishing I didn't smell like cigarette smoke.

"That's fine, sir," she said with a smile. "If you need anything, please let me know." She turned and started to walk away.

"Wait a minute," I said. "There is something you can help me with. Where are the textbooks for your math classes?"

"Right over here," she said. I followed. I found Fontaine's text on fractal geometry, removed one from the top of the stack, and opened the cover: $44.95. I put it down and clutched my chest as if having a heart attack. She laughed.

"I'll take it," I said. I handed it to her and followed her to the register.

"Will that be all?"

"Trust me," I said, "this'll keep me busy for a while."

I walked back to Douglas Hall and heard faint music from Bartels's room, but my knock went unanswered. I gave the knob a gentle twist and peeked inside. Disaster area. Clothes and fast-food wrappers everywhere. Bartels and his roommate had built a loft to make better use of the space, and I noticed a young man asleep on the bunk. I rapped the open door a few times with my knuckles and he began to stir. A dark-haired young man sat up, rubbed his eyes, and tried to focus. He wore beige shorts and a T-shirt with "Just Do It" printed across the front.

"Are you Ronald Bartels?"

"Yeah," he said. I guessed he was six feet tall. About one hundred sixty pounds. He was a handsome kid, but had one of the worst haircuts I'd ever seen. It looked like someone had just taken scissors and snipped their way around his head to create a poor replica of Ringo Starr circa 1964.

"My name's Pepper Keane. I'm a private investigator." That caught his interest. "Lieutenant Gilbert suggested I talk with you." He stretched his arms.

"Sure," he said, "no problem. Sorry about the mess. We've been taking finals all week." He made no effort to climb down and both chairs were covered with clothes, so I took the liberty of sitting on a footlocker that evidently doubled as a coffee table.

"I'd like to talk about Professor Fontaine. I'm trying to determine if there is a connection between his murder and the deaths of two other mathematicians."

"Yeah, the FBI mentioned that when they questioned me. Weird, huh?"

"When was that?"

"I don't know, a month or two ago."

"What did they ask you?"

"Which time?" he replied.

"They questioned you more than once?"

"Yeah," he said. "Two agents from Spokane came down here maybe six or eight weeks ago and spent a day with me. Then an agent from Denver interviewed me by phone, maybe a week or two later, and asked the same questions all over again. I told him I'd already been interviewed, but he didn't want to hear it."

"You get his name?"

"No, but I should have. He was kind of a dick." An agent from Denver. Kind of a dick. That sure sounded like Polk. Why would Polk reinterview a witness who had been questioned at length and in person by two Spokane agents? Standard practice would be for those agents to prepare a Form 302—"FBI Interview Summary"— and forward it to the office handling the investigation. I put that question aside and continued questioning Bartels.

"I'm sure they asked you whether Professor Fontaine had had any contact with Carolyn Chang or Donald Underwood?"

"Yeah," he said, "they asked about that. I told them I wasn't aware of any, but I was just his student assistant."

"What exactly does a student assistant do?" I had never been a student assistant, though I had earned a little extra money in law school as a bouncer at a place called the Grizzly Bar.

"Grade tests, work with freshmen who are having problems."

"Do you get paid for that?"

"Not enough," he said. I smiled.

"What about his research and writing, were you involved with those things?"

"A little. We were always getting comments about the textbook, and one of my jobs was to organize those and make notes about changes we might consider in the next edition. Sometimes he'd ask me to get articles from the library or proofread something, things like that."

"When was the next edition scheduled to be published?"

"There wasn't a firm date, but it was still several years off. I think the last edition came out a few years ago." I felt the footlocker starting to sag a little under my weight, so I stood and faced Bartels.

"Was Professor Fontaine working on anything new before he died? Anything he hadn't written about in the past?"

"Not that I know of. To be honest, I never saw him on campus last summer. He spent most of his time managing the farm."

"How do you know that?" One of the most important questions an investigator can ask.

"I stayed here last summer and worked the harvest for him. He loved that farm; if a combine or tractor broke down, he'd be out there with a toolbox. Wouldn't let anyone else work on 'em."

"He just gave up academics for the summer?"

"For the most part. He'd read the *Wall Street Journal* every day, but that was like a hobby. He enjoyed charting his stocks and following the market."

We talked another twenty minutes and he gave me his story. A native of Missoula, he was finishing his junior year and would work for the Fontaines again over the summer. Long-term plans included graduate school and a career in engineering.

When I couldn't think of any more questions, I gave him my card and asked him to call me if he thought of anything that might be relevant. I was just leaving when I heard my name. "Mr. Keane?"

"Yes?"

"Who's paying you to do all this?"

"My client was a friend of one of the victims," I said. I didn't tell him she was a math professor. Or that she lived in Boulder. Someone was killing mathematicians; I didn't know who or why, but I didn't want to draw unnecessary attention to my client. Wouldn't be prudent.

When I returned to the motel in the late afternoon, a man in a gray suit was waiting for me. My size, my age. The odds were two to one that he was the FBI's resident agent in Walla Walla. "You must be J. P. Sartre," he said with a smile. I approached my room and opened the door. He followed me, but stopped just outside the doorway. I removed my tie and began to unbutton my shirt. "I'm Wallace Gibbs," he said. He removed his credentials from his suit pocket and held them out for me. "I'm the FBI's resident agent in Walla Walla."

"Sounds like a cush job," I said. "I've been here two days and haven't seen a single federal crime."

"It's a good gig," he admitted. "Mind if I ask about your interest in Paul Fontaine?"

"You must be friends with Edna down at the courthouse."

"She knows my number," he said. I continued changing into casual clothes, even though the door was wide open for all the world—or at least all of Walla Walla—to see my Scooby-Doo boxer shorts. "I'm guessing you didn't pay cash for the rental car," he added, "so I can get your real name out at the airport if you don't want to tell me."

"My name's Pepper Keane," I said. "I'm a private investigator from Colorado." I handed him one of my cards. "Tell Polk I said hi."

"You know him?"

"Since law school."

"I went to high school with him. Had our twenty-fifth reunion last year."

"Was he a dick in high school?" I asked.

"Yeah, he was," he replied. "And he hadn't changed much when I saw him last year." I pulled a pair of khaki shorts from my suitcase and said nothing. "Care to tell me the identity of your client?" he asked.

"Nope."

He sort of grinned and nodded his head up and down. "Well," he said as he began walking away, "it was good talking with you." I began to close the door. "Hey," he added, "I really enjoyed *The Age of Reason*."

8

How was Walla Walla?" asked Scott.

"It's 'the city so beautiful they named it twice.'"

"Is that what they say?"

"That's what it says on the police cars."

"That's better than 'to serve and protect.'"

"It says that too."

"Oh." It was a sunny Wednesday morning and we were enjoying bagels and coffee in Boulder at Moe's Bagels, on Broadway. Wearing shorts, sitting at an outside table. Moe's is located in an old strip mall that has managed to thrive by embracing its 1950s architecture and leasing space only to trendy stores and restaurants. It's a popular place.

"I hit it off with the detective up there," I said. "Another ex-marine." I summarized what I'd learned.

"Two million dollars is a lot of money for a math professor," he said.

"He invested wisely." I handed him my copy of the inventory of assets. He studied it.

"We should be in the wheat business," he said.

"Yeah."

"Bought stocks instead of mutual funds. Kind of risky."

"A couple of people told me he liked to play the market. Can't argue with the results."

"Guess not," he said as he handed the document back to me.

"What did you learn?" I asked.

"You owe me," he said.

"Noted."

"Getting into the databases was easy, but lots of people have passed through the doors of those schools since seventy-seven, so I had to design a little program to search for matching names and Social Security numbers. I found three people who fit our parameters. Then I went back and dug up as much as I could on each of them."

"I might have to promote you to vice president for information services," I said. He bit into his bagel, then retrieved some notes from his portfolio.

"Number one is Gail Olgilve. Majored in math at Whitman and graduated in ninety-two. Did graduate work at Nebraska for two years, then on to Harvard for her doctorate. Now teaching in Madison, Wisconsin. She never took classes from Carolyn Chang, and her academic trail suggests she never had much interest in fractals or any other type of geometry."

"I don't think our killer's a woman," I said, recalling that Carolyn Chang had been raped.

"Me either, but I wanted to be thorough." He went inside for more coffee, then struck up a conversation with a sophisticated-looking blonde at another table. In her early thirties, wearing a great tan, a little too much makeup, and lots of gold jewelry. Her German shepherd lay at her feet as she perused the Boulder *Daily Camera*. Scott began by asking the dog's age, then used his Brad Pitt smile to get the basics. "She's single," he said when he finally returned.

"High maintenance," I said. "Tell me about the other two." He looked at me as if to say, Suit yourself, then glanced at his notes.

"The next name that pops up is Mark Sweeney. He spent a year at Whitman, but finished his undergraduate work at Harvard, where he too majored in math. Graduated in eighty-seven. Joins the navy's nuclear submarine program and spends his life doing something that is not just a job, it's an adventure." He handed me some documents. They were copies of Sweeney's officer-effectiveness reports.

"How in the hell did you—"

"Proving once again that no good deed goes unpunished, the navy rewards Sweeney's outstanding performance by sending him to Nebraska to teach ROTC for three years. While there, he takes graduate classes from Carolyn Chang. He earns his master's and goes back to driving subs. Does that for eighteen months, then lands an assignment at Annapolis. By this time, he's a lieutenant commander."

"Jesus, Scott, that's great work."

"I thought so."

"We'll want to take a hard look at him."

"No need to," he said. "He's dead. Struck by lightning last August. Plenty of witnesses." He handed me a newspaper article he'd downloaded describing the incident. Sweeney had caught a lightning bolt while jogging.

"How'd you learn he was dead?"

"Navy officers get effectiveness reports every six months, so there should've been another report in his file. That made me curious, so I called Annapolis and pretended to be an old classmate. A lady in the math department told me what had happened."

"Death," I said, "the ultimate alibi."

"Cheer up," he said, "I haven't told you about bachelor number three."

"By all means."

"Guy's name is Thomas Tobias. Majors in math at Whitman and earns graduate degrees at Harvard. Despite his credentials, he can't find a tenure-track position, so he takes a temporary appointment at Nebraska. After that, he returns to Whitman for a year to take the place of a professor on sabbatical. Then he lands a job at NYU."

"Let me guess," I said. "African bees stung him to death at Yankee Stadium just hours before Fontaine was murdered?"

"No," he replied, "Tom's case is considerably more interesting than that."

"Why is that?" I asked. He leaned forward.

"Because the son of a bitch has disappeared from the face of the earth."

Later that morning I broke down and called the High Country Clinic. The Sinus Infection from Hell had returned with a vengeance and I'd decided it was time to go nuclear on it. I'd never had reason to visit Nederland's only clinic, but they got me in that afternoon. I completed my health history, told the receptionist I'd quit my HMO as a result of a billing dispute and would just pay cash, then considered the case as I sat in the waiting area.

Scott had done first-rate work. The database maintained by Harvard's alumni office had alerted him to Tobias's employment at NYU. He'd then phoned NYU and learned Tobias hadn't taught there since the end of the school year a few years ago. He'd made no other telephone inquiries, but tried several commercial locator services, coming up empty each time. He'd even run Tobias through Social Security's master death file. He'd offered to keep on it, but without knowing more about Tobias, Scott's skills would be of limited value. At a minimum, I'd have to disregard the uncertainty principle and make some phone calls. Worst-case scenario, I was going to New York.

The doctor was behind schedule, so I picked up *Being and Time* and continued plodding through it one page at a time. Heidegger's technical expression for man is "*Dasein*," which means "being-there." *Dasein*, Heidegger declared, is the only being capable of raising questions about existence. We are unique because our existence is an issue for us. He wrote:

The being that exists is man. Man alone exists. Rocks are, but they do not exist. Trees are, but they do not exist. Horses are, but they do not exist. Angels are, but they do not exist. God is, but he does not exist.

I read that passage several times, and I understood the difference between a man and a horse, but I couldn't help but wonder if the horse wasn't better off because it didn't have to wonder about the meaning of life or the inevitability of death—issues that had followed me for years, particularly since Joy's death.

A door opened and I heard my name. I followed a female LPN to an examining room. Young and reasonably attractive, but seemingly detached. She took my blood pressure, said it was a little high, then asked the reason for my visit. I told her the cuff wasn't big enough for my arm, then gave an abbreviated history of my illness. She took it down, then left and promised that the doctor would be along shortly.

The doc turned out to be a slender young carrot-top named Cameron Edwards who had agreed to practice in a rural area in return for the state's assistance in paying for his education. Instead of sending him to some godforsaken outpost on Colorado's eastern plains, the state had set him up in a town twenty-five minutes from Boulder and five minutes from a ski area. I described my symptoms and told him I had a sinus infection.

He examined me, then said, "We see a lot of allergies this time of year." I assured him I had no history of allergies, but he felt the best plan was to start me on an antihistamine and a decongestant. He seemed like a decent young man, but I'd spent a good chunk of one year fighting a sinus infection that had ended in surgery. I recounted that experience and suggested that if he wasn't going to prescribe an antibiotic, he'd darn well better take X rays, draw blood, and perform a throat culture. After a brief lecture on the dangers of overusing antibiotics, he relented. I was glad he didn't take my blood pressure then. I might've popped the cuff.

Being a private eye is not what it once was. I've never had to stand on a dark corner in a trench coat with a revolver in my pocket, and I've never had a sultry blonde sashay into my office and lay down a wad of cash. This being the Information Age, I spent that evening preparing letters to the Alabama Department of Public Safety, the Wyoming Department of Revenue, and forty-eight other state agencies sandwiched between the ends of the alphabet. Not to mention the District of Columbia. Requesting driver's license information on Thomas Payne Tobias, date of birth 2/5/66.

And that was about as glamorous as my evening got because when all fifty-one envelopes were stamped and ready to go, I settled into my black recliner with a green highlighter and my newly purchased copy of Fontaine's *Fractal Geometry*. It wasn't light reading, but it wasn't any worse than *Being and Time*. The first edition had been published in 1984, but a second had been issued in 1992, and a third just a few years ago. That's what I had. Like the author of every textbook ever written, he'd ended the preface to the first edition by acknowledging the assistance of numerous colleagues. Nobody from Harvard or Nebraska. Same story with the preface to the second edition. The preface to the third edition began with a discussion of the growth of fractal geometry since the publication of the second edition:

Fractal geometry has blossomed in ways hardly imaginable when the previous edition of this text was published seven short years ago. What began as an attempt by Mandlebrot to define a geometry of nature today finds application in fields ranging from astronomy to medicine, from cinematography to cartography, from engineering to urban planning, and even in the world of finance.

It ended like this:

Finally, I'd like to thank Donald Underwood, associate professor of mathematics at Harvard University. Professor Underwood's insights were invaluable, particularly in connection with chapter twelve.

A quick look at the table of contents told me chapter twelve, the final chapter, was devoted to the use of computers in fractal geometry. And a quick look at chapter twelve told me that trying to understand it would be a waste of time. I recalled Gumby's words: "Far as we know, they never spoke with each other, never corresponded." Yet there it was, right there on page viii of the third edition.

It was past nine. I put the book down, let the dogs out, went into my office, phoned Ronald Bartels and told him of my discovery. He stood firm in his belief that Fontaine had never corresponded or spoken with Underwood concerning the textbook or anything else as long as he'd been at Whitman. Fontaine kept all comments on the third edition and had always tasked his student assistant with organizing and maintaining such letters. "I was still in high school when the third edition was published," Bartels said, "but when the FBI became involved, we dug out that file and went through it page by page. There was nothing from Dr. Underwood."

I thanked Bartels for his time, then thumbed through my Rolodex. Found what I wanted and punched in the number. "Hello?" A woman's voice.

"May I speak with Tim?"

"Who's calling?" The new wife sounded younger than the old one.

"Pepper Keane."

"It's for you," she said, "someone named Pepper." There was a brief pause.

"Does this concern national security?" asked Gombold.

"Tim, sorry to bother you, but I just came across something I think you should know about."

He sighed. "This on your fractal case?"

"Yeah."

"Fire away."

"You told me the bureau had been unable to find any evidence that these people had ever phoned each other or corresponded?"

"That's right."

"I was reading Fontaine's textbook—"

"That's a sad comment on your social life."

"I know," I said. "Anyhow, in the preface to the most recent edition, Fontaine credits Underwood as one of the people who read it and provided feedback."

"Yeah?"

"Yeah."

"When was that published?"

"Couple of years ago."

"Interesting. If there was correspondence between them, it's possible they trashed it after the book came out."

"Maybe, but Fontaine obviously knew and respected Underwood. Seems unlikely they'd go for years without talking or trading letters."

"Yeah, it does."

"Who checked the phone records?" I asked.

"Wasn't me, so it must have been Polk."

"That's what I was afraid of. He probably spent five minutes on the phone with some minimum-wage clerk at the AT&T subpoena center." He laughed.

"Pepper, I know you don't like the guy, but he's not stupid."

"Just the same, will you take a look at it?"

"Yeah," he said, "I'll take a look at it."

9

AFTER AN EARLY RUN AROUND THE LAKE with Buck, I spent Thursday morning putting the finishing touches on an appellate brief I was writing for Big Matt Simms. A former offensive lineman at Colorado State, Matt stands six-two and must weigh two-seventy, most of it ego. He has a taste for the finer things in life, as is evidenced by the fact that he buys a new car every year. This year it was a Mercedes.

Because Matt won't turn away any prospective client with money, he frequently finds himself with more work than he can handle. Once in a while he asks me to write a brief for him. He pays me seventy-five dollars an hour, in cash, but the client never knows I exist. He bills the client at his normal hourly rate as if he had done the work. Matt prides himself on having one of the highest hourly rates in Denver, but the client gets a first-rate brief and I earn a little tax-free spending money without having to tolerate the daily indignities of practicing law.

Shortly before noon I drove to the post office, mailed the brief to Matt, bought a large diet Coke at the B&F, and returned home to begin my search for Thomas Tobias.

People who intentionally disappear tend to fall into one of three categories: those running from the law, those running from their creditors, and those running from themselves. If you have a name and a Social Security number, it's pretty easy to determine whether someone falls into either of the first two categories. I phoned Gilbert, told him about Tobias, and asked him to run an

NCIC check. That would reveal Tobias's criminal history, if any, as well as information concerning any outstanding warrants. "How'd you find out about this guy?" Gilbert asked.

"You don't want to know," I said.

"Probably not," he agreed.

When Gilbert and I had finished talking, I phoned Matt, explained the situation, and asked him to have the firm's collection agency obtain a copy of Tobias's credit history. "That's illegal," he deadpanned, "I can't be a party to that."

"Yeah, right," I said. "Just fax it up to me when you get it."

"I'll put it on my ever growing list of crap to do," he said.

"Thanks, Matt."

"Hey, Pepper," he said, "when are you going to ditch the investigative bit and get your ass back down here? I'm telling you, man, we're raking in money like never before."

"You're still young," I said. "I figure you've got about five more years until burnout."

"They are a pain," he said, referring to his clients.

"But you love the money and seeing your name in the papers."

"But I love the money and seeing my name in the papers."

"You're an addict," I said. "You need to find a twelve-step program. That's the only way to free yourself from that kind of thinking." He laughed and promised to fax me Tobias's credit history as soon as possible.

By two o'clock I knew Tobias had no criminal history and wasn't wanted for anything. By three I knew he'd had exceptional credit before disappearing. He'd paid his bills in full in May of ninety-seven and hadn't used a credit card since. I'd have to dig deeper. I dialed information for the Big Apple.

After identifying myself as an IRS agent, in violation of 18 U.S.C. § 912, a woman in NYU's accounting department told me Tobias had left a forwarding address in Erie, Pennsylvania, but that his W-2 for last year had been returned with "No Such

Address" stamped on it. The address had probably been bogus from the start; Tobias had chosen Whitman for his undergraduate education, and I had a hunch he'd grown up in the Pacific Northwest.

I called NYU again, this time asking for the dean of the college of arts and sciences. I got the associate dean, Maria Santos. I gave my true name and occupation, then told her I was trying to locate Thomas Tobias. She was initially reluctant to provide any information, but opened up when I explained that Tobias had fathered a child out of wedlock and now owed more than twelve thousand dollars in back child support. "That's awful," she said. "What can I do to help?"

I asked if Tobias had completed an employment application or emergency information card. She put me on hold, but returned a few minutes later and told me he had filled out an employment application and an emergency notification card. She promised to fax them.

"Did you know Professor Tobias?" I asked.

"I'd met him."

"Any idea why he left? Was he in trouble with the administration?"

"No, not at all. He left on good terms." I heard her thumbing through papers. "His letter of resignation is somewhat vague; he felt he needed to take some time off for personal reasons."

"Couldn't he have taken a sabbatical?"

"No, he would've had to teach several more years to be eligible for a sabbatical."

I thanked her for her time, and she wished me luck in tracking down my deadbeat dad. I took a break to pump some iron in my basement. I've accumulated a great deal of weight-lifting equipment over the years, mostly items my brother no longer needed at his gym. It was a leg day, so I did squats, leg presses, lunges, knee extensions, ham curls, step-ups, and calf raises. By the time I had finished, my legs were fried, but I love that feeling. It's a natural high.

I went upstairs and made a protein shake, then checked my fax machine. True to her word, Ms. Santos had faxed copies of Tobias's employment application and emergency notification card. I examined the notification card first. In case of emergency, Tobias had instructed NYU to contact his mother, Iris Tobias, of Bend, Oregon. I debated calling her, but there was a practical problem. If I did, she might notify her son. There was also a moral problem. If a person truly wants to disappear, he has to give up his past life entirely. I'd hate to call Iris if she hadn't heard from her son in two years. I'd have to think it over.

The employment application presented no such problems. It listed three references. Two were mathematicians at Harvard. The third was Paul Fontaine.

10

FRIDAY AFTERNOON. I was in my client's office, waiting for her to return from a meeting.

My first move that morning had been to phone Ms. Santos once more. I asked if Tobias's references had provided letters of recommendation. "No," she said, "but the hiring committee conducted telephonic interviews with them, and they all spoke in glowing terms." So much for that theory. A poor recommendation from Fontaine might've indicated bad blood between the two, and that would have given me some basis, however weak, to suspect Tobias had played a role in Fontaine's death.

I studied my client's bookcases. Analytic geometry, non-Euclidean geometry, Riemannian geometry, fractal geometry. She even had Euclid's *Elements* and a three-volume treatise on the history of geometry. I was still taking inventory, head cocked to the side like a curious collie, when she entered. She was carrying the latest issue of *USA Today* and in it there was a story about the latest terrorist attack on the other side of the world.

"Sorry I'm late," she said. She sighed and extended her lower lip at the same time so that the dark strands of hair hanging gracefully over her forehead flew up for a split second. I wasn't sure if she was frustrated or exhausted. She wore tailored slacks the color of butter, a white cotton blouse, and her trademark pink lipstick.

"That's okay," I replied, "it gave me a chance to check out your books." She stood next to me, looked at her bookcase, and sipped coffee from a foam cup.

"I wish I could tell you I've read them all," she said, "but I'd be lying. The textbook companies send them free of charge."

"Hoping you'll use their books in your classes?"

"Yes." She sat down behind her desk and I took one of the chairs opposite.

"You seem frustrated," I said.

"It's been a hectic day," she said. "I'll just be teaching one class this summer, but I'm on three committees, including the tenure committee, and I'm just stretched to the limit." I thought that a funny phrase for a woman of her height, but I kept it to myself. "I'm sorry," she said, "you don't need to hear my problems. What can I do for you?"

"I wanted to give you an update and ask a few questions."

She offered coffee and I declined. "You sound better," she said.

"I finally saw a doctor," I said. "After I flew up to Walla Walla."

"Really?" Despite her admonishment not to concern myself with her finances, I read her mind.

"Don't worry," I said, "it didn't cost much. I had more frequent flier miles than I knew what to do with."

"Wouldn't you have rather used them for a vacation?"

"I don't practice law anymore," I said. "Every day is a vacation." She gave me a half smile, but said nothing. "Besides, I had to do something to get things moving. The detective who investigated Fontaine's death is another ex-marine and we hit it off when we spoke on the phone. He invited me up."

"What does he think?"

"We're both pretty certain what happened at Fontaine's house wasn't a robbery." I told her about the execution style of the murder and the many valuable items the killer had neglected to take, then summarized my efforts in Walla Walla.

"This Lieutenant Gilbert, does he believe Professor Fontaine's death is related to the other two?"

"He's suspicious," I said, "and he's willing to help, but I don't think he feels comfortable with the mathematical aspects of the case. He's leaving that to us."

"What about the other deaths? Have you learned anything about them?" I told her I'd spoken with the detective in Lincoln, Amanda Slowiaczek, but that she'd been unusually hostile. I promised to keep on it.

"And Professor Underwood?" she asked. I'd been dreading this conversation. I took a deep breath and told her the police felt he had accidentally hanged himself while jerking off. My language was a bit more clinical, but she got the idea.

"I've read about that," she said. "Does it happen often?"

"Yeah," I said, "it happens a lot."

"I guess that explains his death." She sighed.

"Not necessarily," I said. "It would be easy to fake. Point a gun at a man, he'll do whatever you say."

"I suppose that's true," she said, "but if you're going to stage a suicide, why make it look like an autoerotic accident?" She finished her coffee and placed the foam cup in the waste basket beside her.

"Making it look like an accident allows the cops to close the case without asking a lot of the questions they normally ask when someone commits suicide." She analyzed that assertion as if considering a mathematical equation.

"Yes," she said, "that makes sense." She seemed pleased I was open to the possibility that Underwood's death had been staged.

"There are two other things I should tell you," I said. I told her about Fontaine's reference to Underwood in the third edition of his textbook.

"My God," she said, "how could the FBI have missed that?"

"Sometimes you miss the obvious because you're not looking for it. I stumbled onto it because I had nothing better to do."

"You're being modest," she said. "Familiarizing yourself with Professor Fontaine's textbook was a good idea."

"There's one other angle I'm working," I said. "I was able to develop a list of people who either taught with or took classes from all three of the victims." I told her about the mysterious Thomas Tobias and my efforts to locate him.

"How were you able to obtain all that information?" she asked.

I smiled. "Persistence," I said. She waited for me to elaborate, but I remained silent.

"Well," she said, "you're making tremendous progress. I don't know why the FBI couldn't have done these things." Still angry because she felt the feds hadn't taken her seriously. I smiled, said nothing. "I'm sorry," she said, "I guess I should let that go. Is there anything I can do to help?"

"Yes," I said. "Ask Mary Pat to plug Tobias's name into the MathSciNet and make copies of all his published articles. It probably won't lead anywhere, but I have to check."

"Consider it done." She started to brew a pot of coffee. "You said you had some questions for me?"

"Tell me more about fractal dimension."

"I'll try," she said, "but what has that got to do with the case?"

"Maybe nothing, but that was the topic of your article and I noticed that term over and over again in the other articles I read. I want to make sure I understand it. Inquiring minds want to know." She smiled and began my lesson.

"In Euclidean geometry we think of objects as being three-dimensional. A line is one-dimensional, a plane is two-dimensional, and a cube is three-dimensional." She paused to make sure I grasped the concept. I nodded to show I did.

"In fractal geometry, dimensions aren't necessarily whole numbers. The dimension of an object can be expressed as a fraction. That's where the term 'fractal' comes from."

"For example?"

"Remember that coastline we talked about?"

"Sure."

"If we drew that coastline on a piece of paper, in great detail, we'd see a very crinkly line, right?"

"Yes."

"In fractal geometry we would say the dimension of the line is greater than one, but less than two. It's greater than one because it isn't straight, but it's less than two because it doesn't consume the entire piece of paper."

"So a line with a lot of squiggles will have a greater fractal dimension than a line with just a few squiggles?"

"Yes. You can think of a mountain the same way. If we try to fit that mountain inside a cube, its dimension will be greater than two, but less than three because it won't consume the entire cube."

"So, how do you measure fractal dimension?"

"That gets complicated," she said. "Think of it this way. If you examined that coastline from a satellite, it would look like a relatively straight line. The closer you get, the more detail you see, and this adds to the length of the line. Fractal dimension measures the rate at which the length of the line appears to increase—the rate at which new detail appears."

"And some guy named Hausdorff came up with a way of measuring this?"

"Very good," she said, "you've done your homework. Hausdorff said you can measure the fractal dimension of an object by—"

"Okay," I said as I held up my palm, "that's enough." She smiled and we shared a brief silence.

For some reason I couldn't fully articulate, I wanted to ask her out. The rules of professional conduct governing attorneys in Colorado prohibit lawyers from dating their clients because of the fear of conflicts of interest, but I was under no such constraint.

"So," she said, having finished the lecture, "you were in the army?"

"Marines."

"I think Mary Pat mentioned that."

"The haircut didn't give it away?"

"I didn't think anything of it."

"It's funny," I said. "When I was young I wanted long hair, but the very mention of it would send my father into orbit. Then I finished law school and joined the marines."

"Why the marines?" she asked. We had clearly finished discussing the case.

"I don't know," I said. "I guess the short answer is, I wanted to see the world."

"Did you?"

"No, but I got to know North and South Carolina real well."

"That doesn't sound bad. I've heard the beaches are wonderful."

"They are, but the Marine Corps always seeks out the places with the biggest swamps and the most snakes."

She must've picked up on something in my voice. "Oh," she teased, "are we afraid of snakes?"

"We detest snakes," I said.

"I grew up in New Mexico," she said. "Rattlesnakes are a way of life. You just have to watch where you step." Maybe so, I thought, but that won't get you very far when you're trudging through a murky swamp inhabited by copperheads and water moccasins.

We talked for another ten or fifteen minutes. The only child of two physicians, she'd grown up outside Albuquerque. A high school basketball star, several major universities had offered her athletic scholarships, but she'd turned them down to attend a liberal-arts college in Minnesota.

I was enjoying this conversation when Finn appeared in the doorway with a lime green bicycle worth several thousand dollars. He wore black spandex shorts and a bright yellow cyclist's shirt. A radio no bigger than a deck of cards was clipped to his belt line. The glistening sweat on his body indicated that he had just completed a strenuous trip. "Great day for a ride," he said to my client. "I just thought I'd stop by and see how you were doing."

"Come in, Stephen," she said, "Mr. Keane and I were just sharing stories." Finn entered, and my immediate reaction was that a man smart enough to graduate from Harvard at twenty should have enough sense to shower after bicycling twenty or thirty miles in the hot sun. I stood up from my chair.

"I didn't mean to interrupt," he said.

"I should be going," I said. "I appreciate your time and patience. I think the women at the shelter will really enjoy this program." I winked at her, but Finn was behind me and didn't see it.

"You're more than welcome," she said with a sly smile.

"Oh," I said, "I almost forgot." I handed her the cassette.

"What's this?" she asked.

"It's music," I said. I'd made a copy of the fractal ballet tape Luther had given me. "Consider it a present." She looked puzzled, but accepted it graciously. Finn said nothing.

I woke up a bit depressed on Saturday. I don't know how to describe it. "Blue" is probably the best word. It wasn't a deep I'm-going-to-kill-myself depression, just a mild sadness. I'd suffered from mild depression since Joy's death, but didn't get the official diagnosis until I was in the service.

I was a captain assigned to the base legal office at Camp Lejeune. I had a fantastic job, good friends, money in my pocket, and a promising future, but what had been periodic bouts of mild depression became increasingly severe. I couldn't let go of Joy's death. Sometimes I'd go two or three nights without sleep because I couldn't stop thinking about her. When I did sleep, I'd dream of Joy and wake up wishing the dream hadn't ended. Few things are more frightening than the realization that you're going crazy, so I sought help from a civilian psychiatrist. The military didn't recognize the doctor-patient privilege at that time, though the rules have changed a bit since then.

After several visits and a battery of tests, the shrink concluded I was genetically predisposed to depression. Some kind of chemical imbalance. This, combined with my obsessive nature and existential angst, was a recipe for permanent sadness. He prescribed medication, but recommended a therapist and encouraged me to sort through my feelings over Joy's death.

I wanted to keep the therapy a secret, so every Tuesday afternoon I told my fellow marines I was taking an hour to get a haircut. I'd spend fifty minutes with the therapist and ten minutes getting a buzz cut at the barbershop. My colleagues couldn't figure out what had gotten into me. Whereas I had previously pushed the envelope of what was an acceptable haircut for a marine officer, I suddenly made Ollie North look like a flower child.

The medication made a world of difference. Things went well until it showed up on a random urinalysis. The navy psychiatrists were satisfied that I was fit as a fiddle and said I could remain in the service, but any kind of mental health history is the kiss of death for a marine officer, so I completed my three-year tour, then returned to Colorado and became a federal prosecutor.

I don't know why I woke up feeling a bit down. My best guess is that I'd read too much Heidegger the previous night. He uses a lot of words like "equiprimordial," and it's always an ego-deflating experience. My other best guess is that it pissed me off to know I was alone while Finn apparently enjoyed the company of Jayne Smyers.

I needed a long run. I took off up Big Springs Road with Buck. As I've explained, Buck is a large dog, and the first quarter mile was like trying to water ski on concrete. Once the pavement ended, I let him run free. We ran eight miles—past the lake, around the recycling center, and back down into town. In other places it's called the dump, but here it's called the recycling center. People ask me if I have problems running at this altitude, but I'll take running at 8,300 feet over the humidity of Camp Lejeune any day of the week.

When Buck and I returned home, there was a message to call Dick Gilbert. "Good news," he said. "I spoke with the homicide dick in Boston and he's going to send me his file. He thinks I'm wasting my time, but he's gonna do it."

"Fantastic," I said. "What about Carolyn Chang?"

"You were right about that Amanda, she's something else. Asked if you'd contacted me."

"Yeah?"

"I told her I had no use for private eyes. That seemed to please her, but when I started asking questions about the murder, she wasn't very forthcoming. Said she'd have to get back to me on making her file available, but I'm not holding my breath."

"Strike you as unusual?"

"Hell yes, we're supposed to be on the same team."

"Maybe she's the killer," I said.

"Yeah, better check that out."

"Thanks, Dick."

"Let me know if you need anything else."

"Will do."

The run and Gilbert's call had buoyed my spirits. I spent the rest of the day cleaning and doing chores. By five P.M., it was time for dinner. Too lazy to cook anything healthy, I microwaved ramen noodles and topped them with a slice of cheddar. That brought back memories. When we were twenty-one, Scott and I had hitchhiked to the Texas Gulf Coast over spring break. By the time we reached our destination, we were pathetically low on funds. We camped in state parks and lived on ramen noodles. Whenever one of us wanted to spend money on something unnecessary, the other would say, "Hey, that's a lot of ramen." It became a unit of currency. A six-pack of beer was twenty-five packs of ramen. I smiled and punched in Scott's number.

"McCutcheon," he said.

"Hey," I said, "you want to take a road trip?"

11

S PEED LIMIT'S FIFTY-FIVE," Scott warned.

"I don't believe bureaucrats in Washington should decide speed limits in Nebraska," I said. "I'm kind of a Republican in that regard."

It was a gorgeous Sunday, and we were zooming over Nebraska Highway 2 at seventy-five miles per hour. Unless I have to be somewhere in a hurry, I avoid the interstate. You see more of the country that way. That's particularly true in Nebraska because I-80 follows the Platte River and deceives you into believing the entire state is flat.

The windows were down, and the sweet voice of Jerry Jeff Walker poured forth from the speakers. Wheat rode up front with us while Buck slept in the back of my truck. It's carpeted and has a shell on it; I've slept in it myself more than once.

"Any luck on Thomas Tobias?" Scott asked.

"A little," I said. I told him what I'd learned from Maria Santos and Tobias's credit history.

"He's got to be using an alias," Scott said. "We're not going to find him unless we talk with people."

"Maybe," I said, "but I'm not ready to do that. Once he knows we're looking for him, our chances of finding him go way down." We had discussed the uncertainty principle many times.

"You're the boss," he said.

It was three P.M. and we were eighty miles above North Platte when we started seeing signs for the Nebraska National Forest.

"Didn't know there was such a thing," Scott said.

"Me either."

The terrain was rough and dry. We were in the Nebraska sand-hills, an area long considered good for cattle and not much else. Every so often we'd see a dozen or so grouped around a stock tank. Scott said the ranchers used windmills to pump water from the Ogallala Aquifer. It was an unlikely place for a forest, but as we continued east, an oasis of pine began to appear.

A quick drive through the designated campsites convinced us we had the Nebraska National Forest to ourselves. We could've made Lincoln that evening, but decided to camp. Scott set up the tent and I built a fire. As Boy Scouts we'd learned to do it by rubbing sticks together or using flint to create a spark, but Coleman fuel is quicker.

We grilled turkey franks and feasted on roasted corn. When I had finished my second ear of corn, I walked back to the park entrance, put our overnight fee in the box, and picked up a forest service brochure. We were in the largest man-made forest in North America. More than 100,000 acres. On the back of the brochure was a map that showed a lookout tower three miles above our campsite.

A clear, spring-fed river—the Middle Loup—ran across the northern edge of the forest. The sun was still up, so we let the dogs swim while we jumped off the bridge into the river. Then we decided to hike to the tower.

The trail was well marked and not particularly steep. Ignoring the signs that said all dogs must be on a leash, I let Buck and Wheat run free and hoped like hell they didn't come across a rogue skunk or porcupine. When we reached the tower, it appeared unoccupied, but the gate leading to the steps was locked. A sign warned:

DO NOT CLIMB TOWER UNATTENDED
UNDER PENALTY OF LAW

"It's the goddamned bureaucrats in Washington," Scott joked. "I'm changing my party affiliation when we get back."

The gate was only chest high. Scott climbed it and I passed Wheat to him. Buck was more difficult, but we got him over it. We climbed the metal steps, slightly out of breath by the time we reached the top. Scott, by the way, is a great athlete. In addition to his martial arts training, he was the place kicker for the Colorado Buffaloes for two years. In one game he broke three toes on his right foot, but still managed to kick two field goals, thus earning the nickname Two Toe.

It was dark now and there was not a man-made light in sight. We enjoyed the stars, sipped hard apple cider, talked of love and life, and listened to a North Platte station on my shortwave radio. The DJ was playing some great old tunes and we cranked up the volume more than once. We sang along when she played "Bottle of Wine" by the Fireballs. If the deer and the antelope minded, they didn't say anything.

After a few hours we hiked through the darkness back down to our campsite. The dogs slept with us. Sometime in the middle of the night a loud noise startled us.

"What the hell was that?" I whispered as I reached for my Glock. He grabbed his one-million-candlepower spotlight—he likes gadgets—unzipped the tent fly, and slowly moved the beam from side to side. We saw that our cooler had been knocked off the picnic table and then eyed the culprit. I put the pistol down.

"It's a fuckin' badger," Scott said.

"Badger?" I said in my best Mexican accent, "we don't need no stinkin' badgers."

The birds woke the dogs before six and the dogs woke us. Took an invigorating swim in the Middle Loup, made blueberry pancakes on my portable backpacking stove, then fired up the truck and headed to Lincoln with Scott at the wheel.

Somewhere along the way we left cattle country and entered the land of corn and soybeans. The scenery consisted mostly of rolling hills and red-winged blackbirds, but we also saw a turtle that must have been a foot in diameter. When it comes to detecting, I'm a lot like the proverbial tortoise, so I considered it a good omen.

We arrived in Nebraska's capital before noon. It was a typical Midwestern city, not much different from Tulsa, Topeka, Des Moines, or Wichita. Wheat sat on my lap, content to poke his small face and pointy ears out the passenger window as we drove around to get the lay of the land.

There was a Best Western on one of the main boulevards a mile or so east of the university. It had an inviting pool highlighted by two inviting blondes in floral bikinis. "Looks like our kind of place," Scott said. He made a U-turn and guided the truck to a stop beneath the portico.

The desk clerk was a rotund man with a German accent. He reminded me of Sergeant Schultz on *Hogan's Heroes*. He saw Buck and Wheat in the truck and said, "No petz." I reached for my wallet.

"The dogs won't be a problem," I said. "They're trained guide dogs." I handed him a twenty.

"Vell, in that case, vee make exception."

I paid cash for the room and registered us as Bertrand Russell and Karl Popper just for the hell of it. "Yeah," Scott muttered as we left the lobby, "guide dogs for the socially impaired."

We carried our backpacks upstairs, guide dogs in tow, then showered to remove the smell of the campfire and the silt from the river. It was one-thirty on a Monday afternoon and time to earn our pay. Scott caught a bus downtown. I reread the news clippings pertaining to Carolyn Chang. The articles had been written by Susan Thompson of the *Lincoln Journal Star*. Forty minutes later I was sitting across from her.

We were at a coffeehouse near the university. She ordered an espresso; I asked for a diet Coke, but had to settle for the house cola. After we'd ordered drinks, she removed a steno pad from her purse, indicating that she wanted to get down to business. "So," she began, "you've got a new angle on the Chang murder?" She was in her late twenties. Long auburn hair, green eyes. About five-six, nice figure. She wore black gabardine slacks and a white silk blouse.

"What do you know about Carolyn Chang's work?" I asked.

"She was a mathematician. Is that important?"

"It might be," I said. "She specialized in a branch of mathematics known as fractal geometry. She was one of the top people in that field."

"I'm listening."

"Three months prior to Carolyn's murder, the man who wrote the book on fractal geometry was murdered in Washington state." I paused to sip my so-called drink. "Six weeks after Carolyn's murder, a Harvard mathematician was found dead in his home. Guess what his specialty was."

"Tell me more," she said.

I gave her the details of the other deaths and explained that I was investigating the possibility that the three might be related. I also explained that I'd been unable to make friends with Amanda Slowiaczek.

"Few people do," she said.

"What's her problem?"

"She's a woman in a man's world, and she's got an attitude about it." A Hispanic busboy came by, saw the lemon in my diet cola, and poured iced tea in it before I could stop him. Probably improved it, but I ordered a new one just to be safe. While waiting for my replacement drink, I told the reporter the FBI had investigated the matter and concluded the deaths were unrelated. "I knew the bureau was involved," she said, "but I didn't know about the other deaths." I folded my hands on the table and studied her face as she sipped espresso. "Now that you've put me onto what might be a good story, what do you want from me?"

"I want to know what you know about the Chang murder. I'm sure you've heard things you didn't print."

"There's a lot you're not telling me."

"I've told you almost everything," I said. I hadn't mentioned Thomas Tobias. "If you help me, I'll tell you more as things develop."

"And if I don't?"

"Ever read *The Little Red Hen*?" I asked. "You only get to eat the bread if you help bake it." She smiled.

"Okay," she said, "I can tell you a few things, but it may not help much. Just bits and pieces I've picked up from contacts in the department." We talked another thirty minutes, then exchanged cards and went our separate ways.

I plugged the meter and walked to the university's admissions office to get a catalog. "Ten dollars," said the clerk. I wanted a list of the math faculty, the schools they'd attended, and their academic specialties. I didn't know why I wanted it, but I did. I paid the ten bucks.

When I returned to the motel, the blondes had been replaced by three scruffy young men playing Frisbee. Their red 1967 Pontiac GTO was parked next to the pool, and heavy-metal music was blaring from the huge speakers mounted beneath its rear window. New Jersey plates.

I walked upstairs to find that Scott had beaten me back and changed into shorts. "Dogs need to go out?" I asked.

"Already done," he said. Wheat was resting on one of the double beds and Buck was on the other gnawing a Bible placed by the Gideons. "It was either that or the Book of Mormon," Scott explained.

"Tough call," I said.

"Mormons allow polygamy."

"Good point," I said. I removed my shirt, placed it on a hanger, then sat on the edge of Buck's bed and untied my shoes. "So," I said, "what's new at the courthouse?"

"Not much," he said. "Carolyn Chang had never been arrested or sued, at least not in this county. There was no probate file. She'd never been called for jury duty, and she was a registered Democrat."

"What about Amanda?" I asked. I took off my slacks and gave Buck a pat on the head.

"She went through a nasty divorce about four years ago. Lost custody of her two boys."

"Why'd she lose custody?"

"Husband claimed she was a workaholic and the judge bought it. You're the expert on this stuff, but from what I saw in the file, his lawyer was in a different league."

"What did the husband do?"

"He was selling real estate, but he moved the kids to Florida two years ago."

I found some khaki shorts in my backpack and put them on. "What about the police station?" I asked.

"You can forget that," he said. "The detectives are on the third floor. We'd never get past the lobby. There's a steel door with a magnetic lock. You can't get to the elevators or the stairs unless someone behind the glass buzzes you in."

"Could we get in at night?"

"No, the place is covered with cameras because the jail's in the same building. Wouldn't matter anyhow; there are detectives in there around the clock."

"I guess that answers that."

"What did you learn?" he asked.

"Couple of things." I put on a green polo shirt. "First, they didn't find any semen, so whoever did it wore a condom. Second, when Carolyn left her office that day, she told a colleague she was going home. Her car was in the driveway, so they're working on the assumption she made it home. Third, there was no sign of a struggle or forced entry at her house." I found my loafers and put them on. "Oh yeah," I said, "she had a big white cat named Snowball, if you can believe that, and it was still in the house when the cops arrived."

"Maybe the guy just doesn't like cats."

"Good theory, but it won't fly. Fontaine owned a dog he kept on his parents' farm, and Underwood didn't have any pets."

"Oh." He went into the bathroom and closed the door. "Sounds like she might've gotten into a car with someone she knew," he yelled.

"Yeah, that's what I was thinking." I heard a flush, then the sound of water running in the sink.

"Anything else?" he asked as he reentered the room.

"Yeah, they found a few unidentified pubic hairs on her body, but that doesn't do them any good until they have a suspect. And they still don't know where she was killed." It was almost four o'clock.

"This music is starting to bother me," Scott said. I sensed it was way past that point. Despite fifteen years in the martial arts, Scott sometimes has a quick temper.

"Forget it," I said, "let's get some pizza and check out that downtown mall."

Every city in America has a trendy area, and in Lincoln it's known as the Haymarket, a few square blocks of hundred-year-old buildings converted into restaurants, shops, and lofts. We browsed and enjoyed a meal that included deep-dish pizza, hot garlic rolls, and cold beer from a local microbrewery, but when we returned to the motel at six, the heavy metal was still blaring. I parked next to the GTO, handed my cassette case to Scott, and said, "Pick a tape." He thumbed through them, selected one, and held it up. I told him it was a good choice.

We went upstairs, took the dogs for a walk around the block, then changed into our trunks and with our ghetto blaster headed for the pool. We grabbed two chaise lounges and positioned ourselves at the deep end of the pool. By the time Tammy Wynette had finished belting out "Stand by Your Man," the riffraff had decided it was time for supper.

The rest of the night passed without incident. No badgers. No blaring music. No blondes.

12

TUESDAY. DAY TWO IN LINCOLN. We began the morning by taking the dogs for a run, then had breakfast at a pancake house across from the motel. Scott had bacon and eggs; I opted for a strawberry waffle.

"So what's the plan?" he asked.

"Figured I'd mosey over to the university and interview Carolyn's colleagues. Figured you'd drive over to her house and talk to her neighbors."

"I can do that," he said. We walked back to the motel. I put on a tie and suggested Scott do the same. As a private investigator, I don't have the authority of a police officer, so I depend on my ability to persuade. My experience had been that people were more cooperative when I dressed professionally.

The academic year having ended, the math department at the University of Nebraska wasn't a hotbed of activity. I found only two faculty members. The first, Gordon Schutt, was the department chairman.

He was in his early fifties and looked like he'd just stepped out of the 1950s. His thick, black hair was parted on the left and held in position with some kind of gel. He wore Buddy Holly glasses, the kind the military issues new recruits. His loose-fitting chinos were secured by a thin black belt. He was a pear-shaped man. Six feet tall, wide hips, not much muscle tone. I introduced myself and told him I was looking into the possibility that Carolyn Chang's death might be related to two others. He invited me in.

"I didn't know her that well," he said.

"Any particular reason for that?"

"No, we just had different interests and lifestyles. Didn't see each other much outside this building." He reminded me of my seventh-grade math teacher, Mr. Folvin. I had spent the bulk of that year sitting in the back of the class perfecting a new paper airplane and shooting spitballs at Lisa Lawlor through a hollow Bic pen. Which probably helps explain why I ended up in law rather than one of the sciences.

"Professor Chang had been here five years?"

"That sounds about right." He removed his glasses.

"I read some of her papers," I said. "They were well written."

"Carolyn had exceptional writing ability. I often used her papers as examples of what professional writing ought to be."

"Do you know whether she was working on anything at the time of her death?"

"No, but I'm sure she was researching or writing something. She always was." I continued down my mental checklist.

"Did Professor Chang have any enemies?"

"None that I know of."

"I saw some graffiti in the men's room that wasn't particularly complimentary." Juvenile stuff, most of it sexual in nature.

"Carolyn could be abrupt with people," he said. "And she was quite willing to humiliate students who were unprepared. Her theory was that they'd either get with the program or drop the class."

"Had she had problems with any male students?"

"She never mentioned any, but she would've tried to handle that sort of thing on her own. She was not a meek person."

"Problems with male colleagues?"

"No, Carolyn got along well with all of us. Outside class, she was very personable."

"Was she dating anyone?"

He laughed. "I'd be the last to know," he said. "I've been married thirty years and don't pay much attention to that sort of thing. You might try speaking with Glenda; I think she's here, and she probably knew Carolyn better than anyone."

We talked for another twenty minutes. I thought about probing him for information about Finn, but I decided against it. He and Finn might still be in contact, and I didn't want to do anything that might make it easier to ascertain the identity of my client. Nor did I want Finn to know the true nature of my business with Jayne Smyers.

Glenda Sarkasian's door was wide open and covered with cartoons. She wore jeans and a powder blue T-shirt she'd apparently earned by running a local 10K. Late thirties, dark brows, long brown hair with strands of gray, tight body, smooth olive skin. Armenian? She had her feet on her desk and was reading the morning paper. Given the cartoons, I figured it was safe to ham it up.

"Excuse me," I said, "that desk is government property. I'm going to have to ask you to remove your feet from it." She put the paper down, removed her feet from the desk, and looked at me.

"Damn," she said, "that's the second time I've been busted this year. One more and I lose my desk." She gave me a warm smile.

"Actually," I said, "my name is Pepper Keane. May I come in?"

"Please do." She motioned me in.

"I'd like to talk with you about Carolyn Chang." I handed her one of my cards and explained the nature of my investigation, then sat down opposite her.

"Yes," she said, "I spoke briefly with the FBI about this, but I was under the impression they had determined the deaths were unrelated."

"They did," I said, "but I get paid to make my own determination."

"Someone must think highly of you," she said.

I didn't comment. "Professor Schutt told me you and Carolyn were close."

"We were friends."

"Good friends?"

"I don't know if I'd go that far. We talked a lot, and went out occasionally, but she was a hard person to get close to." She was sitting up straight now, arms folded on her desk. Serious.

"Did you ever discuss her social life?"

"A little."

"Was she involved with anyone at the time of her death?"

She studied my face. "I told the police and the FBI, so I might as well tell you. For the past year or two, Carolyn had been seeing one of the professors in the business school, a man named Dale Hawkins."

"Do you know him?"

"I've met him a few times."

I detected something in her voice. "And?"

"I don't know. He's tall and good looking—"

"I hate him already."

"He's just so—" She paused. "I don't know, I can't put my finger on it, but there's something strange about him."

"Can you give me an example?"

She thought for a moment. "Yes," she said. "Sometime last fall we were at a party. Dale kept trying to impress me, telling me he'd been a CIA analyst and all sorts of ridiculous things. I felt he was coming on to me, but it only happened once, so I never mentioned it to Carolyn."

"Nothing unusual about a man trying to impress a woman," I said. "Had he been drinking?"

"No," she said, "he's not much of a drinker. Maybe I'm being unfair."

"What else can you tell me about him?"

"Not much," she said. "Like most economists, he thinks he knows everything."

I smiled. "Anything else?"

"It's just my opinion," she continued, "but I think he has a real need for recognition."

"Why do you say that?"

"It's just the way he is. He likes to be the center of attention. Sometimes I think he spends more time generating publicity for himself than he does teaching. He gets his name in the paper more than any other faculty member I know." She laced her fingers together. "He even has a weekly show on public television here. It's called *This Week with Dale Hawkins.*"

"Impressive," I said.

"He lives to impress," she said.

"Who else knew about them?"

"I don't know," she said. "I don't think anyone in the department knew. Carolyn insisted they keep a low profile."

"Why?"

"She didn't want people to perceive her as being involved with someone. She wanted the option of seeing other men."

"Did she?"

"I suspect she did."

"Why?"

"Women know these things," she said.

I took her word for it. "How would Dale have reacted if he'd learned she'd been seeing another man?"

"He's not violent," she said. "He would've kept it to himself. He knew he had a good thing with Carolyn—sex without commitment—and he wouldn't have risked losing it by confronting her." She paused. "Besides, I suspect he was seeing other women." Women know these things.

"Sounds like they never planned on getting married and raising a family."

"I think that's accurate."

"What about Carolyn's professional life? Was she working on anything at the time of her death?"

"She was always working on something—she loved to write—but we didn't talk shop much. I know very little about geometry and even less about fractals."

"This is a shot in the dark," I said, "but did Carolyn have an interest in the arts?"

"Yes, how did you know?"

"One of her papers had to do with fractals and the arts."

"I remember that paper. Yes, Carolyn enjoyed painting and was quite good. She did that one behind you." I turned around and saw a farmhouse surrounded by colorful hollyhocks.

"It's beautiful," I said. Watercolors are usually too subdued for me, but Carolyn's work was alive with color. She'd captured the early morning light perfectly.

We spoke for more than an hour. If threats had been made against Carolyn, Glenda was unaware of it. She'd never heard of Paul Fontaine or Donald Underwood until questioned by the FBI. As I had with Gordon Schutt, my inclination was to refrain from asking her about her former colleague Stephen Finn, but I'd established a good rapport with her and some inner voice was urging me to probe a bit.

"Stephen Finn," she said with a smile. "There's a name I haven't heard in a while. Is he involved in all this?"

"I don't think so," I said. "Why are you smiling?"

"Stephen was funny," she said. "He was a fine teacher, but he was young and seemed lonely. I don't think there was a woman in the department he didn't try to hit on."

"Carolyn Chang?"

"They went out a few times."

"Were they an item?"

"Not that I know of," she said. "Carolyn might have slept with him—just for the novelty of having a fling with a younger col-league—but it wouldn't have been an ongoing thing. He would've been too clingy for her." There was an awkward pause and we both smiled. The conversation had run its course, but I liked Glenda Sarkasian and I think she liked me. I would have asked her out if Jayne Smyers hadn't been floating around in the back of my mind. "I hope I've been helpful," she said.

"You've been very helpful," I said as I stood to leave, "and I know you were under no obligation to speak with me." A final question occurred to me as I neared the door. "Just out of curios-ity," I said, "how many times did the FBI interview you?"

"Twice," she said. "Once in person and once by telephone."

"Let me guess. Two agents from Lincoln interviewed you here and an agent from Denver called you a week or two later."

"Yes," she said.

"The one on the phone make any kind of impression on you?"

She thought about it. "He seemed a bit high on himself," she offered. I shook my head up and down knowingly and said good-bye.

I walked back to the motel, changed into shorts, took the dogs around the block, flopped on my bed, and clicked on CNN. I lis-tened to the anchorwoman highlight the day's events as I paged through the university's catalog. Dale D. Hawkins, associate pro-fessor of finance, had received his B.S. at Duke, his M.B.A. at the Wharton School, and his doctorate at the University of Chicago. He'd been at Nebraska six years.

Scott came bopping in an hour later holding a large white T-shirt with "Nebraska Football" emblazoned across it in big red letters. "Might as well blend in with the locals," he said. "Got one for you too." He tossed it to me.

"Jesus," I said, "let's just buy some overalls and John Deere hats while we're at it." He removed his pants and changed into shorts.

"What'd you learn?" he asked.

"Buddy Holly is alive and Carolyn Chang was dating a business professor. What'd you learn?"

"Carolyn Chang was a harlot."

"A harlot?"

"That's what one of her neighbors called her. Little old lady who spends all day listening to some AM station preaching hellfire and damnation. Said sometimes Carolyn wouldn't come home at all."

"The slut."

"Sometimes a man would stay at her house until the wee hours of the morning."

"Same man?"

"Same guy for the past year."

"She describe him?"

"Tall, trim, dark hair, always wears a tie."

"Dale Hawkins," I said. "M.B.A. at the Wharton School."

"That's his name?"

"Yeah. You talk with anyone other than grandma?"

"Yeah. It's an older neighborhood. A lot of the houses are rented by students. I talked with as many as I could, but a lot of them weren't living there last winter. Of those who were, a couple of people remembered seeing a sedan in front of her house around six that evening."

"The cops have that?"

"Yeah."

"You get a description on the car?"

"Nothing firm. It was dark and cold and nobody was paying attention. The consensus seemed to be it was a big Ford or Mercury. Dark blue. Brand new. Definitely a four-door. Possibly with Nebraska plates, though one guy insisted it had Colorado tags."

"Anyone get a plate number?" I asked.

"The guy who thought it had Colorado tags said the first three letters were A-M-K. He remembered because those are his initials."

"That's a Denver prefix," I said. "I wonder if anyone checked that."

"If it was a Colorado plate, that would narrow it down to ten thousand vehicles, at most." In Colorado, the first three characters on most license plates are letters, the last four are numbers.

"Out of every ten thousand cars, there can't be that many brand-new Ford or Mercury four-doors that are dark blue."

"Be nice if this broad Amanda would talk with us."

"That's not going to happen," I said. "What else did you get?"

"Nobody saw anything. Nobody heard anything. But a couple of people swore up and down she would never get into a car with a strange man. She was real rape conscious. Carried pepper spray and wasn't afraid to confront strangers who looked out of place in the neighborhood. She was like a mama bear to all the coeds in the neighborhood."

"She would've fought like a bobcat if someone had tried to force her into a car."

"That's the impression I got," he said. "You want to go visit this Hawkins tonight?"

"Let's catch him tomorrow," I said. "I'm sure the cops have interviewed him and obtained pubic hair samples, so I'm assuming he's not a suspect."

"I was hoping you'd say that."

"Why's that?"

"The blondes are down at the pool." I closed my eyes because I knew what was coming. At a minimum, I was going to drink more than I should. I didn't even want to think about the worst-case scenario. "C'mon, marine," he yelled as he changed into his new shirt, "the party's just getting started." What could I do? I put on my new shirt and followed my pal to the pool.

Except for the blondes, the pool was deserted, but Scott laid claim to a table right next to them. Real subtle. The table was protected from the sun by a giant green-and-white umbrella. "We're albinos," he explained as we sat down. "Can't take much sun." They laughed. "My name's Wally," he continued, "and this is my friend Theodore."

"My friends call me the Beaver," I said from beneath my aviator's glasses.

"Monica," said the taller of the two.

"Mindy," said the other.

We gave them our true names and got their story. They had just completed their junior year at USC and had been driving home to Ohio when the fuel pump on Mindy's '79 Duster gave out. They'd been stuck in Lincoln since Sunday, waiting for the right part, and hoped to leave the next day.

"So," Monica said, "what brings you to Lincoln?"

"We're private investigators," Scott said. "We're on a case."

"Give me a break," said Mindy.

"We are," he insisted. He turned to me and said, "Show them one of your cards."

"First of all," I said, "I don't keep business cards in my swim trunks. Second, *I'm* a private investigator; *he's* an unemployed astrophysicist who just likes to hang out with me."

"A groupie," Mindy said.

"Exactly," I said. "That's what he is. A groupie." I stood up, removed my shirt, and dove into the pool. By the time I emerged, my flirtatious friend had convinced them we were, in fact, investigating the mysterious fractal murders.

The four of us spent forty-five minutes discussing everything from the Nebraska National Forest (they had never heard of it) to their majors (economics for Monica, anthropology for Mindy). When we'd been there an hour, Scott asked if they'd like to join us for dinner. They looked skeptical. "You'll be safe," he assured them. "We were Eagle Scouts."

They knocked on our door just after six. Both were clad in tan hiking shorts; Mindy wore a blue short-sleeved shirt and Monica a thin white shirt with a mandarin collar. They were somewhat surprised to see that we were sharing a room with Buck and Wheat. "I thought they didn't allow pets," Mindy said.

"We're not very good with rules," I said.

"The Eagle Scouts?" Monica teased.

"We do pretty well," I said, "with trustworthy, loyal, helpful, friendly, courteous, kind, cheerful, thrifty, brave, and clean, but we've always had problems with obedient and reverent."

"That's still eighty-three percent," Scott said.

13

I woke up in bed with Buck and saw Scott's tousled hair poking out of the covers on the bed opposite mine. The sun was bright, and he was slowly coming to life. The digital clock read 8:37 A.M. I sat on the edge of my bed, then slowly walked to the sink. I assembled my morning regimen of vitamins, then opened my briefcase, found my Motrin, and added four of those to the mix. Without removing the protective wrap, I filled one of the motel's plastic cups with water and swallowed the pills.

"Too much to drink?" Scott asked.

"Nothing I can't run off," I said. I splashed cold water on my face, combed my hair, then rummaged through my backpack for my jogging shorts and running shoes. "Get your gear on," I said, "it's time to pay the piper." Ignoring me, he turned over on his stomach. I took the dogs for a walk around the block, but when I returned Scott was still on his belly with the covers pulled over his head. "Let's go," I said. He gave me the finger.

I grabbed the ice bucket, walked to the machine at the top of the stairs, filled it with ice, returned to our room and added some water, then took great delight in dumping the entire contents on him. He made a loud reference to our Lord and Savior, but got geared up to run.

"You know," he said as we trotted through the city, "either one of those girls would've slept with you." The four of us had dined at a Mexican restaurant, then started a process of drinking, club hopping, and dancing that had lasted until two A.M.

"Wouldn't have been a good idea," I said.

"Why not?"

"Some variant of the incest taboo."

"Fuck the incest taboo," he said. "That's just the bureaucrats in Washington trying to run our lives again."

I gave in to a smile. "The other thing is—and this is going to sound really weird—but I would've felt like I was cheating on my client."

"I knew that was coming."

"How'd you know?" I asked.

"I've known you since the Cuban missile crisis. I can tell when you're stuck on a woman."

"It's probably a moot point. I think she's got something going with this guy Finn."

"What's he like?" Scott asked.

"I've only met him a few times," I said. "He's young, maybe twenty-six or twenty-seven. Competes in triathlons. A little high on himself, but I was too at that age."

"You think?"

"Just a little," I admitted.

"Ask her out," he said. "We can always kill him if we have to." I laughed.

We continued running and I thought about Jayne Smyers. She was pretty, no doubt about that. And she was certainly smart. But some other quality was drawing me to her. She possessed a certain perky optimism—something I felt I lacked. I tried to put her out of my mind, but I kept hearing that Sam Cooke song. Maybe by being an A student, I could win her love for me.

Even at that hour it was warm and humid. I was covered with sweat, and it felt good. I estimated we'd gone six miles when the Best Western came into view. I sprinted for it and Scott took off after me, but I'd been a college sprinter and I've always been fast for a man my size. By the time he reached the parking lot, I had my hands above my head and was catching my breath. He did the same. Eventually we got control of our breathing and stopped walking.

"So, what's the plan for today?" he asked.

"We eat breakfast, visit Hawkins, and get the hell out of Dodge."

Parking at the college of business wasn't a problem; there were plenty of meters beside the faculty lot. We scanned the lobby directory, found what we needed, and went upstairs. His door was open, and he was reading a text placed flat on his desk.

"Professor Hawkins?"

"Yes." He pushed the book to one side.

"Hi. My name is Pepper Keane and this is my associate, Scott McCutcheon. We'd like to talk with you about Carolyn Chang." He seemed neither surprised nor afraid.

"Come in," he said as he rose from his chair and extended his hand. He stood six-two and weighed about one-seventy. Fiftyish. He was handsome and possessed the trim waist of a department store mannequin. His hair was mahogany, dark brown with a red tint. He wore gray slacks, a white shirt, and a maroon tie. A gold-plated pen graced his monogrammed pocket. A matching gray jacket hung on a hook behind his door. It was a conservative suit. We shared the same taste in clothes.

"Are you with the police or the FBI?" he asked. Lying was a felony. More to the point, it was an easy-to-prove felony.

"Neither," I said. "We're private investigators." I handed him a card and he studied it. "We're looking into the possibility that Professor Chang's death may have been related to several others." He sat down and invited us to do likewise.

"The FBI mentioned that," he said. I removed a clipboard and legal pad from my briefcase.

"We want to be as thorough as possible, so we're interviewing everyone who might have relevant information." I surveyed the room. His many degrees and awards were double matted and proudly displayed in matching chrome frames on the wall behind him. An ego wall. One of Carolyn's watercolors hung on the wall to his left.

"You've come a long way," he said. "I'll do my best to answer your questions, but I've got to leave by noon. I'm speaking to the Chamber of Commerce." I promised we'd be done long before then.

"We understand you'd been dating Professor Chang."

"For about two years," he said. I thought I noticed a trace of a Southern accent.

"How did you meet?" I asked.

"We met by chance, actually." The memory made him smile. "I had gone to a movie and noticed her as I was leaving. I knew she was a faculty member and asked her to join me for coffee."

"I assume the police questioned you about your whereabouts on the night of her disappearance."

"Yes, they did. I was at a faculty dinner." I said nothing. "They also requested saliva, blood, and pubic hair samples, if that's what you're wondering, and I provided those."

"When did you learn of Professor Chang's death?"

"A detective contacted me. Amanda something. Carolyn disappeared on a Friday, I think, and the detective contacted me the following Monday."

"Had you tried to call her between Friday and Monday?"

"No, we didn't talk every day. Carolyn valued her time alone, and I tried to respect that." That seemed reasonable, but something bothered me.

"What did you know about Carolyn's work?" I try to ask open-ended questions—the kind that can't be answered with a yes or no.

"I knew what her field of expertise was, and that she loved teaching, but beyond that I can't tell you much."

"What do you teach?" I asked.

"My doctorate is in economics, gross national product and things like that, but I teach finance and investments."

"I read some of Carolyn's papers," I said, "and I'm told she liked to write. Was she working on anything at the time of her death?"

"Not that I know of, but we seldom talked about work."

I continued down my mental checklist and when I'd run out of questions about Carolyn Chang, I asked him about himself. He'd spent his early years in North Carolina, but he'd grown up in Chicago. He'd been at Nebraska six years. He'd taught at a number of different schools and admitted liking the academic lifestyle. "I could earn more in the private sector," he said, "but teaching offers greater freedom." I stood up, ready to depart. Scott took the cue and did likewise. Then I thought of another question.

"You said you also spoke with the FBI?"

"Yes," he replied.

"How many times?"

"Just once."

"Local agents?"

"I think so," he said.

"Did anyone from the bureau phone you after that to conduct a second interview?"

"No," he said. "I told them everything I knew the first time around."

We thanked him for his time and walked out into a blast furnace. It was going to be a hot one in Nebraska. As we crossed the faculty lot, we stopped to admire a silver Jaguar, then noticed the license plate. DDH PHD. "I'd say he's doing pretty well in the public sector," said Scott.

We boarded the truck and rolled down the windows. "So what do you think?" I asked.

"I liked him," he said. "Except for all the crap he had on his wall, he seemed like a pretty regular guy."

"Me too," I said. "He has a certain charisma."

"The one thing I thought was strange was that he didn't try to call her. I don't care how casual their relationship was. I've been in a lot of relationships like that, and we always talked two or three times a week. Hell, before Bobbi moved in, she'd get pissed if I didn't call every night."

"Something's bothering me about that too, but I can't put my finger on it." I loosened my tie, pulled onto the main boulevard, and headed for the motel.

"He never mentioned the CIA," Scott joked.

"He might've been with the CIA," I replied. "They hire economists. If some bureaucrat wants to know what the price of carrots in Finland is going to be next month, I guarantee you the agency has someone who can provide a damn good guess."

We pulled into the motel lot, exited the truck, and headed to our room. "Something bothering you?" Scott asked. "You've got that deep-in-thought look."

"It's probably nothing," I said.

"What?"

"I just thought it strange that he never asked who our client was."

"What do you mean?"

"We barge into this guy's office and announce we're investigating the possibility that his girlfriend's murder may have been related to two other deaths—a theory the FBI already rejected— and he doesn't even ask who we're working for. It just seems odd."

"Yeah," he said, "I guess it does. You think someone told him to expect us?"

"I don't know who it would've been," I said. "Nobody knows we're here, except Bobbi and my brother."

"Who knows we're on the case?"

"Nobody who would've called Hawkins," I said. "I think we can rule out Jayne Smyers, Gumby, and Dick Gilbert."

"What about the professors you spoke with?"

"The department chairman didn't even know about Hawkins. The lady professor knew about him, but it didn't seem like there was any love lost between them."

Scott shrugged and removed his tie. "Hey," he said, "why'd you ask him how many times the bureau had interviewed him?"

"I don't know," I said. "A couple of witnesses told me an agent from Denver had reinterviewed them by phone, and I think it was probably Polk."

"That's not normal procedure, is it?"

"No, but Polk isn't exactly what you'd call a team player, so it wouldn't surprise me if he made some follow-up calls."

"Why wouldn't he do the same thing with Hawkins?"

I shrugged. "Who knows with Polk? Sounds like the physical evidence pretty much clears Hawkins, so maybe there was no need."

We returned our room keys to Sergeant Schultz, then headed west on US 6. Wheat sat on Scott's lap and poked his head out the window. He seemed in heaven as the oncoming air hit his muzzle and blew back his pointy ears.

We were less than twenty miles out of Lincoln when I popped my palm to my forehead as if to say I could've had a V-8. Instead I made a U-turn and said, "Jesus, I am a dumbass."

"Where we going?" Scott asked.

"Manhattan," I said.

"Cheaper to fly," he joked.

"Kansas."

"You want to see where the body was found?"

"I want to talk to that sheriff. I'll bet you dollars to doughnuts he's got a copy of Amanda's file."

As it turned out, we didn't have to drive all the way to Manhattan. The body had been found in Marshall County and the sheriff's office was in Marysville. We made it in less than two hours. A sign at the edge of town welcomed us to "The Black Squirrel City." Sure enough, in the middle of town there was a small park filled with black squirrels.

"This trip has been a real education," Scott said. "First I find out there's a national forest in Nebraska. Now I learn there are black squirrels in Kansas."

"I think the politically correct term is 'squirrels of color.'"

The town seemed dead, but anyone with a choice was probably inside, seeking shelter from the scorching Kansas sun. We ate a late lunch on a concrete picnic table at an A&W, then set out to find the sheriff's office. It wasn't difficult given that Main Street was only four blocks long. I guessed it was the building with the flagpole and patrol cars in front of it.

I guided the truck into one of the diagonal parking spaces. I stepped out of the truck and made sure the dogs had water. The building appeared to have been an addition to the much older courthouse. We entered, and at the front desk a beefy female deputy in a brown uniform asked if she could help us. About thirty. Lots of makeup, no smile. I told her we were private investigators and asked if we could speak with the sheriff. She instructed us to have a seat on some orange plastic chairs, then picked up her phone.

The Sheriff emerged from his office within a minute or two. "Darlene tells me you fellas are private investigators," he said. He stood six-five or six-six. Late fifties or early sixties. Little bit of a paunch on an otherwise rangy body. He wore no uniform, but sported cowboy boots, tan slacks, and a Western-style short-sleeved shirt. His badge was on his belt. "Lee Bowen," he said as he extended his hand. I introduced us, handed him a card, and asked if we could talk in private. He led us into his office and invited us to sit down. The walls boasted a dozen awards from civic groups and an eight-by-ten glossy of him shaking hands with Bob Dole.

"Sheriff," I began, "we'd like to talk about Carolyn Chang. We believe her death may have been related to two others."

"FBI already investigated that," he said. I was tired of hearing that. He leaned back in his chair, put his feet on the desk, and laced his fingers together behind his head.

"At the risk of sounding cocky," I said, "I don't think they did a very good job."

He smiled. "Law degree qualify you to make that judgment?" He had noticed the J.D. on my card.

"I was a federal prosecutor. I know what a good investigation looks like."

"You fellas got sort of a cocky look to you," he said. He paused to mash some tobacco into an old pipe. "Course, a certain amount of that ain't a bad thing in law enforcement."

I noticed a small black-and-white photo of a football team on the wall behind his desk. The players were all white and had crew cuts.

"You play football?" I asked.

"Little bit," he said. Darlene knocked on the door and asked if the sheriff could step outside. While he was gone, I examined the photo. It was the team picture of the 1965 Philadelphia Eagles. He was in the third row.

"Jesus," said Scott.

The sheriff reentered and closed the door. "One of our nutcases," he explained. "Wanted to tell me she'd seen two suspicious-looking strangers in town. Driving a green F-150 with Colorado plates."

"Want us to help look for them?"

"I didn't even want this job," he said. "Only reason I ran was because old Duncan Grimm was gettin' too big for his britches.

Started wearing four stars on his collar and hauling kids into court for swimming at the quarry."

"What did you do before?" I asked.

"Did a little farming, drilled wells with my sons. But that's not why you're here." He lit his pipe. The aroma was sweet and pleasant.

"No," I said. "To be blunt, we were hoping to inspect your file."

"You seem pretty sure these deaths were related." He leaned back in his chair and placed his feet on his desk.

"We're not sure," I said, "but the odds of three math professors—"

"I understand where you're coming from," he said. "My training is in geology and both my boys are geologists, so this old cowpoke actually knows a little something about fractals." He puffed on his pipe. "But what makes you think you're going to find something the FBI missed?"

"I already found something the FBI missed," I said. I told him about Fontaine's reference to Underwood in the third edition of his textbook. He smiled. I got the impression there'd been some friction between him and the bureau. "Sheriff," I continued, "we've done a lot of work on this case." I summarized our efforts, including my trip to Walla Walla, our visit to Nebraska, and our search for Thomas Tobias. "The problem we're having now is that this detective in Lincoln won't let us see her file, so we were hoping we could get a look at yours."

"Yeah," he said, "she's a charmer." He took his long legs off his desk, sat up straight, and hit the intercom button with his pipe hand. "Darlene," he said, "bring that Chang file in here, will ya?"

"Right away, sir."

"I guess it wouldn't hurt to let you boys see what we've got. We took all sorts of pictures and interviewed lots of folks. County coroner did the autopsy, but we had it reviewed by a forensic pathologist from Wichita."

"Would you have copies of the reports from Lincoln?"

"Should have," he said. Darlene walked in, handed an accordion file to the sheriff, and remained standing behind him. He placed his pipe on his desk and started flipping through the file. "Bingo," he said, "we do have some reports from LPD."

"Fantastic," I said. He handed the file to Darlene.

"Darlene," he said, "show these fellas where the copier is and let 'em copy whatever they want. Then check and see if we ever arrested a man by the name of Thomas Tobias. They'll give you the info."

"Sure thing, Sheriff." We followed Darlene and made copies of every document and photograph in the file. The copier didn't have a document feeder on it, so we were able to copy only one page at a time. It took nearly twenty minutes. Darlene sat at her desk and didn't smile once. We were saying good-bye to the sheriff when she appeared in his office. "No arrests on Thomas Tobias," she said.

"That help you fellas?" the sheriff asked.

"Sheriff," I said, "we can't thank you enough."

"Do me a favor," he said, "keep me informed. I'd love to see you prove the bureau wrong."

"We will," I promised.

We took our newfound treasure, walked past the suspicious Ford pickup, then crossed the street and headed to the park. A black squirrel was playfully chasing a gray squirrel around a tree. "If only people could get along like that," Scott said. We sat on a bench and began to read.

Carolyn Chang's body had been found in a ditch on a farm about nine miles south of Marysville. Near the Big Blue River—a body of water that, judging by what I'd seen, should have been named Little Muddy Creek. She'd been dead thirty-six to forty-eight hours, and they'd been lucky to find her that quickly. Her body had been dumped in midwinter, a time when farmers are seldom in their fields. Had not one of the farmer's cows escaped, her body might not have been found until spring.

From the angle of the stab wounds, the pathologist had concluded her killer was probably left-handed. There was little blood at the scene, indicating she had been killed at some other location. Presumably, she'd been killed somewhere between her home and the ditch where her body had been found. Wherever it had been, the elements had probably long since washed away any visible traces of blood.

There was no doubt Carolyn had been raped prior to being stabbed. As Susan Thompson had suggested, the pathologist's report concluded her assailant had worn a condom. She had put up a good fight; there were multiple bruises and lacerations on her face and arms, and skin particles beneath her fingernails. Tests on those particles, and on the unidentified pubic hairs found on her body, suggested there had been only one assailant.

Despite his laid-back manner, it appeared Sheriff Bowen had done a good job. He and his deputies had grilled every local resident and every known transient with any history of violence or sex offenses, but this had produced no viable suspects.

The Lincoln Police Department had provided copies of its reports to Sheriff Bowen as a courtesy, and I paid particular attention to those, but for the life of me I couldn't figure out why Amanda had been so reluctant to share information. The documents consisted mostly of statements from Carolyn's colleagues, friends, and neighbors. With one exception, they didn't reveal anything we hadn't already been able to learn or guess at.

Dale Hawkins had voluntarily provided pubic hair samples, but they didn't match those found with the body. A list of Nebraskans owning a dark, late-model Crown Victoria or Marquis had been cross-checked against a list of violent felons, but this too had produced no viable suspects. Amanda had also checked with the Colorado DMV, but there were no vehicles with an A-M-K prefix matching the description of the sedan seen in front of Carolyn's home on the night of her death.

The only new bit of information was that Carolyn Chang had filed a harassment complaint with the Lincoln Police Department a few years prior to her death. Amanda's report did not provide the details of the allegation, nor did it identify the subject of the complaint. She wrote:

> The evidence developed to date indicates the harassment complaint filed by the victim several years ago bears no relationship to the offenses, which are the subject of this investigation. (See Report # CC-154783-1.) The suspect in that case is not a suspect in the victim's murder.

Report # CC-154783-1 had not been provided to Sheriff Bowen.

When Scott and I had both read all the documents, we looked at our copies of the crime scene and autopsy photos. I'd seen plenty of such photos during my legal career, and I'd even attended a few autopsies, but gruesome photographs were a new experience for Scott. He just shook his head and said, "This guy was sick."

"Or wanted us to think that."

"That's even more sick."

"Yeah." We sat for a few minutes, then I clapped my hands and said, "Let's hit the road."

I started the truck, popped an old Merle Haggard tape into the cassette deck, stopped to buy a pop, and headed west for Colorado on US 36. We could've made Boulder in eight hours, but it was almost four and we decided we'd drive just halfway.

We arrived at Prairie Dog State Park just before eight. It was still hot, but we were on the high plains of Kansas now and the humidity was considerably lower than it had been in Marysville.

Located just east of Reager, the apparent reason for PDSP's existence was a reservoir. We found a secluded area by the lake and pitched our tent while the dogs frolicked in the water.

As the sun went down, we built a fire and later dined on ramen noodles beneath the stars. "Brings back fond memories," Scott said. I nodded agreement.

When darkness came I wasn't the least bit tired, probably because of all the pop, so I dug out the Coleman lantern I'd purchased in 1978 and sat in the back of the truck reading *Being and Time*.

Heidegger argued our man-centered view was responsible for mankind's abuses of nature and for many of the problems of the modern world. "Listen to this," I yelled to Scott, who was sitting on a picnic table looking at stars. "'One type of being, the human being, believes that all of Being exists for it.'"

"Heidegger would have a lot more credibility with me," he replied, "if he hadn't been a fucking Nazi." Like me, Scott has an interest in philosophy. You can't be an astrophysicist and not have an interest in philosophy. He walked to the back of the truck to retrieve his toothbrush from his toilet kit.

"'A foolish consistency is the hobgoblin of little minds,'" I joked. But he was right. There was no denying that Heidegger, generally considered one of the great philosophers of this century, had been a Nazi until the end of World War II. He later called his involvement with the Nazis "a blunder," but never attempted to account for his support of the party. I put the book down, climbed out of the truck, and prepared for bed.

It was still hot, so we opted to lie on top of our sleeping bags rather than inside them. Except for the mosquitoes, we could have slept under the stars. The dogs, of course, shared the tent with us, smelling just like wet dogs should.

"So what does this math professor look like?" Scott asked.

"I don't know," I said, "sort of like a tall version of Courteney Cox or Elizabeth Vargas."

"That ain't bad," he said.

"That's just like you," I joked. "You're concerned only with how a woman looks. Me, I try to look at the whole individual."

"Sleep tight," he said.

"Seriously," I persisted despite my own laughter, "you're so shallow. Why can't you see people for their inner beauty?"

"Fuck you," he said.

I laughed and turned over onto my stomach.

After our obligatory swim the next morning, we stopped in town for coffee and some breakfast. It was a little mom-and-pop version of the Waffle House. The glass-enclosed entry contained a few gumball machines and was plastered with notices of upcoming rodeos and farm auctions. The restaurant was nearly empty. A few old-timers sipped coffee at the counter. Five men wearing overalls and ball caps shared a large table toward the rear. It wasn't quite seven.

When nobody had greeted us after a few minutes, we seated ourselves at a booth in what was labeled the "No Smoking" section. Anything to the left of the entryway was the no-smoking section. A waitress in jeans and a white cowgirl shirt finally noticed us and said, "I'll be right with ya." Her name was Pammy, according to her name tag, and she looked to be a sophomore in high school.

She brought us water and coffee while we waited for breakfast. Locals started to filter in over the next twenty minutes. Just after my pancakes arrived, three bikers in their mid-thirties sauntered in and occupied the booth next to ours. All of them smoking. The smallest one, who I dubbed Tiny, stood six-one and must've weighed two-eighty. All wore ragged jeans and black leather vests. Long, greasy hair. Tiny wore a blue bandanna on his head and had a small teardrop tattooed at the outer edge of his left eye, meaning he'd done hard time. Another had "White Power" tattooed across his forearm. Scott looked at me and rolled his eyes.

We ignored the smoke, but Pammy didn't. "You men'll have to put those things out," she told them. "There's no smoking in this part of the restaurant." Two of the men took a final drag, then extinguished their smokes, but Tiny decided to give her a hard time.

"Hey, cute thing," he said, "I'm the kind of man has to have something to suck on. Know what I mean?" Quick as a viper, Scott turned and back-fisted him—hard—on the upper arm.

"Hey," Scott said, "can't you read the sign?"

"Yeah, I can read the fuckin' sign," the man roared as he maneuvered his beefy body out of the booth and came at Scott. In one fluid move, my friend slid out of our booth, stood, grabbed the man's right wrist with both hands, let out a shrill scream, and bent the wrist back in some kind of joint lock sending the attacker instantly to his knees. I stood up just in case. Shocked, Pammy came to my side. All eyes were on Scott.

Before Tiny's pals could exit their booth, Scott looked at them and said, "Don't even think about it or I'll break every bone in his wrist. There's eight of 'em if you count the navicular." Both of Tiny's pals looked at me.

"You a karate man too?" one asked.

"No," I said, "but I have a lot of anger left over from childhood." Dumbfounded, they resumed their seats.

"Should I call the sheriff?" Pammy asked.

"I don't think it'll be necessary," I said.

Scott looked down on his attacker. "Apologize to the girl," he said. He bent the man's wrist back just a tad more to provide motivation.

In obvious pain, but unable to move, the man looked up at Pammy and said, "I'm sorry."

"Good," Scott said. "I'm going to let you up now," he continued, "and you're going to sit down with your buddies and pretend this never happened, agreed?" With a grimace on his face and gritted teeth, the man nodded. "And if you or your pals so much as flinch in my direction, I'm going to kill the one nearest me. Not hurt, kill. You understand?" The man nodded again. Slowly, Scott relaxed his hold on the man's wrist and allowed him to stand. Then he let go entirely and watched as Tiny rejoined his companions. Keeping his eyes on the trio, Scott resumed his seat.

"You might want to ease up on the coffee," I said.

"Fuckin' pinheads," he said. I just laughed and poured more syrup on my pancakes.

When we had finished, Pammy brought our bill, thanked Scott for his chivalry, and told us to pay at the register.

I still had my checkbook in my hand when we climbed into the truck and I noticed a three-year calendar on the back of the check register. I studied December for the previous year. "I just figured out what's been bothering me about Hawkins not calling Carolyn."

"What's that?" Scott said.

"Carolyn disappeared on Friday the nineteenth and Hawkins didn't find out about her death until the next Monday."

"So?"

"The nineteenth was the last day of school before the Christmas break. Most couples would've had things planned for that weekend."

"And even if they didn't, they would've talked to make plans for Christmas Eve or Christmas Day?"

"Exactly," I said.

"Must've been a strange relationship," he said.

"Must've been," I said.

I started the truck and headed for home. Scott promptly fell asleep. We crossed back into Colorado. "Where are we?" he asked when he woke up two hours later.

"I don't know," I said, "but I've been waiting almost twenty years to say this."

"What's that?"

"Two Toe, I have a feeling we're not in Kansas anymore."

14

Here's the deal," Gumby said, "deregulation has made the whole phone-records issue a nightmare." He was dressed impeccably. Olive suit, starched white shirt, red-and-gold striped tie, new cordovan wing tips. "AT&T keeps records for only eighteen months. Most of the smaller long-distance companies don't even do their own billing; their charges show up on your monthly statement from the local phone company."

"So, in that situation, it depends on the policy of the local company?"

"That's the problem. Some of them keep records for ten years; most of them store the information for only a year or two." He sipped from a tall glass of iced tea. "Polk did it by the book. His report indicates he checked the phone records for the home and office numbers of all three victims, and their cell phones as well. Dittmer audited that report himself. The bottom line is, any phone records that might have connected these people have been destroyed." It was 11:20 on a Friday morning. We were at the Chop House, a yuppie favorite in downtown Denver. The lunch crowd was filing in. We'd been smart to come early.

"The detective in Walla Walla had a technician examine Fontaine's computers," I said. I buttered a hot roll. He understood that I was asking a question.

"Carolyn's only computer was in her office," he said. "By the time we got involved, the university had given it to someone else and he'd installed a bigger hard drive, so there wasn't much we could do. Our people inventoried her floppy disks, but didn't find anything." Our waiter arrived with salads and offered fresh pepper. Gumby accepted, I declined. Despite my name, I'm not big on hot spices.

"What about Underwood's computers?" I asked.

"Had one in his office. Our people examined it, but couldn't find any evidence that Underwood had ever corresponded with the others." He picked up his salad fork and casually speared a tomato slice. "For that matter," he added, "he couldn't find much of anything. The guy had a two-zillion-gigabyte computer, but only used it to trade e-mail and surf the Internet."

"Speaking of the Internet," I said, "was there any indication Underwood ever used his computer to visit pornographic web sites?"

"What's that got to do with anything?"

"If the guy was kinky enough to put a rope around his neck and masturbate, I figured he might've been into that sort of thing."

"No, we didn't find anything like that."

"What about secretaries?" I asked. "If Fontaine and Underwood exchanged letters concerning the textbook, you'd think there would be someone who remembers typing the correspondence."

"We checked that," he said, "but a lot of these professors do their own typing. None of the people we interviewed could connect one victim to another. The 302s are in the file." A complete copy of the bureau's file was contained in an accordion folder resting at my feet. I picked at my salad as I struggled to make sense of what I'd learned.

"Thanks for sharing all this," I finally said. "I know you didn't have to."

"You got my curiosity going with that textbook thing."

We continued eating and talked about matters unrelated to the case. Things like my life in Nederland and his recent second marriage. It was also a chance to catch up on the gossip I had enjoyed when I'd worked in the federal building.

"So," I said, "what's happening at the FBI? Got any good gossip?"

"Not that I can share," he said. "I'm already in trouble with Dittmer. He's from the old school, and lately he has been one tough son of a bitch. He'll cut my nuts off if he finds out I gave you this shit. He was pissed that we had to waste manpower on it in the first place."

"What's his story?" I asked. "I heard he was some kind of spook in 'Nam."

"He doesn't talk about it much," Gumby said, "but he won the Silver Star. Speaks fluent Vietnamese. Did some clandestine stuff over there. One of those Green Beret types who can kill you a dozen different ways. Been with the bureau twenty-five years. His next assignment was supposed to be in D.C., but the director chose a woman with nine years on the job, so you can imagine how he feels about being here."

"Yeah, you told me that," I said.

"Then his wife gets cancer."

"Why are you in hot water?" I asked.

"We did a bank robbery case last year," he said. "Now we can't find the gun, so everyone involved is under the microscope."

"Who logged it in?"

"This'll make your day."

"Polk?"

"Yeah." He caught my smirk and smiled to himself.

"Do you need the gun?" I asked.

"No, we've got the guy on video, and he confessed anyhow, but he had a religious conversion in jail, and Allah's telling him to take it to trial. Losing the weapon makes us look bad—and you know how the bureau feels about that." The last remark was a reference to the Big Crow case.

As an assistant U.S. Attorney I'd been tasked with prosecuting a tribal member charged with molesting a three-year-old girl on the Ute reservation in southern Colorado. Walter Big Crow had confessed, so it seemed like a slam dunk, but he later sought to suppress the confession, claiming two FBI agents had beaten it out of him. I'd heard such claims often and didn't put much stock in them, but he'd been smart enough to have the medical personnel at the jail document his injuries. I started an investigation and learned that one of the agents had bragged about the incident to Mike Polk. Big Crow's confession was thrown out and the case against him dismissed.

Relying on Polk's reluctant testimony, I obtained indictments against the agents on civil rights charges. They were no longer in prison, but the bureau had never forgiven me. As a sad footnote to the whole affair, Big Crow had later raped an eight-year-old girl.

"What are you thinking about?" Gumby asked.

"Nothing," I said. He didn't push it. We continued enjoying our lunch and eventually our waiter presented the check. Gumby reached for his wallet, but I grabbed the check and said, "It's on me." I had picked up $750.00 in cash from Big Matt earlier that morning for my work on the appellate brief.

"Going back to this fractal thing," Gombold said, "are you making any progress?"

"A little," I said. "I've got the name of a mathematician who studied or taught with all three of the victims, but he's disappeared."

"Anything I can do?"

"No, the detective in Walla Walla already ran an NCIC, but there was nothing."

"What if you can't find him? Where do you go from there?"

"Damned if I know," I said.

*   *   *

I was in the Boulder Bookstore on the Pearl Street Mall. I'd spent the day waxing my truck and performing chores around the house. Lacking anything better to do on a Saturday evening, I'd driven to Boulder.

Pearl Street is an eclectic district and consists of much more than the mall, but the mall is the heart of it. Four blocks long, the outdoor mall is a collection of high-end shops and galleries complemented by an ever changing array of trendy restaurants. Jugglers, musicians, and others with varying degrees of talent performed as people strolled the redbrick walkways. Street vendors hawked everything from felt hats to falafel. The well-kept gardens added color to an already colorful scene and gave the air a pleasant sweetness.

This was my second bookstore of the evening. I was in the philosophy section when I heard her voice. "Mr. Keane?" I turned around. It was Jayne Smyers.

"Hi," I said. I looked like crap. I was clad in tan shorts, the Top Cat shirt my brother had given me for my birthday two years ago, and some old running shoes. At least I'd had the good sense to run an electric razor over my face and slap on some Old Spice.

She, on the other hand, looked like a model in an L.L. Bean catalog. Pleated seersucker shorts the color of rose petals. White sleeveless cotton shirt. Brown leather sandals. Pink lipstick.

"Are you a big fan of Top Cat?" she teased.

"He's the indisputable leader of the gang," I replied.

"As I recall," she said, "his intellectual close friends get to call him T.C."

"Provided it's with dignity," I said. We laughed. Two well-educated adults sharing lyrics to a cartoon theme song neither had heard in decades.

"Do you know any others?" she asked.

"All of them."

"I didn't know Top Cat was into philosophy."

"An unfortunate habit I picked up in college."

"Really?"

"I even took graduate classes," I said. "Thought I might like to teach, but a year of symbolic logic cured me of that. What brings you here?"

"Oh, I don't know. Just killing time. Looking for a good read."

"Looks like you found some." She had several books under her arm.

"Too many."

"That's the way I am," I said. "They turn out good books faster than I can read them." I didn't know what to say next; I'm not much for small talk.

"What's happening with the case?" she finally asked.

"Pay for your books," I said. "I'll buy you a cup of coffee." We walked downstairs, each scanning the new paperbacks as we neared the cashiers' counter. After she'd made her purchases, we strolled east along the mall.

"I apologize for the way I look," I said. "I did chores all day and didn't plan on running into anyone tonight." Some Eagle Scout. I had forgotten the Boy Scout motto—"Be Prepared."

"You look fine," she lied. "It's refreshing to see a Boulder man who prefers Top Cat to Ralph Lauren." We passed a mime and approached Ben & Jerry's.

"How do you feel about ice cream?" I asked.

"I love it," she replied.

She ordered one scoop of lemon sorbet and I ordered two of pistachio. The total came to $6.32, but that was cheaper than Häagen-Dazs.

We found a table, and I related the details of the trip to Lincoln, leaving out anything having to do with Monica and Mindy. I told her I'd sent inquiries concerning Thomas Tobias to the DMV in all fifty states and the District of Columbia, but so far hadn't received any positive responses. "I can't believe what you've accomplished in such a short time," she said.

"It was a good trip," I admitted. "We obtained some useful information."

"I wonder if Stephen knows Professor Hawkins."

"I want to keep Finn out of this," I said. "He may be in touch with his colleagues in Nebraska and I don't want them to know you're my client. The fewer people who know about this, the better I'll feel about your safety and mine."

"I won't say anything," she assured me. I had finished my ice cream, but she was picking at her sorbet with a plastic spoon. "By the way," she said, "I listened to the tape you gave me. Where did you get it?"

"One of my neighbors is a musician."

"It took me a while to figure out the significance of it. Essentially, the composer relied on fractal patterns to create three-dimensional music, using pitch, duration, and volume as the x, y, and z coordinates."

"That's what I thought," I said. It took her a second to realize I was joking.

After she had spooned up the last of her sorbet, we stepped outside. It was past nine and the sun had set, but the temperature was comfortable. A guitarist played across the way. He looked like a young Frank Zappa, but played mostly Elton John and John Denver. We shared a wooden bench and enjoyed the music. "You know," she said, "on nights like this, I could just sit outside for hours."

"I do that all the time," I said. "Not much else to do in Nederland."

"What made you decide to live there? I thought Nederland was mostly counterculture types."

"It's a long story," I said, "but I'm finding I have a little of that in me."

Our troubadour took a break. We stood, and I placed two dollar bills in his guitar case. "I think I'd like that coffee now," she said. "Or do you need to be getting home?"

"I'd love the company," I said. "My dogs are great companions, but their conversational skills are limited." We continued walking east.

"What kind of dogs?" she asked.

"One's a schipperkee and the other is a cross between a Rhodesian Ridgeback and a Great Dane."

"What's a schipperkee?" she asked.

"Picture a black fox," I said.

We ended up at a coffeehouse several blocks east of the mall. We talked more about the case, and when we'd exhausted that, I encouraged her to tell me about herself. She was grateful for the opportunity, sharing stories of growing up in New Mexico. Her grandparents had owned a ranch, and she had fond memories of the times she'd spent there. As our conversation progressed we discovered neither of us had ever been engaged or married, and this led to a discussion of family.

"Mary Pat told me about your parents," I said. "That must have been difficult."

"It caused me to reevaluate some of my beliefs," she said. "I'm no longer a pacifist." I steered the conversation away from politics by asking if she had any siblings. She said no, then switched topics on me by asking, "Is Pepper your real name or just a nickname?"

"It's my real name," I assured her. "It's on my birth certificate."

"Is there a story behind that?"

"Not that I know of," I said.

"Well, Pepper Keane, tell me about yourself."

"Not much to tell," I said. "Grew up in Denver. Went to school in Boulder. Joined the service, worked as a prosecutor for a few years, then went into private practice."

"Why did you give that up?"

I thought about it. "The law is a confrontational profession," I finally said. "At first I enjoyed the competitiveness, but after a while I felt I was in a constant state of battle. I was burned out, so I decided to move to the mountains and start over."

"What about your parents?" she asked.

"They'll probably outlive me."

"What do they do?"

"My dad's retired," I said.

"What did he do?"

"He was a junior high principal and a brigadier general in the Marine Corps Reserve," I said. "He lives in Vegas and listens to Rush Limbaugh every day. Still has one of those 'I'm Not Fonda Hanoi Jane' bumper stickers on his car. Seventy years old and still runs five miles a day. My mother's a nurse in Barrow, Alaska. She's what you might call a free spirit."

"Brothers and sisters?" she asked.

"One brother. He owns a gym in Denver."

"Troy Keane's Gym, that's your brother?"

My brother's picture is on half the buses in Denver. "Yup."

"My God, does he really look like that?"

"No," I said. "That picture was taken a long time ago." And those muscles were the product of a lot of steroids.

She smiled and finished her umpteenth cup of coffee. It was eleven-thirty, and we decided to call it a night. "Can I walk you to your car?" I asked.

"I walked," she said. "My town house is only a few blocks away."

"I'll walk you home."

"You don't have to," she said.

"It's a nice night, I don't mind." We walked west on Pearl Street, past the Indian restaurants and bicycle shops, into an area occupied primarily by Rastafarian wanna-bes and kids with pierced body parts. The dreadlock crowd was drinking it up and banging away on their drums as they sat on the sidewalk. The yuppies hadn't yet captured that block of Pearl Street. It's lined with Depression-era apartments and older houses converted into rental units.

"I'm glad you came with me," she said as we passed the last of the rowdies and entered the more fashionable end of Pearl Street.

"Most of them are harmless," I said.

"I try to be tolerant," she said, "but I don't see how they can live like that." I said nothing. Dwelling on it would only get me worried about the gene pool and the future of civilization.

We continued west. "That's mine," she said as we approached her condo. It wasn't a few blocks away; more like ten blocks. Right up against the mountains. She lived in a three-story unit with a small brook running behind it. The entrance was in the rear.

"This is nice," I said.

"I love it here," she said. "The sound of the water is so soothing. I used to see deer every morning. I don't know why they stopped coming."

"It's the Russian olives," I said. There were a couple of dozen beside the brook.

"The trees?"

"Yeah, those things are the arboreal equivalent of cancer."

"Really?"

"They're thorny as hell and grow like wildfire. Sooner or later, they choke out everything else."

"I had no idea."

"They're not native to this area," I said. "Farmers used them as windbreaks during the Dust Bowl days, and they've just gotten out of hand."

"What makes you so smart?" she teased.

"I read a lot," I said. She opened her purse and searched for her keys. "Who owns that land?" I asked as I pointed toward the offending trees.

"I don't know," she said. "The owners' association, I suppose."
She found her keys, opened the door, and switched on an overhead light. Finn was not there and I saw nothing to indicate she
was sharing quarters with him or anyone else. She turned to face
me. "I'm glad we ran into each other," she said. "I enjoyed talking
with you, Pepper." She was no longer referring to me as Mr.
Keane.

"Me too," I said. I slept well that night. I was on a first-name
basis with Jayne Smyers and it felt good.

15

Monday. I'd spent a good chunk of the weekend immersed in the FBI file Gumby had provided. I hated to admit it, but it looked like Polk had done a thorough job of checking the phone records. In each case the service provider either did not retain records for more than one year or, due to internal glitches, was unable to locate any records. Not only had he checked all the long-distance and cell-phone providers, but he had even checked with the various colleges and universities to see if they kept hard copies of their telephone bills. In each case the answer was no.

I'd been on the case for three weeks. Despite my success in gathering information, I felt stymied. The FBI file had provided some useful background information and saved me a lot of tedious work, but it hadn't suggested any new avenues of investigation. Tobias remained my only real lead. I dialed information for Bend, Oregon, to verify that Iris Tobias still lived there. She did. If something didn't break soon, I'd have to put in a call to her and everyone else her son had ever known.

A formidable wall of clouds was forming to the west, but it was warm in Nederland. I decided to jog to the post office before the afternoon storms arrived.

There was a letter from the Colorado Supreme Court informing me I had to complete three hours of continuing legal education within ninety days in order to avoid administrative suspension. CLE is mandatory in Colorado. Attorneys must accumulate forty-five credits every three years, and my three years had evidently just expired. I made a mental note to call Matt. The library at Keane, Simms & Mercante is filled with CLE tapes. Most lawyers don't even listen to the damn things. They're too busy. They just send in the affidavit certifying that they completed the course. You can't blame them. It's a stupid requirement. Good lawyers will always strive to expand their knowledge of the law, and bad lawyers will be bad lawyers no matter how many CLE classes they attend.

The only other piece of mail was a large package from Dick Gilbert. True to his word, he had obtained O'Hara's file on the Underwood suicide and forwarded copies of everything to me. I tucked the eleven-by-fourteen envelope under my arm and jogged over to Wanda's.

"Mornin', Pepper," she said as she reached for my mug.

"Mornin', Wanda."

"Try a hot Danish?"

"Not today," I said. "Have to watch my figure." I didn't have any money on me because I was in my running gear, but she knows I'm good for it and told me to help myself to coffee. I put a little cream in it, gave Zeke a pat on the head, found an empty booth, and began to read.

It didn't take long to realize that the Boston cops hadn't done much in the case of Donald Underwood. They'd taken photographs, interviewed his wife, friends, and colleagues, then labeled it a case of autoerotic asphyxiation and closed the file. I can't blame them; at the time they'd investigated the incident, they'd had no reason to know of the other deaths and therefore no reason to suspect foul play.

As the news clippings had indicated, Underwood had been a thirty-seven-year-old math professor at Harvard. After they'd separated, his wife and their two sons had moved to Longmeadow, an upscale suburb of Springfield in western Massachusetts. They'd been apart ten months at the time of his death. Sara

Underwood told investigators the decision to separate had been hers. After twelve years of marriage, she felt ambivalent about the life she'd chosen and wanted time to sort things out. She returned to the area of her upbringing and accepted a position as a high school art teacher.

Though the couple had been separated nearly a year, Mrs. Underwood said they'd been talking of reconciling and her husband's spirits had been good. He'd visited their sons, ages ten and eight, nearly every weekend, and periodically the couple had enjoyed sexual relations throughout their separation. She insisted he had never demonstrated any aberrant sexual behavior or shared any such thoughts. Nor, she said, had he ever been treated for any form of mental illness, a claim his medical records seemed to confirm.

The file contained more photographs than I needed. Underwood had been found hanging in his spacious walk-in closet. The nylon cord around his neck ran over a metal water pipe along the ceiling. The cord showed no wear and tear and was of a type only recently placed on the market, according to a forensic expert. Underwood wore only briefs. The coroner's report indicated he had not ejaculated. No suicide note had been found.

I jogged home and showered. While I was in the shower, Mary Pat left a message indicating she had copies of every professional article Thomas Tobias had ever published. She sounded excited, but before driving to Boulder, there was something I wanted to do.

I couldn't get Underwood out of my mind. I wanted to do some quick research and the only place in Nederland likely to have what I needed was the High Country Clinic. The receptionist was a frumpy woman in her forties. I told her I'd like to glance at a book or two on psychiatry. She gave me a curious look, then asked me to wait while she disappeared into the rear of the suite. She returned in less than a minute with Dr. Edwards, the carrot-top, beside her. Seeing them together, I realized he was taller than I had thought. Thin, but close to six feet. He'd gotten a haircut since my last visit.

"Mr. Keane," he said as he extended his right hand over the Formica counter, "how are you doing?" I noticed my file in his other hand.

"Much better," I replied. "The antibiotics seemed to do the trick."

"Glad to hear it," he said. He didn't seem to bear a grudge. "Mrs. Sullivan tells me you have an interest in psychiatry?"

"Can we talk in private?" I asked. I nodded toward a mother and her young son seated in the waiting area.

"Certainly," he said, "let me show you my office." He gestured toward the door to my left, opened it from his side, and led me past some examining rooms to an office with a Berber carpet. It looked and smelled brand new.

"Redecorating?" I asked.

"Yes, we hope to have the entire office done by the end of the month." There was an antique rolltop desk against one wall. He sat down in an executive chair beside it and began to tap a pencil. I remained standing.

"I know you're busy," I said, "so I won't take much of your time. I don't think I mentioned this when I saw you, but I work as a private investigator." I handed him one of my cards.

"No, you didn't, but I'd heard there was a lawyer in town who did that type of work."

"I'm working on something right now and I want to learn about autoerotic asphyxiation." He seemed to want more, so I gave him a thumbnail sketch of the case.

"Now I understand," he said. He set down the pencil. "Don't take this personally, but sometimes people with mental health issues feel compelled to read up on those issues, and in the end it usually only results in increased anxiety. The history you completed indicates you take medication for depression—"

"I figured it was something like that," I said. I told him I'd been taking medication for more than a decade and still saw a psychiatrist twice a year. It hadn't stopped me from holding a top-secret clearance or obtaining a concealed-weapon permit. Satisfied that I was telling the truth, he turned toward a bookcase and handed me two large volumes.

"Kaplan and Sadock, *Comprehensive Textbook of Psychiatry*," he said. "This is the bible." He invited me to use his office while he attended to the little boy. It didn't take long to find what I wanted:

Masturbatory practices have resulted in what has been called autoerotic asphyxiation. This practice involves masturbating while hanging oneself by the neck to heighten erotic sensations and the intensity of orgasm. Although such persons release themselves from the noose after orgasm, an estimated 500 to 1,000 persons per year unwittingly kill themselves by hanging. Most persons indulging in this practice are male; transvestism is often associated with the habit, and the majority of deaths occur among adolescents. Such masochistic practices are usually associated with severe mental disorders, such as schizophrenia and mood disorders.

It wasn't conclusive, but it strengthened my suspicion that Underwood's death might have been staged. He wasn't an adolescent, had no history of mental illness, and no female garments had been found in his home. Moreover, if he'd been in the habit of engaging in that type of behavior, it seemed curious that the nylon cord appeared to have been recently purchased.

Mary Pat was at her mentor's desk. She wore cutoff jeans and a pale green top. The pro-choice button was still there. "Hello, Mr. Keane," she said. She was beaming, obviously proud of something.

"Hi, Mary Pat. How are you?" I sat down.

"I'm fine," she replied.

"What have you got for me?" I asked. She passed me a stack of papers.

"Thomas Tobias wrote sixteen articles," she said. "I read them all."

"Do any of them have anything to do with fractals?" I asked.

"Nope."

"Then why are you grinning like a Cheshire cat?"

"His specialty was the history of mathematics," she said.

"And?"

"He wrote a series of ten articles for the *Journal of Mathematical Thought*. Historical pieces. He used a pen name for each one, and always chose the name of a mathematician from the relevant era. He'd write the piece from the point of view of the mathematician he'd chosen for that article." I saw what she was getting at. I thumbed through the articles noting names such as Leibniz, Pascal, and Wittgenstein.

"You sure you want to teach math?" I asked. "You might have a future as a detective." She smiled and did the sexy head twist she had developed to keep her hair out of her eyes. "Do you think Professor Smyers would mind if I borrowed a book or two on the history of mathematics? I'll need to make a list of famous mathematicians."

"Not at all," she said. She stood, went to one of the bookcases, selected two titles she thought might be useful, handed them to me, then resumed her seat. "Do you think he's living under an assumed name?"

"Probably," I said. Forty-six states had indicated no record of issuing a driver's license to anyone named Thomas Payne Tobias. "What you've found may offer a way to reduce the number of possible aliases to a manageable level."

"Can I do anything else?" she asked.

"Work on your thesis," I said. "I'll take care of this." She seemed disappointed, but there was nothing she could do. "I'll let you know if I find anything," I promised. I placed the articles and books in my briefcase.

"I hear you ran into Jayne Saturday night," she said.

"She ran into me."

"She said she had a nice time."

"So did I," I said. I pushed the door shut. "While we're on that topic," I added, "how serious is it between her and Finn?"

"What do you mean?"

"Their relationship, how serious is it?"

"Relationship? That's a hoot."

"I'm confused."

"You must be. Their only relationship is that she's on the tenure committee and he's obsessed with tenure."

"He sure works hard at creating the impression they're involved."

"He likes being seen with her," she said. "He follows her like a puppy—he's always inviting her to lectures and things like that—but I don't think she's interested in him. Not romantically."

"They're not an item?"

"God, no. She'd die if she knew you thought that."

"Well," I said, "let's just keep it our little secret."

Using Tobias's articles and the books Mary Pat had allowed me to borrow, it took only a half hour in my office to compile a list of thirty-four famous mathematicians. I excluded Archimedes, Euclid, Ptolemy, and anyone else traditionally known by only one name. The decision I faced now was what to do with the list. Gumby had the resources of the federal government behind him, but he'd already taken a big risk for me and there were probably only so many favors left in the Gumby Bank. I punched in Scott's number.

"McCutcheon," he said.

"Turn on your computer," I said. We had already agreed Tobias was probably using an alias, but now I had a plausible theory as to the types of names he might be using. I told him about Tobias's articles and his fondness for pseudonyms.

"Where do you want me to search?" he asked. "Some of these commercial locators charge a hundred bucks for a single name."

"Can you bust in?"

"It's hit and miss," he said.

"Use your imagination," I said. "Start with the math and science chat rooms and message boards available through AOL and CompuServe, and see if anyone's adopted one of these names as a nickname. He might've combined the first name of one person with the last name of another. I'll fax you my list."

"What are you going to do?" he asked.

"I'm going to phone Gilbert and ask for some help on the driver's license angle, then I'm going to start calling directory assistance. I'll start in Oregon and work my way east."

16

We found the gun," Gilbert said. It was Tuesday morning and I was in my office. I had called to ask him to run multistate driver's-license checks on my mathematicians, but he beat me to the punch.

"Where?"

"In the Columbia River, forty-five minutes from here. Some crazy kids decided to try to swim across the thing. Got about a hundred yards out and decided it wasn't such a good idea. The current carried them down a good ways. As they were crawling out, one of them found a thirty-eight lying in the mud."

"Any doubt it's the right gun?"

"No, the mud preserved it well. It fired the bullet that killed Fontaine."

"Serial number?"

"Filed off, but it was a five-shot—not a six—and we're trying to match it against similar weapons sold or stolen in the region."

"Who manufactured it?"

"Taurus."

"Taurus five-shot," I said. "That ought to narrow it down."

"Bet your ass," he said. "What can I do for you?" I told him about Tobias's articles and asked if he could use his influence to run my thirty-four names through the driver's-licensing agencies in nine western states. "That'll take some time," he said.

"'Even a journey of one thousand miles begins with a single step.'"

"That's profound," he said. "You come up with that on your own?"

"I think it was Lao-tzu or Confucius," I said, "but it might have been Charlie Chan."

"I'll do what I can," he said. That was all I could ask. I turned my attention to the task of calling directory assistance.

Excluding Alaska and Hawaii, there are nine states located entirely in the Mountain or Pacific time zones. By my count there were twenty-nine area codes. Multiply that by thirty-four names and I might have been looking at 986 calls to directory assistance. Fortunately, several companies had recently started offering nationwide directory assistance.

It was a hell of a way to spend a morning and it made for some interesting conversations. "I need a listing for a Joseph Fourier."

"What city?"

"Every city. I want every listing." Pause.

"I'll have to charge you for each listing, sir."

"I figured you would," I said. "That's okay." And so it went.

Most of the operators refused to search more than one or two names per call, so I had to call back each time I wanted listings for a new name. The woman who answered when I asked for every René Descartes in America must've known something about mathematics because she hung up on me, but I hit redial and drew someone else.

By noon I had the information I wanted. The sun was out, but I didn't feel like a long run, so I rode my bike up to the high school and ran a series of sprints. Races are measured in meters now, and most tracks are four-hundred-meter ovals, but I pretend one lap is a quarter mile. We used to call them 440s. Half a lap was 220 yards. I did some of those too, then ended with ten sprints between the goal posts. The process wore me out, but it felt good.

I had no sooner arrived home than the phone rang. It was Gumby. "What are you doing this afternoon?" he asked.

"What do you want me to do?" I replied. I was dripping with sweat, and Wheat was doing his best to lick it from my calves.

"Polk somehow found out this math professor hired you and told Dittmer. Polk's got him convinced you're a loose cannon."

"You want me to meet with Dittmer?"

"I think it would be a good idea. I told him you were a professional, but he'd like to meet you."

"This afternoon?"

"That'd be great."

"Four o'clock?"

"Perfect."

"I'll work out with my brother, and see you at four."

I got cleaned up, let the dogs out for a few minutes, then headed down the mountain to Denver. It didn't take a genius to know that the agent in Walla Walla had contacted Polk to let him know I'd taken a look at Fontaine's probate file, but how had Polk learned the identity of my client? If Polk knew *someone* had hired me to investigate the three deaths, I suppose Jayne Smyers was the most obvious candidate.

I saw no suspicious yellow Ryder trucks in the vicinity of the federal building, so I figured it was safe to fulfill my promise to meet Gumby at four. The nearest open meter was three blocks away. Between the sprints and my workout with Troy, three blocks was about as far as I cared to walk.

I entered the building, passed through the metal detector, and noted the President's smiling mug. I didn't vote for him, but I thanked God it wasn't Al Sharpton, Tom DeLay, or any one of a dozen other boneheads I could have named. I got off the elevator on eighteen and entered the Denver regional office of the FBI. A black receptionist sat behind a thick glass barrier. Pretty in a 1960s sort of way—like a young Diana Ross. I picked up the phone on my side of the barrier. "May I help you?" she asked.

"Pepper Keane," I said. "Here to see Tim Gombold."

"Please be seated," she said. "Someone will be with you shortly." Very professional, which is not always the case when you enter a government office.

I selected a recent *Newsweek* from the magazine rack and sat down on one of the tan leather couches. After ten minutes a side door opened and Gombold appeared.

"Sorry about this," he said. He handed me a visitor's badge and I clipped it to my lapel. I wore a black suit, white shirt, silver tie, and black wing tips. You don't need a color consultant to select your clothes when you've been blessed with black hair that has a white stripe.

"Don't worry about it," I said. I followed him through a maze and into the main workroom, then down a hallway to Dittmer's office.

The door was open. Gombold knocked on the door, then stepped in and said, "Sir, this is Pepper Keane." Dittmer was tall and lean, with broad shoulders. Wearing a short-sleeved broadcloth shirt. Early fifties. Weathered face, intense blue eyes, square jaw. Sandy hair, almost as short as mine. No smile. Everything about him said tough hombre.

"Bo Dittmer," he said as he stood and extended his arm. He sounded like he might be from the South. Not the Deep South; more like Virginia or one of the other border states.

"Pepper Keane," I said. We shook hands, and I noticed a long scar running the length of his forearm. His paisley tie hung loose around his neck. He motioned for me to sit down. Gumby sat next to me and stared out at the mountains. Dittmer had a corner office with a magnificent view of downtown and the Rockies.

"Agent Gombold speaks highly of you," he said.

"I pay him well," I said.

"Tim tells me you're taking a second look at a case we worked."

"That's right," I said. Stacks of files covered his desk, some nearly a foot high. An American flag on a wooden pole stood behind one corner of the desk. His walls boasted his college degrees, numerous army and FBI awards, and a number of photographs depicting him shaking hands with political heavyweights from both parties.

"I can't say I like the fact that you've become involved in the case," he continued, "but it's a free country and if this lady professor wants to pay you to dig around, I can't stop you." I said nothing. "I give you credit for finding that reference to Underwood in Fontaine's textbook, though," he added. "It's not enough to warrant reopening the case, but that was good work." He seemed sincere.

"Thanks."

"My concern," he said, "is that you don't create a panic in the press or in the mathematical community as you go about doing whatever it is you're going to do. Rumors get started, next thing you know Pierre Salinger's on the fucking Internet claiming the bureau's engaged in a cover-up."

"I've been pretty discreet so far," I assured him.

"I appreciate that," he said. "Can you tell me what else you've learned?"

I gave him the highlights, leaving out our discovery of Thomas Tobias because I didn't want him asking how I'd obtained Tobias's name. The conversation took about twenty minutes.

"Any leads on the gun?" he asked.

"No," I said. "They know it was a Taurus five-shot, but the serial number had been filed off." He just nodded and switched topics. "Tim says you were a marine?"

"Judge advocate," I said.

"You like it?"

"Loved it," I said.

"Why'd you leave?" Strange question given that I'd just met the man, but the question had been asked before and I knew how to respond without revealing my battle with depression.

"That's a good question," I said. "If I'd stayed in, I'd be four years away from retirement." He nodded. It was my turn to switch topics. "How about you," I asked. "You must have been in the service." I pointed to the awards on the wall.

"Army. Seventy to seventy-four."

"Vietnam?"

"Yeah, and parts of Cambodia and Laos. The lines were a bit fuzzy in those days. You ever in combat?"

"Nope."

"A lot of good men died," he said, "but sometimes I miss it. I swear, there are times I'd rather be back in the jungle than sitting behind this desk with baby-faced bureaucrats riding my ass." Gumby glanced at me as if to say, See, I told ya. "But, that's my problem," Dittmer added, "not yours."

He ended our conversation at precisely four forty-five. He promised he'd consider reopening the case if I came up with something concrete. To his credit, he never mentioned my prosecution of the agents involved in the Big Crow case.

"Thanks for stopping by," he said as we stood. "I'm glad we had the chance to meet."

"Me too," I said. We shook hands again, and he turned his attention to some papers on his desk, leaving us to see ourselves out.

"That went well," Gumby said.

"Think so?"

"Yeah, you convinced him you know what you're doing, and that's all he wanted. And I think he likes the fact that you're prior military."

"Good."

"I'll walk you out," he said. He led me through the maze and into the main work area. There were dozens of desks, federal agents working diligently at many of them. It was a symphony of fluorescent lights, telephones, fax machines, copiers, and typewriters. As we approached the other end of the room, Polk came around a corner and nearly walked into us. A tall man with immense shoulders, blond hair, and movie-star looks, Polk is six-five and must weigh two-forty.

"What's he doing here?" Polk said to Gumby, making no effort to hide his contempt for me. His sleeves were rolled up and he wore a leather shoulder holster with a .357 in it. A combination Robert Redford and Dirty Harry.

"Surprised to see you here, Pokey," I said. "I thought they still had you working the Kennedy assassination."

"Kill anyone lately?" he asked. "I never understood how you figured it was okay to kill people, but not animals." Polk is a big hunting enthusiast—birds, deer, big game—and I'd given him plenty of grief about it over the years.

"Just some people," I said.

"Same old Pepper," he said. "If it wasn't for your tendency to indict federal agents, I'd shut that smart mouth of yours once and for all."

"I'm not a prosecutor anymore," I said as I set my briefcase down. "Let's do it right now."

The room was silent. Every agent and secretary was locked in on us. Polk stepped toward me, but Gumby stuck out his hand and said, "C'mon, guys." Polk's left fist was clenched and his face was the color of boiled lobster.

"Go ahead, Pokey," I said, "take a swing at me. I've been waiting twenty years for you to get up the courage."

We stared at each other, then he brushed past me and said, "Your day's coming, asshole."

"Focus on the grassy knoll," I shouted as he walked away. "That's the key."

17

I can't believe anyone would name their son Isaac Newton," said Bobbi. Of the 157 listings I'd obtained from directory assistance, there were three Isaac Newtons. One in Vermont, one in New Jersey, and one in Ohio.

"Who's George Boole?" Bobbi asked as they continued scanning the notes I'd prepared. Of the thirty-four mathematical names I'd chosen to work with, that was the most common. I had telephone listings for twelve George Booles.

"Boolean algebra," I said.

"What's Boolean algebra?" Bobbi asked. She wore cut-offs and a red sleeveless top that accentuated her ample bustline.

"It's a system of symbolic logic," Scott said. He was focused on my notes, so it came out sounding like her question had been a distraction.

"Oh, that's right," she said. "I remember learning that when I studied for my broker's license." She elbowed him playfully. He smiled, put my notes aside, and reached for a bagel.

"Thank God these guys all have unusual names," he said. He wore a white tank top and green running shorts.

"There was one named Henry Smith," I said, "but I decided not to bother."

It was nine o'clock on a Saturday morning. We were in Scott's kitchen eating bagels from Moe's and enjoying Bobbi's gourmet coffee. Aspen Blend, or something like that. Bobbi was in the process of updating the kitchen, so the wallpaper had been stripped from the walls. Buck and Wheat played in the backyard. Outside, it was shaping up to be a gorgeous day.

Inside, it was shaping up to be a tedious day. In addition to the 157 phone listings, Gilbert had faxed seventy-two driver's license abstracts. I handed those to Scott, then began to spread cream cheese across a garlic bagel.

"Why the red and green marks?" Bobbi asked. I'd sorted the abstracts into two categories.

"Red means the license was issued before Tobias disappeared. We can forget those people."

"How many green ones are there?" Scott asked.

"There were seventeen," I said, "but I eliminated ten based on age, race, or height." Tobias was thirty-five years old and white. His employment application had listed his height as five-eleven. I'd culled any man under twenty or over fifty. I'd also cast aside anyone shorter than five-seven or taller than six-three.

"These are just the Western states?" Scott asked.

"Yeah," I said. He put the abstracts aside and poured more coffee for all.

When she'd had her fill of bagels and coffee, Bobbi carried her dishes to the sink and said, "You boys have fun today. I'm off to the farmer's market." Boulder hosts a farmer's market every Saturday from May through October. She gave Scott a peck on the cheek. He responded with a pat on her rear and asked her to buy some fresh corn. We heard her Porsche start, then resumed our discussion.

"I showed you mine," I said, "now show me yours."

"I took your suggestion," he said. "I monitored the math and science forums every night this week, but they were deader than dead. I spent four hours on-line last night and found one chat room open. There were two people in it."

"Jesus." Scott subscribes to AOL and all the other services, so I knew he'd covered all the bases.

"I went through a shitload of message boards and BLOGs too, but the only people using them are computer geeks and graduate students."

"Any mathematical nicknames?"

"One guy called himself Alex the Great, but he lives in Ontario."

"How'd you learn that? I thought all you could get from message boards was the person's e-mail address."

"It's called extraction," he said. "If you have the right software, you can retrieve the on-line service's billing information for anyone who's been in a particular forum or section. Marketing companies use it all the time to develop mailing lists for people with specific interests."

"So tell me about Alex the Great."

"He's not our man," Scott said. "He and some other guy were trading messages about the pros and cons of a new programming language, and a math professor would've known the answers to the questions he was asking."

"Thanks for trying," I said. I stood and took my dishes to the sink.

"I'm not done," he said. "I didn't think of it until Wednesday, but it occurred to me we're looking for someone with an interest in the history of mathematics, so I visited a lot of web sites and posted as many messages as I could. Said I was a high school senior writing a paper on the history of mathematics and wanted to learn as much as possible about it."

"Get any responses?" I resumed my seat.

"Eight as of last night."

"Anyone using a nickname?"

"No, but I got a billing address for each of them, and I figure we might as well check them out."

"Might as well," I said.

He gulped the last of his coffee. "How do you want to start?" he asked.

"Let's start with the phone numbers," I said. "Of those hundred and fifty-seven listings, only forty-eight are in the Western states. There's an on-line crisscross service that will give us a street address for each phone number. We'll compare those with the driving abstracts to avoid duplication, then take a look at the people who responded to your messages and come up with some sort of master list."

"Okay," he said, "let's get to it." I followed him downstairs to what had become known as the War Room. Scott's basement contains more computer and electronic equipment than any home office I've ever seen. The floor is covered in beige carpeting and the walls are finished with wood paneling, but with all the maps, scientific tables, and astronomical charts he has tacked up, the room resembles a military command post.

The crisscross service turned out to be more useful than I had anticipated. In addition to providing a street address for each of the forty-eight phone numbers we'd submitted, we were able to learn how long the person had been receiving phone service at that address. By eliminating those who had obtained service prior to Tobias's disappearance, we shrank the list of possibles from forty-eight to eleven.

By noon we had sorted through all the information and created a list of fourteen men. Fourteen men in the nine Western states known to be using one of thirty-four names prominent in the history of mathematics. Fourteen men who had obtained a driver's license or phone service after Tobias's disappearance.

"The scary part," Scott said, "is that all this assumes he's in the Western states."

"And that he has a driver's license or phone service," I added. I didn't say it, but most frightening was the possibility that Tobias might not even be the killer. We really had nothing on him.

"Now what?" Scott asked.

"On Monday I'll start calling county officials and learn as much as I can about these people. Anyone who registered to vote before Tobias disappeared is off the list. Anyone who paid property taxes before Tobias disappeared is off the list. Anyone who registered a vehicle before Tobias disappeared is off the list." Scott turned off the computer he'd been using, then stood and stretched.

"Boy," he said, "being a private investigator sure is glamorous."

18

C'MON," TROY URGED, "push it, push it." I squeezed out two more reps, then set the bar down on the rack. My fifth and final set of squats. "Not bad for a geezer," he said.

"My legs are fried."

"You'll need that leg strength if Polk comes after you," he joked. I just laughed.

It was Monday afternoon, and we were finishing our workout at Troy's gym. The first day of June. I'd spent the morning on the phone with county officials throughout the West, and I'd trimmed the list of potential Thomas Tobiases from fourteen to six:

George Cantor, San Anselmo, California
John von Neumann, Scottsdale, Arizona
David D. Hilbert, Orem, Utah
David T. Hilbert, Irvine, California
Karl Gauss, Mora, New Mexico
Hermann Weyl, Seattle, Washington

"Want to grab a bite to eat?" I asked after we had showered and changed. It was almost five, and I didn't relish driving home during the rush hour.

"Can't," he said. "We've got Boy Scouts." Troy's son, Andrew, had joined the Boy Scouts a year ago and Troy had volunteered to serve as an assistant scoutmaster. "Want to tag along and talk about the exciting field of investigations?"

"Probably not a good day for me to speak on that topic," I said.

I bid my brother farewell and walked around the fashionable Cherry Creek area, where his gym is located. Not surprisingly, I ended up at The Tattered Cover, the largest bookstore in the Rocky Mountain region. It's supposed to be a great place to meet intelligent women, but tonight I was just looking for books. I didn't purchase any, but if anyone ever writes *Heidegger for Dummies* or *Idiot's Guide to Phenomenology*, those are two I'll buy.

I left the bookstore around six-thirty, found my truck, and headed home. The Rockies were in town that night, so most of the traffic was coming into downtown while I was heading out. Once I got past Thirty-eighth, it was smooth sailing.

It was 7:40 when I arrived in Nederland. I hadn't checked my mail that morning, so I stopped at the post office before going home. There was plenty of junk mail, a few bills, and one letter with a return address in Dayton, Ohio. Who did I know in Ohio? The only person I could think of was a former client, an embezzler serving time at a federal penitentiary. I opened the envelope. It was a handwritten letter from Monica:

Pepper:

As you can probably tell, Mindy and I made it back to good old Dayton. I'm working in a department store, and I'm already itching to get back to school and sunny California.

I found the enclosed article while unpacking and I thought it might interest you. It contains a discussion of the use of fractal geometry in predicting the behavior of economic markets. Thought it might help you catch the bad guys.

Say hi to your groupie.

Fondly,
Monica

The article was entitled "Frontiers of Finance" and had been published in *The Economist*. I put it in my shirt pocket and drove home.

I let the dogs out, cleaned up the house, and wondered what to do with myself. *Monday Night Football* would return in a few short months, the Broncos would begin their annual quest for a Super Bowl title, and all would be right with the world. My problem was what to do for the next few hours. I considered driving to Barker Reservoir and throwing a few lures in the water, but it would be dark soon. Besides, over the past few years, I'd found myself thinking more about animal rights, with the result that I was now somewhat ambivalent about fishing.

I suppose I could've read the article Monica had sent, but I'd done enough for one day and just wanted to relax. I scanned my collection of CDs and selected Peter, Paul and Mary. Then I did something I do once every six months—I tamped some tobacco into a pipe my father had given me, then sat on the front deck while I enjoyed the music.

After forty-five minutes or so, Buck started barking and I saw Luther and Missy walking up the path to my home. They had a dog with them, the same shepherd mix I'd seen in their yard a few weeks ago. It wasn't unusual for Luther to stop by, but Missy seldom accompanied him. Buck trotted over and extracted the requisite amount of affection from each of them.

"Hey, kids," I said, "what's up?" We exchanged greetings and I invited them to sit down. Missy's long gray hair was in a bun and she looked distraught. She took the other rocking chair and Luther sat on the porch steps.

"Missy saw something today," said Luther, "that I think you should know about."

"What's that?" I asked. She seemed hesitant.

"Go ahead," urged Luther.

"Well," she began tentatively, "a few days ago I saw a man park on the road and walk up to your house, but I didn't pay much attention to it."

"What kind of car?" I asked.

"I don't know," she said. "A big car."

"What did he look like?"

"I didn't get a good look at him," she said. "He was tall."

"Tell him what you saw this afternoon," Luther interjected.

"Well," she started, "this afternoon I saw a man walking around your house like he was inspecting it. He parked on the road and walked around your house a couple of times."

"A meter reader?" My pipe had died, so I relit it.

"No," she said, "he was wearing a tie."

"What did he look like?" I asked.

"He was real big and had blond hair."

"The same man you saw a few days ago?"

"It could have been. I'm not sure."

"Did you get a better look at the car?" I asked.

"It looked new," she said. "One of those big luxury cars."

"A Cadillac? A Lincoln?"

"I'm not very good with those things," she said. "Sorry."

"That's okay," I said. "What color was it?"

"Dark blue."

"Did he visit any other houses?"

"No," she insisted, "he came to see your house. He even looked in your windows. Buck was going nuts this afternoon. That's what caught my attention."

"Did he see you?" I asked.

"I don't think so," she said.

"Did you get a license plate?"

"I wanted to," she said, "but I couldn't get close enough without letting him see me."

Big guy with blond hair. Wearing a tie. Driving a late-model sedan. It could've been a Realtor prospecting for new listings, but they usually leave a card or a brochure. Luther interrupted my thoughts.

"Does this mean anything to you?" he asked.

"It might," I said. "Thanks for being alert. If you see anything else unusual, let me know." They assured me they would, then walked away hand in hand.

I mulled over Missy's story as I continued listening to Peter, Paul and Mary. I tried to think of an innocent explanation for what she'd witnessed, but couldn't. If Polk had bugged my house or tapped my phone, he was about to feel the hammer of justice. I'd hammer in the morning. I'd hammer in the evening. I'd hammer all over this land.

"Mornin', Wanda," I said.

"Mornin', Pepper," she replied. "Earliest I've seen you here in a while. You wanna try a fresh bear claw?" She reached for my Foghorn Leghorn mug.

"Sure," I said. I have to buy something once in a while to avoid giving the impression that I don't like her pastry.

I poured myself some coffee, waited for the bear claw, then found an empty booth. It was six-thirty Tuesday morning. I'd stayed up well past midnight. The stranger had not entered my home, but I'd conducted a visual search for bugs just the same. Then I'd used a portable radio in an attempt to detect hidden batteries. If you hear static or interference as you pass the radio over something, that can be indicative of a low-level signal or a power source, but I had been unable to find anything.

I'd finished the process that morning by combing the exterior of the house and the yard for transmitters. Now, as I scanned the *Rocky Mountain News,* I felt confident there were no listening devices in place. Yet.

I finished the paper, poured more coffee, and tried to examine the situation in a logical manner. The threshold question was whether it had been Polk. If so, what had his purpose been? One possibility was that he had intended to search my home or place listening devices inside it, perhaps in an attempt to learn how my investigation was progressing. But the FBI had closed the case, so why should he care? Another possibility was that he was still smarting from our encounter at the federal building and wanted to finish it, but that seemed unlikely. He wouldn't risk his career for that, and it appeared he'd purposely waited until I'd left my house.

I put the incident out of my mind and began reading the article Monica had sent. It described the evolution of a school of thought that holds that the behavior of financial markets is fractal in nature. Using a coastline as an example, Jayne had explained that two things are characteristic of fractal objects. First, each point in a fractal object is correlated with the points next to it. Second, the shape of the object remains more or less the same no matter how closely you examine it.

Applying those criteria to a financial market, the authors pointed out that in a financial market, each day's price depends, at least to some extent, on the previous day's price. Moreover, markets appear to show self-similarity at different scales. For example, a study of foreign-exchange markets had established that the difference between price movements over one day and two days is, on average, the same as the difference between price movements over one year and two years.

Because market patterns appear to be fractal, a growing number of observers believed market behavior could be predicted. Nobody claimed fractal geometry could be used to predict market performance with precision, but many felt it could provide guidance as to trends. To make it work, you need vast amounts of data showing every trade on your chosen market for several years, a library of past patterns, and a computer program to compare the geometry of the data with the past patterns. You also need a device to compare your data with your theory to find the coincidences—a neural network.

Underwood had written about neural networks. I hadn't considered it significant at the time, but I was beginning to see a pattern of my own. I bid Wanda and Zeke farewell, then drove home.

It was unusual for my message light to be flashing at eight A.M., but I played the message, then phoned Scott.

"What's up?" I asked.

"You want the great news or the good news?"

"Start with the great news," I said.

"I think I found our boy."

"What's the good news?"

"He lives about six hours away."

"How'd you find him?" I asked.

"He responded to my message using the name Karl Gauss. He highly recommended a series of articles by Thomas Tobias."

"That would be Karl Gauss of Mora, New Mexico?"

"Yeah."

"Might as well head down there and get his story," I said.

"You want company?" he asked.

"Sure."

"When do you want to leave?"

"How about this afternoon? We'll spend the night with Crazy Uncle Ray and visit 'Karl' first thing in the morning."

19

We got a late start Tuesday, and that meant we'd be approaching Crazy Uncle Ray's shack at night. Probably unannounced. I'd left a message at the store in town, but there was no way to know whether he'd received it. My mother's youngest brother lives five miles out of Blanca, Colorado. Population 272. About four hours southwest of Denver. Not far from where Jack Dempsey grew up.

Ray is fifty-nine years old. He spent forty of those years as a drunk, but sobered up five or six years ago and bought five acres on a land contract. He pays $75.00 a month. The property is located in the shadow of scenic Blanca Peak; the view is wonderful, but the only vegetation consists of cacti and yucca plants. There's no water, no electricity, and no phone.

"You think this is it?" Scott asked. It was dark out, but the outline of a shack was visible in the distance off to the right. It looked familiar.

"I think so," I said. We were stopped on what might charitably be called a dirt road. I let the dogs out one last time because we'd be leaving the road and there would be no place they could romp without risking stickers in their paws. After a few minutes, I got them into the truck, then shifted into four-wheel drive and guided the vehicle over the scrub until we were fifty yards from the structure. Ray had built a "cabin" out of plywood. A former merchant seaman, he had always dreamed of owning land and being self-sufficient.

I gave the horn two long bursts, climbed out of the truck, and yelled his name. A flashlight beam moved inside.

"Who dat?" he yelled.

"It's Pepper," I shouted.

"Pepper, dat you?"

"Yeah, Uncle Ray, it's me."

"C'mon up he'yaw," he shouted. I climbed back into the truck and drove toward the shack. Ray had spent most of his life in New Orleans, so "here" sounds like "he'yaw." As we neared the shack, I saw him holding a large-gauge shotgun.

I exited the truck and shook hands with my uncle. I didn't smell any booze. My mother likes me to check up on him once in a while. "You remember Scott, don't you?" I asked.

"Why sho I do," said Ray. They shook hands. "Son, how you doin'?" Ray's about five-seven and might weigh one-forty dripping wet. His hair is gray and he always sports a bristly crew cut. He hadn't shaved in a day or two and his face was covered with stubble.

"Real well," said Scott. We followed Ray inside. It has never been my dream to live in an eight-by-twelve plywood shack, but if I had to, I'd want Ray to build it. He's a magician with tools. His place is airtight, which keeps the snakes out, and he's even got a wood stove. He lit a lantern and offered water. His water supply consists of a few dozen gallon jugs he fills in town. We accepted the water and sat down. Scott and I took the folding chairs; Ray sat on the bottom bunk.

"What you boys up to?" he asked. He has a scratchy voice, the result of having smoked Camels most of his adult life. I told him we were on our way to New Mexico to interview a potential witness in a murder case and gave him a thumbnail sketch of the case. There was no point in confusing him with details about such things as fractal geometry.

"Dis fella's prob'bly a drug dealer," he said. "Dat's why he don't want no one to find him." In Ray's world most people fall into one of two categories: drug dealers or devil worshipers.

I asked how things were going, and he said pretty fair. Some "Mexkins" had stolen his bicycle, but he'd finally gotten his privilege to drive reinstated and didn't need it anymore. After a while he started talking about the Bible, and that's when we decided to call it a night. He planned to stay up and read the good book awhile. He insisted we sleep on the bunks. "I'll lay me a sleepin' bag on the flo," he said, "and be just fine."

With no mountains to the east and no trees to provide shade, the morning sun hits Ray's shack early. We were up before six. Ray made coffee on the wood stove and offered some tiny cans of franks and beans, but we said we'd get breakfast on the road. "Y'all be careful," he said. "These drug dealers'll kill ya for five dollahs." That's one of his favorite expressions. In Ray's world, pretty much anyone would kill ya for five dollahs.

We'd been on the road an hour. Moving along in silence at a pretty good clip and sipping coffee. "Who the hell was Karl Gauss?" I asked after we had crossed into New Mexico.

"He was like the John Elway of math and science two hundred years ago," Scott said. "He invented number theory. He applied mathematics to gravitation, electricity, and magnetism. He helped build the first telegraph. He even predicted the path of an asteroid that was hidden behind the sun. You ever hear of the Gaussian distribution?"

"I went to law school to avoid learning such things."

"He basically invented the bell curve."

"And the bell curve does what?"

"It describes any random process. If you flip a coin a hundred times, it may come up heads two or three times in a row and it may come up tails two or three times in a row, but by and large you won't see many runs like that. The flat tails of the curve represent those rare extremes and the bell portion represents the more typical occurrence."

"Thanks for clearing that up," I said.

"Don't make fun of statisticians," he said. "They'll kill ya for five dollahs." I smiled and guided the truck off I-25 and onto State Highway 120.

Mora sits thirty miles north of Las Vegas, New Mexico. It's in the mountains, on the edge of the Santa Fe National Forest. Most of the buildings on the main street were adobe structures. My map indicated a population of 4,264, but the streets were empty. We found a hole-in-the-wall restaurant and had an early lunch. We were the only non-Hispanics in the place. We appeared to be the only non-Hispanics in town.

Our address for Gauss was Route 1, Box 66. That didn't help much, so we stopped at the post office and asked directions. The postmaster, an older Hispanic man with a laid-back manner, drew a map and wished us a nice visit.

"So what's the plan?" Scott asked as I drove out of town. "We just gonna stroll in there and ask him if he killed three people?"

"Something like that," I said.

"If it's all the same to you," he said, "I think I'll take old Betsy with me." He began loading his .45 automatic. My Glock was already loaded. I don't have a name for it.

Gauss lived in an old adobe place about two miles south of town. A quarter mile off the main highway on a dirt road. The nearest neighbor a quarter mile away. I slowed down as we neared his home. Nobody visible in the yard or in the house, no cars in the driveway. One mountain bike on the porch. The front yard small, but manicured. A ceramic donkey pulling a cart filled with flowers stood in the center of the closely cropped lawn. To one side was an enviable vegetable garden protected by chicken wire, but the rest of the land wasn't being used. A shallow irrigation ditch ran along the edge of his property on the side where the gar-

den was. I continued past his house for about a mile, then turned
the truck around and brought it to a stop beside a field where
cattle grazed.

"This place is so tranquil," Scott said.

"It is," I agreed. I put my shoulder holster on, then donned a
light jacket so my Glock wouldn't be immediately visible. Scott
had no holster. I put the truck in gear and headed back. When we
were within three hundred yards of the house, I stopped the truck,
killed the engine, retrieved my binoculars from behind the driver's
seat, and scanned the residence.

"See anything?" Scott asked.

"Just one guy walking back and forth inside the house a few
times. Too far away to say for sure whether it's him." We sat there
for forty-five minutes. When it was apparent there was only one
man in the house, we decided to get it over with. I fired up the
truck, put it in gear, slowly drove the final three hundred yards,
and guided the truck into the gravel driveway.

I stepped out of the truck and Scott did likewise. He tucked his
pistol into his jeans, at the small of his back. We were dressed
casually, but looked as respectable as might be expected given that
we'd spent the night with Crazy Uncle Ray and hadn't showered
that morning.

The front door was a solid slab of dark wood. I knocked. Two
strong knocks. I heard footsteps. The door opened. "May I help
you?" the man asked. He matched the description of Tobias. Early
thirties. Just under six feet. Much thinner than I'd expected; one-
forty at the most. I took one look at him and knew he wasn't the
killer.

"Mr. Gauss?"

"Yes." He had stringy brown hair and a pale complexion. He
wore chinos, a white polo shirt, and old penny loafers. No socks.

"My name's Pepper Keane," I said as I handed him a card.
"This is Scott McCutcheon. We're private investigators. May we

come in?" He studied my eyes and realized I knew his true identity.

"I suppose you'd better," he said. I scanned the room, but there didn't appear to be anyone else in the house. He gestured for us to enter. "Would you like something to drink?" he asked. "I can offer water, tea, or lemonade." He was soft-spoken and deferential.

"No, thanks," I said. The living room boasted a hardwood floor, but a large Navajo rug covered much of it. The matching sofa and chairs had been constructed from aspen logs and the cushions were covered with a bright Southwestern fabric. Jayne Smyers would've loved it. I sort of liked it myself.

"What can I do for you gentlemen?" he asked. He sat in one of the chairs. I went to the sofa. Scott walked back into the kitchen to make sure nobody else was in the house, then claimed a chair across the room to make sure Gauss/Tobias was between us.

"We know you're Thomas Tobias," I said. He looked down for several seconds.

"I can't imagine who might have hired you to find me," he finally said.

"We weren't hired to find you," I said. "We're looking into the deaths of some mathematicians, and your name came up."

"My name?" He seemed genuinely surprised.

"Did you know Paul Fontaine?" I asked.

"Of course," he said.

"Carolyn Chang?"

"Sure," he said, "she was at Nebraska."

"Donald Underwood?"

"What's this about?"

"They're dead," I said.

"All of them?"

"Yes."

"Murdered?"

"Two were murdered," I said. "Underwood's death might have been a suicide. We're not sure." I gave him time to process it.

"They each specialized in fractal geometry, didn't they?"

"Yes."

"And you're searching for people who worked with all three of them?"

"Worked or studied with them," I said.

"How did you find me?" he asked.

"It wasn't that hard," Scott said. A little hostile. I don't think he'd figured it out yet.

"You think I killed these people?" he said, incredulous.

"We have to check every lead," I said. "Just give us a rational explanation for the disappearing act. If it's not related to our case, we're out of here."

"I have AIDS," he said. He crossed his left leg over his right.

"I'm sorry," I said. There were purple lesions on his skin. I saw Scott's hostility fade.

"I'd been HIV positive for some time, but when the symptoms began to appear, I decided to live my dream. Buy a place in the Southwest, plant a garden."

"You couldn't do that as Thomas Tobias?"

"I'm gay," he said. "Mother's a devout Christian. She never accepted my lifestyle. I don't have any other relatives. I didn't want to spend my last years listening to her sell me religion. I just wanted to start over. It's better this way." I didn't know what to say. "Don't feel sorry for me," he said. "My medications are working. I have friends here. It's a good life."

I told him about our case and how we'd tracked him down. "You worked hard to find me," he said. "I'm sorry it was all for naught."

"It wasn't," I said. "We've eliminated you as a suspect." I stood and Scott followed suit.

"Would you like to stay for lunch?" he asked. "I'm preparing vegetable soup and salad."

We'd already eaten, but he seemed to want our company, so we accepted his offer. Though New Mexico's growing season is long, he'd constructed a small greenhouse behind his home to enable him to garden all year long. The soup and salad, he explained, were made with vegetables he'd started inside and transplanted a month ago. His pride in his vegetables was obvious.

When we had finished, I asked him to keep what we'd told him to himself. He said he would and asked us not to reveal his whereabouts to his mother or anyone else he'd known. We gave our word and climbed into the truck for the long trip home.

"What's Heidegger got to say about that?" Scott asked.

"I haven't gotten that far," I said.

20

THURSDAY MORNING IN Nederland. With Tobias no longer a suspect, I felt dejected. I'd been searching for a common thread and Tobias had been it.

A few tufts of white cloud punctuated an otherwise blue sky. Perfect running weather. I took Wheat for a morning run, hoping the exercise would clear my mind. Just to be different, I headed up Caribou Road. It will take you to the Continental Divide, if that's what you want, but the first few miles are easy. The dirt road rises gradually and follows a meandering creek.

Two miles up the road is a pasture where donkeys graze. That's usually where I turn around. I picked up my pace as we approached it. One of the reasons I seldom run on a track is because it's too easy to quit. If you start at home and run three miles out a country road, quitting isn't an option. You still have to get home. It was like that with my case. Despite feeling the investigation had stalled, there were at least three reasons not to quit. First, I felt in my gut that the deaths were related. Second, I had nothing else to do. Third, I wanted to know Jayne Smyers better and quitting didn't seem likely to help my cause. I had to finish what I'd started.

Wheat reached the pasture before me. He ran under the barbed-wire fence, but stopped short of the big animals. "Hello, donkeys," I said as I did a wide turn and began running back toward Colorado 119. I've always liked donkeys and mules. They're reputed to be stubborn. Maybe I see a bit of myself in them.

Running downhill required little effort, and I found myself thinking about something I'd been toying with since reading the article sent by Monica. Fontaine had enjoyed following the stock market. Carolyn Chang had been keeping company with an economist. Underwood had written about neural networks—computer programs apparently useful in predicting market behavior. It wasn't much, but it was a thread. And it was all I had.

So I spent the rest of the morning doing some on-line research. By eleven-thirty I knew Fontaine's portfolio of nineteen stocks had beaten the S&P 500 every quarter for the past three years. Sometimes by as much as 7 percent. His portfolio had outperformed some of the hottest funds in the world.

I made some phone calls unrelated to the case, then closed my eyes to consider my next move. I needed more information about the use of fractal geometry in economic forecasting. I started my truck, slipped an old Bob Dylan tape into the cassette deck, and headed to Boulder.

I parked at a meter by the University Memorial Center and walked north to the Norlin Library. Norlin is the main library at the University of Colorado. Joy and I used to seek refuge there when we wanted to escape the law school crowd. It had been years since I'd been inside, but the only difference was that computers had replaced the card catalog. They were everywhere.

The semester had ended, but there were a half dozen students working quietly in the reference section. I claimed the nearest vacant terminal and began reading the instructions. Articles in magazines or academic journals were indexed in sixteen different databases. I could search by subject, title, or author. I was familiar with MathSciNet, but there was also a business and economics index, and that's the one I chose.

I first searched for articles written by Fontaine, Chang, or Underwood. Nothing.

Then I typed "fractals." The monitor indicated my search had found thirty-seven articles. I scrolled through the abstracts just to get a sense of the literature. Many sounded highly technical, but I had expected that. What I hadn't expected was an article by Dale Hawkins. His contribution, "Weather and the Fractal Structure of Crop Markets," had been published shortly after he would have met Carolyn Chang.

Sadly, technology had not yet advanced to the point where I could press a button and print all thirty-seven articles. I could print the list, but I'd have to find the articles in the stacks and copy them individually. In for a dime, in for a dollar. I hit Print.

A dot-matrix printer two tables to my left suddenly came alive. It was noisy and painfully slow, a fact that caused everyone present to look up to determine who had printed thirty-seven abstracts. I retrieved the printout and was about to head upstairs to the periodicals when I decided to conduct one more search. Might as well see what else Hawkins had contributed to the literature.

It took only a minute to learn that he had authored six other articles, all prior to meeting Carolyn Chang. From the abstracts, it didn't appear they had anything to do with fractals. I hit Print once more, took the printout, purchased a twenty-dollar copy card, and began the tedious task of finding and copying the articles. I eliminated some that appeared unlikely to further my education. "The Fractal Nature of Urban Japanese Population Patterns" seemed like one I could safely skip.

It was past four when I finished copying. I left the library and headed in the direction of the math building. Clouds were building over the mountains and afternoon thunderstorms seemed a distinct possibility.

I hadn't read the articles—I would do that at home—but I found it curious that Hawkins had written an article incorporating ideas from fractal geometry. Perhaps I hadn't asked the right questions, but he had conveyed the impression he knew little about the subject: "I knew what her field of expertise was, and that she loved teaching, but beyond that I can't tell you much." He'd also insisted he and Carolyn had seldom talked about their work. Yet the only article he'd ever authored having anything to do with fractal geometry had been written after they'd started seeing each other.

The door to Jayne's office was closed and nobody responded when I knocked. I scribbled a note on my legal pad and slid it under the door.

My truck was four miles up the mountain when the rain began. By the time I reached Boulder Falls, it was coming down so hard I had to pull off because I couldn't see. I leaned against the driver's door, swung my feet up, and treated myself to a brief nap.

The rain subsided within a half hour. I got home, let the dogs out, and ordered a pizza from Backcountry. There are three pizza places in Nederland, but Backcountry is the only one that delivers. I could drive to any of them within three minutes, but sometimes it's nice to have them come to you.

I clicked on the TV just in time to catch the start of the *CBS Evening News*. Some say Dan Rather has a liberal bias, but I don't see it. Besides, he's an ex-marine, and that's more than you can say for Tom Brokaw or Peter Jennings.

A dreadlocked kid delivered the pizza just after six. I tipped him two dollars, ate three slices, and put the rest in the refrigerator. The prospect of reading several dozen articles on economics didn't excite me, so I channel-surfed till seven, then tuned to the *Thursday Night Fights*.

The first bout was a four-round match between two lightweights of moderate talent. The second fight, another four-rounder, was somewhat more interesting, if only because the fighters were women. The main event started around eight-fifteen. It featured an up-and-coming heavyweight from Montreal against a journeyman from New York. Both black. The younger one was taller and in better condition, but kept his fists too close to his head in a peek-a-boo style, like Floyd Patterson used to do. It's good to keep your hands up for protection, but you have to keep them out far enough that they offer some value as shock absorbers. They were in the fourth round when my phone rang. I hit Mute and picked up the cordless.

"Pepper Keane," I said.

"Hello, Pepper Keane," she said, "this is Jayne Smyers."

"Hi, Jayne."

"What are you doing?" she asked.

"Just reading," I said. It was a little early in the relationship to spring my passion for boxing on her. "How about you?"

"Laundry." I was absorbed in the fight and didn't respond. "Are you still there?" she asked.

"Yes," I said. "I'm sorry." I clicked off the TV.

"I can call back."

"No, that's fine."

"Anyhow, I got your note, so I thought I'd call. Do you have some news on the case?"

"I do," I said, "but that's not why I asked you to call."

"Really?"

"I wondered if you'd like to do something this weekend?"

"What did you have in mind?" she asked.

"I don't know," I said. "Maybe go hiking."

"Sounds like fun," she said.

After firming up our plans, I told her the disappointing news about Thomas Tobias and summarized the angle I was now pursuing.

"That's interesting," she said. "I don't know much about fractal geometry in the business world, but if you need help sorting through the literature, let me know."

"I will," I promised. We talked for a few more minutes, then said good night, but when I clicked on the TV, the cable network had switched to stock-car racing—a sport in which men compete to determine who can execute a specified number of left turns in the least amount of time. I still don't know who won the fight.

21

WHERE'S AURORA?" Gilbert asked.

"It's a suburb of Denver," I said. "Why?" I had just finished lift-ing weights in my basement.

"The gun we found traces to a pawnshop there."

"I thought the serial number had been filed off."

"It was," he said, "but whoever did it should've done a better job. The forensic people at the state patrol did some work on it, used solvent to clean it, then ran it through some kind of high-tech X-ray machine. They're certain they've got the last four digits."

"Fantastic," I said.

"Ever hear of Saul's Pawnshop?"

"No, but I'm guessing it's on Colfax Avenue."

"Gold star," he said.

"There's a dozen of them on that stretch," I explained. "It's not a good neighborhood."

"Old Saul did his best to keep it that way," he said. "He sold a five-shot Taurus to a career hoodlum named Delbert Gaffney a few years ago."

"The last four digits match?"

"Yup."

"Any leads on Gaffney?"

"He ain't the guy. The feds caught him selling crack last July, and he's been in custody ever since." Fontaine had been murdered in September.

"Did you get the FBI reports?"

"Yeah, but he was unarmed when they busted him, so nobody asked him any questions about guns."

"They search his house?"

"No weapons there either."

"That's a first," I said. I'd prosecuted dozens of drug cases, and I'd almost always been able to add two or three firearms charges. "Where is he now?" I asked.

"He's in the federal correctional institution in Florence, Colorado, wherever that is."

"It's west of Pueblo," I said.

"I figure he sold the gun on the street or loaned it to one of his gangsta friends before he got busted."

"Maybe some crackhead stole it from him," I said.

"Maybe," he admitted. "Why don't you take a drive down there and ask him?"

"The city won't pay for you to fly down and question him?"

"Kid's twenty-three and doing a mandatory twenty. Why's he gonna talk to me?"

"Why's he gonna talk to me?"

"You're a lawyer," he said. "They love talking to lawyers. It'll take him a full day just to tell you all the mistakes *his* lawyer made." I laughed.

"That's a maximum-security facility," I said, "but I'll give it a try." It was eleven-thirty on a Friday morning.

I spent the afternoon eating almonds and reading the articles I'd copied on Thursday. The crossing of economic and mathematical theory had yielded a bumper crop of jargon, but the upshot of everything I'd read was that the random walk theory popular in the sixties and seventies had been discredited. Whereas many economists had once considered market trends no more predictable than the outcome of a coin toss, the development of fractal mathematics had convinced most that market behavior is not random in a mathematical sense.

This was good news for Wall Street. Taken to its logical extreme, the random walk theory suggested that a blindfolded lemur throwing darts at the financial pages could select a portfolio that would perform as well as one selected by experts. Consequently, Wall Street had never accepted it. Dismissing the random walk theory as nonsense spouted only by out-of-touch academics, Wall Street had long been divided into two camps: the fundamental analysts and the technical analysts.

Fundamental analysts seek to determine the true value of a stock by examining earnings per share, book value, price/earnings ratio, and so forth. Technical analysts, on the other hand, focus on the psychology of the market. They assume the price of a stock is determined by the expectations of all buyers and sellers. Relying on past price movements, they try to predict what a given stock (or the market as a whole) will do in the future. Because they chart the past in order to predict the future, technical analysts are also called chartists.

To fundamental analysts, the belief that you can predict stock trends or market behavior by studying the past is absurd. For this reason, they had long viewed chartists with disdain. To them, the difference between the two schools was like the difference between astronomy and astrology.

But the discovery and growth of fractal geometry had bestowed new respectability on chartists. Using theories borrowed from fractal mathematics, empirical studies had confirmed that economic markets possess a type of memory. When volatility is low, the market follows trends: It rises or falls for longer than random. When volatility is high, trends persist for shorter than random. In either situation, the market is partly predictable. Economic markets do not conform to the Gaussian distribution.

This came as no surprise to chartists. A market consists of

people second-guessing one another. The more people share a belief, the more the belief is likely to come true. Suppose a stock has traded at $50.00 to $60.00 a share for several months. A chartist would call these the stock's resistance levels. If the price suddenly rises above $60.00, the chartist concludes something has happened to change investors' perceptions. The breakthrough convinces investors that other investors believe the stock is undervalued. As a result, investors buy the stock and drive up the price. It's a self-fulfilling prophecy.

It was interesting reading, but for my purposes the most interesting aspect of it was that fractal mathematics had resulted in the computerization of Wall Street. Today's brokerage houses and fund managers are constantly processing vast amounts of data and searching for recurring patterns. And that led me back to the article Monica had sent. Neural networks. Underwood.

The alarm went off at five. By seven I had deposited the dogs at Troy's house for the day and was cruising south on I-25. It was Saturday, but traffic was heavy. I could remember when there was nothing between Denver and Colorado Springs; now there's little open range. It's one subdivision after another, including the one my brother lives in, Highlands Ranch. I call it Little California.

I rolled down my window and listened to a tape I'd purchased from the Smithsonian, a collection of classic American country music dating all the way back to the 1920s.

I had spent Friday evening reviewing the writings of Dale Hawkins. The thesis of his most recent effort, "Weather and the Fractal Structure of Crop Markets," was simple. The price of a crop is determined by supply and demand. Supply is largely a factor of the weather. Weather patterns are fractal in nature. Therefore, weather patterns are at least partly responsible for the fractal structure of crop markets.

That weather affects crop prices was hardly an original thought, but Hawkins's thesis wasn't what intrigued me. What intrigued me was that the writing in his most recent article was so much better than that displayed in his previous writings. I toyed with the implications of that as I continued south, then cranked up the volume as Elvis began "Blue Moon of Kentucky."

Arriving in Florence shortly after ten, I found the prison and parked near the visitors' entrance. Like all modern prisons, it was a concrete fortress with narrow slits for windows, the outer perimeter marked by multiple electric fences, each topped with razor wire. Wearing khaki pants, a blue short-sleeved shirt, and cordovan loafers, I walked across the newly paved lot to the front door and pressed the red button with my thumb. A deep male voice came through the speaker, but the sound was fuzzy and I couldn't understand a word that was said. "I'm an attorney," I said. "I'm here to see a client." I heard a metallic click and gave the door handle a good pull.

I walked down the concrete steps into a belowground passage leading to a waiting area. The room consisted of rows of black metal benches bolted into the concrete floor. The room was empty, meaning I'd had the good fortune to arrive outside visiting hours and had thus been spared having to view dozens of pitiful women waiting to see their respective men. A uniformed guard sat behind a counter at the far end of the room. He looked to be about fifty and was grossly overweight.

"Pepper Keane," I said. "Here to see Delbert Gaffney." I displayed my driver's license and bar registration card. If he noticed my registration had expired, he didn't say anything.

"Supposed to call in advance," he said.

"I know," I said. "I just got appointed by a federal magistrate to represent this turkey in some bullshit habeas corpus action and I'm not real happy to be here. If you want me to go home and tell the judge I couldn't meet with my client, that's fine by me." The last thing any jailer wants is to be accused of denying an inmate access to his attorney.

"Sign here," he said. He slid a clipboard toward me, and I completed the required information. He looked it over, then pressed an intercom button and said, "Attorney here to see Gaffney." He instructed me to stand near a steel door at the far end of the room. When I heard the click, I opened the door and was met by another guard, this one younger and black. Denzel Washington.

"How are you doin' today?" he asked with a smile. Friendly considering he worked in such a depressing place.

"Great, how about you?"

"I'm just fine," he said. I followed him at a leisurely pace to a small room. Perhaps six by eight. "You can have a seat in there," he said. "We'll bring Gaffney right down."

I sat down on one of two plastic chairs beside a sturdy wooden table that had seen a multitude of messages carved into it over the years. Denzel left the door slightly ajar. Like the others, it was made of steel. The walls were concrete but had been painted with semigloss buttercup. There was one window, a rectangular sheet of thick Plexiglas, but the only view was of the hallway and guard station.

Twenty minutes later another guard, white and wiry, escorted a young black man to the room. He wore a tan jumpsuit that was unbuttoned down to his navel. Shaved head. Big scar on his left biceps, like he'd been branded with an iron. Solid build. Washboard stomach. About five-nine and a hundred sixty-five pounds. "This fool ain't my lawyer," he said.

"Just appointed by the court," I told the guard as I rose from my chair. "He probably hasn't received the papers yet." I offered Delbert my hand. He refused it, but he entered the room. We remained silent until the guard had locked the door and disappeared from view.

"The fuck are you?" Delbert asked. "Damn sure ain't my lawyer."

"I'm not anyone's lawyer," I said, "but that's another story." I sat down, opened my wallet, and placed a crisp hundred on the table. "I'm going to ask a few questions," I said. "Give the right answers and that money is yours."

"You a cop?"

"If I were a cop," I said, "I wouldn't lie my way in here and offer you a hundred bucks."

"You a sherlock, I got nothin' to say."

"I'm a private investigator," I said. He sat down.

"Ain't gonna rat on my homies," he said.

"Don't worry," I said, "the guy I'm looking for only kills math professors. I doubt he spends much time in the 'hood."

"What you want?" he asked, surly.

"You bought a thirty-eight-caliber pistol at Saul's Pawnshop a few months before the feds busted you. I want to know where that gun is."

"The fuck you talkin' 'bout?"

"You signed an ATF four-four-seven-three when you bought the gun," I said. "One of the questions on that form is whether you've ever been convicted of a felony." He broke eye contact. "You lied," I said, "and that's a felony." I hadn't seen the form, but I knew what had happened because I'd seen it so many times. "The feds don't know about it," I said. "So the question is, do you want to do another five years for making a false statement in the purchase of a firearm or do you want to earn a quick hundred bucks?" He looked at me and laced his fingers together on the table.

"What you want to know 'bout that gun fo'?"

"Someone used it to kill a man up in Washington," I said. "I'm looking for the killer."

"Don't know nothin' 'bout that," he said.

"I believe you," I said. "Just tell me about the gun."

He looked at me for several seconds. "I sold that fuckin' gun to my cousin," he said. "Don't know what he did with it."

"What's his name?"

"Bailey."

"His first name?"

"That's his first name. Bailey Green."

"Where does he live?" I asked.

"He in jail."

"Where?"

"Denver somewhere," he said. "They holdin' him for armed robbery or some shit."

"Did he use the gun in the robbery?"

"Don't know, I wasn't there."

"Did he say why he wanted the gun?"

"Protection." Stupid question.

"When did you sell him the gun?" I asked.

"Right before I got busted," he said. "July, I think."

"How long has he been in jail?"

"He been in since August, man. Trial's next month. Can't plead because he lookin' at a bitch." Another conviction would qualify Delbert's cousin as a habitual offender.

"You're sure he's been in since August? It couldn't have been September or October?"

"Pretty sho," he said. "Don't know 'zactly 'cuz I been locked up."

I slid the hundred across the table. "You can take it," I said, "or I can deposit it in your account when I leave." He picked it up, folded it in half, and tucked it into his breast pocket. I rapped my knuckles on the door a few times to let the guards know we were done. "You be quiet about my visit," I said. Denzel came and unlocked the door. "He doesn't want my help," I told the guard, "so I guess I won't be seeing you anymore."

22

I can't believe I've lived here this long and never been up here," said Jayne. "This view is fantastic." Boulder was almost directly below us and a good chunk of eastern Colorado, including Denver, was visible to the east.

"I discovered it in law school," I said. "I used to run up here."

"I'll bet that was fun," she said.

"Going up was a bear, but coming down was a natural high." It was two o'clock on a gorgeous Sunday afternoon and we were standing on top of one of the flatirons, large formations of red rock that rise out of the mountains overlooking the city. Our hike had taken more than an hour; the vertical rise is several thousand feet. "Ready to eat?" I asked.

"I thought you'd never ask," she said. "I'm famished." We found a level spot and sat down on the hard rock. From my nylon knapsack I removed the hoagies I'd made, then poured white zinfandel into two clear plastic cups. I shifted my weight in an attempt to get comfortable.

"Hard rock cafe," I said. She smiled and bit into her sandwich. French bread, lettuce, onion, tomato, thin slices of provolone, all topped with Italian dressing and a dash of salt.

"These are delicious," she said. "Are you a vegetarian?"

"More or less," I said.

"You don't look like one," she said. I wasn't sure if she was referring to my build or my haircut.

"A few years ago," I said as I finished chewing a bite, "I

represented a meatpacking corporation that got into some trouble with the government over allegations of unsanitary conditions. In order to do my job, I needed to understand the process from start to finish, so I toured a slaughterhouse and—"

"It's an animal rights thing?"

"I don't know," I said. "It's just something I've been struggling with."

"My grandparents were ranchers," she said. "To them, there wasn't much difference between a vegetarian and a communist."

I laughed. "I don't have it all figured out," I said. "I don't have any problem with killing an animal to survive, but I'm not sure it's right to breed animals for the sole purpose of killing them."

"I never thought of that," she said.

We continued eating and enjoyed the Colorado sunshine. She looked great in olive shorts and a white sleeveless top.

"What are you thinking?" she asked. She poured more wine for each of us. I was thinking she had great legs, but couldn't say that.

"Still thinking about the case," I said. I'd brought her up to date during the drive from her home to the trailhead. "I want to call Gilbert tomorrow and see if he can get some information on Bailey Green."

"What kind of information?"

"What was he arrested for? Did it involve a gun? When was he busted?" I could probably get all that myself, but Gaffney didn't even know what agency had arrested his cousin; all he knew was that Bailey was in jail in "Denver somewhere." It would be quicker to let Gilbert do it.

"Anything I can do?" she asked.

"Come to think of it," I said, "there might be. Do you know anyone who teaches linguistics?"

"Sure, why?"

"I'm convinced Carolyn Chang helped Hawkins write that

article, but it would be nice to have an expert compare their writing styles."

"There's a woman in the English department, Maggie McGuire. I'll call her first thing in the morning."

"That would be great," I said. "I've got the articles in my truck. I'll leave them with you tonight."

"Oh, look," she said. I followed her index finger and saw a brave soul piloting a hang glider several thousand feet above us. Hang gliding is popular in Boulder because of the thermals that rise from the base of the mountains and provide constant lift so a glider can remain aloft for hours.

"He's up there," I said. We watched as the pilot circled higher and higher.

"I went parasailing once," she said. "Have you ever done anything like that?"

"My brother and I used to skydive a lot," I said, "but his parachute malfunctioned one time and we took that as a sign it was time to find new hobbies."

"My God, was he hurt?"

"No," I said. "He slammed into a wet corn field at thirty-five miles an hour, but walked away without any major damage." With that image in mind, I poured the rest of the wine into my nearly empty cup, then removed a second bottle from my knapsack. "He's also been struck by lightning and bitten by a rattlesnake, so we figure he's got six lives left."

She laughed. "Is that true?" she asked.

"Swear to God," I said. She sipped her wine.

"So what's your new hobby?" she asked.

"Going on hikes with good-looking women and getting them drunk."

She smiled. "Well," she said, "you're doing pretty well on the drunk part. This is good wine."

"I think I'm doing pretty well on the good-looking part too."

She blushed and we settled into a comfortable silence as blue jays darted from tree to tree and chipmunks scurried about. "Ask you a question?" I finally said.

"Sure."

"I'm curious about that poster in your office."

"Poster?"

"'A woman without a man is like a—'"

"I should take that down," she said, embarrassed. "I put it up in anger. A man I thought I loved turned out to be married, and that launched my all-men-are-scum period."

"When was that?"

"About five years ago." She pulled her knees in and wrapped her arms around them. This had the salutary effect of revealing a good deal of thigh. "You're sure you're not married?" she joked.

"Never married, never engaged," I said. "We covered that at the bookstore, remember?"

"Thought I might trip you up by asking again." She gave me a playful pat on the arm.

"I lived with a woman once," I said, "but she died before we ever got around to talking about marriage."

"I'm sorry."

"It was a long time ago," I said. "She was one of my law school classmates."

"Did you love her?"

"Yes," I said. "As much as I could at that age."

"How did she die?"

"Car accident. She went dancing with some classmates on a night when I had to work. A few of the guys got really drunk, so she drove them home. When she stopped for a red light, one of them accidentally spilled beer in her lap. She inadvertently hit the accelerator and another car broadsided her."

"That's horrible," she said. "Was anyone else killed?"

"No, everyone else walked away from it."

"What happened to the man?"

"Nothing," I said. "It's not a crime to be drunk and stupid when you're a passenger in a car."

"I hope he's not out there practicing law."

"He's not," I said. "He's an FBI agent."

23

I spent Monday morning spraying a mixture of linseed oil and paint thinner onto my house with a high-compression sprayer. It's a messy task, but it has to be done once a year to protect the logs from the harmful effects of moisture and ultraviolet rays. I hadn't planned on doing it Monday, but I'd had it on my list of things to do and the weather was ideal. Temps in the high seventies, clear sky, no wind.

That kind of physical labor differs from investigative work in at least two ways. First, it allows you to see the fruits of your efforts immediately. Because it requires little brainpower, it also gives the mind a chance to wander. So there I was, standing on top of a sixteen-foot ladder, slowly moving the metal wand from side to side, and musing about Sunday's outing with Jayne Smyers.

She had invited me to stay for supper and we had continued talking in her kitchen while I made a salad and she put together a green bean casserole. I told her I'd disliked Polk long before Joy's death and she asked why. "He was the most arrogant person I'd ever met," I said. "Thought he was tougher than everyone else and saw himself as God's gift to women."

Her smile showed amusement. "He is arrogant," she said, "but something tells me one reason you disliked him so was that you too thought you were tougher than everyone else."

"I'm sure that's part of it," I admitted.

"Did you also see yourself as God's gift to women?" She sprinkled almond slivers across the top of the casserole.

"No," I said, "I never suffered from that delusion."

"Strangely enough," she said, "I believe you." She placed the glass casserole dish in the oven. "You somehow project confidence without appearing egotistical."

I guess she viewed that as a good trait in a man because our date had ended with a better-than-expected good-night kiss. Not the kind that compels people to immediately shed their clothes and go at it, but luscious enough to make me believe there was some interest on her part.

I thought about that as I continued spraying, but the phone rang and I hurried inside to get it. It was Maggie McGuire.

"You work quickly," I said.

"Jayne said it was important." She was all business. From the sound of her voice, I guessed she was in her late forties.

"When can we get together?" I asked.

"I have some time at three o'clock."

"I'll be there," I said. After receiving precise directions to her office, I returned the cordless phone to its cradle and resumed spraying.

It took only a half hour to complete the project, but cleaning up took longer.

It was past two when I got out of the shower. I dressed casually, let the dogs out for a few minutes, then headed to Boulder. Before pulling out of the driveway, I stopped to admire my work. No longer faded, the logs appeared rich in color. The entire house projected the kind of warm glow it had possessed when I'd purchased it.

Maggie McGuire was a professor of English. Because it generated little grant money, the English department was located in one of the oldest buildings on campus. Her office was on the second floor. The door was open.

"Professor McGuire?"

"You must be Mr. Keane?" She was a mildly obese woman in her mid-forties. Her long hair was a frizzy mixture of red and gray. She wore no makeup and possessed a freckled complexion. She wore a long brown skirt, a beige blouse, white socks, and the expensive leather sandals so popular in Boulder. She motioned for me to sit and I did. "Thank you for doing this on such short notice," I said. Instead of saying "You're welcome," she sized me up in the dimly lit room. The only light was that provided by the tall, narrow window behind her wooden desk. I guessed she wasn't a fan of fluorescent lighting. Maybe she taught medieval literature and just liked the ambience.

"I must say I'm intrigued," she finally said. "It's not every day a private investigator asks me to compare the writings of two academics."

"Did Jayne explain the nature of my investigation?" I asked.

"No, she was quite circumspect, but it doesn't matter." She slid the stack of articles I had given Jayne to the center of her desk. "Did you read each of these articles?" she asked.

"Oh yeah," I said.

"And you believe Professor Chang helped Professor Hawkins with his most recent article?"

"Yes."

"Why?"

"His other articles are disorganized and full of jargon. His latest one is crisp and clean. The writing seems similar to the style I noticed in Carolyn Chang's articles."

"What similarities did you note?" she asked. I felt like a doctoral candidate defending a dissertation.

"The ideas were organized in a logical sequence," I said. "There was no jargon, and the author used as few words as possible."

"And that's why you believe Professor Chang helped write this article?" She held up a copy of Hawkins's "Weather and the Fractal Structure of Crop Markets."

"That and the fact that Carolyn was an expert in fractal mathematics. I don't think Hawkins—"

"Was?"

"She's no longer with us," I said. I realized Jayne hadn't told her anything.

"I see."

"Would you like some background?" I asked.

"No," she said. "I can tell you what you want to know without knowing why you want to know it." She laced her fingers together and placed her elbows on the desk. "Your instincts are good," she continued. "The author of this paper employed a style nearly identical to that used by Professor Chang."

"You sound certain," I said.

"Professor Chang has—had—a unique writing style. She employed a style called E-Prime."

"E-Prime?"

"Yes, it's a form of English that discourages using any form of the verb 'to be.'"

"What's the theory behind that?"

"Those who use E-Prime believe the word 'is' promotes sloppy thinking. Instead of saying, 'The cat is white,' they feel it's more accurate to say, 'The cat has white fur.'"

"That's interesting," I said. "Is this widely used?"

"No," she said. "The primary proponent of E-Prime is a group called the International Society for General Semantics, but they've had little success outside academic circles." I nodded and wrote ISGS on my legal pad. "I can't say with certainty that Professor Chang wrote this article. All I can tell you is that, for the most part, the style used is identical to that used in her writings."

"For the most part?"

"There are passages where E-Prime was not employed. And the overall structure of the article appears to have originated with Professor Hawkins. My best guess is that Professor Chang or some other proponent of E-Prime coauthored or edited the article." That didn't prove anything, but it strengthened my belief that Hawkins hadn't been completely truthful with me.

"Thank you," I said, "you've been a big help."

24

It was cold Tuesday morning. The remnants of an Arctic air mass had pushed through overnight. The thermometer outside my kitchen window showed thirty-four degrees at seven A.M. Not frigid, but not what you'd expect in the second week of June.

I zipped through an early weight workout in my basement, then sliced an orange for breakfast and contemplated my next move. The weather being what it was, it seemed like a good day to work the phone. I called Susan Thompson, the reporter in Lincoln, and asked her to send as much background material on Hawkins as she could get. I called the International Society for General Semantics and confirmed that Carolyn Chang had been a member. Then I called Scott.

"That's the way things work these days," he said. "You kiss on the first date; you're tying each other up on the second date." After updating him on the case, I had recounted my Sunday with Jayne Smyers.

"Not like the good old days," I joked.

"It's like we're living in the Victorian era," he said. I smiled to myself, then suggested we resume our discussion of the case. "What about Fontaine and Underwood," he said, "did they use this E-Prime?"

"No, I reread their articles last night." There was no conversation for several seconds, but that's not unusual when we brainstorm.

"If Carolyn helped write the article," he said, "why didn't she insist on being listed as a coauthor?"

"I've thought about that," I said, "and the only answer I can come up with is that she didn't want her name on it."

"Is it that bad?"

"No," I said, "but the thesis isn't particularly original. It doesn't break any new ground. When you sift through it, there's not much scholarship."

"That's your opinion as an economist?"

"That's my opinion as someone who has read far too many journal articles during the past month."

We talked about various aspects of the case for another fifteen minutes. "Anything you want me to do?" he asked.

"Can't think of anything," I said. "The reporter in Lincoln is going to send me some background material on Hawkins."

"Keep me posted," he said. I promised I would.

It was too early to check my mail, so I drove to Wanda's for some coffee and a chance to read the paper. Someone had already snagged the *News,* so I began with the Boulder *Daily Camera.* I was surprised when I turned to the sports section and saw Finn's smiling mug staring at me. The young professor had finished third in a local triathlon, and the paper had devoted a quarter page to a feature story on him. I read it, then refilled my coffee. That's when I saw Missy.

"Hi, Pepper," she said. She was standing near the register in faded jeans and a white peasant blouse with colorful embroidery around the neckline and sleeves.

"Hi, Missy, how are you?"

"I'm great," she said. One of Wanda's female helpers handed her a cup of Red Zinger tea.

"Where's Luther?"

"He's in Aspen," she said. "The band's there all week."

"Why didn't you go?" I asked.

"Didn't want to miss my group," she said. "We're exploring our past lives." I nodded to show I understood. No tables were available, so I invited her to share mine. "Hey," she said as she noticed the newspaper, "that's the guy." She pointed to the photo of Finn.

"What guy?"

"The guy at your house," she said. "That's him."

"That's the man you saw walking around my house?"

"Yeah, I'm positive." She had described the stranger as being "real big" and having blond hair. Missy was about five-two. Finn stood six-three. Though I would have described him as lanky, I realized someone like Finn might seem "real big" to Missy. I questioned her again about what she had seen, but learned nothing new. One of her female friends—another aging earth mama—joined us and they started talking about a candlelight vigil they were planning to protest something or other. I said good-bye, stopped at the post office to collect my mail, then drove home and noticed the flashing message light. I let Buck and Wheat out, listened to the message, then phoned Gilbert.

"Congratulate me," he said, "I've got another grandchild."

"That's great, Dick. Is it a boy or a girl?"

"Little boy," he said. "Eight pounds, seven ounces."

"A linebacker," I said. He laughed, then said he had to put me on hold. The phone system was set up so I could listen to Paul Harvey while waiting, but Gilbert came back on the line within thirty seconds, so I never learned the "rest of the story."

"Sorry about that," he said.

"No problem."

"Anyhow," he said, "I did some checking on Bailey Green, but something's not right."

"I'm listening," I said.

"Green's a federal prisoner. He was arrested in Denver last August for bank robbery. Walked into a bank in broad daylight and stuck a gun in a teller's face. Feds found him in his apartment two hours later with red dye all over him."

"What about the gun?"

"The reports indicate he used a five-shot Taurus, and the last four digits of the serial number on the weapon they confiscated match the one we have."

"How many were manufactured with those as the last four digits?"

"Just one," he said. "I checked with the manufacturer."

"Which raises the question of how a handgun seized in Denver last August was used to kill a math professor in Walla Walla in September."

"I thought that was a pretty good question myself. So I called the bureau in Denver and spoke with one of the agents. Laid it all out for him. He called back ten minutes later and told me they had Green's gun in their evidence room. Said our forensic people had made a mistake."

"Who'd you speak with?" I asked.

"Some guy named Polk. You know him?"

"Yeah, I've known him since law school. He's one of the ones who worked on the fractal case."

"He never mentioned that, but I suppose they've moved on to bigger and better things." I said nothing because my mind was racing. "I don't know," he muttered, "maybe our people *are* wrong about the serial number."

"Think so?"

"I'll have them take another look at it."

"Can't hurt," I said. But I knew there had been no mistake.

I called Gombold that afternoon to confirm what I already knew. My stated purpose was to pick his brain concerning the use of E-Prime in Hawkins's most recent article. He agreed it was suspicious.

"So, what's new in your neck of the woods?" I asked when we had finished kicking it around.

"Same old shit," he said, "but more of it." He sounded fatigued.

"Dittmer has us working extra hours to take up the slack caused by the increase in counterterrorism ops, and some congressman wants us to investigate a waste-removal firm that put Smokey the Bear on its trucks without the secretary of agriculture's permission." I laughed.

"Don't laugh," he said. "That's a federal offense. You can get six months in prison for that."

"Glad you warned me," I said. "Hey, before I hang up, whatever happened with that case where you couldn't find the gun? What was that guy's name, Green?"

"Yeah, Bailey Green. He pled guilty last week. We never did find the weapon, so the U.S. Attorneys agreed not to file a habitual offender rap on him. The powers that be figured that was a small price to pay to keep the missing gun out of the papers."

"Probably just as well," I said. "You don't want to do anything that might alert potential jurors to the fact that the bureau sometimes makes mistakes."

"God help us if that ever gets out."

"Get some sleep, Tim. You sound tired." I hung up and began writing a list of things to do.

There was no shortage of work. In addition to gathering as much information as possible on Hawkins, I wanted to learn more about Polk. For reasons unknown, he had lied to Gilbert about the missing revolver. And he had tried his best to discredit me with Dittmer when he'd learned Jayne had hired me. So I wanted to dig into his background. On top of all that, the image of Finn sneaking around my house kept making its way into my mind. I tried to let it go, but I wanted an explanation.

Hawkins. Polk. Finn. I'd have to learn more about each of them.

25

I couldn't believe it. I actually found a parking space in the visitors' lot nearest the math building. It was eleven-thirty on a sunny Wednesday morning. The warm weather had returned as quickly as it had vanished, and I had a lunch date with Jayne Smyers.

There were few people in the building. I took the steps to the third floor. Finn was not in his office, but the door was open.

Jayne was seated behind her desk wearing camel slacks and a powder blue top with a scoop neck. Pink lipstick. Finn sat in the chair to her right, Mary Pat in the one to her left. They were talking departmental politics.

"Hello, Mr. Keane," said Mary Pat. She wore tan shorts and a yellow oxford-cloth shirt with the sleeves rolled up.

"Am I early?" I asked.

"No," said Jayne, "you're right on time." Finn turned and looked at me, surprised.

"Saw your picture in the paper," I said. "Congratulations." I extended my hand and resisted the temptation to squeeze as if I had been blessed with extra tendons.

"Thanks," he said. He wore navy Dockers, a white short-sleeved shirt, and a maroon tie.

"Yes, Stephen," said Jayne, "that was a wonderful article. We're all so proud of you." Let's not overdo it, I thought.

"Everyone in the department is talking about it," offered Mary Pat.

Finn somehow interpreted all this as an invitation to talk about the race in detail. We listened politely as he recounted his swim-run-bike adventure in far too much detail. When he had finished, I looked at Jayne and said, "Shall we do it?"

"Absolutely," she said with a smile. She reached for her purse, then stood and walked around her desk to my side. It then hit Finn that the two of us had a lunch date, but he did his best to appear indifferent. "I'll be back by one," Jayne announced. I smiled at Mary Pat, gave Finn a polite nod, then gently touched the back of Jayne's elbow as I escorted her from her office. It was a subtle gesture, but I made sure Finn saw it.

"Where would you like to eat?" I asked as I held open one of the glass doors at the entrance to the building. She stepped through and I followed. The sun was bright, so I removed my aviator's glasses from my shirt pocket and put them on.

"Let's eat at the grill," she said. "I've got some things to do on that side of campus anyhow." That sounded fine, so we made our way around various buildings and grassy commons to the University Memorial Center.

There are a number of food vendors in the UMC. One of the most popular is the Alferd E. Packer Grill, a cafeteria named after the only American ever convicted of cannibalism. I hadn't been there in years, but it didn't appear to have changed. I thought briefly of lunches enjoyed long ago with Joy.

The line was long but moved quickly. I ordered clam chowder and a diet Coke; Jayne opted for a large salad and iced tea. She offered to treat, but I had my wallet out. "I'll pay," I said, "you find a table." The academic year had ended, but there were few empty seats in the enormous dining area.

I collected my change from a grandmotherly cashier and briefly wondered whether my aging mother might someday be forced to work in a similar capacity. I scanned the room and saw Jayne at a small table against the far wall. She noticed me and waved. I picked my way through the crowd like a running back dodging oncoming tacklers, then set my tray down across from her. "Is it always this crowded in the summer?" I asked.

"No," she said, laughing, "there must be a conference." I sat down and we began eating. "Did Maggie call you?" she asked.

"Yes," I said, "we met yesterday." I summarized what I had learned.

"E-Prime?" she said. "I've never heard of that. I'll have to experiment with it."

"I've been playing with it since yesterday," I said. "It's a challenge."

"Well, I'm glad Maggie was able to help." She speared a cucumber slice with her fork. "Is that the new development you mentioned?"

"No," I said. I related what Gilbert had learned about Bailey Green, then recounted my conversations with Gombold.

"My God," she said, "what do you make of that?"

"I'm not sure," I said. I paused to sip my drink. "One thing I plan to do is learn more about Polk, but I need your help."

"What can I do?"

"Polk went to law school here," I said. "I want his records. Application, grades, everything."

"The registrar will want a release," she said.

"Make something up," I said. "Tell them he's applied for admission to the graduate program and the department lost his application. Act embarrassed, but make it seem urgent. Do it at noon when the supervisors are likely to be at lunch. If that doesn't work, let me know." She raised her glass to her lips and looked at me as she sipped her tea.

"I don't think I'd want you mad at me," she said.

"I'll take that as a compliment," I said. "Will you try?"

"I think I intended it as a compliment," she said. "And yes, I'll try."

I got up and refilled our drinks and the conversation turned to matters unrelated to the case. "I called the owners' association about those Russian olive trees," she said, "but the man I spoke with didn't seem too concerned."

"The best way to get rid of them is with a flamethrower," I said. "That kills all the seeds. I don't suppose you have one." She laughed and we continued talking about nothing in particular. Her summer, my summer, and so forth. At one point there was an awkward silence, but she broke it by saying she'd had a good time Sunday. I assured her I'd enjoyed the day as well. I wanted to ask her out again, perhaps to dinner or a movie, but I didn't. Before traveling too far down the road to relationshipville, I felt obligated to disclose one or two things, and I wanted to think more about the best way to do that.

She glanced at her watch. "Oh," she said, "it's almost one. Walk me to the admin building?"

"Delighted," I said. It was a bit out of my way, but I enjoyed being with her. We walked along Broadway to the administration building, then said good-bye. I never mentioned Finn's visit to my house. I had my own plan for him, and she didn't need to know about it.

The man who cuts my hair is a funny old guy. Milt owns one of the last neighborhood barbershops in Boulder and still proudly displays his old union card. My lunch with Jayne had been shorter than expected, so I'd decided to stop for a haircut. He was engrossed in the sports section when I walked in.

"Wake up, old man," I said, "I'm tired of looking like a freak."

"Pepper Keane, the lawyer marine."

"Can you drag yourself away from the baseball stats long enough to give me a haircut?"

"It's almost touching your ears," he said. "You got cash?"

"Always," I said. He sprang out of his chair with the pep of a man fifty years younger. I had no trouble believing he had once been a welterweight prospect.

"Don't take checks," he said.

"I know," I said. Milt knew exactly how much income he could report each year without having to accept reduced Social Security benefits.

I stepped up into the black chair and let Milt do his thing as he expertly analyzed the Rockies' pitching woes and brought me up to date on the latest happenings at the VFW. "Ten bucks," he said as I stepped down.

"That's robbery," I said.

"Then go to Super Clips next time," he shot back. "Let one of those homos cut your hair." I handed him twelve dollars and told him I'd be back in a few weeks. Lit up the truck, popped in a tape of old Motown tunes, and headed for Denver.

I arrived at Troy's gym just before three. There were a few hardcores pumping iron, but the overall volume was low. I opened my locker, stripped to my boxers, and weighed myself. I was still on the scale when my brother and Jeff Smart came up behind me. "Two-fifteen," my brother observed. "Maybe you ought to think about liposuction."

"Five-eight," I said. "Maybe you ought to think about elevator shoes." Troy laughed and I stepped off the scale. "Good to see you, Jeff," I said as I extended my hand. "It's been a while." He grew up in our neighborhood and has been one of my brother's best friends since grade school. "I thought you were in Chicago," I said as I donned green workout shorts and a white tank top.

"Moved back a year ago," Jeff said.

"Still flying the friendly skies?"

"Not anymore," he said. "A buddy and I leased a Learjet and started a charter service. It's called Smart Charter. All we do is fly executives around."

"Beats getting a real job," my brother said.

"The Keane family motto," I said. They waited patiently while I put on my running shoes. "In the words of Gary Gilmore," I said as I finished tying the laces, "let's do it."

With that, we began a thorough leg and back workout. Squats, dead lifts, bent rows, dumbbell rows, knee extensions, ham curls, calf raises, and more squats. Jeff kept up well, but used less weight for most exercises. He stands six-one and probably weighs one-seventy. It's the perfect build for the sport he enjoys most—skirt chasing.

Jeff has been a womanizer since puberty. In addition to being outgoing and fun loving, he has a look some women find attractive. He has a dark complexion—probably the result of his Jewish ancestry—and dark, curly hair, which he wears just slightly longer than is today fashionable.

We finished our workout with a short jog through the tree-lined streets of the Cherry Creek area. There were plenty of young women out—shopping, jogging, doing yard work—and Jeff didn't miss a one. "How many ex-wives are you up to now?" I teased.

"Still just the two," he replied. I had represented him in his second divorce, a nasty affair despite the short duration of the marriage and their lack of children. It had been policy at Keane, Simms & Mercante to refuse domestic cases of any kind, but handling such matters for friends and relatives is just part of being a lawyer. You can't avoid it.

Troy's gym came into sight as we neared the end of our trot. We had jogged about a mile. "You guys want to go out for a beer?" my brother asked.

"Sure," I said.

"I'll go, but I can't drink," Jeff said. "We're flying to Boston tomorrow and takeoff is at zero five hundred."

"Beats getting a real job," my brother reminded him.

"How long are you going to be in Boston?" I asked.

26

The cockpit of a Learjet 45 XR is designed to allow the pilot and copilot to work efficiently and in comfort, but the engineers had not anticipated that thick-limbed private eyes might also ride up front, so I sat on the floor. Jeff and his copilot/partner had agreed to let me bum a ride, but I had to remain in the cockpit so the six executives in the passenger cabin could have the privacy they were paying for.

We took off at 5:07 A.M. It was still dark, but hints of dawn were evident on Colorado's eastern horizon as indigo gave way to pale blue. "Is this legal?" I asked as the aircraft leveled off.

"No," Jeff replied. "You're not even on the manifest, so we're violating at least two FAA regulations."

"If we go down," said the copilot, "the extra body is gonna confuse the hell out of the NTSB." Jay was a few years younger than Jeff, perhaps thirty, and looked like one of the Beach Boys. He stood about five-nine and was trim like a pilot should be. Blond hair, blue eyes, nice tan.

We continued east and my lack of sleep caught up with me. I'd risen at 3:00 A.M. to give myself time to drop the dogs at Troy's and get to the airport. "Take a nap if you want," Jeff said. "Won't hurt our feelings."

"I think I will," I said. My only luggage was an overnight bag I'd been holding in my lap. Using that as a pillow, I let my head rest against the door and closed my eyes. I slept a little more than an hour. "Where are we now?" I asked.

"Closing in on Des Moines," said Jeff. I nodded and decided to resume my struggle with Heidegger's *Being and Time,* a self-imposed chore I'd been neglecting lately.

For any man, "*Dasein,*" in the world, Heidegger felt there are three possible modes of existence: undifferentiated, inauthentic, and authentic. A man in the undifferentiated mode never questions the meaning of his own life or faces up to the fact that his existence is defined by the culture fate threw him into. He never recognizes his own "thrown-ness," but blindly accepts the existence he has inherited. If anything, I had questioned the meaning of my life way too fucking much, so the undifferentiated mode clearly did not describe me.

A man in the inauthentic mode recognizes that his existence is a result of coincidence—recognizes his own thrown-ness, but simply substitutes some other role for the life he inherited, not recognizing that both roles were created by the culture he was thrown into. I had left the Marine Corps for civilian life, and I had left the congestion of Denver for mountain life in Nederland, but I recognized that both roles existed within the American culture I'd been born into. I knew that if I'd been born in China, I'd have turned out to be a thick-limbed Chinese private eye, so I definitely recognized my own thrown-ness, and the inauthentic mode didn't describe me either.

A man's recognition of his own thrown-ness sometimes leads to what Heidegger called "anxiety." He begins to think about death. When a man is unable to face up to the possibility of his own nonbeing or nothingness, Heidegger referred to this as "fallen-ness." Instead of dealing with his anxiety, the man who experiences fallen-ness returns to the inauthentic mode.

But some who experience anxiety do face up to their own thrown-ness and their own death, and in so doing they accept responsibility for their own lives. Heidegger called this "care." In caring for the world, each man makes the most of his own possibilities—even if those possibilities were originally dictated by the culture he was thrown into. A man who adopts this attitude lives in what Heidegger called an "authentic mode of existence."

I closed the book and put it down. Then I remembered the dream I'd had in Walla Walla. And I think I understood it. Joy hadn't been shouting, "Dozen"; she'd been shouting, *"Dasein."* The image of me falling to earth indicated a state of fallen-ness. I had changed my outer life, and I was happier, but I still hadn't found a way to deal with death or the fear that there is no God and life is meaningless. And Joy had been carrying a CARE package. Had she been trying to tell me how to pull myself out of my state of fallen-ness?

"You're awful quiet," Jeff said. "Whatcha thinking about?"

"Falling," I said.

"We're not going to go down," he said, "but if we do, at least you know you've got good genes for it." A joking reference to the fact that my brother had walked away from his parachute mishap. I laughed.

We landed at Logan Airport just after ten o'clock local time. I had less than twenty-four hours to work with. The execs wanted to leave early the next morning so they could be back in Denver in time for Friday's doubleheader at Coors Field.

Jeff offered to share a room, but I wasn't sure where events would take me and declined. He gave me the number of their motel in case I changed my mind and told me where to meet them Friday morning. I bid them farewell, then found the nearest airport men's room. To avoid taking a hanging bag, I had worn a suit. I put on a tie to complete the look, cleaned my black wing tips with a paper towel, then stepped outside and hailed a cab. "Harvard University," I said.

"You a professor?" the driver asked. He had an admirable beer gut and a thick New England accent. White, early fifties.

"Not in this lifetime," I said.

"Where you frahm?"

"Colorado."

"What brings you to Bawston?" Great, I had drawn a talkative cabbie.

"Quick business trip," I said. Before he could ask my line of work, I asked about seafood. He fancied himself an expert and described six or seven restaurants as he navigated through heavy mid-morning traffic.

"Hahvad University," he said as we rolled through a yellow light. I looked to my left and saw several Georgian buildings constructed of redbrick and covered with ivy. To my right were two coffee shops, two bookstores, one Kinko's, and a body-piercing parlor, all with apartments above. "Where you want out?" the cabbie asked. "I'll getcha as close as I cahn."

"This'll be fine," I said. He guided the cab to a stop beside the body-piercing place. I paid the fare, tipped him, and thanked him for the ride. A display in the piercing-shop window caught my attention and I decided to take a closer look. Dozens of photos of satisfied customers were taped to the plate glass, each proudly displaying a safety pin or stud in a nipple, tongue, or other body part. It frightened me to think some had probably achieved a perfect score on the Scholastic Aptitude Test.

I crossed the street and began walking the campus perimeter in search of a directory or a map. It was a typical campus, though I noticed more political literature than I'd ever seen in Boulder. Chess seemed popular; I observed people playing on benches as well as outdoor tables designed specifically for the game. I don't enjoy chess, but it wasn't a bad day for it. About seventy degrees and cloudy. A bit muggy by Colorado standards, but that could be said about the entire Eastern Seaboard.

Summer or not, the math department at Harvard was alive with activity. Instructors lectured, small groups congregated in halls for impromptu discussions, and graduate students worked diligently in small offices or cubicles. I located the departmental office on the third floor, introduced myself to a trio of young secretaries, and stated my purpose. The consensus was that mine was a matter for the chairman's secretary, Mrs. Rutherford.

I found her at an executive desk at the back of the room, immediately outside the chairman's office. She was in her late fifties. Tall and thin, her gray hair feathered in a short, but attractive, style. She wore reading glasses and a green knit dress. She was proof-reading a thick document, red pencil in hand, when I appeared.

"Excuse me," I said. She continued scanning until she came to the end of a paragraph, then folded her hands and looked up at me with the presence of a marine colonel.

"If you're here about the teaching position," she said, "applications were due yesterday."

"I doubt I'm qualified for it," I said. I set my bag down and handed her one of my cards. She studied it, then allowed a barely noticeable smile.

"I should have known," she said. "You're too well dressed to be a mathematician."

"I'm looking into the death of Donald Underwood," I said.

"One of the few gentlemen in this department," she remarked.

"Do you have five minutes?" I asked. "I was told you were someone I might want to speak with."

"I suppose so," she said. She stood and removed her glasses. "We'll use the conference room. Leave your bag behind my desk."

I accepted coffee—I was still tired—and followed her to a small and unimpressive conference room where I explained that I was investigating the possibility that Underwood's death might have been related to the deaths of two other mathematicians. "I'm familiar with that," she said. "The FBI interviewed a number of people here."

"So I'm told," I said. I had read the interview summaries, but I planned to pursue a somewhat different line of questioning.

"I never put much stock in the suicide theory," she continued. "That dear man wasn't the least bit depressed and, even if he had been, he loved his sons far too much to take his own life." I let a few seconds pass as I pondered how to broach the next subject.

"I spoke with the detective who investigated this case," I said, "and he suggested Professor Underwood's death might have been an accident."

"I've heard those nasty rumors," she said, "and I don't put much stock in them either." Mrs. Rutherford wasn't shy about making her opinions known.

"Why not?"

"Mr. Keane," she said, "the man was a mathematics professor at the most respected university in the nation. I should think he'd be smart enough not to inadvertently hang himself." I nodded and moved on, asking a litany of questions on topics ranging from Underwood's personality to her familiarity with E-Prime. She described him as polite, soft-spoken, and laid back. She was familiar with E-Prime, but said nobody in the math department was particularly fond of it. "Mathematicians frequently use the verb 'is,'" she explained. "Two plus two *is* four."

Despite her abrupt manner, it was clear that Mrs. Rutherford remembered Underwood with genuine affection. When we returned to her desk and I asked for the names of colleagues Underwood had been close to, she produced a printed list of the department's faculty and placed red marks next to a half dozen names. "Since your time is limited," she said, "I suggest you start with these six." She handed me the list. "I'll instruct them to cooperate fully." Thus assured, I asked if I could leave my bag and began my journey through the mathematics department.

I first spoke with a computer science professor named Singh. Mrs. Rutherford had already contacted him by the time I arrived. He was from India and had a dark complexion accented by jet black hair. Six feet tall, thin build, love handles developing on the waist. "It's a shame about Donald," he said. "We miss him very much." I asked some questions to gain a sense of Singh and his relationship with Underwood, then turned to more specific matters.

"Professor Underwood specialized in fractal geometry?"

"Yes, he was quite well known in that field."

"I read his articles," I said, "and I noticed one of them concerned neural networks."

He smiled. "Donald and his neural networks."

"Is that something which interested him?"

"Neural networks are simple programs," he said, "but they fascinated Donald."

"Why is that?"

"Donald was consumed by a desire to demonstrate the usefulness of fractal geometry in the real world, and neural networks offer one way to do that. With sufficient data, a neural network can recognize patterns and assist in predicting the future behavior of certain phenomena."

"Things like the weather?"

"Precisely."

"What about economic markets," I continued, "did Professor Underwood ever attempt to apply his knowledge to business or economic issues?"

"Ah," he said, "you should talk with the people at NPS."

"NPS?"

"New Paradigm Systems. It's an economic consulting firm. Donald did some work for them. They'll tell you all about neural networks and economic markets."

"Did you tell the FBI about this?" I asked.

"The gentlemen never asked," he said.

By midafternoon I had interviewed five men and a diminutive woman who could've been Donna Shalala's twin sister. All agreed that Underwood had not seemed depressed prior to his death. All denied knowledge of any kinky side to his personality. Three mentioned New Paradigm Systems. I hailed another cab.

New Paradigm Systems was located in a nicely landscaped office park in the Boston suburbs. The building was five stories of greenish marble and smoky glass. A young security guard at an octagonal black kiosk near the entrance asked me to sign in. I told him I had business with NPS and he directed me to the fifth floor. Large metallic letters above the entrance to the suite spelled out "New Paradigm Systems." Smaller letters beneath that announced the company's line of work—"Economic Consulting."

The suite had been decorated by a professional. Glass doors led to a reception area with scarlet linen wallpaper, rich walnut paneling, and elegant French provincial furniture. A highly polished receptionist's desk was centered in front of the rear wall, but there was no receptionist. A heavy wooden door to the receptionist's left guarded the rest of the suite. I noticed security cameras in two corners. I started toward the door, but it opened before I reached it.

"I hope you haven't been waiting long," the man said. "I just noticed you on the monitor." He was my age, a few inches taller, and thin. Gray slacks, blue oxford-cloth shirt, no tie. He had something resembling a Roman haircut, and it was short enough that I could see the tops of his ears, which tapered to rounded points. "I know," he said, "I look like Spock." I smiled to show appreciation for his self-deprecating humor.

"I just walked in the door," I assured him.

"Good," he said. "What can I do for you?" He used his left foot to prevent the door from closing.

"My name is Pepper Keane," I said. "I'm a private investigator." I handed him a card. "I'd like to speak with someone about Donald Underwood." He noticed the J.D. after my name.

"I used to practice law," he said. "Hated it."

"It's an illness," I said. "Like gambling or alcoholism. I'm thinking of founding a twelve-step program for lawyers who want to get out of it."

He grinned. "That's good," he said. "I'll have to remember that."

"Do you have a few minutes?"

"We really liked Don," he said, "so I'll be happy to talk with you, but I'm not sure I'll be much help."

"I'm not either," I said. "I'm just trying to cover all the bases."

"Russ Seifert," he said as he extended his right hand. "C'mon back." He held the door for me, then led me down a hall. Considerably less had been spent decorating the suite's interior; it was modern and functional. There were workstations and offices, but most were unmanned. Much of the space was occupied by a glass-enclosed, climate-controlled computer room.

Except for the stock quotes scrolling across the digital display on the wall opposite his desk, Seifert's office was much like that of any moderately successful insurance salesman. He had a nice view of the parking lot and much of the office park. One wall was dominated by framed etchings of old clipper ships. His desk held some nautical trappings, including a brass barometer, and I guessed he might have a thing for sailing. He motioned for me to sit, then fell into an oxblood leather executive chair behind his desk. "I thought the Underwood thing had been put to rest," he said.

"The local cops and the feds have put it to rest, but—"

"The feds?"

"Let me explain," I said. I repeated the story for the umpteenth time: Two other specialists in fractal geometry had been murdered and I was looking into the possibility that the deaths might be related.

"I had no idea," he said.

"I'm surprised the FBI didn't interview you," I said. "I spoke with some of his colleagues at Harvard, and it's no secret he did work for your company."

"He designed software for us."

"You paid a Harvard professor to write code?"

"It's sophisticated software," he said.

"What exactly does your firm do?" I asked. "'Economic consulting' is a broad term."

"In essence," he said, "we analyze data and try to predict what a market or security is going to do in the future."

"Using principles borrowed from fractal geometry?"

"Fractal geometry, chaos theory, nonlinear statistics. It's all intertwined."

"You're the president?" I asked. I took a card from his gold-plated holder: "Russell J. Seifert, M.B.A., J.D., LL.M."

"I started the company five years ago," he said. "I practiced law on Wall Street for eight years and decided there had to be an easier way to make money."

"Looks like you've found one."

"We've done well," he said. "When I started, it was just me. Now we have ten employees." One of them, a bookish woman in jeans, stopped at the door immediately opposite Seifert's office, entered a code in the keypad, and stepped into what looked like a small library. "That's Dr. Long," he said. "She's an economist."

"Why all the security measures?" I asked. All the doors had keypad locks.

"It's a very secretive business," he said.

"Why is that?"

"We're not the only ones doing this," he explained. "There are other firms offering this type of service. Some of the larger banks and brokerage houses have in-house teams doing exactly what we do." I nodded.

"All of these firms," he continued, "have access to the same information. What matters is what you do with the information."

"I'm not sure I follow you," I said.

"We rely on certain theoretical ideas we have about market behavior—part of Underwood's job was to design software to implement those ideas—and those are all that distinguish us from the competition."

"You're afraid someone might steal your ideas?"

"It happens," he said. "You can't put a value on a good theoretical model."

"What makes one model better than another?"

"Consistency," he said. "Nobody can predict the future with certainty. We don't measure success by how much money we make; we measure it by how often we're right. When you provide investment advice to people managing hundreds of millions of dollars, you'd better be right more often than you are wrong." I massaged my temples and thought about what he'd told me.

"You said you can't put a value on a good model, but I'm trying to get an idea of what one of these models would be worth. Suppose I came to you and tried to sell you on a model I'd developed. How would we arrive at a value?"

"It doesn't work that way," he said. "In order for me to evaluate the model, you'd have to reveal it to me and show me data to prove it works. And once you'd done that, I wouldn't need you, though I might offer you a job if I felt you'd be an asset to the firm."

"So," I continued, "if you're in the business of developing these theoretical models, you can't really sell them door-to-door?"

"Correct," he said. "You can't copyright an idea."

"I could copyright the software," I said.

"Yes, but the model is what has value. If I liked the model, I could buy the software from you or pay someone else to design it."

"So if I develop the mother of all theoretical models, how do I make money on it?"

"You go into business for yourself," he said. "Either that or you publish and hope to win the Nobel Prize."

The economist exited the library and stepped into Seifert's office. Her chestnut hair was brushed back and held in a ponytail by a rubber band. About thirty-five years old. "Excuse me, Russ," she said, "the computer just came alive. It's saying we should short the yen against the dollar. We have to do it now."

"Do it," he said. She called for someone named Maurice and disappeared down the hall. "We also do a little trading on our own," he explained.

"How many other firms are doing this sort of thing?" I asked.

"We don't know for sure," he said. "We think there are about a dozen in the United States. One of them's out in your neck of the woods. It's called the Koch Group." I heard his words, but didn't really process them because something had just clicked for me.

"These theoretical models," I began, "if someone was determined to steal them, would it be necessary to get into your suite or could it be done from a remote terminal?" He leaned forward and thought about it.

"They'd have to break in," he said. "Even if they managed to gain access to our mainframes—which isn't likely—it wouldn't do them much good. Computers are just tools. Ultimately, everything we do is the result of human ideas."

"And those ideas are on paper?"

"You bet," he said. "Our library is filled with memos, studies, and all sorts of analytical papers. I've got most of them right here." He swiveled and pointed to a built-in bookcase stuffed with three-ring binders, bound reports, and stacks of papers.

"How would you know if something was missing?" I asked. He considered the question for a long time, then looked at me.

"We wouldn't," he said. "Not until we went to find it."

* * *

The Adams House is an upscale seafood restaurant on Boston Harbor. I arrived before six and secured a table by a window facing the water. Now I was working on a piping-hot bowl of clam chowder, watching the gulls, and wondering how to spend my evening. Before leaving New Paradigm Systems, I had phoned Underwood's wife, but there had been no answer, so I'd decided to have dinner before trying again. Three different cabbies had recommended the Adams House.

It turned out to be a good choice. A giant bowl of chowder was followed by a generous salad with homemade garlic croutons. Another glass of wine. Then the lobster arrived. I suppressed my ambivalence about eating other creatures and reached for the butter.

I paid, snagged a few mints as I walked past the hostess, and tried Underwood's wife again. Still no answer. I could rent a car, drive to western Massachusetts, and hope she was home when I arrived, but it looked like a two-hour drive and I wasn't eager to do it without some assurance that she'd be there. I could try to get together with Jeff, but chances were better than fifty-fifty he'd already latched on to some woman. In the end, I took my fourth cab ride of the day. "Head for a cheap motel near the airport," I told the driver.

I ended up at a Motel 6, which was fine because it was clean and I've always liked Tom Bodett. They had left the light on for me—just like it says in the ads—and before turning it off, I phoned Troy to check on the dogs, then called Scott to update him on the events of the past few days and ask a favor. "What do you think Finn was doing at your house?" he asked.

"I haven't a clue," I said. "We'll deal with that when I get back." I told him my plan. "In the meantime, if you get a chance, stop by the Denver courthouse and get as much information on Polk as you can. He just got divorced a week or two ago."

"Sure."

"I'll see you Saturday," I said.

27

You gain two hours flying from Boston to Denver, so I made it to Troy's house before eleven. He and Trudi were at work, and the kids were in school, but I had my key. Buck and Wheat greeted me as if I'd just returned from a one-year combat tour. I let them out into the spacious suburban backyard, then searched the kitchen and found my brother's Fritos. I left a message apologizing for my theft, noting that corn chips are rich in saturated fats and suggesting he try rice cakes. Loaded the dogs into the truck and headed for home.

The flashing red light alerted me to messages from Dick Gilbert, Susan Thompson, and Jayne Smyers. On the theory that Jayne was the only one I wanted to date, I called her first.

"Where've you been?" she asked. "I've got copies of Agent Polk's records."

"Took a quick trip to Bawston," I said.

"Boston?" she exclaimed. "I must owe you more money by now."

"I flew free," I said.

"Say that five times fast."

"One of my friends owns an air-charter service. He happened to be going to Boston, so I tagged along."

"Did you learn anything?" she asked.

"A few things," I said. I told her of Underwood's work for New Paradigm Systems and the existence of an industry using mathematics and computers to predict the behavior of financial markets.

"That's interesting," she said. "That strengthens your theory about the economic connection."

"A little," I said. "What about Polk's records, anything there?"

"Not that I can see, but I'm not sure what you're looking for."

"Me either," I said. "I'm just trying to obtain as much information as I can."

"I can fax them if you like, but it will take a while. There are quite a few documents."

"Tell you what," I said casually, "maybe we can get together this weekend and you can give them to me."

"We're having our annual retreat for the women's shelter this weekend, so it would have to be tonight."

"I happen to have an opening tonight," I said. "Why don't you come up? I'll make dinner and we'll enjoy the mountain air."

"What are you making?" she asked.

"If it's just me, macaroni and cheese. If you come, I'll put more effort into it."

She laughed and said she'd be delighted, so I gave directions and said good-bye. Wheat came into my office and jumped in my lap. "We're having company tonight," I said as I rubbed his ears, "so I want you and Buck on your best behavior." He said nothing. I deposited him on the floor and phoned Gilbert.

"The forensic people say they're one hundred percent certain on the serial number," he said.

"Polk lied to you," I said. "The gun you have was taken from the FBI's evidence room sometime after Green's arrest and hasn't been seen since."

"How do you know?" he asked. I told him the story: Gombold had made an offhand remark about a missing gun, and I'd later confirmed it was the one used by Bailey Green.

"Why didn't you tell me?" he asked.

"I wasn't sure until Tuesday. After we got off the phone, I called Gombold and he told me the U.S. Attorneys had just offered

Green a sweetheart deal because the bureau still hadn't found the weapon."

"Why'd Polk lie?" he asked.

"I don't know," I said, "but it's been bothering me since Tuesday."

"Maybe we ought to go to the bureau," he finally said. "A weapon taken from *their* evidence room was used in a murder up here."

"I'd hold off," I said. "I'm digging into Polk's background, and some other things are starting to come together. Once we go to the bureau, it's out of our hands."

"I suppose," he said.

"Matter of fact, I'd take that gun out of your evidence room and store it in a safe place. I don't know what's going on, but now that the bureau knows you have it and you've tied it to a murder, someone may come looking for it."

"You're a cautious bastard, aren't you? It may just be that some janitor at the federal building stole the damn thing."

"Not likely," I said. "I used to work there; they don't let janitors roam around like that. And that wouldn't explain Polk's lie."

"All right," he said, "I'll put the gun someplace else. Now tell me about these things coming together."

I outlined the economic thread connecting the three deaths and recounted my trip to Boston. Then, for the first time, I vocalized a theory I'd been toying with since leaving New Paradigm Systems. "Think about it," I said. "Your killer could've walked out of Fontaine's house with volumes of documents or dozens of disks, and we'd have no way of knowing."

"Okay," he responded, "suppose Fontaine developed some sort of model he used to pick stocks. Why kill him? Why not just steal the information and get the hell out? Better yet, why not copy it when he's not around?"

"I don't know," I said. "Maybe the guy needed Fontaine's help to find what he was looking for. Once he gets it, he doesn't want

Fontaine around to ID him. Or maybe having the information isn't enough; maybe he wants to claim the model as his own."

"That's a lot of maybes."

"Just a theory," I said.

"Well," he said, "since I don't have a better one, I may reinterview a few people and see if it leads anywhere."

"That would be great," I said.

"Let me know what you find out about Polk."

"Will do," I said. I hung up and dialed Susan Thompson. She wasn't in, but the receptionist transferred me to her voice mail. Her recorded greeting was short and to the point. So was my message. "This is Pepper Keane," I said. "We're playing phone tag, and you're it."

Jayne arrived at six-thirty with a bottle of Merlot in one hand and Polk's records in the other. She wore tan slacks and a white cotton blouse with short sleeves. The dogs raced to the door to greet her. "This is Buck," I said, "and this is Wheat." She handed me the wine, then extended her right arm and let Buck sniff her hand. When she sensed he was comfortable, she ran her palm along the side of his massive head.

"Yes," she said in that silly voice people use when talking to animals, "you're a handsome fellow." He licked her hand. Wheat became jealous and began whining. "Oh, you're handsome too," she said as she knelt to meet him.

"He'll shake if you ask him," I said.

"Can you shake hands, little dog?" She offered her hand and he responded. "He's darling," she said, "but how did you come up with 'Wheat'?"

"His name was Blackie when I adopted him," I said. "He had been abused, and I wanted to give him a name he wouldn't associate with his previous owner. I already had Buck, so Wheat was the obvious choice."

"Buckwheat," she said as she stood up. "Cute."

"I could have named him Tooth," I offered.

"Or Shot," she replied. She smiled, handed me the documents, and surveyed my home. "This is beautiful," she said. "You must've done well practicing law." I let that pass without comment and offered to give her a tour. I had spent several hours cleaning, so the prospect didn't frighten me too much. We began in my office. "You have a lot of books," she observed.

"Can't bring myself to get rid of any of them. I still have all my college textbooks."

"I'm the same way," she said. "Each book is like a little trophy." I nodded and we continued on, through the bedrooms and the lofts. I assured her the basement was not worth seeing, but she insisted. Because my brother owns a gym, I have accumulated an enviable assortment of exercise equipment over the years, including an Olympic weight set, stair stepper, stationary bike, and stretching machine, but what caught her eye was the heavy bag. She positioned herself in front of it and threw a playful jab. The bag didn't move, but she smiled like a child who has just discovered a new toy.

"We'll have to work on that," I said. She threw several more light punches, then started laughing. "'Yo, Adrian,'" I said. I rolled my head in the direction of the stairs. She followed and we concluded the tour in the kitchen.

"Something smells good," she said.

"Macaroni and cheese," I said. She put her hands on her hips and gave me a look. "It's Kraft," I assured her. She gave me a playful slap on the shoulder. "Vegetarian lasagna," I said.

I opened the wine and poured some for each of us. We sipped it while I put the finishing touches on dinner. Aside from lasagna, I'd prepared a mushroom salad and garlic cheese bread consisting of more cheese than bread.

"This is delicious," she said after sampling the main course. "Did you put clove in it?"

"A little," I said.

"Do you like to cook?"

"Sometimes," I said, "but it's not a passion."

We continued eating and talking. We were at ease with each other, and I was glad. "I called the owners' association again," she said.

"About the trees?"

"Yes."

"And?"

"The man I spoke with said the trees are on open space owned by the city of Boulder. So I called the open-space department. They said the trees belong to the association." I laughed.

When it was clear neither of us would eat more lasagna or bread or salad, I served generous slices of carrot cake purchased at Wanda's that afternoon. Although I'd taken the larger piece, I finished first. "This is yummy," she finally said, "but I can't eat another bite."

"Too rich?"

"No," she said, "I'm just stuffed." She pushed her dessert plate toward me.

"I've had my fill," I said. "Buck and Wheat will have to help us." I prepared a plate of morsels for each of them, then began clearing the dishes. She offered to help, but I told her cleanup was a one-man job and asked her to pick out some music.

After I had loaded the dishwasher, I poured more wine and we adjourned to the porch where we each took a rocking chair. I thumbed through Polk's law school records as we listened to Sinatra. "That's interesting," I said. "I should've remembered that."

"What's that?"

"He did his undergraduate work in Seattle. Went there on a basketball scholarship. Earned a degree in economics." She leaned over and looked at the document I was viewing.

"The University of Washington," she said. "Why is that interesting?"

"It's interesting only because one of the murders took place in Washington." I continued through the documents and found his law school application. "Looks like he grew up there," I said. "He went to high school in a town called Richland."

"I've never heard of it. Have you?"

"No," I said, "but I've got an atlas in my office." I retrieved the atlas, returned to my chair, and found the map of Washington. Jayne moved her chair closer and leaned over to look at the map. She was right next to me and I caught a hint of perfume on her slender neck.

"There it is," she said. "It's not far from Walla Walla."

"No," I said, "it isn't." It was on the Columbia River. About forty-five minutes from Walla Walla. Right where the gun had been found.

28

THIS WAS YOUR SECOND DATE, right?" We were seated beside
each other on the concrete floor, legs outstretched, our backs sup-
ported by an equally uncomfortable concrete wall.

"I guess so," I said. Not counting one lunch date and our chance
encounter at the bookstore.

"How'd it go?" Scott asked.

"We didn't do it, if that's what you mean."

"There goes my theory about the second date."

"We fell asleep on the couch," I said. A fly landed on his left
forearm; he smacked it with his right hand and flicked the
remains away. "It's probably just as well," I added. "I want to have
the D and M talk before things go too far." He looked at me.

"D and M?"

"Depression and manslaughter."

"I've got a news flash for you," he said. "If you two were curled
up on the couch, things have already gone too far." He was right,
of course. I had selfishly refused to disclose things Jayne had a
right to know because I hadn't wanted to put a damper on a
delightful evening or a potential relationship. He glanced at his
watch. "Almost midnight," he said.

Saturday was about to become Sunday and we were alone in a
musty boiler room in the bowels of the mathematics building at
the University of Colorado. We'd been there since seven, waiting
for an assortment of die-hard instructors and students to go home.

We wanted to be the only ones in the building before starting phase two. Now we were talking about the case.

"Assuming," Scott said, "these three developed some kind of wonder model, it just doesn't make any sense that there's no evidence of them communicating with each other."

"My theory is that whoever did it destroyed anything that might've linked the victims to the model or to each other."

"Before he kills them, he makes them hand over all the documentation on the model and all their correspondence with each other?"

"Yup."

"Why?"

"Two reasons," I said. "First, he wants to claim the model as his own. Second, if he eliminates any evidence linking the three victims, the murders are more likely to be treated as three unrelated crimes. That's why he used a different MO for each murder; he wanted them to appear unrelated." Scott pondered that.

"How do you eliminate records of phone calls over a period of years?" he asked. "They had to be talking with each other."

"The bureau checked all that," I said. I explained what I had learned from Gumby about the lack of any uniform policy on the retention of billing records by telephone companies. "I read Polk's report on all that line by line. His boss double-checked it. If there were ever any records, they're gone now."

We sat in silence on the concrete for a few more minutes. "Something else doesn't make sense," Scott said.

"What's that?"

"I'm the killer," he said. "I get into Fontaine's home and force him to give me all the documentation and correspondence. A lot of this stuff has to be on his computer. So we go upstairs and he gives me the disks. But some of what I want is on his hard drive, so I have to identify those files before I kill him. Then I have to copy them onto a disk and delete them from the hard drive."

"Okay."

"You said the police checked Fontaine's computers and didn't find any files linking him to the other two?"

"Yeah."

"They must not have done a very good job," he said.

"What do you mean?"

"I mean, if you're right, the information is still on his hard drive."

"What?"

"When you delete a file," he said, "it doesn't just disappear. The information remains stored on the hard drive until there's so much new data that the machine has to overwrite the deleted material. You can recover the deleted file by using a simple utilities program."

"I guess I knew that," I said. "So if our killer wanted to completely eliminate that evidence, how would he do it?"

"Only two ways to do it," he said. "You reformat the hard drive or remove it from the computer and grind it into dust."

"But he couldn't do either of those things because that would've told the police something about his true purpose."

"It sounds like the police just inventoried the files they found on the hard drive, but made no effort to recover the deleted files."

"I'll call Gilbert tomorrow."

"Have him check the computer in Fontaine's office too. If your theory is right, the killer had to bust into Fontaine's office before or after he killed Fontaine to find whatever documentation might be in his office."

"It wouldn't have been hard to do," I said. "There was a bike rack that could've been used as a ladder right outside the building. And some of the windows in that building were wide open."

"You might want to ask this cop in Walla Walla if there's any evidence of a break-in."

"Okay," I said. "Speaking of busting into offices, one of us should go take another look."

"I'll do it," he said. He stood and began walking down the dark corridor.

I closed my eyes and tried to do some meditation, but my mind kept coming back to Jayne Smyers. Her delicate features. The scent of her perfume. The taste of her kisses. It was too early to call it love, but it was something I hadn't felt in a long, long time.

Ten minutes later I heard Scott approaching. I knew it was Scott because nobody else would be whistling "Jambalaya" under such circumstances. "Those kids finally took off," he said. "It's just us." The last holdouts had been some students in a seminar room on the second floor.

"Took 'em long enough," I said. I stood, but my legs were asleep. I laughed and jumped up and down a few times to get the blood flowing. When the tingling sensation ceased, we donned surgical gloves and began a cautious journey to the third floor.

"I feel like E. Howard Hunt," Scott whispered. We were just outside Finn's office.

"Let's hope we do a better job than those jokers," I said. Scott knelt to examine the doorknob and keyhole. "You can forget that," I said. I pointed to the suspended ceiling. He understood immediately. I assumed a squat position. When he was firmly on my shoulders, I stood. It took him less than thirty seconds to pop one of the ceiling panels, climb over the threshold, remove a panel on the other side of the door, descend into Finn's office, and open the door for me.

The first thing we did was replace the ceiling panels. "Now what?" Scott whispered. The room was dark.

"You go to work on his computer," I said softly. "I'll check the filing cabinet and desk." I removed a penlight from my shirt pocket. It looks like an expensive writing instrument, but emits an adjustable beam of red light.

"What are we looking for?" Scott asked.

"I don't know," I said. "Anything that might explain why this guy was snooping around my house."

"Why not just ask him?" he said. "I've got a blowtorch you can borrow if he won't cooperate."

I smiled. "I may talk to him," I said, "but first I want to learn more about him." He shrugged and sat down at the computer. I went to the black metal filing cabinet. It consisted of four drawers. I slid the top one out and began going through it. The files were in alphabetical order, each identifiable by a typed label. I opened every file, but found only mathematical articles on topics of interest to Finn.

"This guy may be a genius," Scott whispered after several minutes, "but he's a functional illiterate when it comes to computer security." I said nothing and opened the second drawer. It contained teaching materials—course outlines, grade books, tests, that sort of thing.

The third drawer was reserved for his research. It contained his doctoral dissertation—a lengthy paper on something having to do with prime numbers—and numerous other files holding papers he'd authored on various mathematical subjects. It appeared he had kept every paper he'd written since entering Harvard at sixteen.

I opened the bottom drawer. Every man has a place to hide his junk, and this was Finn's. The drawer's contents included several dozen issues of *Inside Triathlon,* six cans of tuna in spring water, two disposable razors, one nearly empty tube of toothpaste, and a toothbrush so yellowed and full of crud I wouldn't have used it on my dogs. I gently pushed the drawer into place, then walked toward the desk, where Scott was hard at work.

"Finding anything?" I asked.

"No files with your name," he said. "None with hers either, but that can be deceptive because people sometimes choose file names that have nothing to do with the subject matter of the file. Unless

I can tell what it is, I'm opening each file to see what's in it. I'm almost done with the hard drive." I gave him a pat on the shoulder and said he was a good man. Then I considered Finn's desk.

There were only two drawers, the top smaller than the bottom. Both on the right. Both locked. Unlike TV gumshoes, I'm not particularly skilled at picking locks, but the desk was cheap and I was able to pop the bottom drawer open without destroying the mechanism. Then we heard footsteps.

I dashed behind the door while Scott hid between the filing cabinet and bookcase. The footsteps grew louder. It was definitely a man, and he wasn't singing "Jambalaya." I looked at Scott and brought my right fist down hard on an invisible foe. He nodded. We had committed a felony, and I didn't plan on spending the next five years sharing a cell with the likes of Delbert Gaffney.

But it didn't come to that. The footsteps faded as quickly as they had become audible. It sounded as though someone had simply walked down the hall and out the fire door at the far end. "Security guard?" Scott whispered.

"Sad state of affairs when you can't even bust into a man's office without worrying about government interference."

"It's the goddamned bureaucrats in Washington," he agreed. I smiled, but my heart was still racing.

Scott sat down at the computer and began inserting disks. I returned to the desk drawer. Again, the files were in alphabetical order. Their contents tended to be of a more personal nature than the documents in the filing cabinet. Correspondence, pay stubs, pension statements. Toward the rear was an accordion folder labeled "Tenure." I removed it and parked myself on a chair beside the desk.

Finn was nothing if not organized. Inside the folder were four files, each with its own label. The first contained the university's policies pertaining to tenure, a thick document obviously drafted by a team of lawyers. The next held Finn's curriculum vitae and copies of his academic publications. The third contained a chronological list of his significant accomplishments, together with supporting documents in the form of letters, awards, and news clippings. The fourth was labeled "Tenure Committee."

For each person on the committee, he had prepared a paper summarizing that person's background and interests. Each concluded with a rating showing his perceived level of support from that person. He had devised a scale from 1 to 5, with 1 indicating strong support and 5 indicating scant support. His dossier on Jayne consumed three single-spaced pages and ended like this:

SUMMARY Because of her people skills and objective manner, Jayne is likely one of the committee's leaders. She is concerned not only with scholarship, but also with teaching ability. Politically, she is left of center on many issues, but she would not allow political differences to influence tenure decisions, particularly in mathematics and the sciences. The one exception may be women's issues. She serves on the board of directors of a local shelter for battered women. She's a staunch feminist, and any candidate perceived as hostile to the cause or unconcerned about such issues stands little chance with her. *Support Rating: 2.*

I told Scott what I had found. "I thought you said she wasn't a femi-Nazi," he said.

"She's not," I said. I reread the document, slowly, and noticed a passage I'd missed the first time:

Social Jayne Smyers is one of the most attractive and delightful women I've ever met, but she has never been married and all her close friends are women. I've made an effort to attend lectures and university events with her, but it's clear she's not interested in more than that. Maybe she thinks I'm too young. Or perhaps she's afraid of becoming involved with someone in her department. I once thought she might prefer women, but she's recently started spending time with a private investigator named Keane—a big gorilla she claims is helping with something at the shelter. I struggle to control my feelings. I must avoid any action that might embarrass me.

I laughed and read it to Scott. "Sounds like he's jealous of the gorilla," he said.

"Sounds like he's got some issues," I said. The last two sentences concerned me.

"I don't mind you dating a lesbian," Scott said, "but this staunch-feminist thing bothers me." I ignored him.

"I wish we had a copier," I said.

"Why? You can't show it to your new girlfriend without admitting you're a burglar and a thief."

"I'd just like to have a copy," I said.

"Maybe he's got it on disk." Scott sighed. "If he does, I can e-mail it to you." I asked him to give it a try, then reviewed the remaining files in the drawer. When I had finished, I stood over his shoulder and watched as he went about his work. "Here it is," he said. It was a word-processing file labeled "TENUREBIOS." I watched as the document appeared on the monitor. It contained all the bios, and they appeared identical to the hard copies I'd found.

"Send the whole thing," I said. We'd been in the office more than forty-five minutes. I wondered what to do while Scott completed his task, then noticed a tattered black address book on top of the desk. I opened it and began turning pages. If nothing else, I might learn who Finn was still in contact with back in Lincoln.

"Okay," Scott said as he shut down the computer, "let's get out of here." But I didn't hear him. "C'mon," he said, "let's go." I debated it for a second, then tore a page from the address book. "Why'd you do that?" he asked. I handed it to him and pointed to the name.

"Amanda Slowiaczek," he said. "Why does that sound familiar?"

29

OUR TECHNICIAN INVENTORIED and examined the files on both computers and all the floppy disks," Gilbert said, "but she never attempted to recover any deleted material." It was eleven o'clock on a Sunday morning. I'd phoned him two hours ago and he was just now getting back to me.

"She had no reason to," I said, "because she didn't know about the other deaths."

"What about the bureau?" he said. "They were supposed to be looking for a connection."

"I reviewed the file this morning. In Fontaine's case, they relied on your technician's report and never conducted an independent examination of his computers. The hard drive in Carolyn Chang's computer had been replaced by the time the feds got involved, so there was nothing they could do there. They did conduct a thorough examination of Underwood's hard drive, but didn't find anything."

"Maybe Underwood did his work at New Paradigm Systems."

"I'll check that," I said. "In the meantime, can you have someone take another look at Fontaine's computers?"

"You bet."

"Did you check with the college about possible break-ins?"

"Yeah, I spoke with their chief of security this morning, but it's not a real sophisticated operation. They pay a student to walk around the campus all night and check the doors on the buildings. No record of any break-in or vandalism. You're right, though. I drove past the campus after you called. Anyone who wanted to could get into that building just by standing the bike rack up under a window."

I said good-bye to Gilbert, drove to the Texaco to buy a large coffee and a copy of the *News*, came home and read the paper, then contemplated the rest of my day. There wasn't much I could do on the case. Finding Amanda's name in Finn's address book had aroused my curiosity, but I didn't want to bother Susan Thompson on a Sunday. I had yet to review the documents Scott had obtained pertaining to Polk's divorce, but those were unlikely to contain anything earth shattering. I decided to take a drive.

"C'mon, boys," I said, "let's go see what there is to see." The tone of my voice told the dogs all they needed to know. They ran straight to the truck. I loaded them, then went inside for a jacket. There wasn't a cloud in the sky, but that can change quickly in the mountains. I grabbed the Polk documents on the theory I might stop to read them along the way. Hit the B&F for a diet Coke, popped in a Turtles tape, and headed south on Colorado 119 with no particular destination in mind.

We ended up near Leadville, a mining town ten thousand feet above sea level. There are four national forests in that area and plenty of dirt roads. I picked one and followed it nearly five miles to an abrupt end. There was one other vehicle at the trailhead, a white Jeep Cherokee with a "Trout Unlimited" emblem on the rear window. Serious fishermen. I studied the topographical map and guessed they had headed north to a small lake. With both dogs off leash in violation of forest service regulations, I wanted to avoid others at all costs, so I chose a different trail—one that didn't lead to any lakes or designated camping areas. It meandered west, at times following a narrow creek.

Our hike took four hours, but the dogs loved it. They sniffed and raced from one curious object to the next. Seeing them frolic in the creek brought joy to my heart. If I accomplished nothing else in life, I had taken care of the two creatures entrusted to me. But I hoped to do more than that. I hoped to be able to care for my parents when the time came. I hoped to marry someday. And I hoped to solve the fractal murders.

As for short-term goals, I hoped to find a restaurant. It was past six when we finished our trek and I was hungry. So were Buck and Wheat. I keep a supply of dog chow in the truck, so feeding them was easy, but I wanted something better than Science Diet for myself. I drove into Leadville.

It was Sunday night and most restaurants were closed. A few taverns on the edge of town were open, but they appeared to cater to bikers. Not the kind who wear spandex shorts. The kind who deal meth and can smell a prosecutor—even a former one—a mile away. I ate at the Tastee-Freez.

The atmosphere wasn't much, but the crinkle fries were good and the fluorescent lighting made it easy to read the documents Scott had copied at the courthouse. I began with the complaint.

Janice Polk had filed for divorce a year ago, citing irreconcilable differences. They'd been married less than four years and had no children. It should have been a simple matter, but Janice had retained J. Bradford Compton, a silver-haired ass who calls himself a "matrimonial attorney."

I had crossed paths with Compton a few times in private practice. He's tall and has a patrician look, but he's as trustworthy as a cobra. And arrogant. Once, just before starting a trial, he sauntered up to me and whispered, "My gal's gonna kill your guy on the stand." I thought about taking him literally and reporting the death threat to the judge, but that would only have pissed her off. Instead, I looked at him and asked if anyone had ever told him he walked like a peacock.

As you would expect in any Compton case, the complaint

concluded with a request for temporary and permanent alimony, an "equitable division of the assets and obligations of the parties," temporary and permanent attorneys' fees, and an order restoring Polk's wife to her maiden name, Janice Ford. I put the complaint aside, ate some more fries, and began reading the decree.

It didn't take long to see that Polk had gotten the shaft. In addition to paying $1,000 a month in alimony for three years, the judge had ordered him to pay Compton's fees and the lion's share of the marital debts. I couldn't believe it, and I wondered how Compton had done it.

The answer became clear as I reviewed the remaining papers. The most interesting documents in any divorce action are the depositions and answers to interrogatories. Those aren't usually filed with the court, but they'd been offered into evidence at trial and Scott had made copies.

Janice's deposition revealed that she held a master's degree in public administration. Throughout most of the marriage she had earned a good income as executive director of a foundation dedicated to wiping out a disease I'd never heard of. But she had begun to experience depression within a year of the wedding. Six months prior to filing the complaint, she'd consulted a psychiatrist. The shrink—almost certainly handpicked by Compton—met with her several times, conducted a multitude of tests, and diagnosed her as suffering from an "adjustment disorder with work inhibition." In his opinion, the prolonged and constant stress of marriage to a federal agent had rendered her barely able to work. The foundation allowed her a leave of absence.

That explained how Compton had achieved the result he had, but I read Polk's deposition just to be thorough. Taken in December, the deposition had lasted four hours. I tried to picture it. Polk, the hulking federal agent accustomed to interrogating suspects, sitting in Compton's conference room high above downtown Denver, biting his tongue, trying desperately not to lose his temper as he answered question after question. I smiled and continued reading. It was amusing until I came upon this:

MR. COMPTON: Aside from your salary as an FBI agent, have you earned income from any other employment during the past year?

MR. POLK: Yes.

MR. COMPTON: Tell me about that.

MR. POLK: I earned approximately five thousand dollars as a consultant for a small corporation.

MR. COMPTON: What kind of consulting?

MR. POLK: Corporate security.

MR. COMPTON: And when was this?

MR. POLK: I started in August or September.

MR. COMPTON: I didn't know agents were allowed to engage in outside employment?

MR. POLK: You have to have permission from the special agent in charge.

MR. COMPTON: Did you have permission?

MR. POLK: Yes.

MR. COMPTON: Did you report this income?

MR. POLK: I'm a federal agent. What do you think?

MR. COMPTON: Please answer the question, sir.

MR. POLK: Yes, I reported it.

MR. COMPTON: Are you still doing work for this company?

MR. POLK: No.

MR. COMPTON: Do you plan to in the future?

MR. POLK: If I'm asked.

MR. COMPTON: What is the name of this company?

MR. POLK: It's called the Koch Group. It's an economic consulting firm.

MR. COMPTON: Is this a local company?

MR. POLK: Yes. It's in the Colorado State Bank Building.

MR. COMPTON: During your career with the FBI, have you
engaged in any other outside employment?

MR. POLK: No.

MR. COMPTON: All right, let's talk about your investments.

The remainder of the deposition was unremarkable. I gathered
the documents together. From my review of them, one thing was
clear—the couple had been living beyond their means. New cars,
vacations in Mexico, a condo near Aspen. Polk had been in financial trouble even before the divorce, and that was interesting, but
his mention of the Koch Group was what stuck in my mind.

"The Koch Group," I muttered to myself. I finished my fries,
bought a soft-serve ice-cream cone for the road, and climbed into
the truck. "Guess what?" I said to the dogs. "One of Daddy's classmates is gonna die by lethal injection."

30

By morning I realized I didn't have that much. And what I had was circumstantial. I thought about it in my kitchen as I ate a mixture of Grape-Nuts and yogurt.

The gun used to kill Fontaine had been logged into evidence by Polk and later taken from the FBI's evidence room in Denver. Polk had falsely told Gilbert that the bureau still had the weapon. The revolver had been pulled from the Columbia River near Richland, Washington. Richland was Polk's hometown. Polk had personally reinterviewed a number of witnesses and had even done some work on the case after it was supposed to have been closed. There seemed to be an economic thread running through the case. Polk had a degree in economics and had done work for a firm that used mathematical models to predict market behavior. Polk had been having financial and marital problems. It was enough to go to the bureau, and maybe I should have, but I wanted to build a stronger case. There were too many unanswered questions.

The first question was motive. If Fontaine had developed some sort of revolutionary model or software designed to predict market behavior, how would Polk have known about it? Why would he have cared? Perhaps the Koch Group had learned of it and hired him to kill Fontaine. If so, it would have had to pay him more than five thousand dollars. And Polk certainly wouldn't have reported the income. Maybe that was just a smoke screen for his real business with the company. If they had paid him some money above the table, maybe they had paid him a lot more under the table.

Even if Polk had killed Fontaine, I had no evidence connecting him to the deaths of Carolyn Chang and Donald Underwood. What would have been his motive? Had the three been working together? If so, how would the Koch Group have known? How would anyone have known? Fontaine had never mentioned anything like that to his colleagues. Underwood had never discussed it. Had Carolyn Chang talked about it with Hawkins? He was an economist, and I knew she had helped him with his most recent paper. I called Susan Thompson.

"You're a hard person to reach," I said.

"It was a busy news week," she said. "And to top it all off, a pair of wolves escaped from the zoo yesterday."

"Good for them," I said.

"They found them soaking up the sun in a cornfield."

"I guess that's why they call them the Corn Huskies."

"You really need help," she said.

"No doubt about it."

"I suppose you're calling about Hawkins?"

"Primarily," I said.

"I don't like the sound of that," she said. I laughed. "I can't tell you much we didn't already know," she continued. "His name's been mentioned in our paper quite a few times. Whenever he receives an award or gives a lecture, he sends a press release. He writes a lot of letters to the editor, mostly arguing against government regulation of business."

"Free-market economist," I said.

"Evidently."

"Anything else?"

"He's been active in Big Brothers since he got here," she said. "He received some sort of award for it."

"That's it," I said, "that's the clue I've been waiting for."

"This might interest you," she said. "He was in the army. He finished an ROTC program at the tail end of the Vietnam War, seventy to seventy-three. The school paper did a story on him when he first got to Nebraska."

"Any idea what he did in the army?"

"He was an intelligence officer, whatever that is."

"That's what they do with you when you're too smart to lead an infantry platoon." Probably drafted and commissioned as soon as the army realized his potential. "I appreciate your help," I said.

"It's not free," she said. "Tell me something to keep me interested."

"I'm wearing only boxer shorts," I said.

"I want a *big* story," she said. I laughed, then told her everything. "Wow," she said. "The FBI loses a gun that ends up being used in a murder. That's quite a story."

"Not as good as the zoo losing a pair of wolves," I said. I asked her not to print anything yet, and promised her first crack at the story when it all came together. She gave me her word.

"So what else do you need from me?" she asked.

"I don't think this has anything to do with the case," I said, "but there's a math professor in Boulder named Stephen Finn. He used to teach at Nebraska and he's somehow connected to Amanda Slowiaczek, but I don't know how."

"Why do you care?" she asked.

"One of my neighbors saw Finn snooping around my house not too long ago."

"F-I-N-N?" she asked.

"Yeah."

"I'll check it out and call you back."

"Thanks, Little Red."

I placed the cordless phone in its cradle, put my cereal bowl in the dishwasher, showered, and dressed for the day. Sat at my desk and pondered the case.

It would be nice to know where Polk had been when the victims died. I could get that from Gumby, but I'd have to lay the whole case out for him and then Dittmer and the bureau would take it away from me. I didn't want to do that if I could avoid it. I'd put a lot of time into it and wanted to take Polk down on my own terms. I still held him responsible for Joy's death, and I wanted to be there when his karma caught up with him. I punched in Scott's number.

"McCutcheon," he said.

"How hard is it to tap into the airline reservation system?" I asked.

"We may not have to," he said. "One of Bobbi's friends owns a travel agency. It's that one over on Baseline. What are we looking for?"

"I want to know if Polk made any trips to Walla Walla, Boston, or Lincoln during the relevant time periods." I told him about the Koch Group and Polk's admission that he had done work for the firm.

"He wouldn't use his real name," Scott said.

"Maybe not," I said, "but let's check it out just the same."

"I'll see what I can do," he said, "but I don't know how those systems work. It might help if I had his Social Security number or a credit card number."

"I think I've got his Social," I said. "Hang on." I thumbed through Polk's law school records, found the SSN, and read it to Scott. He read it back to make sure he'd written down the correct number. I promised to work on the credit card information.

"By the way," I added, "there aren't any direct flights from Denver to Walla Walla, so you might as well check Seattle, Portland, Spokane, and Boise. Better check Omaha too."

"I'm on it," he said. "What are you up to today?"

"I've got to make some calls," I said. "Then I'm thinking about visiting the Koch Group and trying to rattle the bushes a little."

"If Polk takes a shot at you as you come out of the building,

I'd say that would be pretty strong circumstantial evidence." I laughed, said good-bye, and thought about the best way to obtain information about Polk's credit cards. I reviewed the records from his divorce, but there were no references to specific account numbers. I punched in the number for Keane, Simms & Mercante, and asked for Big Matt.

"I'm sorry," the receptionist said, "Mr. Simms is in court right now. May I take a message?" I doubted my former partner was in court at eight-thirty on a Monday morning. Matt hates talking with clients, but he wants them to think his advocacy skills are in such high demand that he's constantly in court. For years he'd been instructing receptionists to feed the "He's in court" line to all callers.

"Tell him it's Pepper Keane," I said. She put me on hold.

"Sorry about that," Matt said, "we have a new receptionist and she didn't recognize your voice."

"That's okay," I said. "I just called to ask another little favor."

"That was a great brief, by the way. Thanks."

"You're welcome," I said. "Listen, I need you to run two more credit histories."

He sighed. "Jesus, Pepper," he said, "I had to really push hard to get our agency to run the last one."

"I wouldn't ask if it wasn't important."

"I know," he grumbled. "Give me the names of these two fuckers."

"First guy's name is Dale D. Hawkins," I said. He wrote it down. "Second guy's name is Michael K. Polk."

"Polk? You want me to ask our collection agency to run a credit history on an FBI agent?"

"He'll never know," I said.

"Jesus," he muttered. I gave him the address for each, their respective dates of birth, and Polk's Social Security number. He promised to do what he could.

I went into the kitchen and poured myself another cup of coffee. It was 8:45 A.M., which meant it was 7:45 in Richland, Washington. I found the number for the high school there on the Internet and dialed it. Without really saying why, I explained that I needed to know the date of the twenty-fifth reunion that had taken place last year. She put me on hold for a few minutes, then returned and said, "It was the first Saturday in September."

My head was spinning. Fontaine's body had been found the first Monday of September and the pathologist's report stated he had most likely been killed on that Sunday. Wallace Gibbs, the FBI agent who had attended high school with Polk, had told me he'd seen Polk at their twenty-fifth reunion last year. I fumbled through my desk until I found the previous year's calendar. The first day of September had been a Friday, so Polk had been in Richland—forty-five miles from Walla Walla—one day before Fontaine's death.

I needed to clear my head. It was shaping up to be a hot day by mountain standards, so I wanted to get my run out of the way. Both dogs wanted to accompany me, but that never works. I wanted to run at least six miles, so I opted to take Buck. I never know when Wheat's paws are going to start hurting.

We ran up to Magnolia Road on Highway 119, then I let Buck off his leash and we continued down a forest service road. A lot of hippie kids were living in tents and old vans, but that happens every summer. Most are harmless, but they tend to leave a lot of trash, and that's been an issue. A few troublemakers stole a local resident's dog last year and the town marshal had to drive up and take the animal back at gunpoint. I pity the fool who ever tries to steal Buck.

We trotted about two miles down the forest service road, then turned around and headed for home. During my shower I made up my mind to visit the Koch Group. But first I telephoned Russ Seifert at New Paradigm Systems.

"Sure," he said, "Don had a personal computer in his office here, but much of his work required the use of mainframes."

"What I'm looking for," I said, "is evidence that he might have been working on some kind of economic forecasting model or some kind of software for such a model."

"In addition to whatever he was doing for us?"

"Right."

"And you think he was working with these other two math professors?"

"Yeah."

"What were their names again?"

"Carolyn Chang and Paul Fontaine."

"I'll take a look at it," he said, "and let you know if I find anything."

"I appreciate it," I said. "By the way," I added, "do you keep all your company's long-distance phone bills?"

"Yeah, we keep 'em until our accountant tells us we're safe from an IRS audit."

The Koch Group was located on the twenty-third floor of the Colorado State Bank Building. I had worked as a security guard in that building during the summer after I graduated from college and visited it a half dozen times for depositions while practicing law. The thirty-story structure had once been one of Denver's tallest buildings, but some of the office towers built during the boom years of the 1980s and 1990s are twice as high. I studied myself in the mirror as I waited for an elevator. I looked professional in an olive suit, white shirt, green-and-gold regimental tie, and black wing tips.

The suite occupied by the Koch Group was all chrome and glass. Brushed metallic letters beside the entry spelled "The Koch Group," but there was nothing to indicate what business the company was in.

A Hispanic receptionist greeted me. High cheekbones, white teeth, fawnlike brown eyes, long dark curls. She wore a fuchsia knit dress and was drop-dead gorgeous. "May I help you?" she asked. I had purposely decided not to call ahead or make an appointment.

"My name's Pepper Keane," I said. "I'm a private investigator." I handed her a card. "I'm working on a case and your company's name came up. I wonder if I might speak with someone about it." She smiled, got up from her desk, and promised she'd return shortly. Her nails were long and the polish matched her dress— she was the kind of woman who spends an hour every day on her makeup. She used her slender index finger to enter numbers on a keypad and disappeared behind a door made of smoky glass. I noticed strategically placed security cameras.

"Mr. Koch will meet with you," she said when she returned, "but it may be five or ten minutes. Please make yourself comfortable." I picked up a recent *Sports Illustrated* from an array of magazines on a glass table, then sat in one of the leather-and-chrome chairs and started catching up on Mike Tyson's latest antics.

Twenty minutes later a man in a gray suit entered the lobby from behind the glass door. About six feet. Early or mid-fifties. Salt-and-pepper hair parted on the right. Piercing blue-gray eyes. Erect posture, military bearing. In darn good shape for his age, but not as big as me. "Mr. Keane," he said, "I'm Alan Koch." He extended his hand and I shook it. His left hand was holding the business card I'd given the receptionist.

"Pepper Keane," I said.

"Ms. Lopez tells me our company's name came up in the course of one of your investigations."

"Do you have a few minutes?" I asked. "It won't take long."

"Sure," he said. "Would you like some coffee?"

"That would be nice," I said. "A little cream, no sugar." He nodded to Ms. Lopez. I followed him through the door, down a hallway, and into his spacious office. The furniture, including a large conference table, was all chrome and glass. No paintings graced the walls, but a variety of large plants gave the room a little color. An impressive array of college degrees and professional awards graced the wall behind his desk. We sat down at the near end of the conference table.

"I have to tell you," he said, "it's not every day a private investigator walks in and tells me my company's name has surfaced in some type of investigation." I smiled.

"I may have given her the wrong impression," I said. "Your company's not directly involved, but it appears to be the only company in Denver using some of the new mathematical techniques to predict market behavior." He asked me to continue, but Ms. Lopez arrived before I got the chance. I surveyed the room again and among Koch's degrees and awards noticed a photograph of a young Alan Koch standing with a famous public official, but I couldn't for the life of me recall the other man's name. Someone from the Nixon/Ford/Carter era. Not William Simon or Elliott Richardson, but one of those anonymous-looking career civil servants. I tried hard not to gawk at Ms. Lopez as she served coffee to each of us from a silver tray and then, with just the right amount of deference, departed with a polite smile. Koch sipped his coffee, looked at me without expression, and waited.

I sipped my coffee, then said, "I'm looking into the possibility that three mathematicians who died recently may all have been murdered by the same person."

"How does my company fit in?" he asked.

"Each of the victims specialized in fractal mathematics," I said. "There's some evidence these murders were related to the use of fractal mathematics in economic forecasting. When I found out your company was right here in Denver, I thought I'd see if you couldn't educate me a little bit."

"I see," he said.

"I'd be happy to pay you for your time."

"That won't be necessary," he said with a forced smile. "What would you like to know?"

"To be honest," I said, "I'm just trying to get an overview of the business. Can you give me a thumbnail sketch?" I wanted to get him talking before I sprang my surprises on him.

"I'll try," he said.

He talked for twenty minutes and told me what I already knew, things I had learned from speaking with Russ Seifert and reading dozens of articles. I played dumb as he explained that the use of fractal mathematics and other mathematical techniques to predict market behavior was a growing, but highly secretive, industry.

"I took some economics in college," I said as I sipped my coffee, "but the conventional wisdom back then was that markets couldn't be predicted because all known information was already reflected in the price."

"What you're referring to is known as the efficient-market hypothesis. Nobody believes it these days."

"Why's that?"

"Well," he said, "even if all known information is reflected in the current price, traders are just people. And each person reacts to information differently. Two people can receive the same information at the same instant and still come to different conclusions about its likely impact on prices."

"But one of them is going to be wrong," I said.

"That's true," he said, "but if you have enough information about how traders have reacted to events in the past, you can use mathematical models to predict how traders as a whole will react to similar events in the future."

"Fascinating," I said.

"It's really nothing more than psychology with numbers," he said.

"I assume you rely on some type of mathematical models to do what you do?"

"We employ several different models, depending on the market we're looking at."

"Do you develop your own models," I asked, "or do you bring in outside consultants for that?"

"It's all in-house," he said. "I hold a doctorate in economics, and we have several other economists on staff." I asked him to explain a little about the industry, and he did.

"This is just fascinating," I said. "I never realized there was an entire industry using mathematical models to predict markets." He smiled politely. "I guess I should be going," I said. "I want to thank you again for your help. Are you sure I can't pay you?"

"Don't worry about it," he said. I stood up.

"By the way," I said, "do you know an economist named Dale Hawkins?" His eyes blinked rapidly for just a second.

"Doesn't ring a bell," he said. "Is he in Denver?"

"No," I said, "just someone I know in Nebraska."

"Is there anything else I can do for you?" he asked. His patience was turning to anxiety.

"No," I said, "but I just want to thank you again for your time."

"I hope it was of some benefit," he said.

"It was," I assured him. He stood and we shook hands. "Hey," I said, "I understand one of my friends did some work for your company."

"Who would that be?" he asked.

"Mike Polk."

"Yes," he said, "Mike's done some work for us. Still does once in a while."

"Mike and I used to work together," I said.

"Really?"

"We go back a long way."

"If I see him," he said nervously, "I'll tell him you were here."

"Yeah," I said, "you do that."

31

By eight o'clock Tuesday morning, the temperature in Ned had already climbed to seventy-seven degrees. It was going to be another scorcher in the high country, so I decided to go running early and took off for the Eldora ski area. It's about five miles each way, and the vertical rise is at least two thousand feet. It was the longest, most difficult run I'd attempted in a while, but I finished it in less than an hour and a half. Not as fast as Finn could've done it, but not bad.

Later that morning Big Matt faxed me copies of the credit reports he'd obtained on Hawkins and Polk. On the fax cover sheet he'd written, "If you need anything else, ask someone else!" He'd also drawn a little cartoon man giving me the finger. I smiled and reviewed the documents. Hawkins's credit was fine. His only debts were what he owed on his home and car, and he'd paid those like clockwork each month. Polk had accumulated a lot of debt, but I already knew that. I faxed Polk's credit report to Scott so he'd have Pokey's credit card numbers.

A teenage girl called around two P.M. and asked how much I'd charge to help her establish a new identity. Her parents were trying to control her life and she just couldn't take it anymore. She was seventeen. I got her name and some other information, told her running from problems is seldom the answer, and encouraged her to see a therapist I know in Boulder. She began to cry, told me I was just like her parents, and hung up on me. I thought about it awhile, then tracked down the girl's guidance counselor and alerted her to the situation. I didn't feel bad about violating the girl's trust. Half the kids these days are crazy, and I didn't want to pick up a newspaper someday and read about her killing herself.

I couldn't think of anything to do in connection with the case, so I cleaned house and did laundry, then drove up to the recycling center where I deposited two large bags of trash and a few weeks' worth of newspapers. The red message light was flashing when I returned. "Pepper, this is Jayne. Please call me at home right away." She sounded distraught. I punched in her number.

"Thanks for returning my call so quickly," she said.

"What's up?"

"Someone's been in my house," she said.

"Anything missing?" I asked.

"Not that I know of," she said.

"Any damage?"

"No," she said, "but someone's been here."

"I'll come right down," I said.

I ran an electric razor over my face, exchanged my shorts for a clean pair of slacks, and splashed on a little cologne. I thought about it and decided to take my Glock with me. I grabbed a blue blazer so I'd have something to conceal the weapon with, then fired up the truck and headed for Boulder.

She was wearing designer jeans, a blue cotton shirt to match her eyes, and leather sandals. "Thanks for coming," she said. Still a bit distraught.

"No problem," I said. "Tell me what happened." I entered and she closed the door behind me. It was approaching one hundred degrees in Boulder, but she had the air-conditioning going full blast.

"I had an easy day," she began, "so I left work around three o'clock. I checked my mail in the box by the street, then came in and put my briefcase down on the kitchen table. I went into my office to check my messages and noticed a few things out of place."

"Like what?" I asked.

"Just little things," she said. "I'd had my Rolodex opened to the card with the number of a women's shelter in Denver on it, but when I returned it was opened to a different card."

"What else?" I asked.

"Don't you believe me?"

"I believe you," I said. "I'm just trying to find out which rooms the intruder concentrated on."

"My office," she said. "He concentrated on my office. My chair was pushed right up against my desk, and I never do that because it scuffs the arms of the chair."

"Have you been through the entire house?" I asked.

"Yes."

"You checked the closets and everything?"

"Yes."

"Let's take a look around," I said. "Show me what's out of place." We began in the kitchen and went from room to room. Now and then she pointed out items she felt had been moved slightly or just didn't seem quite right. Nothing really concrete. I quizzed her on the contents of each room, but she assured me nothing was missing.

We ended up back in the kitchen. She was calming down. She offered lemonade and I said that sounded great. Before taking a seat beside her glass dining table, I removed my blazer and hung it over the back of one of the chairs. She noticed the Glock, but said nothing. She handed me a tall glass of cold lemonade, then sat down in the chair to my right with one of her own. Bright yellow lemons with green leaves adorned each glass.

"Do you think this is related to the case?" she asked.

"Seems a good bet," I said. "Nothing's missing and it comes at a time when we seem to be making progress." It also came only one day after I'd visited the Koch Group.

"I was afraid you'd say that," she said. She gave me a feeble smile and I put my palm on top of hers in an effort to reassure her.

"Does anyone else have a key to your unit?" I asked. There were two ways to enter the town house. One was the front door, the other was through the garage. None of the doors appeared to have been tampered with, but the lock on the front door wouldn't have been difficult for an intruder with any skill. There wasn't even a dead bolt.

"No," she said.

"The owners' association?"

"No," she said, "just me." I sipped my lemonade. "What could they have been looking for?" she asked.

"Maybe someone was hoping I'd given you some written reports concerning the case."

"Why do you say that?"

"Just a guess," I said. We sat in silence for several minutes. I knew she didn't want to be alone, but I wanted to question the neighbors before the trail became cold. "Stay here a few minutes," I finally said. I stood and put on my blazer. "I'm going to knock on some doors and see if anyone saw anything." She nodded, but I saw the fear in her eyes. "Lock the door behind me," I said. "I'll be back soon."

Jayne's town house was one of eighteen three-story units. My first six knocks went unanswered. On my seventh try I was greeted by two grade-school boys waiting for their mother to come home from work. They were playing Risk and hadn't seen anything. I continued around the complex and noticed an older man kneeling in a flower garden in front of one of the town houses. He was in his mid-sixties, but tan and fit. Silver hair. He wore a white T-shirt, blue shorts, running shoes, and a tan golf hat. No socks. "How are you doing?" I said.

"Can't complain," he said.

"You live here?" I asked.

"Sure do," he said.

"Nice garden."

"Thanks."

"A friend of mine lives in that unit over there," I said as I pointed, "and we—"

"The math professor?"

"Yeah."

"Nice lady," he said. He stood up and faced me. He was about five-eight and possessed a hawkish nose.

"We're wondering if you saw anything unusual or suspicious here today?"

"You a policeman?" he asked.

"Just a friend."

"Used to be a homicide detective," he said. "Retired five years ago. Thirty-four years on the force, so the bulge under your coat caught my attention. Men packing heat are the only ones wearing getups like that on a day like today."

"I'm a private investigator," I said. I handed him a card.

"Lawyer, huh?"

"It's a long story," I said.

"You may be the first private investigator I've ever met with half a brain," he said.

"Jury's still out on that," I said.

"I did see something unusual this morning," he said. I kept silent. "About eight-thirty a dark blue sedan pulls up and parks out there on Pearl Street. Crown Victoria, four-door. Fella gets out, sees me, and starts walking in the opposite direction. Big fella, about your age, maybe a little older."

"Tall and skinny or tall and muscular?" I wasn't going to make that mistake again.

"No, he had muscle," the man said. "Must've weighed two-twenty at least." That eliminated Finn.

"I knew the guy was on the job right away. He had that look about him, and the car had all sorts of antennas on it. Figured the guy must be federal because I didn't know him and the federal boys always drive big Fords these days. Didn't think much of it at the time."

"How long was his car here?" I asked.

"No more than thirty minutes."

"Did you get the plate number?"

"Colorado plates," he said. "A-M-K 8115."

"A-M-K?" The prefix one witness claimed he'd seen on the car outside Carolyn Chang's home the night of her disappearance.

"Yeah."

"You sure?" I asked.

"Positive," he said. "I've got a knack for remembering those things." I wrote it down. "It won't do you any good," he said. "I'll guarantee you it's a dummy plate. They use them for undercover operations and things like that. That info's not available to the public."

"Could you run it through your connections?" I asked. He assessed me and his conclusion must've been favorable.

"Sure," he said. "Give me a day to work on it."

"What's your name?" I asked.

"Thomas Hammond," he said. We shook hands and I told him a little about my background, then thanked him for his help. "Is your lady friend in trouble?" he asked.

"She hired me to look into something, and that's evidently making some folks nervous. Looks like someone broke into her home and searched it while she was at work."

"I'll keep an eye on it," he said.

* * *

Jayne looked through the security eyepiece in the door, then let me in. She seemed more composed. "Did you learn anything?" she asked.

"I think you might have had a visit from our friend Polk." I took off my blazer and related what I'd learned from Hammond.

"Wonderful," she said. "That man was creepy even before I knew he might be a killer."

"This will all be over soon," I said. I didn't know that with certainty, but at the time it seemed like a good thing to say.

"I don't want to stay here tonight," she said.

"You're welcome to stay with me," I said.

"What if he tries to get into your house?" she asked.

"He won't," I said. "He knows I've got a weapon and the will to use it." She eyed my pistol. "Besides," I said, "Buck would wake up the entire town before Polk got within a hundred yards of the house."

"I'll follow you in my car," she said. She walked upstairs, packed an overnight bag, and followed me up the mountain in her silver Saab 900.

It was just after six when we arrived. I let the dogs out, then clicked on the *CBS Evening News*. Jayne made herself comfortable on the sofa.

"You want a glass of wine?" I asked.

"Sure."

"Red, white, or pink?"

"Anything with alcohol," she said. I poured us each a glass of white zin and sat down beside her.

"Hungry?" I asked.

"A little."

"Pizza okay?"

"Sure."

I picked up the cordless and called Backcountry. "What do you want on it?" I asked.

"No anchovies," she said. I ordered a large pizza with mush-rooms and garlic, then let the dogs in and fed them.

After we'd eaten and consumed more wine, we channel-surfed for fifteen minutes, but we agreed that there was nothing worth watching, so I clicked off the TV. The wine had helped her re-lax. She noticed my CD collection and walked over to see what I had. "This may be the most diverse collection of music ever assembled," she said. "I mean, to see *Stirring Marches of the Amer-ican Services* right next to *Hollywood's Singing Cowboys* boggles the mind." She was teasing me, but in an affectionate way. She finally selected a collection of songs by Nat King Cole, then turned off the overhead lights, returned to the couch, and cuddled up to me.

We talked and enjoyed the music. I kissed her. She kissed back. Always a good sign. It went like that for an hour. Under the cir-cumstances I figured I could miss *SportsCenter*. At ten-thirty she yawned and said, "Let's go to bed." I was pretty sure she meant the same bed.

I let the dogs out a final time while she disappeared with her overnight bag. When she came out of the bathroom, she was wearing a powder blue camisole with matching satin shorts. Buck and Wheat looked betrayed when I closed the bedroom door before they could enter.

I brushed my fangs, stripped to my boxers, then took Jayne in my arms. "You look wonderful," I said. She blushed, and we stood there holding each other.

"Something wrong?" she asked.

"I want you to do this because you want to, not because you're afraid and need to be with someone."

"I want to," she said. She tapped the tip of my nose with her index finger to emphasize the point.

When we had finished making love and were about to fall asleep in each other's arms, I realized I'd forgotten to take my medicine. I gave her a peck on the cheek and climbed out of bed. "Where are you going?" she asked.

"Forgot to take a pill," I said. I opened the bedroom door to head for the kitchen, and when I did the dogs rushed past me and onto the bed. Jayne laughed and pulled the covers over her head so they wouldn't lick her to death. I took my pill with a little water and returned to the bedroom. "They usually sleep with me," I explained. "You want me to evict them?"

"No," she said, "it's a big bed." I climbed in next to her and turned out the light. We were facing the same direction, me on the outside, her on the inside. Our bodies fit like two pieces of a perfectly cut jigsaw puzzle. I covered her neck and shoulders with light kisses and debated whether to bring up the big D.

"I've been wanting to tell you something," I said.

"This would be a real bad time to tell me you're married," she joked.

"Nothing like that," I said. She turned to face me and waited for me to continue. "I suffer from depression," I finally said. "I have to take medication for it. That's why I had to go take a pill."

She smiled and said, "You had me worried for a minute."

"If we're going to be spending time with each other, I felt you had a right to know." I told her I'd suffered from depression since Joy's death, but that the medication worked wonders for me, and I was generally as happy as the next existentially pained ex-lawyer.

"Lots of people suffer from depression," she said. "At least you're doing something about it."

"It doesn't bother you?"

"Not particularly," she said. She caressed my cheek. "Sounds like it bothers you."

"The whole thing is sort of a blow to my male ego," I said.

"Even Pepper Keane can't be perfect," she whispered. She kissed me good night and we drifted off to sleep.

The alarm went off at six-thirty and we made love again. Then we lay on our backs, her head resting on my chest, both half asleep. The phone rang and I wondered who would be calling so early in the morning. I picked up the receiver. "Pepper Keane," I said.

"You sound hungover," Scott said. "Too much wine last night?"

"It wasn't wine that I had too much of . . ."

"It was a 'double shot of your baby's love'?"

"Yeah."

"You were dying to say the whole thing, but you couldn't because she's right next to you?"

"Right."

"Who did that song?"

"The Swingin' Medallions," I said. "What do you want?"

"You're gonna love this," he said. "Seems our boy Polk flew to Boston the Sunday before Underwood died. He flew under his own name and used a government credit card to pay for the ticket."

"You're gonna love this," I said. "He attended his high school reunion in Richland, Washington, one day before Fontaine was murdered."

"Jesus," he said.

"Can you place him on any flights to Omaha or Lincoln?" I asked.

"Not so far," he said. "The whole thing was a bit more complicated than I thought it would be. You can't just go into a travel agent's system and retrieve past reservations made by people who didn't use that agent. I had to worm my way into the billing database for each airline, and it took some time." I remained silent a moment. Jayne got out of bed, let the dogs out the door from my bedroom to the backyard, then removed her pajamas and went into the bathroom where I heard her start the shower. Then she used her index finger and gestured for me to come hither. "What do we do next?" Scott asked.

"I'm going to take a shower," I said. "I'll call you back."

32

I NEVER GOT THE CHANCE to return Scott's call. Soon after Jayne headed down the mountain for the math department, Susan Thompson phoned me and told me the connection between Amanda Slowiaczek and Finn. I punched in the number for the Lincoln Police Department.

"Detective Slowiaczek," she said.

"Amanda," I said cheerfully, "how are you?"

"Who's this?" she demanded.

"Pepper Keane."

"Do I know you?"

"Limp-dick lawyer turned private eye," I said.

"Oh," she said, "what do *you* want?"

"I was going through your reports on the Carolyn Chang murder—I got copies from Sheriff Bowen down in Kansas—but I seem to be missing a few. I was wondering if you could fax me a copy of the paperwork on the harassment complaint Carolyn filed a few years"—she hung up on me—"ago."

I smiled to myself—few things are more satisfying than making someone eat their words—and I pondered what to have for breakfast. I was in the process of slicing a whole-wheat bagel in half when Russ Seifert called.

"I searched Don's office from top to bottom and couldn't find anything like what you described," he said, "but this may interest you."

"What's that?"

"I got to thinking about your theory and I remembered that a day or two before Donald's death, we had some problems with our security cameras."

"What kind of problems?"

"The power went out in our building one night that week and the cameras were out of service for about an hour."

"Don't you have batteries or generators?"

"We have backup generators for the mainframes, but not the security system."

"Anything taken that night?"

"Not that we know of, but if your theory's right, an intruder wouldn't have been looking for our materials. He would have been looking for something Donald had been working on. We wouldn't even have known it existed."

"Yeah."

"Does that help?" he asked.

"It's not the connection I was hoping for, but it's mighty suspicious."

"Let me know if I can do anything else."

"I will," I said.

I ate the other half of the bagel, then went downstairs to work the heavy bag. I usually start out sluggish and finish sharp, and this morning was no exception. After a few minutes my punches were quick and full of snap. I felt good when I came upstairs. Things were falling into place.

Then Jayne called and said, "We need to talk." She sounded distant.

"What's up?"

"You weren't completely honest with me."

"What are you talking about?"

"While you were being so honest with me about your depression, it didn't occur to you that I might like to know about your manslaughter trial?"

"Who told you?" I asked.

"Stephen."

"It was self-defense," I said. "I was acquitted."

"That's not the point," she said. "I had a right to know."

"Yes," I said, "you did." She remained silent. "I wanted to tell you," I added, "but I was waiting for the right time."

"And when would that have been?" I had no good answer and said nothing for a moment, then asked if she would like to hear the story.

"Maybe in a day or two," she finally said.

"Okay," I said. "Let me know when you're ready. And call me if you need me."

"Good-bye," she said.

"Jayne, I'm—" Click. I placed the receiver in its cradle.

I sat in my office and tried to organize my thoughts. I should've been focused on the fact that Mike Polk looked like a pretty good bet to be a player in the fractal murders. Instead I found myself thinking about Jayne. And the more I thought about it, the more I wondered why Finn had been at my home and why he had taken it upon himself to dig into my past and tell Jayne about it. I thought I knew the answer, but I wanted to hear it from the triathlete's mouth, so I headed to Boulder.

The math department was busier than normal, but I managed to reach Finn's office without being seen by Jayne or Mary Pat. He was at his desk, wearing Dockers and a blue poplin shirt. He looked up at me. "Mr. Keane," he said, "what can I do for you?" I closed the door behind me, then sat down on one of the two wooden chairs in front of his desk. I took a deep breath and let it out in order to relax.

"One of my neighbors saw you snooping around my house a few weeks ago. I was hoping you could explain that to me."

"I don't know what you're talking about," he said. He removed his wire-rimmed glasses and set them on his desk.

"She saw your picture in the paper and she can identify you," I said. "Let's put that issue aside for a moment. Perhaps you can tell me what prompted you to dig into my past, and why you felt compelled to share my manslaughter arrest with Jayne Smyers this morning."

"I don't like your tone," he said. He began to stand and I again noticed the multitude of blue veins in his sinewy arms.

"Sit down," I said. The command startled him. "You may be a better athlete, but you don't want to fight me." He gave me a hard stare, but sank back into his chair.

"Let me tell you what I think," I said. "You had a thing for Carolyn Chang when you were at Nebraska. Am I right?" He said nothing, but I had his attention. "You had some fun times with her, but you wanted more than that and she didn't. Maybe you were just too young for her to take seriously." I paused, but he again said nothing. "When she got tired of you," I continued, "you couldn't let go. You became obsessed. You called her constantly, bothered her. You wanted her to explain what had happened. Maybe you stalked her. Eventually she filed a harassment complaint with the police. Ordinarily, your career would've been over, but Carolyn didn't know your big sister was a detective. Amanda pulled some strings and worked it out so you could leave quietly and start over somewhere else. How am I doing so far?" He set his elbows on his desk and buried his face in hands.

"Things were going pretty well for you here, but you developed a little crush on Jayne Smyers. You became curious when you learned she was working with a private investigator. The more you saw us together, the more worried you became. You feared it might have something to do with the decision on granting you tenure. You thought I might be looking into your problems in Lincoln. So you went to my home. I'm not sure why. Maybe you wanted to talk with me. Or maybe you planned to break in and see if you could learn what I was up to. My dogs or my neighbor scared you away. Then, when it became clear that Jayne and I were developing a friendship, jealousy got the best of you. You've always been sweet on her and you wanted to do whatever you could to sink the relationship."

"It's all conjecture," he said without looking up.

"It's not conjecture that Amanda Slowiaczek is your sister," I said. "And it's not conjecture that Carolyn Chang filed a harassment complaint with the Lincoln Police Department shortly before you left Nebraska. I even have the report number. It's the one report your sister didn't give the sheriff in Kansas after Carolyn Chang's murder."

"What do you want?" he said, glaring at me. In his eyes I saw a mixture of hatred and shame.

"You have some issues to work on," I said. "Your IQ is in the stratosphere but you got thrown into the adult world before you were ready for it, and now it's catching up with you." He broke eye contact and his face began to turn red. I stood there, silent. Tears began to form in his eyes.

"Christ," he said, "going to your home was stupid. I don't even know why I did it. I just wasn't thinking." He sighed. "I've really messed things up this time." He gazed at the floor and let out a pathetic laugh, as if he couldn't believe the extent to which he'd ruined his own life.

"Not necessarily," I said. He looked up at me. "The consensus seems to be that you're a good teacher. So I'm not going to share any of this with Jayne, your sister, or anyone else." He looked at me in disbelief. "On two conditions," I said.

"What are those?"

"First," I said, "get into counseling. Once a week for at least a year. You pick the therapist, then send me a canceled check or receipt every so often so I know you're sticking with it." He nodded. Hatred and shame were turning to respect and relief.

"What's the other condition?" he asked.

"Don't get between me and Jayne Smyers."

I spent the afternoon at Troy's gym and worked off some aggression. The heavy bag was Polk's body, the speed bag Finn's face. I was still mad at Finn because of my problems with Jayne. My brother hadn't seen me work that hard in a long time. "You coming out of retirement?" he joked.

"Why not?" I said. "I'm younger than Foreman and Holmes."

When I returned home I had a message to call Dick Gilbert. It was just after five. I punched in his number. "What's up?" I asked.

"You're a smart son of a bitch," he said in his gravel-edged voice.

"Mind if I quote you in my next yellow pages ad?"

"We hit the jackpot," he said. I could tell he was working on a cigarette.

"Tell me about it," I said.

"I had a technician from the state patrol check Fontaine's home computer and the one he had in his campus office. They used some type of utility program to recover deleted files."

"Keep talking."

"The hard drive on the office computer contained portions of letters he'd apparently written to the other two concerning some type of project they were working on."

"That's great," I said.

"It gets better."

"Yeah?"

"After the state patrol guy told me what he'd found, I got to thinking about your theory. I figured if these three had developed some sort of model to predict the stock market, and if it was good enough that someone was willing to kill them for it, maybe Fontaine would've kept another set of documents or disks or whatever. So I drove out to his parents' farm and spoke with that kid Bartels. Turns out Fontaine had a little office at the farm. Just a small room in one of the barns where they keep some of the combines and tractors. We found all sorts of correspondence between Fontaine, Underwood, and Carolyn Chang. It looks like she developed the model and shared it with the other two. I don't really understand the technical stuff, but I sent you copies of everything by overnight mail. You'll have it tomorrow."

"That's fantastic," I said. "We're closing in on this thing."

"There's been one other development," he said.

"What's that?"

"The bureau requested the gun."

"You didn't give it to them?"

"Hell no."

"Where'd the request come from?"

"Denver."

"Who requested it?"

"Polk."

"It didn't come from the agent in charge?"

"It came from Polk," he said.

"They'll probably hit you with a lot of paperwork real soon," I said. "We need to wrap this thing up before some federal judge threatens to hold you in contempt."

"It would be a welcome vacation," he said.

"I'll wait until I get the documents tomorrow," I said, "then I guess we have to think about going to the bureau."

"You really think this guy Polk is capable of this?"

"We found out he flew to Boston just before Underwood's death."

"Christ."

"The weird thing is, he flew under his own name and paid with a government credit card."

"When was that?" he asked.

"Just before Valentine's Day," I said.

"Hang on a second," he said. He put down the phone and I heard some background noise. The rustling of papers, the opening and closing of file cabinet drawers. "Here it is," he said. "There was a big conference on sex crimes in Boston that week. I was gonna go myself, but I canceled because of my daughter's health problems."

"Polk goes to a sex crimes seminar. Underwood's death is set up to be autoerotic death."

"I still don't have enough to charge Polk with Fontaine's murder," he said.

"No," I said. "You don't have his prints on the weapon and you can't place him in your area at the time of the offense."

"How'd you find out he was in Boston?" Gilbert asked. I told him. "I'll see what I can do on my end," he said. "Maybe I can place him here or in Nebraska."

33

Mornin', Pepper," Wanda said. She reached for my Foghorn Leghorn mug.

"Mornin', Wanda," I said. As always, the place smelled wonderful, the aroma of just-baked treats saturating the air.

"You look happy," she said.

"Been waiting a long time for something," I said, "and it looks like it's finally going to happen."

"Glad to hear it," she said. I treated myself to a hot pecan roll, poured some coffee, left three dollars on the glass counter, and found an empty booth. It was ten-thirty A.M. and I'd just come from the post office.

Gilbert had sent the documents in one of those large bubble envelopes. I tore it open and began studying its contents. The letters, memos, graphs, and other papers had been jammed into the package in no particular order. It took nearly two hours to arrange them in chronological order and review them. I ignored some passages that were simply over my head, but I understood enough to learn what had brought Paul Fontaine, Carolyn Chang, and Douglas Underwood together.

At about the time she started dating Dale Hawkins, Carolyn Chang developed an interest in the possible applications of fractal mathematics in the business world. She immersed herself in the literature and learned that many academics and investors were already using fractal mathematics and related concepts to predict market behavior.

As Carolyn became more familiar with the subject, she realized that everyone who had written on the topic had treated the concept of time in the same fashion. A second was a second, a minute was a minute, and so on. Identical units of time each received the same weight. This was the conventional approach, but Carolyn thought it simplistic.

In real life, Carolyn knew, activity frequently occurs in clusters. Little happens when people sleep, for example, but much happens during the day. She wondered whether models designed to predict market behavior might be improved if time periods filled with activity received greater weight than those during which nothing happened. She called this approach "intrinsic time" and formalized her idea in an unpublished paper entitled "The Use of Intrinsic Time in Predicting Market Behavior." In explaining her concept, she wrote:

Quite simply, intrinsic time compresses time when little happens and expands time when much happens: Seconds consume less time during the Asian lunch break than during the American lunch break, for example, because American traders eat lunch at their desks while continuing to trade.

She shared her idea with Fontaine because she knew him and knew of his interest in the stock market. Fontaine liked Carolyn's concept of intrinsic time and helped her refine it. He urged Carolyn to contact Underwood because of Underwood's ability to develop software to implement her theoretical ideas.

Working together the three developed mathematical models and corresponding software designed to predict the behavior of various economic markets. For months they monitored various markets and sent highly technical papers back and forth. Their preliminary studies demonstrated that Carolyn's concept of intrinsic time had tremendous potential. They continued to refine the idea and finally decided to subject it to a more rigorous "real world" test.

To test Carolyn's idea the three decided to focus on one particular market index. Fontaine suggested they use the S&P 500. Using Fontaine's theoretical ideas about market behavior, Carolyn's concept of intrinsic time, and Underwood's skill in creating computer programs, the three developed a model designed to predict the behavior of the S&P 500. Underwood created a sixteen-gigabyte database containing every tick in the S&P 500 dating back to 1983. Then he put his neural networks to work and started looking for fractal patterns.

He found them. In one year of testing, the Chang-Fontaine-Underwood model had beaten the S&P 500 threefold. Intrinsic time worked. That fact established, they began working on a paper intended for publication. After again explaining the concept of intrinsic time, they wrote:

> Having redefined time in this way, the computer then draws a series of graphs incorporating assumptions about how the different traders in the market will react to a price change in intrinsic time. Each graph has the same overall shape, but with different slopes according to each trader's time horizon or risk profile. The model assumes each trader will react in a nonlinear way: little at first to a price rising above its moving average, then with increasing interest, and finally to slacken off as he thinks he has invested enough. The computer merely adds up these models and arrives at an estimate of how the market as a whole will react to an event. It does not work with normal time, but it works quite well in intrinsic time.

Nothing in the documents suggested that the three had ever attempted or even considered selling their idea to a brokerage house or consulting firm. I remembered asking Russ Seifert how one who had developed a good model could make money if it wasn't really possible to sell the model. "You go into business for yourself," he had said. "Either that or you publish and hope to win the Nobel Prize." But what if making money had never been their goal?

Nothing indicated that the three had ever considered going into business for themselves. They had intended to publish their work for all the world to see. Their correspondence contained no mention of seeking the Nobel Prize or any other award. Maybe they never felt their contribution was that significant.

But someone had learned of their work and concluded that the idea was valuable. Worth killing for. I didn't know who that someone was, but as an economist and Carolyn Chang's occasional lover, Dale Hawkins seemed a good bet.

"Hey, Wanda," I said from my booth, "can I use your phone?" My cell phone does not work in Nederland because there are no cell phone towers up here.

"Sure," she replied. I dialed Scott.

"McCutcheon," he said.

"You got any time this afternoon?" I asked.

"I have to help Bobbi put down some mulch, then I'm free."

"Two o'clock at Moe's?"

"I'll be there," he said.

"It's an interesting concept," Scott said as he finished reviewing the stack of documents. He wore tan shorts, a white T-shirt with grass stains on it, leather sandals, and a baseball cap with the National Rifle Association's logo on it. He's not really a member, but he gets a kick out of wearing things like that in the liberal enclave of Boulder. I'd summarized the chronology of events for him, then allowed him to study the model and test data while I read the *News*. We were seated at an outside table on a warm but overcast afternoon. "How much do you think you could get for something like this if you sold it to one of these consulting firms?" he asked.

"You probably wouldn't sell it," I said. "You'd probably go into business for yourself." I told him what Russ Seifert had told me.

"Doesn't look like they were planning to go into business for themselves."

"Looks like they planned to publish their research in some academic journal," I said. "I'm guessing Carolyn shared her work with Hawkins. He saw dollar signs and decided to claim the idea as his own. We find the connection between Hawkins and Polk, we solve the case."

"What about Underwood?" he asked. "He worked for an economic consulting firm, didn't he?"

"New Paradigm Systems."

"Maybe he presented the model to them and they decided they wanted it."

"I thought about that," I said, "but the guy who runs that company didn't strike me that way. And I'm not aware of any connection between New Paradigm Systems and Polk. We know there's a connection between Polk and the Koch Group."

"So in addition to connecting Hawkins and Polk, we have to connect Hawkins with the Koch Group."

"There's a connection," I said. "Koch got real fidgety when I asked if he knew Dale Hawkins."

"I can work on the connections," he said, "but you're talking about phone records and bank records. The bureau can do that a lot easier than we can."

"I know," I said, "but let's see what we can do on our own in the next few days." He gave me a skeptical look; he knew I had a long history with Polk and wanted to go as far as I could on my own. I went inside to refill my drink.

"Oh, by the way," Scott said as I resumed my seat, "I think I've about exhausted the airline reservation angle. I can't find any evidence that Polk flew to Nebraska before Carolyn was murdered. If he did, he didn't use his own name and he didn't use any of his credit cards."

"He might have driven to Nebraska," I said. "I can't believe I forgot to tell you this."

"What's that?"

"There's a retired homicide detective who lives near Jayne. He told me the federal agents all drive Crown Victorias now. He saw a dark blue one, brand new, park near Jayne's town house the day she called me about the break-in. The guy driving it fits Polk's description. Guess what the plate prefix was."

"A-M-K."

"Yeah. He thinks it's a dummy plate—the kind they use for undercover ops—but he promised to run it for me."

"Why would he drive to Lincoln?" Scott asked.

"Gives him mobility while he's there," I said. "And it eliminates the risk that someone on a commercial flight might remember him."

"If he flashes his badge at Carolyn, that might explain why she'd get into his car so willingly."

"It would also explain how the killer got into Fontaine's house and Underwood's apartment without breaking anything and without a struggle." Scott nodded, went inside, and emerged with a glass of iced tea and another bagel. To the west I noticed the afternoon clouds thickening. Thunderstorms were certain.

"So how are things with you and the math professor?" Scott asked.

"Not so good," I said. I told him about Finn's disclosure of my manslaughter arrest to Jayne. I also told him about Finn's relationship with Amanda and how I'd handled Finn the previous morning.

"You let him off easy," Scott said. I shrugged. Thinking about my problems with Jayne was bringing me down and Scott could see it.

"What are you doing this weekend?" he asked.

"No plans," I said.

"I'm thinking of going camping. Bobbi bought me some night-vision goggles for my birthday, if you can believe that, and I'm dying to try 'em out."

"That sounds like a plan," I said. "I could use a little rest and relaxation."

"We can leave tonight if you want."

"No, I want to talk with Jayne. Let's leave tomorrow."

Jayne wasn't home, so I parked the truck and sat on the cement slab leading to her front door. I stared at the Russian olive trees beside the creek and wondered what idiot had brought them to the United States in the first place. My cell phone rang. It was Tom Hammond.

"It's a dummy plate," he said. "The car belongs to the Denver office of the FBI."

"I guess that's no surprise," I said, "but thanks for your efforts."

"Sure thing," he said. I almost hung up, but decided to ask one more question.

"Hey, Tom?"

"Yeah."

"If a law enforcement agency in Nebraska had asked the Colorado DMV to provide a listing of all vehicles meeting that description with an A-M-K prefix, would the DMV have given out the information about the car registered to the bureau?"

"Not right away," he said. "The DMV gets these requests all the time. The clerks who handle them don't even have access to that information, so the decision on disclosure has to be made at a higher level."

"Okay," I said. "Thanks again." I couldn't blame Amanda for sloppy police work. She'd had no reason to believe the FBI might own the mystery vehicle.

It was three-thirty P.M. My butt was sore from sitting on the concrete. Jayne showed up around five. She wore tan slacks and a white sleeveless shirt. She wasn't happy to see me.

"Hello," she said. I stood. She walked past me and unlocked the door, but I didn't follow her in and she didn't invite me. I saw her set her briefcase and purse down on the kitchen table.

"Let's take a walk," I said from the entrance. "I'll tell you about it." She removed a pitcher of water from the refrigerator and poured herself a glass. When she had finished drinking it, she walked toward me and pulled the door shut behind her.

We started walking east on Pearl Street. "I thought I'd bring you up to date on a few things," I said. She didn't respond, but she continued walking with me, so I summarized the latest developments in the case. She listened patiently and, despite her anger toward me, I sensed a certain satisfaction. We hadn't pieced it all together yet, but we had effectively established that the three deaths were related. I told her we'd have to turn it over to the bureau sooner or later.

"You've done a good job," she said. "Do I owe you any more money?"

"No." We turned right on Ninth Street and walked south to Boulder Creek. A pedestrian path follows the creek, and some high school kids were tubing in the clear water. I knew they'd have to call it a day soon because of the approaching storm.

"You remember my dog Wheat?" I asked.

"Yes." She didn't look at me.

"I adopted him a few years ago," I said. "He'd been abused and I read about him in the paper." I pulled a photocopy of the article from my shirt pocket and handed it to her. She stopped to read it.

Denver—A Denver man was arrested on charges of cruelty to animals when his roommates reported him to the police after they found his puppy whimpering and unable to walk.

Blackie, a three-month-old schipperkee, was found in its owner's, Melvin D. Dawson's, rented room with limp front paws, unable to walk and in obvious pain.

The puppy was taken to a local veterinary hospital by Denver police officer Wayne Simmons and found to have a swollen brain and concussion. The veterinarian confirmed the animal had been abused.

Dawson's roommates, who claim they had witnessed him throw, kick, and hit Blackie daily, decided they had seen enough and reported the problem to police. The two roommates also claim Dawson kicked their dog down some stairs on another occasion.

Simmons was told that the roommates had to break into Dawson's room to get to the dog since his doors were locked. Also, despite Dawson being at work, music was turned up in the room, apparently to mask the puppy's cries.

It was explained by Dawson that the dog had been biting on an electric cord a few days earlier so he hit it with his hand to discipline the animal. He said he did not take the dog to a vet because he felt it would be all right.

Dawson said he only hit the puppy with his hand and never kicked it. Dawson also explained that he disciplined the dog when it defecated on the floor.

Simmons arrested Dawson so there would not be any problem with retaliation against the roommates. Both Dawson and the roommates who reported him have been evicted, as no animals were allowed in the house. Subsequent investigation revealed Dawson had several outstanding warrants on various other misdemeanor charges.

She folded the article, handed it back to me, and said nothing. As we passed beneath the bridge over Broadway, I continued the story. "I adopted the dog," I said. "Later I learned Dawson had skipped town and that a warrant for his arrest had been issued, but cruelty to animals is a misdemeanor, so the cops weren't making any effort to track him down.

"A couple of months went by and I forgot about it. The dog seemed to be doing well and I considered myself lucky to have him. Then one day I was in line in a grocery store down near my brother's gym. The guy in front of me was a scruffy-looking doper and I noticed the name on his check—Melvin D. Dawson. I figured there couldn't be that many Melvin D. Dawsons in Denver and this guy just looked like the type of sick loser who would abuse a puppy. So I followed him out to his motorcycle and yelled, 'Melvin.'

"He just looked at me and climbed on his motorcycle. 'Hey, Melvin,' I say, 'c'mere, I want to talk to you.' 'Fuck you,' he says. I keep walking toward him. 'You've got some outstanding warrants, Melvin, so why don't you climb down off the bike and we'll go take care of them.' He gives me the finger and starts his motorcycle. I don't want him to get away so I run to him and yank him off the bike, but his jacket's slick and I lose my grip. The bike falls over and he comes up with a big spring-loaded knife.

"I've had some self-defense training, so I manage to avoid the knife, but that's just making him angry and he keeps circling me, trying to cut me. The cops still aren't anywhere to be seen. Finally he corners me between two cars and comes at me. I sidestep him and redirect his arm downward, and the knife slides into his belly. It severs an artery and he bleeds to death before they can save him." I heard the first crack of thunder. We continued walking.

When she finally said something, it was, "Why didn't you just walk away?"

"I've thought about that a lot," I said. "I don't have a good answer." I felt a light raindrop on my arm.

"You don't sound very remorseful," she said. Her anger was slowly diminishing.

"I could've walked away," I said, "and maybe I should have, but once I started it, I did what I had to do." I paused. "And the world's probably a better place for it," I added. "I know that sounds cold, but there are evil people in this world."

"I think I know that better than most people," she said. A reference to the deaths of her parents.

"I suppose you do," I said. A loud crack of thunder stopped us in our tracks for a moment. More raindrops began to fall. We turned around and began walking back toward the mountains in silence.

"You should have told me," she said as we neared her home.

"I know," I said. "I was afraid to. Afraid I might scare you off. Afraid you'd judge me without really knowing the whole story." The rain came harder and faster.

"So," I said as we reached her door, "what's the status of Pepper and Jayne?"

"I don't know," she said. "I need some time." My instincts told me not to press her.

"I'll call you in a day or two to update you on the case," I said. She nodded, went inside, and closed the door behind her. I glanced toward the creek and noticed the damned Russian olive trees again, then walked to my truck and headed for home.

34

SATURDAY NIGHT. Our second night camping. Scott and I were sitting on opposite ends of a small fire in a dry riverbed eighty miles east of Denver. That's right, east. Trying to camp in the mountains west of Denver in the summer is a poor way to get away from it all. The national parks and forests are just too crowded. Even in the primitive areas you can't hike more than a few miles without running into other backpacking enthusiasts.

When we were kids we used to ride our bikes out east of Denver to the old Lowry Bombing Range. The air force kept junk planes there, and we used to explore abandoned missile silos and Japanese internment camps. That was in the late sixties and early seventies, and most of that area is now the suburban cancer known as Aurora, Colorado—a suburb that will one day run clear to the Kansas border.

So now we just keep going farther east—out onto the high plains. It was a clear night; you could see the Milky Way. The dogs were quiet. Scott looked up at the stars and said, "Jesus, I needed this."

"Why?"

"Bobbi's still on this decorating kick," he said. "Wants to paint every room in the house. Every ten minutes she's busting into my office with paint samples and asking me which I like better, plum orchard or raspberry creme."

"Tough choice," I said. "I like the ambience of plum orchard, but raspberry creme has a certain audacity." He took a swig from a pint bottle of Jack Daniel's and handed it to me. I stared at the flickering flames, but said nothing. It would be nice to have Scott's problem. He must've read my mind.

"Things any better with the math professor?" he asked. "I know you like her." I thought about that line from Gordon Lightfoot's song—"a movie queen to play the scene of bringing all the good things out in me."

"A little better," I said. "We'll see how it goes."

We spent hours recalling old times. Grade school, junior high, high school, college. We stared at the orange coals of our campfire. The flames had died down, but we didn't want to build the fire back up. We were on some rancher's property and didn't want to draw attention to ourselves. We'd left my truck on the road with the hood up so people would think we'd developed car trouble and headed for the nearest town.

"What are you thinking about?" Scott asked.

"When I went to visit Koch, there was this photo in his office. Koch looks really young in it, college age, and he's standing in front of the American flag shaking hands with a famous public official—and I should know the guy's name but I just can't remember it."

"Was it a recent photo?"

"I just told you—he looked *really young* in the photo."

"And he's what, fifty now?"

"At least."

"So how long ago was the photo taken?"

"I don't know," I said, "twenty-five years, maybe more."

"Wish I could help," he said, "but without seeing the photo it's pretty hard."

"I know," I said. I took a sip of whiskey and stared at what was left of our fire.

"You give any more thought to going to the bureau?" Scott asked.

"First thing Monday morning," I said. "We've done as much as we can."

"Don't feel bad about it," he said. "Polk would have gotten away with it if not for you." I nodded and stirred the coals with a stick.

"Strange thing is, in a way Jayne actually helped him out."

"How do you mean?"

"She reported it to the FBI in Denver. It should've been investigated by someone out of Boston, Seattle, or Omaha, but the call came into Denver and Polk grabbed it so he could cover his ass."

"Hadn't thought of that," Scott said. "He was lucky."

I took another sip of whiskey. "Pass me the cheese and crackers," I said. "I'm not used to drinking like this."

"Colby or cheddar?"

"Fuck," I said. "William Colby."

"What?"

"That's the guy in the picture with Koch."

"The former director of the CIA?"

"Yeah."

"If Hawkins really worked for the CIA," he said, "that could be the connection. Hawkins and Koch are both economists, and both may have worked for the CIA."

"Now we just have to figure out how Polk fits in." I handed him the whiskey and resolved not to drink any more that night. Whatever my future with Jayne Smyers, there was no point in destroying my health. I found some aspirin in my pack and swallowed them with water from a metal canteen.

"Preventive medicine?" Scott said.

"Yeah."

The coals died down as the night went on. We pissed on the fire, gave the dogs some water, then crawled into the tent. It was warm on the high plains and there was no need to zip the sleeping bags. I wore only boxers and a T-shirt.

I was dreaming of Joy when I felt Wheat's moist nose poking

my face. I sat up. Buck was tense, his ears erect. Something was out there. I grabbed my Glock and peered through the screen, but saw nothing. I tapped Scott's shoulder a few times and signaled him to be silent. "Someone out there," I whispered.

"Sheriff?"

"I don't see any lights." Scott's rifle was in the truck, but he had the night-vision goggles. He placed the evil-looking device on his head and looked through the mesh door of the tent.

"One man," Scott said. "With a handgun. Automatic. About a hundred yards out. Coming right at us. Not in uniform. And he ain't a rancher."

"Check the back side," I whispered. He crawled to the back side of the tent and shook his head to indicate he'd seen nothing. I quickly tied my running shoes. "I'll try to flank him and get him from behind," I said. I handed Scott my Glock. "If he starts to raise the pistol, put some holes in him."

"Count on it," he said.

I slowly unzipped the tent's back door and began crawling over sand and brush to a position where I'd be able to take the stranger. My head hurt, but I had to suck it up. As I slowly circled away from the tent I hoped like hell I didn't crawl across a prickly-pear cactus or stumble into a den of slumbering rattlesnakes.

The stranger was within ten yards of me. I lay perfectly still. By now my eyes had adjusted to the dim light of the stars and I could see that his back was to me. He started to raise the pistol, apparently planning to fire blindly into our tent. I quietly raised myself into a sprinter's stance and exploded forward. He turned and fired one shot, but missed. I launched a flying tackle and knocked him to the ground. I struck his arm as I hit him and the force of my blow sent his weapon off into the sagebrush. "Got him," I yelled.

Scott emerged from the tent, flashlight in his left hand, pistol in his right. The man struggled, but I must've outweighed him by fifty pounds. Scott found the weapon—a Sig Sauer nine millimeter—while I wrestled the intruder over onto his back and brought a few hard rights down on his face to stop his struggling. Scott shined the light directly on the man's face.

"I wonder who this sorry fucker is," he said.

"His name's Alan Koch," I said.

"I'll have the rancher's deluxe," Scott told the waitress. She had auburn locks and was on the wrong side of forty, but was built like a burlap bag full of bobcats. Big Matt would've loved her.

"'I'll have a diablo sandwich and a Dr Pepper,'" I said. "'And make it fast, I'm in a goddamned hurry.'" She just stared at me. "It's a line from *Smokey and the Bandit*," I explained. "Jackie Gleason said it. I've always wanted to use it." She didn't see the humor in it. "I'll just have a short stack and some coffee," I said sheepishly. She wrote it down and walked away with an unamused look on her face.

"Fuck her if she can't take a joke," Scott said. We were in a greasy spoon in the ranching town of Strasburg, Colorado. It was Sunday morning. Koch was under some GI blankets in the back of the truck with enough duct tape around his legs, arms, and mouth to attach the wings to a 747. We'd given him a pretty good beating, but he'd stubbornly refused to tell us a thing. Scott had wanted to take it further, but I'd reminded him that torture is against the law.

We'd found Koch's Lexus parked behind my pickup. Someone had planted a tracking device on the rear bumper of my truck, and the equipment to follow its signal was inside the Lexus. It was the type of high-tech equipment Koch could only have obtained from the FBI or a similar agency. Scott punctured the underside of Koch's radiator hose to make it appear as though he had suffered car trouble.

"Maybe we shouldn't wait till tomorrow to go to the bureau," Scott said.

"If we try to set up a meeting today," I said, "Polk might learn about it and God only knows what he'd do. I think we just lay low until tomorrow morning."

"He probably knows something's up," Scott said. "If this dickhead had succeeded in killing us, don't you think he would've called Polk to tell him the mission had been accomplished?"

"Probably," I said.

"So where do we spend the night?" I looked out and noticed a combination truck stop and motel on the other side of the interstate.

"'The Old Home Filler-Up An' Keep on A-Truckin' Cafe,'" I said. That was the title of a song by C. W. McCall.

35

We woke to the sound of cranking diesels early Monday morning. Enjoyed breakfast at the same greasy spoon, then returned to our room. It was almost eight. I phoned the FBI on my cell phone and asked for Gombold. The receptionist asked my name, but I declined because I didn't want Polk to know I'd called the bureau. She put me on hold for what seemed like an eternity. "Agent Gombold," he said.

"Agent Keane," I said.

"Pepper," he said, "why the hell didn't you give her your name?"

"I need to set up a meeting with you and Dittmer this morning."

"What about?"

"I think Polk murdered the three math professors."

"You out of your mind?"

"You won't think so when you hear the evidence." I gave him a detailed summary of the evidence we'd developed. The gun, the car, everything.

"It's circumstantial," he said, but his tone suggested he knew the bureau had cause for concern.

"We've gotten indictments with less," I said.

"How soon can you be here?" he asked.

"Little more than an hour."

"Okay," he sighed, "I'll set it up. Dittmer's gonna love this."

"Don't tell Polk," I said. "The son of a bitch sent one of his coconspirators out to kill us a couple of nights ago."

"You're shittin' me?"

"The guy's tied up in the back of my truck," I said. "Tried to off us with a nine millimeter. I'll bring him with me if Scott doesn't kill him first."

We checked out of the motel and drove several miles down a desolate country road until we found an old shack, then helped Koch out of the truck so he could empty his bladder. He was wearing the same clothes for the third day and sharing the back of the truck with the dogs, so he smelled like a bum, but that was the least of my concerns.

We arrived downtown at nine-thirty and parked in an all-day lot. We left Buck and Wheat in the truck with our prisoner, then walked the two blocks to the federal building. I phoned Gombold from a pay phone in the lobby and asked him to come down. "Why don't you just come up?" he asked.

"I'm not inclined to surrender my weapon," I said. "Figure you could help us get past security." He sighed but said he'd be right down.

He stepped off one of the elevator cars two minutes later. Navy suit, white shirt, solid green tie. Saw us, said a few words to one of the security people, and motioned for us to walk around the metal detector. "You've looked better," he said as he led us into one of the elevators. I hadn't shaved in a few days and my forearms were covered with abrasions from crawling around in the brush.

"Felt better too," I said. "You say anything to Dittmer yet?"

"Just that there had been some developments that might impact the bureau. Told him you seemed kind of itchy to discuss them."

Dittmer was at his desk wearing a white oxford-cloth shirt with the sleeves rolled up and a leather shoulder holster. A paisley tie hung loose around his unbuttoned collar. He looked haggard. His weathered face bore a stoic look—one of those men who had seen it all and consequently had toughness etched into his features. Gombold escorted us in and closed the door behind him. I introduced Scott and we all took chairs in front of Dittmer's massive mahogany desk. Scott was the only one not wearing a shoulder holster; his gun was tucked into the small of his back.

"What's this all about?" Dittmer asked. "Tim said there had been some developments."

"I think Polk killed those math professors," I said. He leaned forward and gave me a hard look.

"I hope you've got something to back that up," he said.

"I do," I said. "I'll start with this. The weapon used to kill Fontaine was a five-shot thirty-eight-caliber Taurus revolver Polk took from a bank robber named Bailey Green last summer. Polk logged it into evidence and, as you know, the weapon later came up missing. Here's the ballistics report from the Washington State Patrol." I handed the report to him. He reached for a legal pad and began taking notes.

"What else?" he asked.

"A witness claimed to see a brand-new Ford or Mercury luxury sedan, dark blue, with Colorado plates in front of Carolyn Chang's home the night of her disappearance. The prefix on the plate was A-M-K. The only Colorado vehicle fitting that description with an A-M-K prefix is an unmarked Crown Victoria registered to your office."

"What's the plate number?"

"A-M-K 8115."

"Yeah." He sighed. "That's one of ours. What else you got?"

It took more than a half hour, but I laid it all out for him. Everything. Polk's lie to Gilbert, his ties to the Koch Group, a man fitting Polk's description breaking into Jayne's town house, Polk's being in Boston at the time of Underwood's death and in Washington at the time of Fontaine's death, and Koch's attempt to kill us the other night. Polk was a southpaw and the man who had stabbed Carolyn Chang had been left-handed. "This look familiar?" I asked. I handed him the tracking device we'd found on my truck. He studied it.

"It's ours," he said, sighing again.

I told him my theory. Showed him the documents Gilbert had found that established conclusively that the three victims had been working together on a model designed to predict market behavior. He was initially skeptical, but I thought I saw his doubts dissipate as the circumstantial evidence of Polk's involvement became overwhelming.

"Jesus Christ," he muttered as he leaned forward and placed his hands on his desk, "a weapon taken from our evidence room is used to commit a murder we're supposed to have investigated." He shook his head slowly from side to side. Gumby just stared out at the Denver skyline. Scott sat quietly and took it all in. I inventoried the military awards and college degrees behind Dittmer's desk. "Where's Polk now?" Dittmer finally asked, the question clearly directed to Gombold.

"He's in the building," Gumby said. Dittmer pressed a button on his telephone set and a young woman's voice came over the speaker.

"Sir?"

"Have Agent Polk come in here," he said.

"Yes, sir."

Several minutes passed before Polk arrived. He wore gray slacks, a light blue shirt with short sleeves, a solid navy tie, and a leather shoulder holster with his howitzer in it. He wasn't happy to see me. "What's this?" he said.

"Close the door," Dittmer said. Polk complied. "I need your weapon and badge," Dittmer said.

"What's going on, boss?" Polk asked. Surprised.

"Your weapon and badge," Dittmer repeated.

"What the fuck is going on?" Polk demanded.

"You're suspended until further notice," Dittmer said loudly as he stood. "Now give me your goddamned weapon and badge."

"Why?" Polk demanded.

"Killing three math professors seems like a pretty good reason," I said from my chair. I was roughly halfway between Polk and Dittmer, and I made no effort to hide my contempt.

"You think I killed them?" he shouted.

"That's where the evidence points," I said.

"We're not discussing this now," Dittmer said. He extended his long arm to signal Polk he still wanted my former classmate to surrender his badge and gun.

"What evidence?" Polk shouted. His denial angered me. I stood up and faced him.

"I'll tell you what evidence," I shot back. "A weapon you logged into evidence was used to kill Fontaine. You lied to the police about it. You're in Boston at a sex crimes seminar when Underwood dies in an autoerotic death, you're in Richland when Fontaine takes a bullet. A blue Crown Victoria with Colorado plates is seen outside Carolyn Chang's home the night she disappeared, and that plate traces to the Denver office of the FBI. Carolyn's killer was left-handed and you're a lefty. Three people who developed a revolutionary way of constructing economic models are dead and you work for an economic consulting company. You reinterviewed witnesses who had already been interviewed by other agents, to make sure nobody was on your trail."

"I was working on the goddamned case!" he shouted. "You think I didn't know something funny was going on? You think I didn't know that I was in the vicinity when all three murders took place?"

"You broke into Jayne's house and—"

"To find out what you knew," he said. "I couldn't get into your house because of your fucking dogs."

"We're not discussing this now," Dittmer repeated firmly, but the situation was slipping away from his control.

"By the way," I said to Polk, "Koch botched the job the other night. We confiscated his FBI tracking device and gave him a good beating. Probably should've killed the fucker, but the prosecutor may need him to testify against you."

"What are you talking about?" Polk demanded.

"We're not discussing this now," Dittmer shouted.

Polk turned to Dittmer. "You son of a bitch," he said. "You set me up."

Dittmer pressed the intercom again and said, "Send some agents in here to take custody of Agent Polk."

"Right away, sir," a female voice replied.

Polk looked at me, then at Dittmer, then back at me. "Don't you get it?" he pleaded. "Dittmer's the one who decided our office would run the investigation. That's why he was so interested in knowing whether the phone records could connect any of the victims."

"You're the one who logged in the gun," I said.

Polk turned to Dittmer again. "You fuckin' set me up," he repeated. He was as angry as I'd ever seen him. Every vein and artery in his neck was bulging. "You got me that job with Koch. You sent me to Boston. Told me to take time off to attend my reunion. You had me drive to Lincoln with you for that stupid meeting. How fucking stupid could I have been? I ought to fuckin' kill you right now." I knew what was about to happen and reached for my Glock. Then everything went into slow motion.

Polk started for Dittmer, his face filled with rage. "You fuckin' set me up," he repeated yet again. Dittmer stepped back and began to draw his weapon with his left hand. Gumby saw what was about to happen and went for his gun, as did Scott, but I got to mine first. I shot Dittmer once in the chest.

36

I'M NOT SURE I CAN explain it," I said. "I guess the idea had been floating around in the back of my mind, but it didn't come together for me until Polk started going off on Dittmer. All of the sudden everything made sense."

"Lucky for you," Gombold said. He wore a gray suit, white shirt, and maroon tie. Black wing tips. Two weeks had passed. We were sharing a booth in an upscale bar near the federal building. It was four P.M. on a Friday afternoon and the place was filling up. He looked at me, signaling me to continue. I'd given a formal statement immediately after wounding Dittmer, but now was our chance to talk in a more relaxed setting.

"I'd been studying Dittmer's glory wall while we waited for Polk," I said. "It struck me that he and Hawkins had both been in Vietnam at about the same time. Both in intelligence. Then I noticed that Dittmer had attended Duke. And I remembered that Hawkins had attended Duke. And even though Dittmer was taking notes with his right hand, he was going to shoot Polk with his left hand."

"And the coroner in Kansas said Carolyn had probably been stabbed by a lefty?"

"Yeah." I took a few cashews from the bowl between us and washed them down with red wine.

"Well," Gumby said, "the important thing is, you were right. The pubic hairs we took from Dittmer match the ones found with

Carolyn's body. It took some work, but we verified that he flew to Seattle and Boston under an alias."

"And he drove to Lincoln with Polk in an FBI car?"

"Yeah, Dittmer scheduled some kind of meeting in Lincoln that week just so he'd have an excuse to go there, and he decided to take Polk with him. Polk says they took the Crown Victoria, and the mileage records seem to support that. They put about fourteen hundred miles on the car during that time period."

"Enough to get you to Lincoln and back, with maybe a little side trip down to Kansas so Dittmer could dump Carolyn's body."

"Yeah."

"What about Hawkins?" I said.

"Picked him up the day after you shot Dittmer. He and Dittmer aren't talking, but we've learned they were fraternity brothers at Duke and worked with each other in Vietnam."

"How is Dittmer?" I asked.

"He was lucky. The bullet punctured his lung but didn't do any serious damage."

"He might have been better off dead," I said.

"Yeah, he might have. I don't condone what he did, but I have to confess I feel a little bit sorry for him. He devotes most of his life to his country, then gets passed over for promotion and loses his wife to cancer. Decides he's entitled to something more than a government pension and ruins his life." I nodded in silence.

"What about Alan Koch?" I asked.

"Told us everything," Gumby said. "Sitting in back of your truck for a few days must have had a therapeutic effect."

"I doubt it," I said. "He probably figures the three of them are pretty good candidates for the death penalty, and he decided to rat out the other two to save his own skin."

"I guess," he said. He grabbed a handful of cashews.

"Don't keep me in suspense," I said.

"Koch had been an economic analyst with the CIA, just like Hawkins. That's where they met. They stayed in touch over the years. Hawkins went to Koch with this intrinsic time model and Koch loved it. Thought it would revolutionize the business and make his firm a lot of money."

"All they had to do was kill the people who'd come up with the model."

"And Dittmer was the man to do it," Gumby said. "With those three dead, they didn't have to worry about the model becoming public knowledge. So, according to Koch, they approached Dittmer and Dittmer agreed to do the dirty work." He motioned for the waiter to bring another gin and tonic.

"Dittmer sure manipulated Polk," I said.

"I don't think he ever intended for Polk to take the fall," Gumby said. "I don't think he even thought of it until after he took Bailey Green's gun from the evidence room. He knew that would cast suspicion on Polk if anyone found out, and he figured, why not set it up so all evidence points to Polk just in case?"

"Then he kept the case in Denver when Jayne Smyers reported it to the bureau."

"Yeah."

"When did Polk get suspicious?" I asked.

"I talked with him a little," Gombold said. "When we were working the case, he thought it was strange that he had been in the general vicinity at the time of all three deaths. He had a funny feeling about it; that's why he reinterviewed so many witnesses after receiving the 302s from the local agents.

"When we got the interview summaries from Lincoln and learned about the big Ford in front of Carolyn Chang's home on the night of her death, Polk wondered whether Dittmer might've been involved, but only one witness claimed the car had Colorado plates and the notion seemed so ridiculous that Polk dismissed it as a coincidence.

"Then when Gilbert called and told him a gun missing from our evidence room had been used to kill Fontaine, he knew something was wrong and decided to do a little investigating on his own. He knew someone in our office was bad, but didn't know who and didn't feel he could trust anyone. That's why he requested the gun from Gilbert instead of routing the request through Dittmer."

"Is that why he broke into Jayne's home?" I asked.

"Yeah, he wanted to know what you knew, but given that you two are like India and Pakistan, he couldn't just pick up the phone and ask."

I took another sip of wine. "What's Polk up to now?" I asked.

"He's been assigned to Montgomery, Alabama. He'll be moving next month."

"Good a place as any for him," I said. "He in any trouble over the break-in?"

"The professor said she didn't want to pursue it, and the bureau sure didn't want to publicize it, so the director gave him an unofficial suspended oral reprimand and sent him to Alabama."

"Punishment enough," I said.

"Haven't you talked with her?" he asked.

"Not lately," I said.

"I thought you two had a thing going."

"It's up in the air," I said.

He switched topics. "That was a quite a write-up in the *News*," he said. I was the best-known investigator in Colorado at the moment. My fifteen minutes of fame.

"I almost got the wrong man," I said. Nobody is harder on Pepper Keane than Pepper Keane.

"Hey," he said as he looked right at me, "you figured out the economic connection. You proved the deaths were related. Polk didn't have any of that. If you hadn't taken this case and stuck with it, Dittmer would have quietly retired and all three of them would be living the good life."

"I suppose," I said.

"Just be glad it's over," he said. I smiled, but it wasn't quite over for me. I still had to win back Jayne Smyers.

We finished our drinks and the waiter brought our check. I paid it. We talked for a few more minutes, then walked out into the late afternoon sun and shook hands.

"Want to join my wife and me for dinner?" he asked.

"Take a rain check," I said. "I've got an early day tomorrow."

"Tomorrow's Saturday," he said. "I figured you'd take it easy for a while."

"I plan to," I said, "but my brother's a scoutmaster, and I volunteered to help him and his kids with a little conservation project." We both donned our sunglasses. "Actually, they volunteered to help me. The kids are working on their conservation merit badges."

"That the one where they have to do so many hours of public service?"

"Six hours," I said.

"What are you gonna have 'em do?"

"We're going to take down a stand of Russian olive trees."

"This on your land?"

"Ownership of the land seems a little unclear," I said, "but the trees are making it hard for the deer to get down to a creek they like to drink from."

"Why do you care?" he asked.

"I don't know," I said. "I just do."